THE SKIES ROARED

BLUFF CITY BUTCHER TRILOGY #2

STEVE BRADSHAW

1st Edition 2013

2nd Edition 2016

ISBN: 978-1-948059-54-1

Library of Congress Cataloging-in-Publication Data

THE SKIES ROARED/Steve Bradshaw

Printed in USA

THE SKIES ROARED© is a work of fiction.

Names, characters, businesses, organizations, places, institutions, events, and incidents either are the product of the author's imagination or use is fictitious. Any resemblance to actual persons, living or dead, events, or locals is entirely coincidental and fictitious.

BOOKS BY STEVE BRADSHAW

The Bell Trilogy
Bluff City Butcher
The Skies Roared
Blood Lions

Evil Like Me

Serial Intent

Terminal Breach

Shared Innocence

THE BELL TRILOGY

Is an utterly plausible genetic solution for life extension woven into a heart-pounding epic battle between good and evil . . .

The Bell Trilogy chronicles a family of great privilege harboring an unimaginable secret and dream that turns into a global nightmare. Elliott Sumner, a world renowned forensic pathologist, struggles to rectify his abandoned beginnings and innate gifts when unexpected paths cross. The serial killer hunter meets the genius psychopath of Memphis urban legend and discovers a secret to life people will kill for. He must protect the greatest evolutionary leap for mankind.

BLUFF CITY BUTCHER – Book one begins with Elliott's chilling, forensic pursuit of a genius, psychopathic serial killer. The heart-pounding hunt for a real monster uncovers a century old mystery and sinister plan with profound, world implications.

THE SKIES ROARED – Book two enters the unfathomable realms of wealth and power where a secret society seizes control of a genetic breakthrough. Stealth armies on an evil mission and an unstoppable killer lure forensic sleuth Elliott Sumner onto a horrific blood trail that crosses three continents. While hunting the deadly force and navigating the startling twists, Elliott must find answers to an utterly plausible threat to mankind.

BLOOD LIONS – Book three is the masterful conclusion to the Bell family nightmare. Shocking pieces of the ill-fated puzzle fall in place. Elliott Sumner and his unlikely allies must secure, formulate, and disseminate the Medino biogenic compound or the greatest evolutionary leap of mankind is lost. Sinister forces seek control waging a secret battle. In the end Elliott must embrace a real monster and call upon his innate gifts to prevail.

For more information on **The Bell Trilogy** *books, visit author website at*

THE SKIES ROARED
Primary Characters

Henderson Bates, M.D.	Shelby County Medical Examiner
Albert Bell	Billionaire Bell Family Patriarch
Alberto Bella	Immigrant
Jack Bellow	Biomedical Entrepreneur
Trenton Brent	Wealthy Memphis hermit
Adam Duncan	Psychopath
Betty Duncan	Mother of triplets
Max Gregory	Retired CIA, Spyglass PI
Alex Harris	Memphis Homicide Detective
Bill Kramer	Davidson County Medical Examiner
Carol Mason	*The Memphis Tribune*
Enrique Medino, M.D.	Geneticist
Melba Montrose	Eyewitness
Marcos Moreno	Son of Dr. Medino
Elliott Sumner, M.D.	Gifted Forensic Pathologist
G.E. Taft	Shelby County Sheriff
Tony Wilcox	Memphis Homicide Detective

THE THIRD DREAM

While Gilgamesh rested his chin on his knees, sleep that pours over mankind overtook him. In the middle of the night his sleep came to an end, so he got up and said to his friend: "My friend, did you not call out to me? Why did I wake? Did you not touch me? Did a god pass by? Why are my muscles trembling? My friend, I have had a third dream, and the dream I had was deeply disturbing. **The skies roared and the earth rumbled; then it became deathly still, and darkness loomed...there rained death.**"

Epic of Gilgamesh, 2000 BC

PART ONE
SCIONS AND DEMONS

ONE

"Evil is just a point of view."
Anne Rice

"Oh God, Elliott. Is there anything you can do for him?" Carol whispered.

Thirty squad cars in a tight circle surrounded the Bell mansion. High beams poured over fresh snow and climbed Georgia marble to the growing, crimson red stain. Statues with badges stood next to smoking metal and spinning blues, arms hung and guns pointed down. Every Memphis cop and Shelby County deputy within five miles came.

Sheriff Taft found the security guards in the gatehouse, guns in snapped holsters and bloody tracks to the gates. Before Taft pursued, he sent out an APB—Bluff *City Butcher is* alive at the *Bell mansion. Come help* if can."

They pulled the serial killer's carcass from the Mississippi

River two months ago. There were not ready for what they would witness on this cold, winter night in east Memphis.

Standing on the balcony, Carol slides her hand under Elliott's coat and around his waist. He pulls her close. Thirty feet away, through floating ice crystals in white light above the packed courtyard of eyewitnesses, Elliott stares at the serial killer he hunted for a decade—now with a seven foot spire piercing his abdomen and protruding from his back. Steaming blood runs from the massive, gut wound down the snow covered roof.

Elliott thinks he knows why the Bluff City Butcher jumped from the balcony onto the razor sharp spire—and it was not a failed escape.

He whispers back into Carol's ear, "Adam made a decision tonight. He saw no other way . . ." Elliott's thoughts drift into the places he must learn to understand, thoughts about the monster he hunted and brother he found.

So this is your moment of clarity . . . suicide your end. I knew one day we would meet, but I would be the one dying, the one crazy enough to hunt a freak of nature, a genius, psychopathic serial killer. An unstoppable, man-eating lion with the brain of an Einstein. Even now I don't know what you can do, all your capabilities. You killed so many and escaped for so long. Elliott's eyes move to the growing crowd in the courtyard. *These people gather not to watch you die, but to witness your next escape. They expect you to pull your bloody hulk from the spire. They want to see you bound across the rooftop and disappear into the night. They wait for you to again return to the curious fog of Memphis legend. But this is your end, Adam Duncan . . .*

Elliott turned to Albert Bell now bent over the balcony rail a few feet away. The drawn face of the billionaire patriarch told the story of the tragic evening. Albert's eyes were empty, and his complexion as white as the clinging snow. Albert's blood left his head and moved to his core to protect the breaking heart.

Are you thinking about the people your illegitimate son killed, Albert? Elliott thought. *How can you reconcile the abominable acts of a monster with the unconditional love of a father? You see Adam dying, and a heinous killer dying. Does the love of a father bridge all . . . ?*

"Tonight I learned Adam is my brother," Elliott said ony to Carol. Their bodies fused. She spoke with her eyes. He felt her inside—the only one he let in. Her long blond hair fell from her sculpted cheekbones, and her wet lips almost touched his. Then they did, but not a kiss. His hand pressed on the small of her back, holding her, pulling her closer, and wanting to protect her.

"Max called from Dallas. He told us everything on Albert's speakerphone. That's when Adam rested his knife on my shoulder . . . my neck. He pressed the blade to my carotid artery. Adam owned the room, Carol. He came to kill Albert and me."

"You were the last names on the kill list," Carol said.

"Max did no know he was speaking to three," Elliott said.

"And why did Max call?" Carol asked.

"To correct information he gave earlier to Albert."

"Information regarding an investigation . . . ?"

"The missing persons investigation—Betty Duncan—Albert's mistress forty years ago."

"And Adam's mother. Now Max claims she is your mother too—twins?"

"Triplets: Adam, me, and Jack Bellow."

"God, Elliott—triplets! Albert Bell is your father? It is all very hard to believe."

"Max possess irrefutable evidence, so he says."

"Hard to swallow the serial killer you hunted the last ten years is your brother," Carol said. "And Jack Bellow is your brother too . . ."

"Max was first to figure it out—that Jack Bellow's body is in the morgue and the Butcher is still out there. Max had a hunch Adam would come for Albert and me tonight."

". . . a county-wide Christmas party crawling with cops, I could not agree more."

"Fits the BCB's modus operandi—use the *impossible* to outmaneuver us mere mortals. "

"And Jack Bellow is certainly the Butcher's double. I saw him," Carol said.

"On the bluff . . ."

"But you don't look like them, Elliott."

"They are identical twins. I'm fraternal."

"What's the difference?"

"In simple terms, Jack and Adam shared an embryo. I had my own."

"Does that stuff really happen?"

"Yes it does. Happens more when fertility drugs are involved. They could have been."

"Fertility drugs were available in the '60s?"

"Hormone *hMG* was in clinical studies in the '60s."

"Forty years later paths cross. I wonder why." She rested her head on Elliott's chest.

He stared at Adam dying on the steep roof atop the now red snow.

"I think someone is pulling our strings."

She stayed in his chest. "It looks to me like Adam Duncan is pulling the strings."

"Two months ago I would agree because I thought we stopped the Butcher. But now a world acclaimed biotechology entrepreneur—who happens to also be my biologic brother—is dead and my *serial killer* brother is taking his own life."

"When you say it that way . . ."

"I must find out why Adam let Albert and me live, and why kill himself?"

Carol studied Elliot's face. "I see your wheels turning."

Their eyes met. "If Jack and Adam messed-up someone's plans, maybe it's my turn. If they were a threat, maybe now I am the threat to eliminate."

"How will you find out?" she asked.

"The answer's in the timeline of events. I need to dig deeper. I need to know more about how Jack died and what led to Adam's change of heart and snap decision."

"You have little to go on, Elliott."

"Something's not right about any of this. It's always been much bigger than a serial killer."

Adam released a primal scream, a cry like a helpless animal being eaten alive. The delirious, rhythmic flow of excruciating pain slowed as the end neared. The iron spire reflected white light from the squad cars. It shot a beam into the black sky and a surreal portal.

"The night the Butcher took you from Beale Street, were you alone in the back of that van? Do you know if he took anyone else into the catacombs?"

"I was alone that night." She felt Elliott's phone vibrate.

"Excuse me." He pushed through the balcony crowd and disappeared into the study.

Carol moved to Albert. When she held his arm, he managed a slight smile. His eyes stayed with Adam writhing in pain, flopping and spewing bright red blood onto the snow. She prayed Adam's death would come soon—the pain and the nightmare needed to be over.

The crowd in the courtyard parted. The ambulance rolled to a stop and paramedics got out slowly—they could not change the inevitable. The monster, who tormented the community for decades, laid in his blood three stories up. The BCB would die before anyone could get near him.

Elliott returned to the balcony. Carol found her nest in his coat. Although a strong woman, she needed a strong man this night. They watched in silence. Elliott seemed pensive when the ladder did not reach the steep roof three stories up. The snow fall thickened. He knew the long-ladder truck on its way would arrive too late. Adam was now still.

"Why did you ask about the night the Butcher took me from Beale?" Carol asked.

Elliott's cell buzzed again. This time she saw the name— Mike Primeaux—one of Elliott's handpicked paramedics used on special assignments. There were two, highly trained and tight-lipped.

Elliott did not hide his conversation.

"Is Dr. Bates with you now . . . ? Good. I'm coming."

Elliott met her stare. "First, why the question about Beale?" she pushed.

"At that time we thought Adam and Jack were one. Now we know they are two. Adam could not have taken you and Jack on the same night at the same time."

"My god. I did not get that far. That means . . ."

"It means Adam had help he did or did not know about." Elliott turned to leave. "There are others in this, Carol."

"You're right. Adam could not do all of it alone." She turned to the crowd in the courtyard. "They're here now, watching him die. They must be shocked at the abrupt change in plans. With the Butcher, kills were never in doubt. This outcome has gotta be disturbing to them."

"Adam's suicide is catastrophic or a blessing. The others came tonight expecting him to do what he always does, kill and escape. This time his task was terminate the Bell patriarch and me, the first male born and sole heir to the Bell family fortune."

They watched a powder-blue Bentley leave the edge of the crowd and crawl up the drive with lights off. When it reached the crest, the lights popped on and dropped out of sight.

"Who would leave now, and like that?" Carol said.

"I don't know. But I need to take care of something. I'll be back."

Elliott left the balcony as the fire truck barreled down the drive with lights spinning and sirens blaring. The turntable ladder would be adequate but never be deployed. Carol returned to Albert's side and surrounded his arm as they both watched the spectacle.

Adam Duncan stopped moving before the small door on the roof opened and a square hole appeared in the snow. William crawled out first and then two paramedics. They unbolted the spire with a sparkling socket wrench and removed it from Adam's stomach. It slid to the edge of the roof as the crowd watched in breathless awe. The three pulled the blood covered, lifeless body of the legendary serial killer inside and the small door closed.

Soon the fire trucks departed and the guests followed. A long line of lights moved from the Bell estate, and were swallowed on Walnut Grove. Sheriff Taft and Deputy Pilsner walked the snow fields releasing each squad car with a handshake and "thanks." The grounds would return to normal except for the blood stain on the north wall of the mansion, and the tire tracks in the surrounding snow fields.

They brought out the body in a black crash bag strapped onto a gurney. Two paramedics crossed the courtyard with heads down and loaded Adam Duncan in the back of the ambulance. The M.E. had examined the body in the attic. He officially ruled manner of death SUICIDE, and cause of death severe, abdominal trauma with terminal exsanguination.

In the crawl space beneath the little door to the roof, Dr. Bates collected the required body fluids for the obligatory toxicology tests. He obtained a full set of fingerprints, dental impressions, and DNA samples. There was no need to bring the the twin to the morgue. An autopsy would not tell them anything new. Dr. Bates withnessed the suicide and pronounced the Bluff City Butcher dead at the scene.

Bates said he did it out of professional courtesy. He released the body to the family to avoid a long, drawn out, meaningless inquest. Bates explained to the press he had more than enough to rule and sign a death certificate. The only one hurt this night was the man committing suicide. His life of offenses had no bearing on his death. Bates declared the circus officially over. The serial killer of Memphis urban legend would no longer threaten the community or use up the ink at the Memphis Tribune. Albert Bell would go forward with private funeral arrangements.

No lights. No sirens. The ambulance pulled out of the courtyard leaving Elliott standing alone in the snow. No one would question the ambulance's destination until later.

He looked up to the balcony where Albert and Carol stood alone. Only Carol noticed the fingers poking out his blazer. Only Carol saw the bloody, white latex gloves worn by the man she adored.

Carol squeezed Albert's arm. He smiled for the first time all night . . .

TWO

"A thing is not necessarily true because a man dies for it."
Oscar Wilde

"Is he . . . ?"

"Yes. Barely."

"How are vitals?"

"All bad."

"But stable?"

"We have never seen anything like . . ."

"I know. How much blood so far?" he whispered.

"Ten units, packed red cells, steady push normal saline," he replied.

"Good, keep it up. How far out now?"

"ETA 22:32."

"You know who will meet you. He's waiting."

"Sir?"

"Yes, Mike."

"I think we are going to lose him."

"I know you do. Tighten the restraints now. All of them."

"Yes, sir . . ."

The Memphis Tribune
Bluff City Butcher Dies Third Time at Billionaire Bell Mansion

Carol Mason, Investigative Reporting

December 24, 2009

At 9:00 p.m. last night a serial killer, thought to be dead, resurfaced. The infamous Bluff City Butcher of Memphis urban legend killed two private security guards at the gates of the billionaire Bell family estate on Walnut Grove Lane in east Memphis. After gaining access to the mansion, Adam Duncan held Albert Bell, and Dr. Elliott Sumner hostage. Memphis Homicide Detective Tony Wilcox and Shelby County Sheriff G.E. Taft were the first to enter the study where the two were held captive. Adam Duncan, forty-year-old Caucasian male (Bluff City Butcher serial killer), leaped from the balcony onto a rooftop spire thirty feet away where he later died.

Thirty squad cars responded to an APB sent out by Sheriff G.E. Taft after discovering the slain guards. Police surrounded the mansion and witnessed the BCB death on the snow-covered roof. A crowd of more than one hundred city and county employees attending the Bell Christmas Gala watched.

On October 18, 2009, Memphis police found a body in Mississippi River after a confrontation on Mud Island with the BCB who was wounded and fell into the river. Twenty-six hours later the body was found by Presidents Island and taken to the county morgue. They identified the body as the BCB. An autopsy confirmed the wounds. DNA matched Jack Bellow who is missing. Police thought the BCB, alias Adam Duncan, was Jack Bellow, the president/CEO of LIFE2 Corporation. Some believe he had a psychological condition (Jekyll and Hyde) giving rise to the serial killer now believed to have taken 150 lives in six states over a twenty-five year period.

Police believe Adam Duncan and Jack Bellow are identical twins. Adam Duncan was the BCB, Jack Bellow was the victim of a Duncan's plan intended to throw off the Memphis police.

Today, Albert Bell told *The Memphis Tribune* Adam Duncan and Jack Bellow are his biological sons. The identical twins were born without his knowledge following a brief relationship over forty years ago. Bell said he had no knowledge of his sons until the night the BCB appeared in his study. Bell said he would release information when more facts were known.

The body of Adam Duncan (BCB) was removed from the Bell mansion by private ambulance and taken to an undisclosed location where a private autopsy may be conducted by the Medical Examiner and forensic pathologist, Dr. Elliott Sumner. The cause of death was ruled exsanguination due to abdominal trauma, manner of death, suicide. Because Dr. Henderson Bates witnessed the death, he released the remains to the Bell family. "An autopsy will not tell us more," Bates said. The names of the two security guards killed at the Bell estate are being withheld until notification of family.

THREE

"Risk varies inversely with knowledge."
Unknown

It was after midnight. Elliott parked five blocks away. He stayed in alleys out of lights and waited until there were no cars or people before crossing downtown streets. He went in through the parking garage, avoiding cameras, and up the back stairwell. After the horrific event at the Bell mansion and suspicions he was next, no one could know his relationship with Carol Mason. Now it was too dangerous for anyone to be around him, especially the girl he loved.

He had a key to Carol's suite on the twelfth floor of the Peabody Hotel. He eased inside and saw her sleeping on the sofa. Elliott put a log on quiet embers and watched a new flame pop up and dance. A warm glass of CLIO waited next to her empty glass. A stack of files leaned against an ottoman. Lids were off rubber tubs scattered around the room. Papers were spread on the dining room table, bar, window sill, and mantel. Carol expanded the research effort after the horrible night at the Bell mansion.

Elliott stood above the lamp at the end of her sofa. He sipped his Cabernet and watched her breathe. Her long blonde hair fell off her shoulder. Her lashes were soft on her cheeks. Her hands were together beneath her head. Her shapely legs were outside the blanket and toes pushed under the cushion.

Even now your beauty, your existence, everything about you, takes my breath. I must break our promise tonight. I cannot tell you everything anymore . . . I need to go away.

When they first spoke a year ago, something touched his heart and calmed his darkness. The evil and pain sucking life from him, stopped. When they met months later, his world changed. She helped him control his demons, the monsters he hunted now living in his head and eating away at his soul. Elliott's perfect, photographic memory would never let him escape the sick details of the demented monsters, or the pain they inflicted upon all the helpless victims.

You touched me like no other, he thought. *You brought me from the edge, stopped me from committing suicide, when I could bear no more. You were the unexpected light in my dark world and more. But now . . . I cannot expose you to the unknowns coming my way. These dangers are far greater than the Butcher. You will not understand. Tonight is our last night together. If anything happened to you, it would kill me. I must go do what only I can.*

By the window at his knees he saw the open tub stacked with papers from the catacombs. In the flickering light the page on top caught his eye. The light touched lines of long numbers and letters, some reversed, some upside-down, and all spaced uneven. He saw a cryptic image with a coded message. The white space and black ink created the obscure pictures only Elliott could discern, images of symbols—peace, infinity, life, death and more.

Maybe these images are a validation of authenticity. Or they separate document from the thousands of decoys, he thought. *Or maybe they're used to group coded messages in the text.*

The month old puzzle remained a mystery.

Documents taken from the Brent catacombs were processed according to a strict protocol Elliott Sumner designd upon request by County Sheriff G.E. Taft. Law enforcement believed, among hundreds of boxes and thousands of documents, they would find imformation on the vicitms of the BCB: identities, dates of death, and locations of remains.

Elliott knew the hidden documents would shed new light on the veiled activities of Dr. Medino, the noted geneticist researching biogenic life extension. Some of the early evidence collected showed Dr. Medino used a section of the catacombs beneath the Brent mansion for organ and tissue procurement. The disturbing information confirmed Medino maintained a guardian-like relationship with Adam Duncan. Elliott wanted to know more about their work together, and the coded documents with the *Gilgamesh* stamp.

Guards were assigned to the catacombs. The rigid discovery and processing program required every single piece of paper be scanned, digitized, categorized, and electronically transfered to a secured VPN cloud before it left the catacombs to a secured location. The protected digital document would be analyzed by an select network of experts and top cryptologists around the world.

"Hi, Elliott." The words floated from the sofa.

Part of him hoped to hear her voice once more before carrying her to bed and leaving. Elliott turned from the window with a distant smile. She peered over the back of the sofa, her hair in sexy disarray, her look in love and inviting.

"Hello there." He came around to her. They embraced. Her arms wrapped tight around his muscular neck, her fingers spread into his thick hair, and her legs wrapped around his waist as he stood like an oak tree. They kissed. They could not get enough of each other. But this night would be different. Elliott's mission would end their relationship.

He sat on the sofa. Each took a glass. He filled hers. "Can you talk about it, Elliott?"

He looked in his glass. "I'm not sure what I'm doing is right."

She touched his arm. "You will know. And when you do, then we will talk. I trust you. I trust your instincts. I am certain you are miles ahead of everyone else, Elliott."

"You're just saying that because you're crazy about me." He pulled her close and they kissed again. "I've got an idea. You talk about your day." He eyed the piles scattered around the room and on the coffee table. "Looks like you've made some of your own headway."

"I'll let you off the hook, for now." The logs delivered by the Peabody concierge were damp. The one Elliott put on the fire started to sizzle and pop. They stared. The brilliant blues and greens with orange tips meszmerized. Elliott poured more wine.

"Okay, Miss Mason, top investigative reporter at the *Tribune*. How was your first day back?" He scanned the room of opened tubs and piles of papers.

"Actually, I've been here all day. Didn't go into the office, Christmas Eve and all, remember? I studied a few hundred documents found in the newest dirt room, number nine."

"They found another room down there?"

"Seems they do every week. These documents are different from the others, Elliott." She reached for the stack on the coffee table.

"Different how?"

"Lets go back to the night the Butcher took me off Beale Street."

"What new have your remembered?"

"Nothing. I'm talking about before he took me."

"You were here, right?"

"Yes. UPS delivered an envelope. It contained a parchment, a sheet of vellum folded twice. It came to me from one of my Washington DC sources."

"You were poking around on Gilgamesh?"

"Yes. The piece of vellum had the Gilgamesh watermark like we've seen on other documents in the catacombs." She opened the file and passed Elliott the fragile page. He held it up to the firelight.

"See the logo. It is the same logo on the vellum."

"Why didn't you tell me about this sooner?"

"After the Butcher kidnapped me, I forgot. Seeing these documents found in dirt room number nine, it reminded me."

Elliott poked at the sizzling log not wanting to reveal his concern. "Tell me more about the parchment, or the vellum as you call it."

"It was a table, five columns and twenty lines. I counted a hundred boxes. Each box had numbers or letters. Some were first initials and a name."

He stared at the fire. *I wish you hadn't seen this . . .*

"Elliott, I saw your name in one of the boxes—*esumner*." Elliott kept poking the fire. "Do you have anything to say about that?" she asked. Elliott shook his head.

"There were other names I recognized: *aduncan*, *jbellow*, and *bduncan*. There were more names and codes, but I did not have time to study them. If you remember, we were meeting for dinner. I planned to go over all of this with you that night."

"And that dinner never happened."

"Elliott, this connects you, your brothers, and your mother to Gilgamesh. I have no clue what it could mean. However, the *someone* pulling the strings may be this Gilgamesh entity."

Elliott returned to the sofa and his glass of wine and said nothing.

Carol pushed her hair back. "What do you think?"

Elliott shook his head and kept staring at the fire.

"I tried to reach my other D.C. source today, the reluctant one. He agreed to do some sniffing around in spite of his discomfort."

"Reluctant because he knows something about Gilgamesh"

"The opposite. Thirty years as a D.C. insider, he never heard the name. It freaked him out."

"What did he have to share?"

"Nothing. He vanished, Elliott."

"*Vanished," Elliott said.* Sounds a bit dramtic. You sure you want to use that word? People don't always do what they say. People go on vacations, change jobs, get sick . . ."

"A career government guy, Elliott. They do not get up one day and quit without telling anyone. They do not just depart without leaving new contact information."

"Sounds suspicious, but may be explainable. I would not assume the worst."

"Please, give me some credit forensic-man. I'm not new."

"Sorry. Continue."

"I asked a friend in the D.C. area to look into this very carefully. I discovered on the day I spoke to my source, he hung up the phone and took an extended vacation to an unknown destination. He never returned, Elliott."

"Extended vacation?"

"Apparently he accumulated nine months of unused vacation time over his thirty years."

"There you have it. He's taking his vacation time."

"Elliott. My friend tol me he was listed in Human Resources as terminating his employment on the day we talked on the phone. On that same day his computer was removed and office sealed. I sent a PI to his apartment. It had been ransacked."

"Sounds like he did something wrong. Maybe fired and investigated. It may not be related."

"They put his apartment on the market the same week he vanished," Carol said.

Elliott had to look away from Carol. She could read him. He held his glass to his lips and stayed on the fire. "It does sound suspicious." *But I can't tell you Adam gave me the vellum, in the crawl space of the Bell mansion before he passed out. I can't tell you what he said to me . . .*

"Elliott, I think Gilgamesh is the diabolical entity behind the deaths of your biological brothers and mother. After last night at the Bell mansion, and these cryptic documents, I am concerned they are now coming for you."

"That's a lot to think about, but it's late. Let's go to bed." He took her hand.

She smiled. "I guess you're right. Merry Christmas, Elliott."

"Let's hope . . ."

FOUR

"When danger calls, the rules change."
Steve Bradshaw

S he slept with her head on his chest. Elliott stared at the ceiling for hours. He could not sleep. If he had, he would have missed the most important call of his life. His cell phone on silent lit-up on the nightstand—an incoming call.

Under the bold words on the screen—U
NKNOWN CALLER—he saw 5:04 A.M. and December 25. *It's Christmas morning. Who has my number now . . . ?*

Everything in his world turned upside-down when he learned he had two biological brothers, and one was the Bluff City Butcher. Elliott would never forget the night in Albert's study. Max told them on the speakerphone. At that moment the Butcher stepped out of the shadows and put his blade to Elliott's carotid artery.

He knew Elliott had come to kill him and Albert, the last two names on the kill-list. But when Elliott looked into Adam's eyes he saw hesitation, confusion. Then the room filled, guns raised. Adam held his knife to Elliott's throat at the balcony doors. Adam whispered in his ear and jumped from the balcony—seconds later impaled on the cold, iron spire. That night a century-old hell storm had gathered. Elliott knew the three illegitimate sons of a billionaire patriarch stood in its eye. He knew Jack was dead and now Adam had killed the monster in him.

Did the unexpected suicide disrupt a sinister plan? Was Gilgamesh the secret entity on some mission? That night Elliott knew he stood alone, the

last surviving member of the elite progeny. He could be the last chance for some and the last obstacle for others. That night Adam Duncan's suicide became Elliott Sumner's unexpected doorway into hell.

He pressed the phone to his ear. *Are you going to be the one to blow this wide open for me?* He thought. *Or are you another dead end?*

He had a raspy voice—*a heavy smoker.* Although gruff and unfamiliar, he wanted to talk about what no one else would. The voice used words like, *soldier,* and *AWOL.* He wanted something from Elliott. In return, he promised information on Gilgamesh. They agreed on a meeting—alone on the rooftop of the Peabody Hotel after sundown, thirteen hours away. The voice said his name, Michael.

The next time the sun set, Elliott smelled a cigarette in the stairwell of the Peabody Hotel on sixth floor. *Not surprising, he thought. Michael's a smoker. He would be early. Who else would use these stairs on Christmas day?* Elliott climbed eight more flights checking at each turn. He stood at the door to the roof—it was ajar. *I hate surprises.*

When he stepped into the cold night air and entered an empty world high above an empty city. Elliott saw the tall, lanky silhouette wearing a hat leaning against the railing on the west side. He was a hundred feet away. His cigarette smoke laced the breeze drifting across the roof.

Elliott approached from behind taking in the surroundings. The man in the hat didn't move. The First Tennessee Bank sat to the north, the other side of Union Avenue, the highest ground. To the northwest a parking garage blocked the view of the river. It had a one-floor advantage and numerous, horizontal shadows for someone to hide. And the *Memphis Business Journal* erecter-set signage loomed above the corner building on Main two blocks west. It provided a plethora of obscure opportunities for snipers.

At twenty-seven paces Elliott passed the Peabody duck house. After twelve more, he took a position at the railing down from the smoking hat. A blast of the dying December day met him as the last of the Memphis sun slid beneath the horizon. Flapping raincoats and snapping pant legs filled the quiet like a regatta coming about. As the sky darkened, the giant white snake that cut the country down the middle melted into the black Mississippi River Valley.

"Nice view, Dr. Sumner. I like your town." Michael said.

"Not my town," he replied. "You want out of Gilgamesh?"

"That's right." He sucked his smoke. "You're a Texan."

"I'm not here for banter. You got my attention. Why should I believe anything you say?"

"Let me make this easy. You don't need to believe me." Michael sucked one more time and flicked the hot orange butt into the air like a bottle rocket. The burning spray was swallowed.

"There's not enough time to get you comfy." He lit another. "This is about sharing. We have information you want, and you have something we need. No time for games."

"We? I see only you."

"There's another, but not tonight. We don't have a lot of time."

"Let's make time. Tell me about me."

"Is this a test?" He turned his head but stayed in the shadows.

Elliott stared at the river and studied Michael in periphery—flat face and fat lower lip, smooth skin and trimmed mustache, wire glasses with crystal-clean lenses, and manicured finger nails. In his mid-forties, the emaciated intellectual hid behind an invented character.

The celestial glow of the city grew, and the downtown lights became relevant. Elliott studied Michael like no other. From the phone to the rooftop, he assessed the most subtle details. He would here the story behind the words, the secrets held close, the overstated and understated, the truths and the lies. Elliott would devour the minuscule facial contortions and fleeting tics. He would catch each misstep, the most revealing voice inflexions, hesitations, stutters, and the telling pauses. Elliott would know more than Michael ever intended to share. His psychological assessments, advanced training, and perfect memory were unparalleled.

The tattered hat Michael wore belonged to a much older man, one who lived a very different life. *Was he an old friend, or is he now a dead pedestrian?* And the long, dark raincoat, two sizes too large. And the cross-country shoes, peeking from under the worn brown khakis, were new. All the articles of clothing were taken, borrowed, or purchased. It revealed a desperate or feeble attempt at a disguise. *This effort is not for me. You're trying to blend in. You're hiding from someone. Is it Gilgamesh? Are they hunting you now?*

"Yes, it is a test," Elliott said. "And you better pass or you'll be finishing your smoke alone." Michael's irritated laughter turned into a hacking cough.

"November 1968, Abilene, William and Martha found a

baby in a basket on their front porch, Dr. Sumner. I know who put you there and why. The feeling of abandonment would shape you more than anything else, more than your adoptive parents or the deranged fiends residing in your genius brain—those demons who tried to kill you in Dallas."

Only three doctors know about . . . How could you know? Do you know about my ongoing battle, the physical toll of an eidetic memory? Do you know I live on the edge of sanity?

"Your adoptive parents were William Sumner, the city prosecutor, and Martha, the family physician. Later in life you took a little something from both—how thoughtful. Out of all the professions you chose forensic pathology, medical/legal jurisprudence. And you became the youngest medical examiner in Texas history, twenty-six when you got started."

Elliott saw movement in the garage. Michael seemed unaware.

"When your brother decided to be a human shish kebab the other night, the proverbial shit hit the Gilgamesh fan. Cell phones buzzed around the world. Big plans changed." Michael lit another cigarette and flicked the spent butt to the steets below.

"Why is Adam's suicide important to Gilgamesh?"

"Short answer, they had some common goals. His suicide changed things."

"Common goals?"

"I assume we're good here." Michael said.

"Yes."

"Sorry. Wasn't talking to you, Sumner."

"Are you wearing a wire?"

"Yes."

"Why?"

"There are two of us, remember? I'm clearing the path, so to speak." He pulled an envelope from his pocket and held it out behind his back. His eyes moved to the parking garage.

"Take this. If you survive the week, you'll need it."

"Gee, I don't know how to thank you," Elliott chided as he took the envelope.

"You will meet Bernardo Yaroslav Kuzma in New York City in four days. This tells you when and where. There is a backup plan in case Mr. Kuzma must abort."

"And who is Kuzma?"

"A member of the founders board. He is one of the twelve running Gilgamesh."

"And tell me why a founder would want to meet with me."

"Mr. Kuzma will answer all your questions."

"That's great. And what about you? Why are you in this, whoever you are?"

"Let's say I'm doing a favor for a friend. Leave it at that." Thee flash across the way caught Michael's eye. "You better go now. Mr. Kuzma confirmed the meeting. We are done here."

"He confirmed the next meeting? What did he have to think over?"

"If he didn't like you, I would kill you."

"Nice to be liked, I suppose. I happy Mr. Kuzma wants to meet me, but I'm not so sure I want to meet him. Tell me going on, Michael."

"Mr. Kuzma knows your life from before birth. He knows your lineage, innate gifts, and reputation. He knows more about you than you know about you. But, he does not know Elliott Sumner, the man you are today. He wanted comfort . . . you are the one."

"The one what?"

"The one to stop Gilgamesh."

"Is he listening now?"

"No. He is gone. It is four in the morning for him."

Elliott put it together. The name and the time zone. *Kuzma's in Russia.*

Michael opened his coat and felt for the gun jammed under his belt. He lit his next smoke off the last and flicked it over the side with the others. Elliott backed from the railing and slid the envelop in his pocket, and held down his coat as the next gust climbed the building.

"Outside of Mr. Kuzma, does anyone know you're here, Michael?" Elliott asked.

"No one."

"Do you see the man's head moving, the dark cement wall in that garage?"

"Yes, I see him. He's been here since I arrived."

"He has a rifle with a scope," Elliott said looking away."

"Are you certian?"

"A McMillan TAC-50, rotary bolt action, 736 mm barrel with a 5-round box magazine."

"You're as good as they say." Michael smiled for the first time. Elliott watched the head drop below the cement wall.

"Let's get out of here."

"You leave now. I'll cover to the door. After that, you're on your own. *You go now!*"

"No. Back away with me. We leave together, Michael. There's no benefit for either staying. You're could be vulnerable."

If they left three seconds sooner, it could be different. Both missed the shooter tied to the back of the MBJ sign. The end of his barrel poked out a letter. Michael had no time to consider Elliott's logical proposal.

The soft pop, a car backfire in the streets below, seemed harmless as it rolled through the empty city. Michael's hat flew off his head, and he turned to Elliott. His eyes were fixed. Michael was dead, but his body did not know yet.

"*Michael . . .*"

Above the cigarette pinched in his lips, at the center of the forehead, a dime-sized hole bled. His legs buckled and he fell toward the railing.

Elliott jumped to him out of instinct, the doctor in him, the medic in the field of battle determined to save life. Elliott did not hear the next, soft pop. The plaster exploded on the piller where his head would have been.

He dropped to the roof and rolled beneath the barrage of pops and pitted explosions following him. He rolled to the west wall of the duck house atop the Peabody Hotel.

Michae's dead, he thought. There're at least two high-powered rifles with scopes, and probably night-vision, pointed at me. I've been hit! The headshot's a graze, a slow bleeder thank God. My calf's killing me. I think the bullet went through—yup. One shot, two holes—it exited. He ripped off a pant leg and tied a compression bandage over the wounds. *That'll do for a while.*

I've got to get out of here. The stairwell's not an option. The elevator's shut down. There's no help. It's Christmas night . . . a skeleton crew in the hotel. These people have all the time they need, unless they think I'm gone. Maybe someone heard the shots? I counted ten. Maybe they're only after Michael. No. This is my introduction to Gilgamesh?

From the shadows he watched. One held a rifle and the other talked on a cell phone. They were new, standing on the roof of the First Tennessee Bank to the north and looking at the MBJ sign. *They're together. But the bank guys don't see me.*

Two more heads popped up on the bank building—now four. *How important is this? How many are you? You still don't see me. The one shooting as I rolled must think I got away. Maybe he shot before the others were in place, a rogue soldier.* Elliott's pocket vibrated. *Can't look now, the light will give me away. Someone's coming . . .*

He tried to use his leg, but it screamed in pain. The stairwell door opened onto the roof. Elliott dragged his useless leg along the south wall of the duck house. Seventy feet out, he eased an eye to the edge. More were coming. Bent down and armed, they moved to Michael's body.

You guys don't know I'm over here. Maybe you think I left the rooftop. Get Michael and leave. I survive this nightmare. Three, four, five, six, seven . . . He stopped counting. Now the small army stood at the west edge of the rooftop. Gilgamesh would not send fourteen to recover one body. Elliott crawled to the southwest corner of the duck house and watched them stuff Michael into a large trunk. Four carried it to the stairwell and disappeared. Ten fanned-out along along the west railing and moved east in a line. One followed the chipped cement trail and would find the blood. It would take him to the duck house.

Elliott had less than a minute to do something, anything. The narrow shadow on the south wall would not do. *They have guns tight to their shoulders, and noses to their barrels, and tiny red dots dancing on the roof. Where they look, their guns point. I'm injured and trapped. I can't get too much farther. There's no way off this roof . . .*

The tip came in at 5:30 a.m.—Elliott Sumner agreed to a meeting on rooftop of the Peabody Hotel, sundown Christmas day. It would be the perfect setting and time. New developments called for immediate and aggressive action. The kill-order went out. The stealth, midsouth team assembled—eliminate Sumner, neutralize witnesses, and remove all obstacles. Bodies and evidence of event to be sterilized—scrub the scene. Transport of bodies to alternate Memphis drop site required, Brent catacombs no longer an option.

No one knew the the dead guy. They took a picture and removed him from the rooftop.

The rusted vent on the south wall of the duck house seemed big enough for a man to squeeze through. Elliott pried it open and went in head first. When he closed the vent, he found an inside latch covered in cobwebs. When he slid it in place, he saw boots through the louvers.

They stood there. Fingers pulled at the vent. It did not move. Elliott held his breath and sunk deeper into the dark, dank crawl space. The flashlight fell short as it moved around the louvers, then went out.

Would they know this is my only option? Did I leave blood . . . ?

"Sumner's not here, sir," the man said and paused.

Who's are you talking to?

"We think enough time between first shooting and our team taking the roof, sir."

You're on a radio . . .

"Yes, sir. Sterilize the area. A team is checking the Peabody and surroundings. No more than an hour . . . out."

FIVE

"What unknown power governs men? On what feeble causes do their destinies hinge?"
Voltaire

"The Bluff City Butcher is dead," he mumbled as he poured a disgusting stream of sugar into his coffee. Director Wade arrived early for the impromptu 8:00 p.m. meeting Christmas night. City streets, parking lots, and the mayor's halls were empty.

"The Bluff City Butcher is dead," he whispered crossing the conference room, an unfriendly place, always cold and dim and smelled like citrus and old dust. He could hear a busy motor somewhere in the bowels of the building. It whined in the air vents without a known purpose.

"The Bluff City Butcher is dead," he boomed, looking out the long, tall windows at the Hernando de Soto Bridge lighting up the river and the banks and a barge and the surface of the coffee shaking in his mug. He could never again look at the enormous structure without seeing the three-headed body swinging on a rope. The police director dreams the same dream every night, the Butcher standing on the bridge smiling at him and saying; *"You're next . . ."*

On April 8th, the monster of Memphis urban legend went public. It was the day the Memphis police had no choice but to tell the world the serial killer existed, the one they knew for more than two decades. Unprepared, Wade turned from the window into the shiny, pinstriped, black suit, stiff white shirt, loud Christmas tie, and Grinch scowl.

"And how sure are you?" barked the mayor with a squinted eye and furrowed brow. *How could such a man climb the ranks of the Memphis Police Department,* he wondered? *And how much longer am I going to keep you around?*

"Good evening, Mr. Mayor. Well, sir, I'm as sure as anyone can be. In the end, the BCB is just a man."

"Don't you think it might be an understatement, Director Wade? This *just-a-man* killed over one-hundred-and-fifty people in six states. He fed on the midsouth for a very long time."

"We didn't know what we were dealing with until the end, sir. We thought an urban legend like Bigfoot. Sightings. When we realized he existed, we got to work."

The mayor leaned closer. "This man killed midsoutherners and took body parts. People went missing. There were bizarre accidental deaths and suicides. He hid everything. When his twisted needs changed, he put his victims on public display and taunted law enforcement. I think then you were forced to accept what our people had been telling you for years, Director."

"There were some who believed we were . . ."

"Isn't it when *you* reluctantly accepted the relentless and urgent recommendations from your top homicide detective, Tony Wilcox? Only after the Butcher went public did you listen to him, and the strong advice from the top forensic pathologist and serial-killer hunter in the world, Dr. Sumner. And Director Wade, isn't it when you were forced to address the extensive findings of Miss Mason, the Pulitzer Prize winning investigative reporter brought to Memphis by Albert Bell to lead the Cold Case Collaboration I demanded be set up?"

"I think the . . ."

"And if we are being completely honest tonight, isn't it true *you* were the *last* person in Memphis, Tennessee, to accept the existence of the Bluff City Butcher?" The mayor straightened up and buttoned his coat. His eyes were on fire.

"As head of the police department, it is incumbent I stay with time-tested policies and procedures. Sir, I brought in the FBI. I assigned Detective Wilcox to the cases. Sir, I engaged Dr. Sumner, and I coordinated the collaboration with the *Memphis Tribune*.

"As you are, I'm first and foremost concerned about the welfare of our community. In my role I must assess moving targets and evolving situations. I process mountains of input from hundreds of people. No one imagined the nature of this beast or extent of the carnage. No one understood who or what we were dealing with until the end—no one but Elliott Sumner. Our department had an impossible mission. We hunted a genius psychopath, a killing machine."

"You made the decision to keep this atrocity behind closed doors," the mayor huffed. "You kept the public in the dark. You allowed a monster to walk the streets of Memphis without warning the people. All rests with you, Director Wade."

"But, sir . . ."

"The BCB controlled you. Our police department and the FBI were no match."

"We had little information to warrant abandonment of standard operating procedures, those used by law enforcement across the country. I still believe conducting police investigations in a low profile and proprietary manner is in the best interest of the public I am sworn to protect. We know when we broadcast our moves and findings, we educate the criminals we hunt. It prolongs the crisis, puts more at risk, and increases our opportunity to fail."

"Apprehending this serial killer took twenty-five years. Are you selling this to me today?" With arms crossed on his chest, he rocked on heels in disgust.

"Back to your first question—*yes*—I think the man who jumped off Albert Bell's balcony on December 23 is the Bluff City Butcher. A terrible thing to watch even if the he's a monster, the most dangerous serial killer in American history. I'm sure you saw the police video of . . ."

With his back to Wade pouring coffee, the mayor finished his sentence. " . . . the man on the roof of the Bell mansion with the seven-foot spire out his back. Yes. I saw the miserable video." He sat down at the end of the long conference table and pointed to a chair.

The director squeezed into a chair across from him. With seething eyes on his coffee cup the mayor growled, "It looked like the Butcher died that night, director. But looks can be deceiving. Are *you* sure the monster is dead? Can you guarantee me our city is safe?"

Wade wrung his hands under the table. *You've never liked me. You've been looking for a way to toss me out on my ass ever since you took office. But you gotta have the support of the people or you're toast. Chances for reelection put at risk. You can beat on me all you want, but I know one thing—asshole—the people believe the Bluff City Butcher went down on my watch. I may have been a problem behind the scenes, but the write-ups make me bulletproof for a while.*

The mayor walked to the window looking at the Mississippi

River. The snow started again. He turned and stared a hole through the director. "This is the third time the Butcher died. You didn't get it right in the past, did you?"

"No sir."

"Each time you thought you got it right. Each time you stopped looking when you were ninety-nine percent certian. Is that a fair statement?"

You want to hang me on the rack tonight so you can finish me off later. Like all political animals, you know the game. There's no way out of this chokehold. "Yes. I was never one hundred percent sure, Mr. Mayor."

Wade thinks I'm trying to get rid of him, thought the mayor. *He's not hearing me. I don't think he has it in him. This is not about him or me. This is about Memphis, the people depend on us. I can't let another mistake be made. The costs have been too great in my city.*

He leaned across the table. "This is why I asked you here tonight. You are the Director of the Memphis Police Department. You are the one responsible. Do you have the Bluff City Butcher this time? Is he dead, or is there another one percent? Is there another unimaginable situation you have not considered? Are we fooled again, Director Wade?"

The director lifted his head and looked straight into the mayor's eyes. With all the strength and conviction he could muster he said, "The Bluff City Butcher is dead. I am one-hundred percent positive. There is no sequel to this horrific urban legend. If I am wrong, I will give you my badge, Mr. Mayor."

"If you are wrong, Director Wade, I will take your badge and run you out of Memphis. That is my promise to you, sir." The mayor turned and disappeared into the hollow hall.

The room smelled like citrus and old dust again. Wade shivered. The whining motor in the vents seemed louder and desperate. The empty building got darker. Wade stayed seated at the long conference table, his eyes on the Hernando de Soto, and now holding a cold coffee. His hand trembled when he set the cup on the saucer. There were a few clicks and then the whining motor took over. Collin Wade's chair was wet—he lied to the mayor . . .

SIX

"Everything you can imagine is real."
Pablo Picasso

"**P**ay attention, Womack," she barked. "And quit looking for ghosts and goblins. Get over here. Give me a hand with this thing."

Deputy Sutter was smaller than her mouth. The five-five, hundred-fourteen pound redheaded firecracker from Omaha came to Memphis with an idiot she divorced six months later. A month before the breakup, she signed on with the Shelby County Sheriff's Office and started training at the academy. Four years later, the idiot lived in Omaha and she made deputy. Her junior status worked her on the night shift Christmas day processing documents underground—not her idea of exciting police work.

Balancing on the edge of a bent stepladder commandeered from a broom closet in the old mansion, Sutter reached out as far as her body would allow. She pulled another cardboard box over decades of dusty cobwebs, rat droppings, and shells of dead things.

"Where in god's living hell are you, Womack?" she called out.

The twenty-two-year-old rookie moved from the dark into the light of the portable flood lamps. He stood there like a boy coming home at suppertime, waiting to be told to clean up. He wore dirty goggles and filthy paper mask. His latex gloves were bunched to his wrists and a layer of powdered dirt covered his curly, black hair. Womack took hold of Sutter's box like a hot turkey coming out of the oven. He set it next to the aluminum table holding two laptops and scanner. Womack sat down on his lawn chair and resumed his vigil.

"This place is creepy," he mumbled.

Sutter took her seat at the other end and leaned over the last of her stack of documents to scan before she would open the new box. The discolored papers were no longer brittle. At the bottom of each box they were damp and moldy. After weeks of experience, she knew how to separate the delicate papers without destroying them in the process. Her unique talent only got her more work. Sutter held the record for assignment to the Brent catacombs.

"How many times you worked down here?" Womack asked with his back to her.

"Thirty-seven now." She scanned the last few papers and placed them in one of the designated rubber tubs going topside at the end of the shift. She wiped dirt off the new box and opened it. Inside were more papers. She stopped reading weeks ago—too many. For processing purposes, she only looked for *sorting words* according to protocol: Butcher, Duncan, Bell, Medino, Gilgamesh, LIFE2, Sumner, and Bellow.

"Womack, are you gonna process any more docs or chase ghosts the rest of the shift?" Sutter pushed the rookie to no avail.

"Hard to believe a serial killer lived down here, right under the nose of the sheriff." Womack stared into the cool darkness of the long, narrow dirt room they designated as #9. The latest discovery of many.

"Get it right, Womack. The house above us sat empty for decades in these woods. County took it over for free, the house and twenty-five acres in the boonies. All I know is the county authorized a build-out to convert the place into a substation for the north county people. It's never been a headquarters, and a lot of the place has been sealed because it's unsafe."

"I'm just sayin' . . ."

"No. You're *just listening* to me. This place has a history. Learn it Womack. Built by the Bell family in the early 1900's. They moved to their new place in east Memphis and sold it to a guy named Brent in the '60s. He was a weirdo hermit. Old man Brent died alone. Ruled cause of death undetermined. Some say the Butcher killer him and made it look like a suicde. This place never sold. Sat empty until it someone decided to give it to the county for a dollar. That's why the county remodeled the place. The sheriff's office needed a north substation. They remodeled two floors of the mansion and sealed off the rest—too much to fix."

"I'm just commenting on the obvious. A serial killer lived here. It's a spooky thing. Just imagine how the Bluff City Butcher killed people at night and dragged them back here. The monster slept under the sheriff's butt during the day. The guy had balls."

"If you ever want to get anywhere with your career, you need to stop this kind of talk. Sounds like you're pointing fingers, saying the sheriff's stupid or something. If the county had money they would have sent in a demolition crew, leveled the mansion, and built a nice place on the free land. They would have found the catacombs and all this stuff."

"Sorry, didn't mean anything by it." He looked back at Sutter.

"You think it's a little scary they keep finding new tunnels and rooms down here, like this room? It tells me they don't have a clue what's down here."

"Sheriff Taft had a hissy-fit when they found the catacombs in the first place." She scanned another document never looking up. "They think this is important stuff down here."

"Like what?"

"Information on the people the BCB killed—names, location of remains."

"Something is down here with us," Womack whispered as he squinted into the darkness.

"They say the Butcher lived down here a few decades." Sutter cleaned her goggles with a single swipe of the forearm. "Last count, he killed one-hundred-sixty-seven. Killed some down here."

Womack forced out a weak chuckle as a drop of sweat left his sideburn to his chin even thought the temperature in the catacombs stayed 67°F year round.

"I'll bet some were killed in this room—number nine—where we are right now. Sutter, we are in a friggin horror movie."

"Cool it, Womack. The Butcher's dead. Stop with the drama."

"Can you imagine being a victim? I heard the BCB moved his knife through the air so fast it looked like a fanning blur. If he didn't decapitate or dismember you, he'd ram an ice pick in your brain, top of your skull, immediate paralysis."

Womack swallowed hard and looked around. "And then he harvested organs." He wiped his forehead, leaving mud streaks like Indian war paint. "And he kept his victims alive a while. You think they watched him cut-up others waiting for their turn?"

"Get back to work or I'm writing you up."

"Bet they were dissected like frogs in biology class. Got pithed, brain scrambled with that ice pick." Womack chuckled, but his hands twitched when he screwed the cap on his bottled water. He leaned and squinted. *Shit. What just moved? I'm scaring myself.*

"Womack. Get back to . . ."

"*Whoa!* Are you kidding me? No way," he whispered. "Sutter, I swear. I saw a humongus shadow move over there." He pulled out his gun. *Please be an illusion . . .*

Sutter ignored him. "Just because you're a rookie doesn't mean you've got to act like one all the time. Put your gun away before you shoot yourself."

Womack holstered his gun and pointed his light into the depths of the dirt room. The meager beam cut ten feet into the soup. *Damn. The dust is stirred.* Without a word he ventured out as Sutter stayed in her last stack of docs, and her mind wandered between her miserable private life and the mysteries in the catacombs.

Must admit, he makes some good points, she thought. The biospeleologists brought in were supposed to map the tunnels. Cost a lot of money. They dropped the ball. The sheriff wanted to get us down here fast anyway—I get it. There's evidence down here. Could help find some of the missin' folks. But we're finding new tunnels and rooms loaded with boxes, seems every week. Womack's right. No telling what else is down here. The man-made tunnels are at least sixty years old. The natural catacombs have been here hundreds of years. This place could have been important to someone—and could still be. Who in the hell is this Gilgamesh I'm seein' on some of these docs?

"Womack," she called out. "I'm not totally disagreeing with you. Just sayin'. I agree this is a lousy place to be right now. Down right spooky at times." She keyed in more data. "But we've got a job to do. Look at this as just one assignment. One day we'll look back and laugh." She hit enter. "The only things down here are you, me, and a few skinny rats." Sutter chuckled and tossed the document into a rubber tub.

She reached for another.

"Okay. Don't be giving me the silent treatment, rookie." She checked her watch and punched numbers on the keyboard. "It's 22:00. After I finish this one, we can take a break. Go topside and get some fresh air."

Sutter looked up from the keyboard. She realized she'd been talking for several minutes and motor-mouth had not said a word. "Womack, talk to me."

She turned. His chair was empty. *"Womack!"*

SEVEN

"Monsters are real, and ghosts are real too."
Stephen King

It was two in the morning. Memphis Homicide Detective Tony Wilcox emerged from the rotted, cellar doors punching numbers on his cell. He stopped on the top step and puked. After sucking in the cool night air, he looked for a tree to piss on.

The manmade ravine behind the Brent mansion dropped seven feet below the rest of the grounds. It ran fifty yards north into miles of thick woods. After the county sheriff's office found the catacombs—the home of the BCB and depository for boxes of curious documents—the ravine's purpose started to make sense. Anyone could enter and leave, day or night, without detection. It was an ideal route from the woods to the Brent mansion cellar. A hole in the wall went to the catacombs. It also explained how the Butcher got around never seen. The catacombs reached under the city and north along the Mississippi River as far as Atoka.

Tony walked into the moon shade of a giant oak and unzipped. Standing at the massive trunk he watched the wind roll the tall grass. He tapped *speed dial* on his cell.

"Elliott, where are you? You did not pick up earlier and you did not get back to me."

"I'm in Millington at the moment."

"At our private medical facility?"

"Yes." *I'm not telling you about my Peabody rooftop experience. Not yet.*

"What in the hell happened to you? Did you go somewhere alone again? I told you to stop that shit—especially during this time of uncertainty. You're not superman, goddamnit."

"We'll talk later. I'm ok. Why the call?"

"We lost two of our people this morning. Two county deputies were killed in the catacomb about four hours ago."

"Who would attack deputies at a secured site on Christmas night?"

"Good question. I just stepped outside for some air. The M.E. is down there now."

"You don't call me on your homicides. What's bothering you about these?"

"Both were carved up bad, Elliott. A lot of blood down there. Lacerations to the neck, chest, and stomach area. I'm talkin' single sweeps of a goddamn razor or sharp-ass knife. The carotids and jugulars on both deputies are cut with same arc. Bates is not a happy camper right now. He is very disturbed over what he's seein' down there. He's taking a long damn time. Getting a close look at those wounds before anybody gets moved."

"That's what he should do, Tee. It's not unusual."

"Bates calls the guy THE SWEEPER, single passes and all. Said each pass got vital targets. Said the killer had experience, skills he's seen only one time before."

"THE SWEEPER?" Elliott said.

"It fits, Elliott."

"Is Dr. Bates reaching conclusions or are those yours?"

"I have only theories with this stuff. I look to smart guys like you for conclusions. Bates kept using words like *precision* and *powerful* and *high-velocity*. Said cut depths were just enough to sever a targeted artery. We know that is a very rare skill." Tony turned. *What was that? Sounded like someone passed by but there's no one here. I'm alone.*

"What else?" Elliott asked. The nurse put the last roll of tape on his leg wound dressing. His calf had been cleaned, the bullet hole irrigated, medicated and stitched. They stuck him with a needle in one arm for the pain and the other with a broad-spectrum antibiotic.

Tony refocused. "The chest wounds on both were left-to-right. Nicked some ribs and cut into the . . . cavity."

"Thoracic."

"Yeah. Thoracic cavity got cut open in places."

"Perforations."

"Yeah. Perforations and the pneumo-thing."

"Thorax."

"Right, the pneumothorax. Goddamn medical terms. Deputy Womack died first, a strong, healthy male. He didn't know what hit him, Elliott. He had a flashlight in his hand and his gun in the holster. Deputy Sutter, a thirty-four, strong female, went down next. Bates believes she got to Womack a few minutes after he went down. She lost her right arm above the elbow, Elliott. Lying in the dirt a few feet from her body."

"Dr. Bates confirm single-pass dismemberment?"

"Yep. Went through bone like a hot knife in butter. No bone chips. High velocity sweep with a razor-sharp knife."

"What else?" Elliott asked.

"Remember the Voss case—out federal agent, 2008? Like

him, Sutter lost an arm. In both cases they were holding a gun. Both got one shot off. Remember?"

"You know I remember everything, Tee."

"Goddamn Elliott. Not all of us have photographic memories. Cut me some slack. This is the way mortals talk. I'm thinking out loud."

"Little edgy tonight. Did you make yourself vomit again?"

"Hell yes. It settles my stomach. Not a big deal. This crap is starting to get to me. I don't know how much longer I can do it."

"Medically, I do not approve of forced regurgitation as a stress-relieving measure. But I understand. And we both know you're not walking away from anything. Neither am I. So tell me what you're trying to say, Tee."

"Deputy Sutter's hand was grippin' the gun tight. She was scared, Elliott."

"Of course she was scared. I would expect nothing less."

"*Shit!* What in the hell?" Tony dropped the cell phone.

"What's going on . . . ?"

He picked it up and moved his hand to his gun as he peered around the fat trunk. "Hey."

"Hey what?" Elliott asked.

"Elliott." he whispered.

"Talk Tony."

"Someone's here. I heard a goddamn stick break, leaves rustle, and some thrashing. But I don't see a damn thing. It sounded close. Wait. Hold on, Elliott."

Tony eased around the base of the tree, his cell pressed to his ear and hand on his holstered gun. He looked up the ravine to the woods—nothing. He scanned the junipers along the back of the mansion—nothing. He studied the ridge on each side of the ravine—nothing.

"I don't get it. I have people crawling all over the catacombs and running around the Brent grounds. Not a soul in this ravine but me."

"Tee, what's happening where you are right now?"

"Nothing I see. I'm under one of three big-ass oak trees."

"You need to get with your people. It's not a good idea to be alone."

"Wait. I hear . . . a faint . . . rustling . . . sound . . . again," he whispered pulling out his gun.

"Tony. You took out your gun. I know you. Listen to your instincts. Whoever killed those two deputies is nearby. You don't imagine things."

"I don't get it," Tony said. "The half-moon is lighting up the place pretty decent." He walked around the oak tree in a wider circle and returned to the base. "Another twig snapped."

"What's happening on the Brent grounds?" Elliott asked.

"The goddamn Normandy invasion. There are no less than twenty squad cars out here and maybe thirty cops with dogs. Our people are all over this place except the marshy ravine—it's not easy to navigate for anyone, and you're visible to anyone looking into the ravine.

"Makes sense, but the bad guy knows that too."

"You know what happens when a cop gets killed? This time two—a rookie and a female deputy. That's pretty damn bad, Elliott. My people are motivated. They want to kill somethin'."

"If your *sweeper* is still there, he's stuck. He hiding and desperate."

"It's quiet now. I bet it was the wind. I'm beat to hell, Elliott." Tony leaned agains the fat trunk holstering his gun.

"Keep an eye open. You may be the easiest exit opportunity for your perp."

"Thanks, Elliott. I'm not a pussy."

"We are sensitive tonight," Elliott chided.

"Did I tell you Deputy Sutter got a shot off?"

"You mentioned that."

"We'll be looking for the bullet after Bates gets done down there."

"Or maybe she got him. Maybe he's carrying the bullet around."

"We can only hope." Tony saw flashlights moving down the ridge to the woods, dogs barking. "You know, with all these people out here I'll bet the sounds are bouncing off the back of this mansion and rolling around in this ravine messing with me."

"Possible. But I would stay with your instincts."

"Elliott, the eyes. The look on their faces. Not typical. It was terror. Like we saw with the Butcher's victims. Do you have anything to tell me?"

"It is not the Butcher. Stop. Come up with another theory?"

"Give me time." Tony checked his watch.

"Who found the bodies?" Elliott asked.

"The next shift. Sutter and Womack worked the night shift."

"Alone? That's not protocol. No one knows what is down there, Tee."

"It's Christmas. We have not had one single incident. And the Butcher took himself out of the equation a few nights ago. Sheriff Taft cut back staffing for the holidays. They did keep security at the same level topside. They guarded the entrance to the catacombs and patrolled the property."

"You mean guarded the known entrances."

"Right. Bates wants you at the inquest, 06:00, in four hours."

"Sorry, not going to work for me this time my friend," Elliott shot back.

"You know you need to be there. The *sweeper* could be another Butcher type."

"I have my reasons."

"Talk to me, Elliott."

"Suffice it to say some people have taken an interest in me. Best I lay low until I figure out who and why."

"It explains your Millington trip. You're injured. What happened in my city?"

"A man died on the Peabody roof around seven last night—high powered rifle. You won't find a body or evidence anything happened up there. These were real pros."

"You met with unknowns on top of the Peabody and did not tell me?"

"I did not expect it to go quite so badly."

"Nothing is predictable until we know more about why the BCB decided to end his life."

"I often meet with informants, people who do not want to be seen. As much as I would like you to join me, you are a recognizeable figure. Tends to change the dynamics of a friendly, stealth get together. I'm working on something I'm not ready to talk about. You've got your job, I've got mine."

"What happened, Elliott? Don't wait too long this time to bring me in."

"They killed the man I met. They tried to kill me. I ruined their day."

"Is this connected to the Butcher's suicide?"

"Yes. Some were not pleased when he failed to kill me and Albert Bell. The Bell scions are being eliminated."

"What the hell is a *scion*?"

"A descendant. Jack Bellow, Adam Duncan, and I are direct descendants of Albert Bell. Two are dead. I'm the last one standing. There is an order for my termination."

"I thought after the hell the Butcher put us through we would have smooth sailing a while. You're the next in line for the Bell family fortune, the next Bell patriarch. Did the man you met tell you who was hunting you?"

"I don't think money is what this is about."

"Fifty billion is a lot of money to everybody, Elliott."

"Not everybody. Based on the resources deployed and the precision operation I witnessed, they have money and are on a mission."

"You got a name?"

"Gilgamesh."

"I've seen it on some documents out of the catacombs. Great. Another damn mystery. You need toget to this inquest, Elliott. I think it's connected in some way."

"Why?"

"These deputies were in a new room. Maybe we're getting close to something Gilgamesh wants kept burried."

"My presence would put people in danger."

"You're a damn genius. Come up with a way."

Elliott waved off the nurse holding a needle.

"You need to see these bodies, Elliott. You will find something."

"Only you and Bates can know I'm coming. Bates must be educated on the risk. Buy in completely. Or there will be consequences."

"I'm texting him now. He already replied, short and sweet. If Elliott wants presence unknown . . . done. Guess he's been through enough with you."

"Good. I'll be there."

"You'll need more eyes on this new mess, Elliott. If fifty billion dollars is not a motivator, your advisory is powerful, driven, and many. Unlimited resources. An enormous network. You need a team this time. Solo, you won't last."

"You may be right."

"The Butcher may be the tip of the iceberg," Tony said.

"If they sent Adam to kill us, I need to know why Adam worked for the entity. His decision to let Albert and me live had to be spontaneous. It had to disrupte some larger plan."

"The way these deputies died worries me. It's like there's another. Someone is picking up where the Butcher left off."

"I hope not. We won't solve this tonight."

"I've got to get back down in the catacombs."

"Later, Tee."

Under the giant oak tree

Tony pocketed his cell and glanced down the ravine. This time he heard rustling of leaves with a swishing sound.

Alone and off the phone

Tony made the same mistakes. He looked in all the wrong places until the final seconds. When he looked up, it was over.

On the way down the ten-inch blade flashed in the moonlight. Tony reached for his gun. The two-hundred-forty pounds of rage dropped from the branches and crushed Tony to the ground, and slashing steel cut through the crisp night air —*swoosh!*

EIGHT

"What in the . . ." Carlson jumped. The giant pneumatic doors gushed open. Everyone in the county morgue walk-in refrigerator was supposed to be dead. Elliott Sumner's six-four frame unfolded from the billowy blast of crystal fog rolling into the desolate hall of scuffed linoleum and ceramic tiles.

"Hello, Robert." He brushed frost from his coat and threw hair from his eyes as if he just stepped off a bus at his stop. "I left you a slightly used crash bag in there."

Still stuck in the surrealistic moment, Carlson muttered, "How did you . . . ?"

"My EMT friends delivered me twenty minutes ago. I laid low a while." Elliott adjusted his cuffs and coat sleeves with snapping tugs and ran the creases of his lapels with sliding pinches.

"Your new man checked me in, but not according to *Hoyle*. If I were you Robert, I would consider reviewing proper procedure with the young man. Didn't unzip my bag to say howdy."

The three hundred and thirty-five pounds dominated the hall like *Jabba the Hutt.* Carlson favored the slug-like alien—the wide mouth, thin-lips, bulging eyes, and hairless bumpy scalp. Now studying his admissions log, his finger stopped and eyes climbed the renowned forensic pathologist and serial killer hunter.

"Ah, your're supposed to be Mr. Gregory Thompson. Says here you're a seventy-two-year-old, white male . . . a natural death. No trauma and no attending physician. You came from Linder Avenue."

"That would be me. No death scene. No field agent report. I'm a routine, natural death brought here for my routine inspection before they put me in the ground. We *naturals* never get the attention we deserve," Elliott teased. He squeezed by Robert and patted his damp back. "Good to see you again. Little chilly in there."

"Dr. Sumner, I'm sure you did this for a good reason."

"Yes, my friend. My presence is stealth. Dr. Bates, Detective Wilcox, and now you are the only to know." Elliott stood by the exit door to the flight of stairs leading to a now empty locker room. His scrubs and surgical paraphernalia would be waiting in the last locker on the south side of the small changing room, compliments of Dr. Bates. To all others attending the inquest, Dr. Sumner would be a gowned and masked visitor blending in with the medical staff.

"It may not be my business, but why the secrecy?"

"It's complicated. Appears I'm a person of interest to some."

"Is it related to the Butcher's recent suicide and your biological father, Mr. Bell?"

"Good to see you're staying current, Robert. That is a distinct possibility."

"And it would be bad for you? I mean . . . is someone trying to hurt you?"

Elliott turned to Carlson. "Some want me to join my brothers. The reason is unclear at the moment. I do not want that to put others at risk should they still be looking for me."

"And the dead deputies are two more pieces of the puzzle?"

"I think so, Robert. What is the status upstairs?"

"Dr. Bates has been there about an hour. The first autopsy—Deputy Womack—started thirty minutes ago. I've not seen Detective Wilcox. I would have thought he . . ."

"Wait. Tony's not here?"

"No. Dr. Bates called a couple minutes ago looking for him."

The basement of the county morgue is one of the most secured floors in the city. Each year thousands of dead bodies spend the night and tell their story. Their visits are required by law when their last breath is suspicious—cause and manner of death unknown. Mountains of related, physical evidence pass through the county morgue basement to be processed and examined by skilled medical, scientific, and legal experts. Only then can the truth have a chance and justice be served. Tampering with the *medical-legal process* alters results, hides truth, and changes lives.

Robert Carlson, a veteran morgue clerk, guarded his basement like a five-star general with a three-day toothache. Elliott met him the day the Bluff City Butcher stepped from the fog of urban legend and killed on Beale Street.

Distracted by thoughts of the pending autopsy, Elliott missed the soft thud in the dark depths of the morgue basement. Instead, he stood under the exit sign holding the cold knob of the battered metal door looking through the narrow, useless window into the dark stairwell. The complexities of the unfolding mystery were churning.

"How is Dr. Bates holding up?" Elliott asked.

Carlson hung the clipboard on the hook and said, "When I left to get the next body, they cracked the chest. Dieners were passing Dr. Bates the organs. I saw a dozen specimens in formalin ready for histology, and a full toxicology rack. I'm guessing in another twenty minutes he'll be ready for number two. He's not himself. I can tell something's bothering him."

"I saw Deputy Sutter's body in the refrigerator." Elliott looked up as if he could see through the two floors of the county morgue and into heaven. "I don't like any of this either . . ."

Carlson waddled closer. Obesity already taking its toll on the thirty-five year old. The slightest move over taxed his heart revealed by cherry red cheeks and beads on his forehead. "Dr. Bates never shows much, but he's scared. He's acting the same way he did when we thought we brought the body of the BCB in here. Freaked out everybody lying on the table after being in the river a day. I remember that long, black leather coat and those legs hanging off the end of the table. Biggest man ever had here. Turned out to be Mr. Bellow. That was a shocker."

"I remember."

Carlson pulled out a balled-up handkerchief and dabbed his forehead. "The man still scared the heck out of Dr. Bates. He's got the same look on his face today."

Turning back to his reflection in the little window on the metal door Elliott asked, "How many people up there?"

"Six in the observation room: two county deputies, one Memphis police officer, and three FBI. The new guy, Greene—took Director Voss's place—is there, and some other man I didn't recognize. There's a lady in a suit. She's new too. They all had FBI badges hanging around their necks."

"And in the autopsy room?"

"Not counting the body, Dan Nelson—the medical photographer—and three dieners. Daryl and Randall you know. John Gray is a new guy. I don't like him." Carlson tucked in his shirttail. It pulled out when he wiped his dripping head.

"Tell me more about John Gray." *You wouldn't say something if it wasn't important.*

"Gray has been here a few weeks. Came from the medical school."

"What about him?"

"For a guy anxious to be a forensic pathologist, he doesn't show me interest."

"What do you mean?"

"He spends more time looking around than he does watching autopsies. It's like he's waiting for something. I don't trust him."

"Thanks for the insight." Elliott put a hand on Carlson's shoulder. "This door is locked, my friend." Carlson hesitated.

"I can arrange for your private inquest, both bodies, Dr. Sumner. It'll be a whole lot safer. I can set it up for you down here tonight."

"Robert, it's important I get to this the first time around. There are things I need to see within hours of death or they're lost."

"I know about the forensic windows.

Guess you're most interested in Sutter."

"Appears she confronted the killer. Her condition may be most revealing."

"I don't like the way things are . . ."

"Sometimes in our chosen profession we do what we must, Robert."

They stood eyeball to eyeball. Carlson slid the master into the keyhole. After a twisting whine, the metal door popped open for the first time in years—no one used the steps anymore, at least not Carlson.

Elliott started to enter the stairwell and Carlson grabbed his arm. "I'll be up with Deputy Sutter in a few minutes. Are you sure?"

"Yes. I'm sure. Thank you my friend." Elliott turned and flew up the stairs. His echo faded, the second door opened and closed.

Carlson locked the exit and turned to retrieve the clipboard with Sutter's paperwork. A soft thud muggled from the end of the long, dark hall. Carlson looked at the double doors into the evidence room. They were ajar.

NINE

"Seeing is different than being told."
African Proverb

Elliott changed closthes in the empty locker room. In a crumpled, brown bag he found scrubs, a neatly folded lab coat, mask, head cover, and tinted eye-shield. The note from Bates said, *"Welcome. Staff looks forward to the visiting Vanderbilt pathology resident."* He saw the name tag pinned over the pocket. Elliott would pretend to be Dr. Robert Durkin.

Standing in the dark hall he looked in one of the small windows on the swinging metal doors opening into the autopsy room. Scanning the room, he tucked hair under the paper cap, tied his surgical mask, and positioned the eye shield.

Although it looked like an oversized surgical suite in a hospital, the county autopsy room was designed to protect the living from the dead.

Four times longer than the thirty-foot width, shiny, white linoleum met polished white ceramic that climbed to the ceiling. An endless row of cupboards with glass doors and metal cabinets and drawers took one side. Above the stainless steel counters and deep sinks were fume hoods and fluorescent lights. Every surface was in use: slide prep station, tube racks, microscopes, beakers, tissue culture flasks, stacks of petri dishes, and white towels lined with surgical instruments, saws, drills and hammers. There were countless disposable dispensers for latex gloves, swabs, gauze squares, tubing, meshes, tapes, disinfectant, soap, and anything else one would need when dissecting a human body.

The observation window was on the other side of the room. The fishbowl held six gawkers. Next to it were long illuminator boxes outside the lead-shielded room dedicated to full body x-rays. In the back were large appliances: incubators, autoclaves, centrifuges, refrigerators, water baths and a freezer for tissue sections. Six giant biohazard bins on wheels made a line. They would be full before ten. A dozen metal carts in the wings held more disposables, towels, and surgical instruments. They would be empty by ten as well. Center stage was the body.

The large stainless steel bed with metal walls and grids and running water and drains was surrounded by five blood-covered gowns and masks. Dr. Bates stood in the center, a diener on each side. A circulator and histology assistant always kept moving—bringing and taking.

White light poured over the naked body of the young, healthy male lying on his back. His chest flapped open like a pair of flank steaks straddling a bloody hole. Gloves reached deep for organs, cut them free with razor-sharp scalpels, and passed them to the M.E.

Next to the adjustable spotlights and UV lamps, laminar airflow filters sucked the nauseous oders of blood, human flesh, and body gases. Dr. Bates peered over his mask at the little window and nodded, eager for Elliott's arrival—the most remarkable forensic pathologist he ever met.

Elliott entered without fanfare, his mask in place, tinted visor down, and pulling on gloves. Bates held the attention of the room. He barked orders at the medical photographer, passed tissue sections to the histologist, and called for Womack's liver. Elliott found a spot behind the M.E. and waited for his introduction to the team—protocol.

"Welcome, Dr. Durkin," Bates said without looking up. "I am pleased you could join us this morning." He paused, straightended his stance, and clasped bloody hands on his stomach. "People, your attention please. I would like to introduce Dr. Robert Durkin. He is finishing up his pathology residency at Vanderbilt School of Medicine down the road—Nashville. In the spring he begins his forensic training. I had the opportunity to meet Dr. Durkin during his decision process. I am pleased he is joining the medical specialty." He turned to Elliott. "Good you could step away from your holiday schedule, doctor. I think we have a few interesting cases for you to observe."

Elliott nodded. "Thank you for the invitation, doctor." He joined Bates next to the body. The staff returned to their duties. The observation room seemed uninterested in the addition. So far the plan worked, anonymity achieved. Elliott Sumner was an irrelevant member of the team.

Bates picked up Womack's liver. He examined and dictated detailed observations. He sectioned the organ like carving a country ham for dinner. He cut quarter-inch filets from one end to the other, fanned them on the table, studied each, and selected one for his histologist.

"Dr. Durkin, as I shared with you on the phone, this Shelby County Deputy is the victim of a knife attack eight hours ago. I do not expect to find disease process. All organs and tissues are those of a healthy, twenty-two-year-old male."

Elliott glanced at the observation window. *Interesting to see FBI engaged early. Hello, Director Greene. Who is your friend?* Both silver haired men sat with long faces in blue suits and narrow ties. *You are determined. One way or another you'll weasel your way into the Brent catacombs still not your business. These homicides will still not authorize justificational access, unless Director Wade caves and invites you in . . .*

Next to them sat a brawny Memphis police officer with small eyes, crew cut, thick neck, and in a bad mood. Standing like pillars behind him were two uniformed sheriff deputies in stiff shirts. They held their hats on their chests with their eyes locked on their comrade. *It's no accident your guns are sitting high on your hips with holsters unsnapped. You're more than ready for anything until justice prevails.* They had black tape across their gold badges and rage in their eyes. Between them sat a woman with glasses writing in a notepad. She was middle aged, plain, but attractive—high cheekbones, short brown hair, an intelligent face, and busy eyes.

The dieners uncoiled ten feet of lacerated intestines. They fed it onto the table like a string of uncooked sausages. When all others in the observation room looked at their feet, the only lady leaned closer.

"I assume you have Memphis homicide detectives in the observation room," Elliott said. *Hopefully you hear my question— where is Tony Wilcox?*

"Actually we're missing our lead man, Anthony Wilcox. We spoke last night at the scene. He left me in the catacombs around 2:00 a.m. and never returned. I assumed he left to do his job. I expected him here this morning.

Apparently he is missing. The Memphis police have been unable to find him. His car is still at the Brent mansion."

My questions can't attract undue attention, thought Elliott. *I don't know who is on the Gilgamesh payroll—if anyone. Jump around with the questions, Elliott. Act like an apprentice, a visitor with no particular interest in any detail. Do not attract attention.* "So the observers are county sheriff deputies and Memphis police?"

"Yes. They often send a representative to homicdes." The diener handed Bates a right kidney after weighing and recording. Bates inspected the organ and fileted as he spoke. "And we have the FBI with us—Regional Director Greene, agent Fortes, and Agent Rice, an FBI pathologist. She is new to the area."

Taft probably blocked the FBI pathologist's participation on the floor, Elliott thought. *What happened to Tony? He could be lying in the weeds behind the Brent mansion, or in the woods somewhere. I have got to get what I need fast so I can get out there.*

"Dr. Durkin, I invite you to take a look at the neck trauma. Gentlemen, please move to your work stations and give us some space." The dieners left the table. The two doctors leaned over the body, their heads inches apart. Bates needed a magnifying glass. Elliott did not. Bates whispered. "Audio is off. We can talk," he whispered under his mask.

Elliott wasted no time.

"Get a message to the MPD. Tony is on the grounds of the Brent estate. He could be injured, unconscious, or worse. We spoke last night. He was concerned when he was outside alone. He thought someone was hiding nearby."

"Got it—when the time is right. Now, take a look at the knife wounds and tell me what you see. We have three sites: neck, chest, and groin. I preserved as much of the chest wounds as possible, but it may be too disrupted for you to reach any new conclusions."

"Forceps . . ." Elliott held out his hand. Bates slapped them in his palm. Elliott lifted a flap of the neck laceration and moved a probe beneath and along the seven-inch path revealing the layers of dissected tissue.

"Turning audio on," Bates said.

Elliott took the cue and started talking medical.

"The left carotid artery is partially severed with the stemocleidomastoid muscle. There is minimal disruption to the levator scapulae and the middle and anterior scalene muscles." He slid his probe further. "The knife partially severed the external jugulars preserving the thyroid." He pushed the tip to the wound depth and moved to the end point, stopping above the right, common carotid artery. "And is the same here as on the left."

And the incision arc is a duplication of the one on Deputy Sutter's neck. Although the light is marginal in the morgue refrigerator, I could see the identical damage to surrounding tissues. There are partial or precise lacerations of targeted vessels. The 'sweeper' is pulling back from a perfect path. It is hesitation? Why do that?

"Very good, Dr. Durkin. Okay, audio is off again. I haven't seen you since that night. You know, when we worked on Adam Duncan in Albert's crawl space."

"We agreed to leave that alone."

"I know. I'm not going there. But I do need to know about Dr. Medino. I've heard some documents coming out of the catacombs are incriminating. Is it true he had a relationship with Adam, the Butcher?"

"I looks that way. But Henderson, this is not the time or place." Elliott leaned close to the wounds with forceps and probe.

"I understand. But is it possible Medino used organs and tissue from the victims?"

Elliott lifted his head from the wound and looked into Bates's eye shield and through the rooster spray of blood. He forcefully whispered, " I will not get into this now. Can we please get back to this autopsy?"

Bates looked down at the wound.

"You cannot deny Dr. Enrique Medino secretly engaged in *life-extension* research. He was a brilliant medical doctor, a geneticist and molecular biologist hellbent on finding genetic secrets to immorality. It is a shame he was killed in a bogus car accident. Murdered."

"We know he accomplished cartilage cell regeneration with his biogenic solution for the treatment of osteoarthritis. The mechanism is a step away from working on any somatic cell in the body. If he was successful, all aged and damaged cells would be readily replaced with new, vibrant cells. But his research is not so unique. Others are looking at the same things. The question remais, how far did Dr. Medino get? Did he find the genetic trigger for cell rejuvenation? So far, no one has found it."

"Is it the secret research of the *LIFE2* Corporation?"

"I don't know." Elliott looked up. "Your audience is stirring. We best turn the mic on and get back to this autopsy?"

Bates looked over at the observation window. Director Greene tapped the glass and pointed to his ear. "Okay. I am turning audio back on. Get medical again."

"And it appears the blade moved sagittal to the midline, a course left-to-right. The feathered edges of the incision are consistent, uninterrupted, an no snags. It suggests the blade was razor-sharp and was a singular, rapid event. The most significant discovery is the accuracy, minimal tissue disruption yet precise laceration of vital arteries."

"Very good, Dr. Durkin. You have good forensic instincts. Please continue."

"The knife tracked at a consistent depth reaching below the hypodermal layer and finding each target vessel with—as I noted —almost no disruption of underlying tissues or structures. The depth of the laceration is consistent from one end to the other with the greatest depths reached at the targeted vessels."

"Seems a very difficult accomplishment.

The killer is highly skilled," Bates said.

Elliott adjusted the light and moved to the chest wound. Both heads tracked the incision inches above the body topography. After all the corpses and carnage experienced in their morbid lives, neither were bothered by the smell or the view.

"What can we learn from the chest wound. The path is less important than the puncture stops at each end of the arc."

"Pneumothorax to elicit a shock response. Instand debilitation of the victim.

The killer understands human anatomy, knows how to cripple with minimal strikes, and has the skill."

Elliott moved to the groin and studied the laceration to the upper leg, another precision strike. Bates followed. "He went for the most accessible bleeders—precision lacerations of the iliac vessels, arterial and venous. He worked from top down."

"Both victims may have these wounds—first the neck, then chest, and then groin."

"And all strikes accomplished within seconds," Elliott said.

"I agree," Bates said acting the sage.

"When I arrived, your morgue clerk allowed me a brief look at Deputy Sutter in the walk-in refrigeration unit."

"Did you see similar trauma patterns?" Bates backed from the corpse, clasping his bloody hands as his staff prepped Womack for removal, and the arrival of Deputy Sutter.

"Yes. Is it your assumption the arm taken first?" Elliott asked.

"Yes. The killer neutralized the gun," Bates said.

"That further supports a theory of skill and accuracy. Each knife pass on Deputy Sutter is accomplished at the same angles as Deputy Womack. Both victims stood erect. Both were surprised by their attacker. Both were dead before they dropped."

Elliott walked back around the body and took a position next to Bates. They viewed Womack and considered the total picture.

"I concur," Bates said. "However, we need a closer look at Deputy Sutter."

Bates turned to the window. "Observers, now is the time for bathroom breaks. We will be ready to start the Deputy Sutter autopsy in fifteen minutes. Officer Crowley, please stay back. Pick up the phone." Bates turned the audio off. "I will suggest the MPD look for Wilcox where you last spoke with him—the ravine behind the Brent mansion."

"Where is Sheriff Taft?" Elliott asked when Bates returned.

"We're good. They will check. Taft . . . his plane is due from Philadelphia at nine. His first stop is here. His second stop is Director Wade to synchronize city and county."

"Vintage G.E." Elliott's eyes smiled behind the visor and refocused as dieners started to clean up Womack's body, washing off the blood and closing the chest.

"Do you know who is after you and why?"

"To early. All I know is I'm a target."

"I can't imagine anything happening at the county morgue. That would be a first."

"We don't need to risk it. My anonymity is best for everyone."

"Elliott, is there any chance the Butcher is responsible for this?"

"No. You know better . . ."

"I suppose. But we've only seen wounds like this on Butcher victims, and we both know it. I hate to think we have another monster out there," Bates whispered.

Without a glove Elliott ran his finger the length of the neck wound, his vision another rare asset, near microscopic magnification. *The tip of the knife tore the epidermis at the onset, but as it plunged one millimeter it was already a fluid transverse cut through the three dermal layers, uninterrupted for seventeen centimeters, descending a few millimeters only at the carotids and jugular. Is it possible there are two with these skills?*

"I see hesitation and control," Elliott said emerging from his complex world.

"You see control?" Bates asked as observers returned to their seats.

"I see more. He tried to pull back. It is like he knows one way. He attempted to modify. I think to minimize damage. He did not intend to kill Womack or Sutter. He tried to ratchet back his moves but failed."

"He only knows how to kill?"

"Deputy Womack came upon him by accidental. The killer reacted instinctively. Sutter appears. I don't think he ever intended to kill these people. If he did, there would be no hesitation in these sweeps."

"Like a professional boxer in the ring, he attempted to hold back the second swing of a one-two punch, the combination he could throw in his sleep."

"Exactly."

"Interesting concept, Dr. Durkin. Audio is off. Say what you really mean." Bates forgot his staff could hear every word.

"This work is what the Bluff City Butcher is known for, his unique skills. Everything is for a reason, no wasted motions. Adam Duncan's work with a butcher knife is extraordinary, unlike anything I have ever seen before or since . . . until now."

The staff turned in unison. They realized the man posing as Dr. Durkin was Dr. Sumner, the man who knew the Butcher better than anyone in the world.

"If it's not the Butcher, and it's not a copycat, then what are we dealing with here?" Bates asked. The people in the observation room were oblivious to what was happening before their eyes on the other side of the thick glass, except for Dr. Rice. She saw the staff standing frozen over the naked corpse and staring at doctor who started to look familiar, his stature and moves. Staff eyes were on Dr. Sumner, their backs to the swinging metal doors.

"I'm saying we are looking at the work of . . ."

The metal doors into the autopsy room exploded open!

TEN

He came into the autopsy room like a wounded walrus headed for deep water. Heads turned as the whale-horse of a man moved into the light that poured off the surgically ravaged carcass atop the stainless steel table. The observation room jumped to their feet. Blood stained scrubs and masks turned. They parted exposing Elliott Sumner alone on the opposite side of the corpse and behind the autopsy table. Robert Carlson stopped five feet away. Two dieners started toward him; they were the first to see his chest. The bright red circle on the white shirt grew.

"I closed them off," Carlson yelled. "I think I stopped them . . . There are three, maybe more. I'm not sure now."

Carlson reached for his head and shook to stave off the

darkness closing-in. His shirt dripped red onto his shoes. In the shock and silence one squeaky wheel got louder on the other side of the metal doors. Carlson dropped his hands to his sides and yelled, "Dr. Sumner, they are coming for you!"

Nothing

made sense—no one dies in an autopsy room.

Carlson's eyes rolled into his head. He started to fall like a giant Sequoia. Two dieners jumped into action but could not stop the toppleing behemoth, or get out of its way. Three-hundred-fifty pounds soon pinned them to the floor where reality set in— they struggled to get free. They too could die.

Sheriff deputies and Memphis police left the the observation room and entered the quiet before the storm. Their guns were aimed on the double doors. The squeaky wheel was silent. Now there were whispers and shuffling feet.

The doors blew open. A torrent of bullets and shooting smoke followed. The autopsy room transformed into a battleground: exploding glass, shattering tiles, metal pelts and pings, whistling ricochets, and bodies falling. Through the dense haze and burning stench and deafening blasts, Elliott saw the gurney wedged between the doors. And he saw Deputy Sutter's naked body used as a shield. The sick, pathetic image, and the shock of an attack at a protected, government facility reavealed the desperation of his adversaries, and the overwhelming firepower showed an unwavering determination to eliminate the next Bell patriarch.

The moment the Butcher died on the spire, Gilgamesh signed my death certificate, Elliott thought. *Why such aggressive, high-risk behavior? Do you fear me more than Adam . . .?*

Bates stood frozen between Elliott and the shooters. E lliott reached over the corpse and grabbed his armpits. He hoisted the two-hundred pound doctor over Womack, and pulled him to the floor behind the metal autopsy table. How they avoided injury only added to the surrealistic moment.

Gunfire flew in all directions, zipping over heads and pelting the fortuitous metal shield for the time being. Through a small crack Elliott located Carlson and two dieners. The bloody pile was still. The bodies absorbed bullets like raindrops on a glass pond. Rescue was impossible and not necessary. The three were dead.

The FBI agents were hunkered down. The observation glass window was shattered. They returned fire in a selective and deliberate manner. Their marksmanship held back the attackers. The sheriff deputies and Memphis police returned fire from behind the rubber biohazard bins.

"*Who are these people*," Bates yelled as he tore off his mask, his head in his chest.

"We can't stay here," Elliott said inches from his face. "What are our options?"

His eyes widened. "Follow me." On hands and knees Bates crawled between supply carts to the darker end of the room. They crunched broken glass beneath flying metal.

I hope you know where you're going. No time for a wrong move. Elliott followed under the rain of shattering tiles. *I don't see a door or window back here . . .*

Bates stopped in the darkest corner, out of sight. He opened the last of a dozen cupboard doors on the bottom row. Bates moved boxes to one side and pushed the inside wall with his feet. It hinged open into more darkness.

"Follow me." They slid through the cabinet into the smells of bleach, detergent soap, and linens. Bates closed the cupboard doors from inside, slid the boxes back in place, and resealed the wall muffling the gunfire.

"Where are we?" Elliott whispered.

Bates slid a small bookcase over their wall entrance.

"We're in a storage closet, southeast corner of the building. It's always locked. The only people with a key are janitorial staff. They won't be back until Monday."

Dim light seeped under the closet door from the adjoining hall. As eyes adjusted Elliott checked his cell phone—no bars, no reception, no help.

The storage closet was a small ten by ten. There were stacks of sheets and towels, boxes of janitorial supplies, buckets and mops, bookcase, and a two-drawer file cabinet. Bates opened the bottom drawer and removed two revolvers. He passed one to Elliott.

"I put these here in 2008. I was not going to let the Butcher get me in my own morgue."

"I can see that." Elliott examined his with fingers in the dark. He did not like guns.

"You were right about people being after you," Bates whispered.

"They won't stop until they see my dead body or think I got away. These guns loaded?"

"I don't believe in keeping unloaded guns around. I figure if I'm going to pick one up, I'll need to use it damn quick." He opened his, blew into the barrel and snapped it closed. They sat another ten minutes before all the shooting stopped.

"Damn determined." The cold linoleum and light under the door were already getting to Bates. "Hope the police get here soon. I'm not good at this stuff. Too damn old."

"Is there another way out of here beside the closet door?" Elliott asked.

"Just the way we came in. Damn legs are starting to cramp. Can't handle the cold floor."

Elliott checked his watch. He set his gun on the floor behind him.

Two days . . . two attempts on my life, Elliott thought. *This medical team, they're dying because of me. If I get out of this alive, I need to disappear. Work from the shadows. I can't put people at risk. I needed to leave Carol for sure. I can't do anything until I understand Gilgamesh and why they want me dead . . .*

Bates whispered, "You never answered my question back there."

"Which one?"

"If Adam Duncan did not kill the sheriff deputies, and you're ruling out a *copycat,* what does it leave us?" Bates pushed.

Elliott touched his lips with one finger. "Someone's in the hall outside our door."

"They can't hear us. And the door's locked—no key. Everyone knows it's a damn storage closet, Elliott. We are safe in here."

"Something's not right," Elliott said.

"No. Stop. You're not going to do this to me. You cannot keep holding back on me, not now, not after all we've been through that night in Albert Bell's crawl space. I'm in this thing deep, much deeper than I ever thought possible. You owe me, Elliott. I want an explanation. I want to know what you know about the thing that killed the two deputies with a knife."

Elliott heard a shoe squeak. It was slow and hesitant. Maybe someone stopped to look. *You're not going to be quiet until I give you what you want. Maybe the closet is the best place for us until this whole thing blows over.*

"All right. Promise me you stop talking."

"Agreed," Bates whispered. His eyes danced.

"You saw those unique lacerations. They are trademark, the Bluff City Butcher."

"It is the Butcher?"

"No. This is the work of a student. The high level of precision and replication is possible if one possesses innate skills and years of intense training.

"What are you saying?"

"The Bluff City Butcher had an apprentice."

"My God, there's another one out there," Bates grimaced.

Elliott held up a hand. Shoes stopped outside the door. A key slid in the keyhole. Bates froze and raised his gun. Elliott reached for his when the lock popped and door opened inches. They watched a hand slide to the switch.

The new diener did not see Bates and Sumner on the floor between piles of folded sheets and towels, until Bates spoke.

"John Gray . . . thank God." Cramping legs required both hands to push up off the floor after he set down his gun.

Elliott's squinted into the new light and found the gun in Gray's hand. *Dieners don't carry guns. Police would not let medical people roam the corridors of a crime scene . . . his* eyes jumped up to Gray's flat face and empty eyes, but it was already happening.

John Gray shot three times pointblank. Henderson Bates fell back onto the cold linoleum and laid still, his eyes wide like a dead fish on a pile of chipped ice.

Elliott reached behind him for his gun—it was gone. Bates must have kicked it. Gray wasted no time. He moved the smoking barrel to Elliott. The world slowed. Ears still rang. Elliott reached for Bates and heard a fourth blast. The fifth and sixth came in the same second.

Carlson said he did not like the new diener . . .

ELEVEN

"Danger can only be overcome by more danger."
Greek Proverb

The first shot got him in the shoulder. He reeled from the impact, but it didn't matter. The second shot got him in the upper thigh—it didn't matter either. There was no more time, a fraction of a second and the outcome would be very different. The third shot got him in the head. He died before he slumped to the floor next to Dr. Bates. The dark silhouette took shape in the doorway, the smoking gun now pointing down, but ready if it was not over.

"Damn, Elliott. You okay?"

"You're late, Tee." Elliott turned Bates over. "He's losing blood. We need help fast. Gotta send someone next door, the blood center, STAT. Got to transfuse or he'll never make it out of this closet alive. And I can't hear. My ears are ringing."

Tony yelled in his face. "They're behind me. We have a lot

injured. EMTs brought blood. Shit, whenever you're around blood is SOP."

Tony knelt over the shooter yelling down the hall. "Hurry you guys. The medical examiner is dying."

Elliott worked on Bates. "He took three, upper chest. Angle gives him a chance. Two bullets deflected, shattered collar bone and exit out his back. Primary bleeders, I can manage a few minutes. One bullet is next to the heart. Don't know damage. Bates is on the edge, Tee. We could lose him."

"How you know missed his heart?" Tony asked, holstering his gun.

"He's still alive . . . !

"Blood loss is starting to trigger shutdown. We've got a lot of bleeders."

Tony flipped the shooter over. Elliott pressed fingers to his neck. "Dead."

Tony removed the gun by the barrel from a clinched fist. "Wonder who this bastard is?" He pulled the wallet from the bloody scrubs as paramedics rounded the corner.

"Going by John Gray. I'm sure it's bogus. Posed as a medical student for a few weeks according to the morgue clerk."

Elliott kept pressure on Bates's chest wound. "Heart rate slow but steady." The EMTs approached as Elliott looked up at Tony for the first time. "What happened to your face?"

"Some bastard jumped on me at Brent's." Tony picked at the tape running across his nose under his black, puffy eyes. A bloody bandage wrapped around his head.

"Leave your bandages alone. Quit picking at it. We'll talk later."

Paramedics squeezed into the doorway.

"Looking forward to it." Tony moved out of the way and got on his cell.

"You know what to do, gentlemen." The three paramedics got

to work lifting Bates onto the gurney, cutting off clothes, and passeing IV needles to Dr. Sumner. He started the first line and they pushed a bag of double reds, O-neg.

"BP dropping. He's going into shock," an EMT said.

Elliott directed the team with steady confidence. "I need another line now. Normal saline. Roll him on his side. Give me ten micrograms epinephrine STAT."

Everything happened before Elliott finished sentences. He injected epi. They intubated. "More RBCs. Someone talk to me —BP and heart rate, please."

"BP coming back in line. Heart picking up, doctor."

Bates stirred. He opened his eyes. "What is . . . My legs, they are . . ."

"You've been shot, Henderson," Elliott said inches from his face.

"Am I going to die? You can tell me the truth."

"You're going to live. Stop talking and let us do our work."

"Thank you, Elliott."

"You can thank Tony Wilcox later. He got the bad guy."

Bates smiled and slipped back under. "There you go. He's good to transport. Keep pushing RBCs and saline. Tell ER we've got two 38 exits and one next to the heart. Any abrupt movement could have consequences, gentlemen."

They secured Bates and headed down the hall. When they rounded the corner and disappeared, Elliott and Tony heard a voice behind them.

"This one is dead." They turned. Leaning over the body of John Gray was another EMT, one new on the job. He was lost in the chaos and was waiting for direction. He did not know he had been working on a killer. Elliott pulled a sheet from the stack and they draped it over the body.

"I think best we leave him here for now," Elliott said. "There's no more we can do. Join the others. They need you, I'm sure." The young EMT nodded as a half-smile returned to his white face. He grabbed the orange tackle boxes and ran down the hall.

You never forget your first body, Elliott thought. *Doesn't matter if it's a good guy or bad. Death is a confusing thing the first time—a body with no one home. Forces you to think about your own mortality. To think, one day your body will be empty too . . .*

Tony gripped Elliott's shoulder. "We are getting out of here now."

"I can't leave, Tony. There'll be questions. I'm the reason all this happened."

"This is not a request. It's an order from a Memphis police officer. Do not make me shoot you." Tony turned and went into the nearest office. Elliott followed. They popped open a window, climbed out, and went to a car parked a few spaces away.

"Whose car?" Elliott asked.

"Not sure. I had to borrow it. Mine's at Brent's place. This is better—nondescript." They eased onto Madison and blended with morning traffic. From behind dark, tinted windows they watched the beehive of activity—Memphis police, Fire, EMTs, and news media setting up. They saw Bates being loaded into an ambulance. "That's a good sign," Elliott said.

"This is pretty bad. Some major shit coming down, now." He turned onto Pauline and headed north of the city. Traffic thinned the farther away they got.

"Where're to?" Elliott asked, as he read a text from Carol. She saw the news. She needed to know Elliott survived the attack. His response was brief; *"Am good. You be careful."*

"Anywhere but here," Tony said.

He pulled onto Ayers and checked mirrors. "We're alone, so far." They escaped the gridlock in time.

"How many hurt?" Elliott asked. "The truth . . ."

"For all the bullets fired there were surprisingly few. I guess no one takes the time anymore to aim their damn guns."

"How many?"

"Four dead . . . three medical staff and one FBI. Three injured . . . two deputies hit in arms and legs. They'll live. The big Memphis cop at the autopsy took one in his side. He pulled the damn bullet out with his fingers and stuck a wad of guaze in the hole. He even took the time to put the bloody bullet in his pocket for evidence. One tough dude."

"You said an FBI agent did not make it."

"Agent Fortis. Caught one in the head. The other two disappeared."

"Do we know if they're okay?"

"We know nothing. It's the way they roll."

"What about the attackers?"

"Come on, I didn't have time to do a total body count, Elliott. I got there and started looking for you. I knew they came for you. If I had not heard Gray's shots, damn."

"You know I appreciate your help."

"I gave him two warning shots—shoulder and thigh. He had other plans. Had to drop the son-of-a-bitch."

"We know anything about the people who raided the morgue?"

"There were seven. We nailed two, not counting Gray. They tried to take their dead with em. We forced the pricks to leave em behind in the lot."

"The other four got away?"

"In a black Bronco."

Tony left Ayers into an empty parking lot—the Union Grove Church. He found a place out of sight, under trees, surrounded by a thick hedge. Leaving the motor running, he cracked a window and adjusted the mirror on Ayers. Tony could see all angles with a slight head turn.

"The dead guys were dressed like cat burglars, black everything. I got a look at the faces, no one I've ever seen. Their weapons are the best money can buy. You're right, they're organized and resourced. What's going on, Elliott? You know you're being hunted. Talk to me."

"It's complicated."

"When is it not?"

"A lot of things are converging."

"Bring me up as much as you can."

"I need to do this alone. I can't expose anyone else. You saw what happens around me."

"You cannot do this alone, Elliott. You're good, but not that good. You will not win and a lot more people will be hurt."

Tony locked eyes on the forensic sleuth waiting for agreement. This time Tony's logic was unshakable. "With help, we get this under control faster and more lives are saved."

Elliott nodded. "It is true. But you're going to have a problem with what I'm going to tell you. I don't have time to convince you of anything. You need to struggle on your own until you catch up."

"Struggle is how I grow, brother." He smiled looking in the rearview mirror. The black Suburban crawled by on Ayers. Tony felt for his gun.

These bastards are determined. You got every cop in the city looking for you, and you're still risking it looking for Elliott Sumner. You boys must be afraid to take a failed mission home with you. I wonder, who are you working for . . .

TWELVE

"All the gods are dead except the god of war."
Eldridge Cleaver

"Adam is not who we thought," Elliott said. Another black car went down Pearce through the ghost town on the cold, gray morning. Saturday, the day after Christmas, people stayed inside. Tony and Elliott hid in swirling snow. Their tracks in the empty church parking lot were already covered.

"Last count, he killed 167," Tony said. "Even if he is your long, lost brother, the dude is a pretty sick guy."

"The people Adam killed are connected."

"We both know when you kill that many people, some will be connected."

"All are connected, Tony."

"That's bullshit. He tried to kill Albert Bell, Carol Mason, me, and you. We're not connected to any of the other victims. He killed the three college boys on the bluff twenty-five years ago.

He killed the Weatherford girl—only five. He killed a damn radio talk-show host and program director. He killed the girl he used on Mud Island, the one who looked like Carol."

"I can't explain everything now. You asked. I'm telling. Take it or leave it."

"Help me some, Elliott. None of the people I just listed are connected. If this is your theory, you are wrong. You may be too close to be objective." His cell vibrated. "Shit. MPD is looking for you. Wade wants me to bring you in for questioning."

"Can't happen, Tony. I'll be dead before I get inside the building."

"Give me more, Elliott. My ass is hanging out here. I've got a lot of dead people in my city and still no answers. I gotta manage Wade. After the killings in the catacombs, I know the man. He's thinking somehow the BCB out there somehow. He's got the mayor all over his ass.

"Wade wants Adam Duncan's body brought to the county morgue immediately. Now, Bates is in no condition to explain away what he did at the Bell mansion that night."

"Neither the director or mayor have the legal authority to order an exhumation. Adam's remains were released to family by the medical examiner in accordance with law."

"They don't buy the actions of Henderson Bates. The law said the body had to go to the morgue for an inquest including an autopsy. And, for that matter, I don't get it either. There are a lot of questions swirling around the departure from standard procedures."

"You tell your boss the only way they can get their hands on the body is a court order."

"They know that, Elliott. It's you and me, we need to be on the same page."

"Regarding Adam, for now you have to trust me."

"I do trust you, but you need to trust me too. Tell me what's going on." Tony leaned closer. Elliott looked up from his hands spread on his knees. It was time.

"Adam Duncan is more than a serial killer. He is killing soldiers."

"Soldiers! What kind of soldiers?"

"An elite, stealth force of highly trained soldiers on a secret mission."

"I don't know about this."

"I am reluctant to discuss it with you. It gets into areas with very different rules. I don't know if you can process what I know."

"Let me get this straight. Adam Duncan is not a sick, serial killer. He is a misunderstood soldier who killed 167 enemy soldiers. Is that what you're telling me?" Tony scratched his head and looked up Ayers.

"Not all 167 dead are Adam's. Others are involved. Adam Duncan is killing with purpose. I am not saying he is a good person. Adam is a psychopath. He may have killed innocent people along the way. His focus has always been on the people who are now trying to kill me."

"This is bizarre, Elliott. You could be too close to see. You can make mistakes."

"The Peabody rooftop, the county morgue, now, I am dealing with trained soldiers on a mission. John Gray posed as a medical student. He had a role. They recruited, developed, and planted him in the county morgue for me when the time came."

"It is logical. They knew you would be in the morgue one day."

"The stealth army belongs to Gilgamesh.

I do not know what's driving the timeline, but it just got shorter. It is possible my biological brothers and I were once important to Gilgamesh."

"Now you're a problem.

And the last one standing."

"They killed Jack. When Adam learned I was his brother, he could not kill me. Gilgamesh had him confused. They drove Adam to his death."

Tony rubbed his head trying to rationalize Elliott's words. "After Adam killed you they would send an army to kill him?"

"I believe they also would terminate Albert Bell. I don't know why they wanted to eliminate current and future Bell patriarchs, but the answer to the question may explain everything."

"December 23rd disrupted their plan," Tony said.

"Where is this going?"

"I don't know yet, but sense enormous consequences on the horizon."

"Sounds apocalyptic."

"A piece of the puzzle fell into place when Henderson Bates asked me about Dr. Medino's relationship with Adam."

"The quirky geneticist someone killed in the car wreck on Austin Peay?"

"Yes. We now know Dr. Medino moved from Dallas to Memphis the summer of 1982."

"And that's important, why?"

"What happened in 1982, Tony?"

"Shit. The people killed on the bluff. The stranger jumped off the Harahan Bridge and the body lost. 1982 was the first experience with the Bluff City Butcher."

"Adam came to Memphis with Dr. Medino."

"It is either a possibility or a coincidence?"

"Dr. Medino was involved in genetic life extension research."

"We know now."

"His termination tied to the progress of his research—files are missing."

"He had a breakthrough?"

"Possible. Jack, Adam and I are involved in some way."

Tony sat up straight. "Let me summarize. Medino brings the Butcher to Memphis. Gilgamesh kills Medino and takes his research. Gilgamesh kills Jack Bellow and tells Adam to kill you and Albert Bell. Then Gilgamesh is going to kill Adam so they can do what . . .?"

"I don't know."

"Getting pretty far out there, Elliott."

"If some entity controlled the genetic secret to immortality, they would have an unprecedented advantage in the world. There would be nothing they could not have or do. Time would always be on their side. They would accumulate knowledge, outlive their enemies, and always operated from a superior position of wealth, geography, and power."

"Why terminate the Bell triplets and Albert?"

"I need to find out why. Tony, I need to disappear. Get with Max. Take a closer look at the Butcher's victims. There's gotta be one common thread. It could take us inside Gilgamesh where all the answers reside."

"If they are soldiers, they would need to meet somewhere for training and instruction. Maybe travel would intersect in a common local. We can look at communications, money transfers, proximity of victims with suspicious deaths, cold cases, and other odd events."

"Protect and be careful around Albert Bell. I don't know his exposures or entanglements. I won't be able to get with him for a while. Not until I know more."

"Where's Carol in all this?"

"I can't pull her into this hell. I can't risk it, Tony."

"She's not that kind of girl, Elliott. She won't step away from you."

"I don't want her here. If they know she's with me, they use her . . . kill her."

"You're forgetting your demons, those monsters in your head

because of your photographic memory. Carol stops them. No one else can. She's special. You know you need her."

"I'm better now. I'm managing it myself."

"It almost killed you in Dallas. I was there. You couldn't handle it then. Your body took over. It shut down. A damn cardiac arrest. Elliott, the doc said you are toast if you experience one more horrific event—you're at emotional capacity. Think about what you're doing. You don't want to kill yourself. "

"I've made my mind up, Tony. Are you going to support me or not? I need to know."

"I don't like it at all."

"Are you or not?"

"I'm with you all the way, but you're making a mistake."

"I need to get out of Memphis . . ."

Tony reached for the key. The black Bronco crawled by again —north. This time the brake lights flashed and the red glow faded in the falling snow. Tony eased onto Ayers with the lights off and headed south.

The Memphis Tribune
Sheriff Deputies Found Dead in Brent Catacombs
Carol Mason, Director Investigative Reporting
December 26, 2009

Two Shelby County Sheriff Deputies were found dead in the Brent Catacombs around 2:00 a.m. this morning. Officials said the deputies were discovered by a relieving shift. "We are dealing with homicides," said one unnamed source at the scene. The bodies were examined in the catacombs by the Shelby County Medical

Examiner, Dr. Henderson Bates, and the scene jointly processed by the county CSI unit and MPD. Details are withheld.

On October 17, 2009, an elaborate maze of tunnels and rooms were found under the eighty-year-old mansion located in north Shelby County, once owned by the now deceased Trenton P. Brent. The catacombs are believed the home of the Bluff City Butcher. They are held as a restricted area by the county. An active investigation is underway. Possible information about victims of the BCB may be found in the catacombs. The two deputies killed early this morning were working an evening shift processing potential evidence when attacked.

Brent, a seventy-six-year-old white male, lived alone in the dilapidated mansion on twenty-five acres in north Shelby County. Brent was found dead August 2, 2002. His death was ruled *undetermined* and later changed to *homicide* by the medical examiner. Brent's killer remains unknown.

The mansion sat vacant from August 2002 until donated to the county in November 2008. In an austerity program, the county renovated portions of the mansion, converting the site into a north substation for the Shelby County Sheriff's Office at a substantial savings. The cellar and attic of the mansion and outbuildings on the property were boarded up by the county. On October 17 Deputy Marty Pilsner found back entrance into the cellar—a restricted area. His investigation led to the discovery of tunnels and rooms and the rescue of Michael Bell, brother of Albert Bell and this reporter.

Memphis Homicide Detective, Anthony Wilcox, was not available for comment. Sheriff G.E. Taft was out of the city, attending a law enforcement conference. Taft is returning from Philadelphia to attend portions of the two medical examiner inquests scheduled to begin sometime today. Names of the deputies killed in the catacombs are being withheld.

The Memphis Tribune

Shooting at Morgue leaves 5 Dead; Medical Examiner in Critical Condition

Carol Mason, Director Investigative Reporting
December 27, 2009

Armed men stormed the Shelby County morgue around 7:00 a.m. Saturday morning and killed four medical assistants and FBI Agent, and sent four to area hospitals in critical condition. One Memphis police officer, two Shelby County sheriff deputies, and the medical examiner—Dr. Henderson Bates—were among the injured.

Dead at the scene were three dieners (autopsy assistants) whose names are being held until notification of next of kin. Longtime morgue clerk, Robert Carlson and a regional FBI Agent were pronounced dead at the scene.

Reliable sources say seven armed men dressed in black shot their way into the autopsy room where Medical Examiner and team were conducting inquests into the deaths of two sheriff deputies found in the Brent Catacombs earlier. The unnamed shooters exchanged gunfire with Memphis police, sheriff deputies, and the FBI. The MPD responded to the urgent call for backup minutes after the shooting began. Two of the unnamed shooters were pronounced dead at the scene; five escaped in a black Bronco.

Anyone with information (or who sees a black Bronco) is to call 888-CAN-HELP. Your call is confidential. For your own safety, do not attempt to intervene.

PART TWO

THE CEDAR FOREST

THIRTEEN

"There is a thin line between genius and insanity."
Oscar Levant

He walked into the Plaza Hotel kicking snow off his shoes and scanning the lobby lounge from a faceless crowd. It was a little after 7:00 p.m. Elliott was tired and in a bad mood. Then he saw Bernardo. Although they never met, he was sure. The chair next to him was open.

"Your people have been busy in Memphis." He sat across from the only rich, old, skinny Russian and gray ponytail in the room. "Killed four innocent people and put the Shelby County medical examiner in intensive care. Got Michael too," Elliott whispered looking straight ahead.

"Are you sure Michael's dead?" asked the voice from the long, narrow face behind the rumpled *New York Times*.

"Hollow point, center of the forehead from a hundred yards. Took off the back of his head before he knew what hit him."

"God! Are forensic pathologists always so graphic?"

"Yes." Elliott glared. "But you're asking the wrong questions. Tell me why I shouldn't turn you over to the NYPD or FBI right now."

Kuzma lowered his paper. Elliott saw his face many times in a morgue—the milky eyes and paper-thin skin draped over edgy facial bones, and the ruptured vessels and age lines. He had the face of the dead. Kuzma had to be late eighties, not long for this world. Elliott started to understand why a meeting now.

"I'm sorry. I meant no disrespect." His slight smile showed brown-yellow teeth.

"That's not an answer to my question."

"They informed me of the Memphis casualties on both sides, all except Michael. The shooting of Dr. Bates is a mistake. The operative is new. Eager to impress."

"You forget I sat next to Dr. Bates. No mistake. Your man was four feet away. He pulled the trigger three times. He knew Bates. Don't tell me it was a mistake."

"I'm afraid we've gotten off badly. Again, I've failed to communicate. I meant to say the shooting of Dr. Bates was a dreadful mistake because our people were there for only one man."

"Me . . ."

"Yes, Dr. Sumner. You are the only target. No one else mattered unless they got in the way. Dr. Bates posed no threat, unless he had a gun."

"Are you suggesting then it would have been okay?"

"I'm sorry. No. They were there for you."

"You knew they were coming for me at the Peabody too, didn't you?"

"No. I had no information on the Peabody. The morgue initiative went through normal channels and according to protocol. You were expected to attend the inquests for the two unfortunate deputies slain in the catacombs. I had no time to warn you, and my attempts to reach Michael were unproductive."

"They were too prepared to make the decision hours before."

"We have people and operations in many places, Dr. Sumner."

"You should have known when you could not connect with Michael."

"I believed our meeting successful, Michael was compromised. He often went into hiding following a delicate assignment, a clever and resourceful man. Michale always got back to me in good time." Kuzma looked around the lounge. "The Peabody was an outlier."

"Outlier?"

"An unsanctioned operation."

"There were a dozen soldiers running around with rifles. They shot Michael with great accuracy. They came after me like taking a hill. They scrubbed the area and vanished."

"Only someone very high-up could deploy resources without my knowledge. If I knew we were breached, we would have aborted. We both have too much to lose."

"Who is Michael?" Elliott asked.

"A close, longtime friend who knew little about Gilgamesh. He was the best way to you—undetected. The leak came from your side," Kuzma said with authority.

"Impossible. I discussed it with no one."

"You didn't have to. You've been watched 24/7 for a long time. If you lost your *tail* that day, it had to be your phone or a bug. Based on the size of the operation, someone liked the opportunity, timing, and location. I suspect downtown Memphis dead Christmas night. You presented many angles and limited escape opetions."

Elliott satisfied himself Kuzma told enough of the truth for him to stay and push for more.

"Why did Adam's suicide attempt December 23 trigger my termination order?"

"Suicide attempt?" Kuzma's eyes widened. Elliott said *attempt* suggesting it failed.

"I meant . . . Adam's suicide."

Kuzma sunk in his chair. "Dr. Sumner, your termination order went out in October."

"The Butcher lured me to Mud Island? Was he working for Gilgamesh?"

Bernardo laughed and downed his vodka. "Your brother was a real monster, and Gilgamesh his enemy for a very long time."

"Why?"

"That explanation will have to wait. Suffice it to say Gilgamesh hunted Adam since 1982. He always managed to kill our people first."

"That makes no sense. You knew Adam lived in the Brent catacombs. The place is full of coded documents with your logo. Gilgamesh used the catacombs, too. You could have sent in a small army and flushed him out whenever you wanted. Why didn't you?"

"We tried, many times. Too many of our people disappeared."

"So you stopped hunting him?"

"No. New interests emerged, interests more important than our desire to eliminate him."

"What new interests?"

"Another topic for later. For now let's just say the Bluff City Butcher was never a friend of Gilgamesh. In November we found some leverage, a common goal. We never controlled Adam. No one controlled him, not even Dr. Medino."

"Enrique Medino was killed in November 2008—your common interes, your leverage."

"Yes."

"Why did Adam kill for Gilgamesh?"

"The kill-list delivered to the Bell mansion in the summer of 2009, it was a list of people Adam believed were working for Gilgamesh. We fooled Adam into thinking he created the list. He killed those people thinking he was sending us a message, he was coming for the board."

Kuzma leaned close and said, "The skies roared, Dr. Sumner. His only friend was dead. So death would rain down upon us . . . just like the story."

"The Epic of Gilgamesh. But many names on the list had no association with Gilgamesh."

"We fooled Adam. He didn't know the Gilgamesh board members.

He didn't know his father, his brothers, or much about his life. The man lived in the dark. The people he killed were sent to kill him. After Medino's death, Adam wanted to end Gilgamesh."

"Why?"

"He blamed Gilgamesh for Enrique Medino's death."

"Why blame Gilgamesh?"

"Because Gilgamesh tried to kill Dr. Medino since 1982. Adam protected him from us."

"Why did Gilgamesh want to kill Dr. Medino?"

"It is complicated . . ."

"You are the monsters," Elliott said pushing elbows into his knees and reaching for his head.

"Adam is one of many tragedies in my life." Kuzma looked into his glass as Elliott slid his fingers up his forehead and into his scalp, his eyes pinched closed and wet. The sharp pain shot from the center of his brain down his spine. A new, dark anger grew within.

"What makes killing *me* important to Gilgamesh, Kuzma?"

"I need to prepare you for . . ."

"*Tell me*," Sumner growled. His seething eyes popped open with pinpoint pupils.

Kuzma backed away in his chair. "This is why I'm here. Why I'm risking my life. You were once an asset. Now you are a liability."

"*Tell me*." Elliott's face hardened. His brow dropped and jaw tightened. A bulging vein climbed his forehead. "I've had a very bad week. It is a good time to give me something." He dropped his hands revealing bloody fingers. "I will finish Adam's work. I am your next nightmare. I know Gilgamesh has a problem with me—now they should fear me."

Kuzma heard the words and saw the fat drop of blood roll down Elliott's forehead. Gilgamesh was a part of the triplet's lives from the beginning. They lived in the shadows ever since: observing, manipulating, and waiting. They knew the three boys were gifted. But there was a problem, they had an unforseen wild side. Gilgamesh feared all three, even though two were unaware and in control. It was a matter of time. Kuzma watched Elliott approach the dangerous edge for the first time in his life. Kuzma knew the deep anger had to be pushed back or everything he hoped to accomplish would be lost.

"Doctor, I need time to explain or . . ."

Elliott got to his feet. He towered over the little who witnessed the raw savagery of the unique lineage. "This will be the last time you see me." Elliott turned to leave. He felt the monster growing inside. He was losing control.

"*You are immortal*," Kuzma said as he cringed on the sofa.

Elliott froze. Conversations stopped and heads turned with vacant stares irritated by the rude interruption. Elliott turned back to Kuzma, his eyes smoldering and face moving to confusion.

"You heard me. I did not want to tell you like this. Please, sit."

You're a crazy old man, Elliott thought.

"You know you have gifts—genius intelligence and acute, sensory perception to name a few. You don't know you and your brothers possess a genetic anomaly that can change the future of mankind. You are immortal," Kuzma whispered with trembling hands.

"You are a liar." Elliott hesitated. He slumped down into his chair.

"Endless cellular renewal. You're a doctor. You know you mature—get better—but do not age. You wonder why. The answer is your aged and damaged cells are replaced. You will never die a natural death, Dr. Sumner. Your genome maintains telomeres and protects your DNA."

"Impossible."

"It is why you have the attention of Gilgamesh.

You and your brothers are evolutionary miracles." The frail, old man folded his *New York Times* over his lap and watched Elliott process the unthinkable.

I see a spark of life in eyes invaded by the biological death march you cannot deny—nobody can deny. Elliott scrutinized Kuzma with every innate gift he possessed. *I see truth and envy in your worn and tired lines. Your facial muscles are coming alive, those dormant until needed for hope and serenity and joy . . .*

"The Gilgamesh mission, from the start, is to find the genetic secret to immortality, the one expressed in your genome."

You're telling a truth, you believe. Is it even possible immortality is one of my gifts?

"Gilgamesh believed their century-long search for the secret to immortality was over. They believed they crossed a threshold of understanding and no longer needed the Bell triplet's genome . . .

"They were presented with the perfect opportunity to kill

Jack Bellow, Adam's identical twin. His body would give Adam a perfect opportunity to kill the world renowned serial killer hunter. Your death would be swift and unchallenged. No inquiries. No investigations. Gilgamesh could then direct all their resources on destroying Adam. Not only do they rid the world of the Bell genome, they take credit for stopping the most horrific serial killer in American history."

"You're sick people," Elliott seethed.

"Adam's suicide was a major setback. Although the illusive monster was no longer a problem, you remained. Gilgamesh sees you as the most formidable foe of all."

"Why? What do they fear?"

"You have all the gifts, Dr. Sumner . . . including the gift of rational thought and creative determination. Only you could stop Gilgamesh from realizing their century-old dream."

"Why would I care?"

"Because Gilgamesh has no intention to share biogenic immortality. They will control the coveted genetic trait. Only the most privileged will qualify. The masses are not worthy. In the end Gilgamesh will control everything. But your existence leaves open the door of enlightenment for the masses. Gilgamesh wants the door closed."

Biogenic immortality is a logical evolutionary step in sophisticated and educated society. Advances in genetic research have made many things possible. Such a goal could attract the the wealthy and the powerful—death and disease are frightening possibilities. Some could be consumed by the dream to live forever. Gilgamesh is a narcissistic, delusional, select collection of billionaires; a far more sinister force than I ever imagined.

"You made me drop this bomb too soon, Dr. Sumner. Allow me to explain why I am here, what it means and what you must do."

"If you are right about the monitoring of my every more, we

should be concerned your people followed me here tonight." Elliott looked over his shoulder.

"Detective Wilcox did a superb job covering your trail out of Memphis. We got you at LaGuardia—you were clean.

"A few of my best protectors are watching over us right now." Bernardo waved to a waitress and touched his lips. "Now, how far did Michael take you before they shot him?"

"He legitimized this meeting." Elliott looked past Bernardo. "Your Gilgamesh world must be falling apart if a founding board member wants to talk to me."

Kuzma smiled.

"My father died in 1947. I received a letter in October from the Chairman of the Board of *Gilgamesh*. The letter gave tribute to my father—I had no idea he was one of the six founders. The letter said his board seat remained with the Kuzma family unless rejected by me, the next patriarch. I received an invitation to the December meeting in New York City.

"Gilgamesh was formed in 1915—a secret society of select billionaires from around the world. In the beginning it was a harmless investment in a hopeful dream. Wealthy people interested in enhancing their lineage and extending longevity joined. Who wouldn't want to live better and longer? Gilgamesh limited membership to ten percent of the 2,000 known billionaires in the world. A portion of our assets were pooled. We merged global networks and organized the effort to pursue an impossible dream.

"I joined in New York City that year. I signed over ten percent of my family's wealth. You see, membership required ten percent of one's net assets every ten years. I suppose I chased the *immortality dream* ever since."

"On the surface it appears to be a legitimate although bizarre union," Elliott said.

"I'm here today because it got out of control a long time ago. I finally got the courage to do what I must. Now, it may be impossible to stop."

Kuzma took a slow swallow of vodka. His boney hands with bulging veins gripped the beaded goblet as he peered over the rim at Elliott. The waitress delivered two more drinks.

"Dr. Sumner, did your research include reading The Epic of Gilgamesh?"

"Of course, an obvious first step."

"The greatest surviving work of Mesopotamian literature, Enkidu's death is painful and life-altering for Gilgamesh, a demigod and protagonist in the story. His great anguish and confusion launched an unprecedented quest for eternal life." Kuzma's eyes danced.

Elliott prodded. "I think we can establish the character—Gilgamesh—went on a long and perilous journey to master immortality."

"The Gilgamesh you seek to understand today is an equally determined entity. Our strategies and tactics can be found in the book. For many Gilgamesh is a private club with big dreams. The concept of living forever is tantalizing. When one has more money than one could ever need, one often spends it on folly.

"Many members failed to see the changes. Over decades we made very little progress. What we did learn, we protected. I suppose we became self-centered. Then we became clandestine. We started to believe we owned *immortality*—we paid for it. We began to see all outsiders as obstacles, nuisances, unworthy, and disposable risks."

"Risks?"

"Yes. Anyone who jeopardized our mission—we neutralized. We got very good at it. Anyone who advanced our mission—we controlled, and they never knew it. Gilgamesh established extensive and elaborate processes, monitoring tools, and analytical systems. We followed biotech research around the world. We had stealth access to all global information reservoirs pertaining to our fields of interest. Gilgamesh had access to private, public, and government data bases anywhere in the world anytime we wanted. Our global network was constructed over the last century."

"And you have unlimited capital."

"That translates into unlimited technology, resouces, and manpower. Gilgamesh capital resources are equivalent to Japan's GNP. But we have only twelve decision makers—no balance of power to slow things down, just consensus."

"Tell me about membership. How many and how do they participate."

"There are 212 members; 200 attend one meeting every ten years. Their rights are inherited. Their only responsibility is to maintain confidentiality. Any breach means release and more."

"More?"

"Two times members disappeared."

"Disappeared?"

"The members know little about Gilgamesh operations. They are told Gilgamesh is engaged in secret, genetic research. Their ten percent investment guarantees their families a place in line, access to any and all breakthroughs.

"The twelve member board runs Gilgamesh. Six are original founders and six are charter members. Charter members are scions—direct descendant of an original founder. There is no difference in powers."

"What does the board do?"

"We manage between $50 and $70 billion in assets. As you have observed, the organization is formidable. We set mission, strategy, and implement tactical elements to achive objectives."

"Is the board global?"

"Yes. I'm the Russian representative. The other countries on the board are China, Japan, Spain, Italy, France, England, South America, Israel, and the United States. Each country has one representative. Except for the United States. I has three."

A shadow grew on Kuzma's left shoulder. He turned and his nose met a tray holding two drinks. The girl hovered—maybe listening. She was new and seemed out of place as a cocktail waitress. Kuzma smiled, took his vodka and Elliott's scotch. They watched her leave.

"We are compromised," Elliott whispered. Kuzma froze. "She carried the empty tray like an evening purse."

Kuzma nodded over Elliott's shoulder. Two large men appeared.

"Thank you for an enjoyable evening. I look forward to meeting again. Give my regards to the family." They shook hands. Kuzma departed along with anything he touched.

Elliott waited, dropped a fifty.

After leaving the lobby and rounding the corner, Elliott sidestepped into the kitchen and held the swinging door to a stop. He went to the back and found the service elevators. Halfway up he got off and took the stairs to twelve. His room, preregistered to Gerald W. Glasgow of St. Louis, faced Central Park.

Elliott left off his room lights. He stood at the window watching the snow drift into the park and rehashing his meeting with Kuzma.

I need more. We didn't make plans. How will I find him? He slid his hand in his coat pocket and touched a folded note. It had a phone number, date, and time. The Gilgamesh logo sat next to the embossed initials—BK.

If it happened, they would meet in three days. Elliott flushed it in the toilet and returned to the window to think. He remembered every word the old Russian uttered. And he remembered the anger that grew inside.

The floating snow seemed to have a calming effect. Another hour passed. Did their meeting go as planned? Did they avoid Gilgamesh?

The only light in his room came from under the door. When someone stopped outside, Elliott knew immediately . . .

FOURTEEN

"If one does not know to which port one is sailing, no wind is favorable."
Seneca

C arol parked on Monroe in front of *restaurant iris*. She swung her long, shapely legs out of the car, her coat flapping open and skirt riding high on her thighs. Albert Bell pulled up behind in a well buffed, black and silver Bentley. He almost bumped her car sidetracked by the most splendid view. A young seventy-seven, he still appreciated a good set of pins, and a pleasant distraction from his worries. She looked up with a gracious smile, adjusted her skirt, and approached.

"Good evening, Miss Mason." Said the tall, willowy man in the dark suit and red tie under the heavy camel hair coat. As he closed the door and turned to her, his wavy silver hair fell across his forehead in a boyish manner. "It is always a pleasure to spend an evening with a beautiful lady, my dear."

She slid her hand through his arm. "And a dashing gentleman." They smiled.

"Well then, so much has happened since your return to Memphis. You seem well tonight."

"I always dreamed of working for *The Tribune*. It is the newspaper I read every day growing up. Do you remember the first time you interviewed me?" she asked. "The day after I got my degree in journalism from Ole' Miss. I was ready to tackle the world."

"Of course I remember, my dear. And I remember suggesting you go tackle that big world and call me after you wrestle it to the ground." They laughed. They enjoyed each others company.

"I found a ten-year challenge. I lived the dream on the west coast, a gainfully employed freelance journalist. Then I get your call."

"You could not say *no* to an opportunity with one of the oldest newspapers in the country."

"I could not say *no* to Albert Bell," she said. He smiled humbly. "And, I could not say *no* to the juicy assignment dangled —an exclusive consulation with the MPD on a decade of cold cases. Really Mr. Bell, no police department agrees to work with a newspaper like that. They prefer to avoid people like us. Whatever motivated the Memphis police department to turn over their cold case files and give unlimited access to their evidence room had to be big."

"I hope you won't judge me too harshly over my clandestine approach."

"You mean hiding the truth? Mr. Bell, if you had told me the mayor wanted a new set of eyes on the most prolific serial killer in American history, I would have been here faster."

"You are too forgiving."

"We got the job done. We managed to live through the experience."

"Now, I am pleased to receive the call from Detective Wilcox. It is time we got together." Albert spoke with renewed strength although he had been through a lot of trauma.

"Before we go in the restaurant, tell me, how are you doing Mr. Bell?"

"I'm much better, Miss Mason. Thank you for your concern, young lady. I suppose a few days of medication and rest helped." He forced a smile and fumbled with his keys. "Do you know if Elliott is joining us this evening? We've not spoken since the terrible night. I know he is a man in great demand."

"Elliott will miss tonight. I wish I knew more. We've not spoken for three days. I know I shouldn't worry, but I do." Carol saw Albert's head drop. *I shouldn't have said that. The life's draining from your face like the balcony,* she thought. Albert's color paled and facial muscles let go of his identity.

"Yes. I too," he said.

That night you learned you had three sons, she thought. One dead and another a monster dying in front of your eyes. Now, losing Elliott is more than your heart can bear.

"Albert, I'm so sorry. I didn't mean to . . ." Carol watched him sink. Then he lifted his head and lost himself in Carol's young and vibrant eyes, the perfect girl in love with his perfect son. *My child . . . you cannot begin to imagine where my thoughts traveled in the span of seconds. You remind me of forty years ago, the only love of my life, the mother of my three boys, the love I lost and think of every day. Like Betty, you are a part of something you do not know, but how could you? How could anyone imagine. When do I tell you? Do I ever tell you?*

"I'm quite all right, dear."

"Hello, Miss Mason." Michael Bell walked up behind Albert.

"What a surprise. I'm so happy to see you," Carol said.

"I'm pleased to be alive," he said.

"I'm sorry to keep you waiting, Michael." Albert put his arm around his brother.

Michael smiled at the girl who shared his horrible experience in the catacombs. "I kept waiting for Albert to release me from the confines of his monstrosity. After a minute of silence, I sensed I was on my own."

"I was swept away by the attentions of this beautiful, young lady brother."

"Well then, you are forgiven, sir." Michael leaned on his brother. "I wouldn't miss this dinner for anything."

The streetlamp peeked through naked winter branches. Soft light fell on Michael's withered body. The once tall, two-hundred-pound man had melted to a skeleton. But he survived his encounter with the BCB. Michael had been taken and held several months with minimal food and water. His miraculous discovery in the final hours beat death . . .

"Miss Mason, did Albert ever tell you we received hundred's of resumés and interviewed dozens of qualified candidates for your position at the *Tribune?*"

"No. He kept that information from me," she teased.

"When Albert found you, he kept you to himself. If you recall, Albert was the only one to interview you, my dear."

"Yes. That is true."

"You should know, and I will tell you now, my brother was so kind as to provide the family with copies of your splendid resumé and robust portfolio of achievements, and most interesting stories you broke across the country."

"Michael, please, I'm sure Miss Mason does not want to hear your dribble on this topic," Albert said trying to turn them up the sidewalk toward the resturant.

"Oh yes, I do. Please, Michael, continue dribbling. This is good for my ego."

Michael struggled to step closer to her with Albert's gentle assistance. The light poured over him. She saw more. The ravaging damage from prolonged starvation and dehydration now appeared insurmountable. Michael could collapse before the night eneded. He could die at any moment with no chance of rescue. Carol reached for the now frail man and found his withered hand on a wobbling cane. She held back the tears out of respect of his determination.

"Miss Mason, things would have been very different around here for a lot of people if you had passed on the *Tribune* employment opportunity. Your courage and relentless investigation broke open this terrible nightmare. Countless times you put your life on the line and walked into a hell no one could have ever imagined."

"Yes, but Micahel, you too faced . . ."

Michael stepped closer.

"Miss Mason, I will not live much longer."

Carol blinked back the tears she had for the man she helped in his most dire moments.

Michael continued. "I've had a blessed life, my dear. Please. I want to be here tonight because I want to thank you and the others before I—well—say goodbye to this world."

Carol kissed his cheek, and Michael stood silent with a wan smile on a face sculpted by the bones beneath paper-thin skin.

Albert ran a finger under his eye before lifting his head and clearing his throat.

"Well then, I hate to break this up." He managed a smile. "Why don't we join Detective Wilcox and our dear friend, Max Gregory. I suspect the two are sipping their third Wild Turkey by now, and I fear if we delay the quality of their participation will be severly limited."

"You've always had a way with words, Albert." Michael turned and broke from his brother's supporting hand. Michael's cane led the way up the shoveled walk as giant flakes started to fall like leaves in a white forest. Carol clung to Albert's arm as they navigated the ice patches. No matter how hard they tried to keep the evening light, the unspeakable terror lurked nearby. Tony called for the meeting, his topic unknown.

On the way to the doors of *restaurant iris*, Albert scanned Monroe Avenue crowded with snow covered cars, except the one parked under a stick tree away from the street lamps. He saw the same dirty, white van in his mirror on Walnut Grove. He saw it ease to the curb when he greeted Carol. The lights snapped off. Now smoke drifted from the tailpipe . . .

FIFTEEN

"Any belief worth having must survive doubt."
Unknown

The doors swung open and the rich aroma of French Creole cuisine bolted from *restaurant iris*. Smells of cannelloni duck, veal sweetbreads, and lemongrass lifted above Natchitoches meat pies, Brussels sprouts with bacon and sherry, and the sweet corn griddle cakes piled high with crab *ravigote*. The three stepped inside. Tarragon, basil, blue feta, and a sizzling strip steak stuffed with fried oysters walked by on a giant silver platter. Guided by the hostess, they moved through the swarm in the heart of the four-star restaurant always booked. Albert Bell made the call the night before to his favorite chef—the private dining room was held for the billionaire.

As predicted, Detective Wilcox and Max Gregory were on their third Wild Turkey. Standing with an arm on the time-worn mantel above the fire, the two were lost in conversation until

Michael entered the private dining room. They had not seen Albert's brother since his ordeal deep in the catacombs. They tried not to appear shocked, although they were.

One wall held hundreds of expensive, dusty wine bottles cradled in a wooden honeycomb that ran the length of the room from the floor to the ceiling. A ladder on wheels hung from a brass rail in the corner. The outside walls of the old building were exposed brick with oak paneling surrounding tall, narrow, small-paned windows, white sheers, teal drapes and gold tiebacks. Fat candles flickered on wrought-iron stands. A gothic, brass chandelier centered in the room brought more warmth.

Next to the fire sat a long oak table with white linens and robust settings of fine china and crystal goblets. The flood of sterling sparkled like riches from an overflowing treasure chest. A glass bud vase with a single red rose adorned Carol Mason's position at the table. At each setting stood a framed personalized menu from the chef welcoming the revered patriarch and each of his honored guests.

Albert sat at the head, Carol and Michael on one side, Tony and Max the other. When the last drink was poured, and water glasses started to bead, and hot yeast rolls steamed in their baskets next to butter-balls iced in silver cradles, the doors opened. The creator and chef of *restaurant iris* glided into the room with the splendor and flair of a U.S. President making an unscheduled stop between meetings with heads of state.

"Mr. Bell, I'm delighted to see you, sir. I welcome you and your friends to *restaurant iris*." His eyes stopped on each visitor. All glasses halted at various stages as they took in the young, accomplished chef with red cheeks, thick curly hair, black horn-rims, and wearing his signature white coat, the top button open.

Albert stood. They embraced. "Chef English."

"I understand you wish to meet with your friends, and then your meal."

"Yes. Thirty minutes together would be adequate."

"Very good. And I would be honored to take care of your food selection for this evening."

"Yes. Of course. I hope your signature appetizer—lobster knuckle sandwiches with tarragon and tomatoes—can find a way into your plan."

"You honor me twice in one night, Mr. Bell. Thank you for remembering. You will have it exactly as you wish, of course."

"Excellent. We belong to you."

The chef smiled and sailed from the room. As the doors closed, all eyes turned to the one who called for the meeting.

Tony stared at his hands, his palms on the table and fingers spread on each side of a half-empty glass. The room fell quiet except for the fire popping and the snow peppering the windows. When he raised his head, his eyes were angry.

"Some bastards are trying to kill Elliott."

"*Kill Elliott!*" Carol gasped, almost dropping her water glass. The others stiffened.

"The shooting at the morgue, they came for him." Tony took a long swallow and set his glass down hard. Michael jumped. His cane slid to the floor.

"It was the second attempt. The first, the night before. The rooftop of the Peabody Hotel Christmas night after sundown. Elliott met with an informant, someone with information about a secret organization he is investigating."

Albert leaned forward. "Do you know who Elliott went to see?"

"*Michael* is the name I got. But he was not a part of the effort to terminate Elliott."

"How could you possibly know that?" Carol asked with growing distress.

"The poor son-of-a-bitch took a bullet in the head. A sniper. High-powered rifle with night vision from another building downtown." Carol set her glass down. Albert's eyes narrowed.

"Elliott's wounded," Tony said.

"*Elliott's shot?*" Carol exploded. "My God, is he . . ."

"He's okay, Carol. He got hit in the leg—the calf. And grazed . . . the head. Don't worry. He got medical attention the same night."

"Were you there, Tony? Are you keeping something from us?" she asked.

"I was not there. Elliott went alone like you people often do with informants."

"Then what happened to your face?" Carol pushed.

"Some asshole jumped out of a tree on my face, Carol. Broke my damn nose."

"When did that happen?"

"Look, It's not related to Elliott and the Peabody incident."

"Just tell us when it happened, Tony," Carol persisted.

"Later the same night. Around two in the morning at the Brent mansion. I was working the two deputies killed in the catacombs."

"I'll bet it was the killer of those deputies," Michael muttered.

"You could be right, but I don't know who it was. Knocked me out cold. I did not have time to introduce myself or take pictures."

"Don't take these comments the wrong way, Anthony," Max said. "Surely the timing of your encounter relative to Elliott's experience is peculiar." Max returned to cleaning his glasses with the edge of the table cloth.

"Someone dragged me into the woods behind the mansion and covered me with leaves."

"You were lucky," Michael said. It rang hollow coming from the most unlucky person in the room. "It probably kept you from freezing to death, detective."

"I woke up around seven with a damn headache, black eyes, and bloody nose. They taped up my face and I got my ass to the morgue for those autopsies. I asked Elliott to be there. He did not want to go. He tried to tell me it would be too dangerous. I didn't listen. I pushed him."

"You can't blame yourself," Max said.

"Yes you can," Carol blurted out. "You should listen to Elliott."

Tony froze. He deserved it. Albert reached over for Carol's hand. She leaned back in her chair on the edge of tears. "I'm sorry," she whispered.

"Your incident sounds peculiar to me, Anthony. It appears the one who killed the two deputies found themself trapped, police and dogs running around the premesis. You could be the victim of wrong place wrong time . . . collateral damage. Why else allow you to live, drag you away to be found later, and cover you with nature's blanket." Max opened his small leather-bound notebook and started writing with his nose close to his pen.

"Max, I'd appreciate it if you would kindly put your damn notebook away. This is a proprietary meeting. No notes. And the catacomb killings is not why I asked you here tonight."

"Is Elliott okay?" Albert asked.

"I can tell you I got him out of Memphis alive."

"How can you be so sure?" Carol asked with sizzling ire, still angry at Tony.

"I was with him at the morgue when it all happened. I put him on a crop-duster in Covington that afternoon."

"I covered the story," Carol said. "Nobody saw Elliott at the morgue."

"He went in disguise—mask, visor, fake name. Elliott pretended to be a visiting doc, an observer. He could get a look at the bodies and avoid the people hunting him. He said the people after him at the Peabody would come for him if they knew his location. Elliott did not want to put other people at risk."

"Was Elliott shot at the morgue, Tony?" Carol asked with a dipping brow. It would be a long while before he got off her list.

"No. I'm telling you everything I know, and it can not leave this room. Seven people died that morning. Dr. Bates may not make it. He is in a coma. Elliott gave Bates a chance at life. No. Elliott was not shot. "

"Elliott was with Dr. Bates when he got shot, right?" Carol pushed.

"I don't see how that . . ."

"Elliott was sitting next to Dr. Bates when he was shot. Tony I can read you." Carol said.

"Okay, fine. Yes. Elliott was there. The shooter shot Bates three times, point blank."

"And the gun moved to Elliott."

Tony looked at his hands. "Yes."

"You saved Elliott's life, didn't you Tony?" Carol said.

"I did my job. That's all." The room gasped. Carol left her chair and went to him. She held his neck. He froze. Then he put his hand on her arm.

"Thank you, Tony. I don't know what I would do . . ."

"I know. He's fine. I promise."

Max cleared his throat. "Where did Elliott go?"

"That I do not know. We agreed it best he move in the shadows a while. Until we know who is after him and why." Tony turned back to Carol. "And that is why you haven't heard from him. He can't use his cell phone. He believes he's being monitored. There was a chance this room was bugged. It's not. Max and I swept it. But Albert, you are being monitored, too."

"Who is pursuing Elliott?" Albert asked.

Tony studied his empty glass and said, "Not sure how to go on from here."

"Tell us Elliott's perceptions at this juncture," Max instructed.

"He thinks a stealth organization is on a mission. They now see Elliott as an threat."

"Does this secret organization have a name?" Max asked.

"Gilgamesh."

Carol said, "Gilgamesh is the organization Elliott and I have been investigating for months."

"Why the interest?"

"The name appears on documents found in the catacombs," Carol said.

"What kind of documents," Max asked.

"Carol, you're getting into classified areas," Tony said with a firm tone.

"I think we are all good here. Max, we've learned nothing. The documents are in code."

"Do you have anything else, Carol?"

"They are well financed, networked, and way underground. We believe Gilgamesh has been around for more than a century. Membership could be . . ."

"And we should stop there," Tony said.

"I would like to talk about the Peabody incident," Max suggested.

Tony nodded. "Elliott told me the man named Michael and he were standing on the west side of the Peabody rooftop when the shooting occurred. They were there maybe five minutes before the firs shot. It struck Michael. He died instantly—the head. The second shot hit the pillar next to Elliott. He dropped to the rooftop and rolled to safety."

"Oh God," Carol gasped.

Max said, "If they were after Elliott, why shoot Michael first?"

"There could have been two shooters. Or, they wanted to

eliminate the professional, eliminate return fire and attracting attention."

"What happened next?" Carol asked.

"Elliott rolled seventy feet avoiding bullets and exploding cement. He made his way to the duck house—the place where the Peabody ducks are kept when they're not in the fountain."

"Wonderful," Carol mused.

"Elliott found a loose grid. Squeezed into the crawl space. Waited five hours. He said more than a dozen with rifles in black fatigues were on the roof that night."

"A small army," Max mumbled.

"Where are you going with this, Tony?" Carol asked.

"I don't know where I'm going, because it does not add up."

"What do you mean?"

"Elliott's story does not add up."

"I'll take it from here, Anthony," Max said. He leaned forward, rested his thick arms on the table, and waited for everyone's attention. The retired CIA operative was comfortable working with loose ends and unknowns. His job was about completing pictures.

"Yesterday, I visited the Peabody rooftop with my people. We combed the area with every scientific, observation gadget available, and some not. We found nothing to confirm a shooting or death occurred at the location."

"I don't understand," Albert said.

"We found no evidence, sir—no blood, no broken plaster, no chipped cement. And we found no signs of a cleanup—no repairs to pillars or rooftop surfaces. We looked at the duck house, the grid described, and the crawl space."

"You saw where Elliott hid?" Carol said.

"On the contrary . What I saw would suggest Elliott could not fit."

"What are you saying?" Michael asked.

"If I had twelve professionals hellbent on finding me, we would have been all over the duck house. There's no other place to hide."

"Are you suggesting Elliott lied?" Carol huffed.

"No." Tony cut in. "I asked Max to take his people and technology up there because I couldn't find a damn thing either. All of us were looking for clues to help Elliott. We were not checking his story, Carol."

"It sounds like you do not believe the shooting occurred," Albert said.

"We don't know what to think. We found nothing, no physical evidence. It makes no sense."

"Obviously they covered their tracks. They're professionals. Did you consider that?"

"We did. And, it is possible. But we looked for a cover-up. If it happened as Elliott said, Gilgamesh possesses significantly more advanced scrub methods than known to the CIA."

"Something's bothering you, Tony. Say it." Carol pushed.

"I did not look at Elliott's leg. Maybe I should have."

"Are you kidding me? You of all people doubt Elliott?" Carol picked up a steak knife. "I can't explain the vanishing evidence, but I know Elliott. I'm sure everything he said is a hundred percent accurate. He is honest and misses nothing."

"This is not about Elliott misrepresenting facts, Carol."

"It should be about the people hunting him. It should be about why they stormed a county morgue and killed innocent people on their way to Elliott."

"It's about that and more," Tony said.

"What *more*?"

"Elliott was talking crazy Saturday morning after the morgue shootings."

"What do you mean, *talking crazy*?"

"We all know he's incredibly gifted. We also know he holds

onto every detail of every sick killer he's hunted. And we know he carries all the painful memories of the victims. He's not like us. He remembers everything and it has taken a toll.

"The doctors in Dallas said Elliott reached emotional capacity. One more significant event could trigger bad things. I know first hand what it did to him—a damn heart attack in Dallas two years ago. Elliott almost died that day. He's had suicidal thoughts."

"What does this have to do with the Peabody, the morgue, and Gilgamesh?"

"Elliott just learned he had two brothers—then he lost them. He learned Albert is his father, after forty years of being alone in the world. Now Elliott is in line to be the next Bell patriarch and heir to a fifty billion dollar estate with all the attending responsibilities. Carol, he fell in love with you, and almost lost you three times in six months. The Bluff City Butcher tried to kill him twice in the last two months. Elliott saves my life with his bare hands last August. Now, he just saved the life of the medical examiner, and looked into the barrel of a smoking gun . . ."

"Tony is making some very important observations," Albert said.

"We carry a fraction of the load this man carries. We've all had our crash-and-burn moments. If we were honest, each of us would admit we there were times we lost our way.

"I know Elliott. He is overwhelmed with personal responsibility. He is on mental overload worrying about everyone. Now he may be hunted for unknown reasons. Elliott is struggling with the heavy emotional weight in his new world."

"What is your bottom line, Tony?" Carol demanded.

"If the Peabody did not happen, it can only mean two things. Best case, Elliott is not thinking clearly and needs our help."

"And worst case?" Carol asked.

"Worst case, Elliott is not who we think he is . . ."

SIXTEEN

"Yet from those flames; No light, but rather darkness visible."
John Milton

"This is Collin Wade. Who is taking the medical examiner's calls?" He pulled out of the MPD garage onto Front Steet and took a left onto Madison. Rush hour traffic was over. Weather permitting, he would get to the Regional Medical Center in five minutes.

"That would be Dr. William Kramer. I can put you right through, Director Wade."

"Hello, Bill Kramer here. What can I do for you, Director Wade?"

"Thank you for taking my call at this hour. I'm finishing up a long day and on my way over to The Med to look in on Henderson Bates and . . ."

"Such a tragedy. I heard today he's still battling, still in critical condition, in and out of consciouness. We're all hopeful. I don't think there has ever been a shooting like this in a county morgue, a very bizarre set of circumstances."

"Yes, we're hopeful too. And I feel the same way about the terrible incident. The world is falling apart. God knows what these people are after."

"I'm sure it's a mystery your people will solve."

"Which brings me to the reason I called. Dr. Kramer, this is an active investigation and there are many unanswered questions. I have some for the medical examiner and know he is in no condition. My visit with him today is strictly personal in nature. I have no expectations, but the Womack and Sutter homicides cannot wait. We have a dangerous killer or killers out there somewhere, and after the shootout we need to move even faster."

"So you believe they're linked?"

"To reach any conclusion now would be premature."

"But it is hard to think otherwise." He located the Womack and Sutter files in the stack and laid them next to each other on the desk in front of him. "What do you need, Director Wade?"

"I've reviewed the paperwork sent over today. I've met with staff. The mayor made a personal visit to express his concern and expectations. I need your help."

"Of course, but you should know I did not attend Deputy Womack's autopsy. I did review and finalize Dr. Bates's work-up and looked at the histology and toxicology. Maybe the better news is I conducted the Deputy Sutter inquest yesterday. That's why you have reports on both cases today."

"Are you a forensic pathologist, Dr. Kramer?"

"Yes."

"Are you a friend of Henderson's or did a procedure bring you to Memphis?"

"I appreciate your scrutiny. Yes, I am a friend, and yes, there is a process. I'm the Davidson County Medical Examiner; have been seven years. Prior to that Spokane,

Washington, and prior to that Ames, Iowa. When we heard what happened in Memphis, I came immediately. The Tennessee M.E. systems have a backup plan. This is the first time we've needed one."

"I see. The information is helpful. Now I can focus on my questions."

"Certainly."

"I am particularly interested in the trauma, the knife wounds. I read both reports. The medical terminology describing these multiple lacerations and the tissue damage seemed to get a lot of attention, but most of it is over my head. I got the sense you and Dr. Bates stumbled onto something of interest to forensic investigators. Can you please translate?"

Kramer opened the Womack file first and turned to the gross examination section containing Bates's observations, measurements, and assessments. "Let's begin with Deputy Womack." Pages turned. "Okay. Here we are . . . lacerations to the neck, chest, and abdomen. No defense wounds. I can confirm the person who killed Deputy Womack also killed Deputy Sutter."

"You're able to reach that conclusion? Are you certain?"

"Yes to both questions. The lacerations are unique and duplicated between victims in terms of anatomical placement and various characteristics of the wounds. The same knife was used to kill both deputies. I believe will find comingled blood evidence when reports come in."

"What else can you tell me?"

"I will speak in layman's terms. The degree of precision tells us the attacker is experienced with knives. Dr. Bates reported detailed measurments taken across each wound. He measured the depth of the cuts at multiple sites, as I did with Deputy Sutter. We independently determined each wound was created by a singular pass of a razor-sharp knife accurately severing vital, vascular targets along a specific path. There was minimal disturbance to underlying tissue."

"Is that significant? Is it an unusual observation?"

"Yes. It is significant because it is rarely seen."

"How so?" Wade pulled up in front of The Regional Medical Center. Snow flurries picked up. Streets were carpeted white and starting to freeze. The trip home would be treacherous.

"I've examined thousands of lacerations and hundreds of knife wounds over my career. I've never seen this type of damage, or level of precision, or perfect reproduction on two bodies. And I've never seen a singular knife pass through skin, muscle, vessels, cartilage, and bone like this. It was like a hot knife in butter. To accomplish what we are seeing on a microscopic level, the knife had to move with a force and velocity impossible for the average man to produce. The arm speed would be at the limits of human capability."

"How can you make a statement like that, Dr. Kramer? How would you know?"

"Cadaver work. Forensic research attempts to recreate wounds on cadavers so we can better understand instruments used by the damage they leave. There has been a lot of research in this area. It is well understood. We know the velocities and forces required to pass a knife through human tissues of varying densities and dimensions without tearing or fracturing."

"I never knew. It makes sense you would study such things."

"Now take this unusual, super human, knife speed and add the incredible accuracy. The two deputies were killed in seconds by a knife moving so fast it would be invisible—a blur. It nailed each underlying vascular target perfectly. Add to that performance equation it took place in a dark cave."

"I'm not sure how to process that information," Wade said.

"Deputy Sutter had identical wounds plus lost an arm—an above the elbow amputation."

"You're saying Deputy Womack had identical soft tissue damage but no dismemberment? Have you ever seen anything like this before?" Wade asked and turned off his car.

"I've never seen this level of precision, force, and velocity before. Few forensic pathologists have. To my knowledge, this has been seen in only six states . . . and Memphis, of course."

"Six states? So if they are still out there we could have as many as six suspects with these skills?" *This can't be possible? Is the nightmare starting again?*

"No. There has been only one with these skills we know. He is known to kill in six states. You know, the Bluff City Butcher. Or I guess it is now, Adam Duncan."

"What?" *No. That's impossible.* He noticed his windows steaming up. The snow melted on his windshild as he sat under the streetlights in front of The Med. "Adam Duncan is dead. The Butcher is dead, doctor."

"If I did not know he died on December 23rd, I would tell you he killed these two."

"Since it is impossible, what is your next best guess?"

"The precision, velocity, and reproduction I'm looking at is not something just anyone can do. This level of execution is unnatural and not easily learned."

"I don't understand."

"Not just anyone can paint a *Mona Lisa*, Director Wade."

"You're losing me, Dr. Kramer."

"Are you certain Adam Duncan is dead?"

"A hundred people saw him die on the roof of the Bell mansion."

"Then, there is another one like him in Memphis."

"That seems impossible," Wade mumbled.

"Did you actually see Adam Duncan's dead body with your own eyes, Director Wade?"

No. I did not see that body with my own eyes. It's that damn one percent question in my gut.

"Thank you, Dr. Kramer. That's all I need . . ."

Wade disconnected and watched the snow in the streetlight. It seemed to be falling sideways. Nothing made sense to him.

SEVENTEEN

"We are never deceived; we deceive ourselves."
Von Goethe

"I'm sorry, sir. You cannot talk to Dr. Bates," bellowed the ICU nurse, her thick hair tightly shaped into a frizzy bun, pointed glasses swinging on a chain above enormous breasts framed by massive shoulders and biceps any linebacker would be proud to claim. If the *female Hitler* had been any smaller, Wade would have pushed by her without a second thought. This one looked like she could whip him. Wade would try the *man card*.

"Do you know who I am . . ." he scanned her name tag, ". . . Miss Fockle?"

"I don't care if you're the president of these United States. You're not getting in my ICU. And the name is not *Fockle*. It is *Fochle* with a *cha*."

"Fine Miss *F o c h l e* with a *c h a*." Wade regrouped. Intimidation got him nowhere, and he had to get to Bates. "I think we got off to a bad start. Allow me to apologize for my insensitive behavior. I am sure we can . . ."

"You're still not getting in. Bye."

"Ma'am, I know you have a job to do. I certainly would not want to be a problem. But I am the director of the Memphis police department. You may have seen me on television or heard my name, Dr. Collin Wade. Henderson Bates and I are very close personal friends, not to mention we carry the weight of the world solving homicides in your city."

Fochle busied herself with charts as Wade built his case.

"He is like a brother to me. I just want one minute to see him, to say a short prayer, our time together. I am so afraid I'm going to lose him. I think my visit will help his recovery."

"Bullshit. Leave. Visiting for Dr. Bates is limited to his wife, daughter, Elliott Sumner, and Tony Wilcox—no one else. I have my orders."

Damn Sumner and Wilcox . . . No damn respect for the damn director, he fumed?

"Yes, I know. It was an oversight. You see, Anthony Wilcox works for me. We are very close. I wish you mentioned his name before. I would have remembered to tell you I'm here on his behalf. Yes, Anthony's been working so hard looking for those who shot Henderson. He is unable to get here today. I let him off work . . . to spend some time with the family hollidays."

"Bullshit. I know Tee. We all know Tee up here. He dates too many of my pretty nurses. Creates all kinds of hell. Sorry, no family either. Goodbye."

"I should cuff you and throw you in jail."

"Fat chance." She slid the glass closed and turned her massive back.

Wade almost exited the ICU waiting room when a *code blue* went over the intercom. He knew it meant someone in ICU had a cardiac arrest. All hell would break loose.

Against the wall he watched the *behemoth in white* with the bun waddle away, stethoscope in hand. The draw bridge opened —the pneumatic doors to ICU gushed wide into the waiting room as a team of greens flew through and caught up with the *gargoyle* at the turn. Before the cage doors closed, Wade stepped inside and eyed the clipboard on the gatekeeper's wall.

Bates was in room seventeen—private—at the opposite end of the chaos. Wade would not be deterred.

Doctors and equipment continued to sweep by as he turned down the empty corridor and counted doors. When he stepped inside the bedlam on the floor was replaced with the sounds of monitors and pumps and aspirators, and TV on a silver dollar speaker clipped to the pillow. Wade closed the curtains and lowered the lights and choked on the smell of mercurochrome, alcohol, poop, urine, and chlorine.

He was on his back on foam rubber pad in a steel bed with a dozen controls. The arm rails were up and the panel of buttons blinked as Wade eased up to Bates bedside. He looked dead or in a coma or asleep. Bates

shoulders and upper torso were bandaged. Drain tubes came out his chest and filled bags with cherry red fluid. A catheter ran from under his sheets into a bulging bag of bloody urine. He had an IV taped to his hand and arm strapped to a board.

Wade noticed the IV bag almost empty. It would soon trigger the main desk. He didn't have long before his favorite nurse-witch would come and beat him. Wade leaned over the nest of wires and tubes and whispered into Henderson Bates's hairy ear;

"Did you see the Bluff City Butcher die?" *Talk to me, you dying son-of-bitch. You were the last one to see that monster after they pulled him off Bell's roof and slid him into the crawl space. I read the damn death certificate you signed: manner of death—suicide, cause of death—acute abdominal trauma and terminal exsanguination. You pronounced him dead at* 10:00

p.m. on the dot. That never happens. Who the hell ever dies on the dot?

Wade leaned in closer. He noticed a change in breathing. BP on the monitor started to climb. "Okay, I know you're in there, Henderson Bates. Talk to me. Tell me about the Butcher. Did he die that night? Now you are dying, Bates. Set things right. You don't want to go to hell."

Why release the body at the scene? Why not take Adam Duncan to the morgue for a full blown autopsy? Yes, it's your decision, but something is fishy. What did you do? Was that monster still alive?

Bates blood pressure continued to rise. Respiration got heavier. His eyes moved under the taped lids. His face twitched.

"Dr. Henderson Bates, did you take part in resuscitating Adam Duncan in the attic of the Bell mansion on the night of December 23, 2009? If you cooperate with me now, you will be permitted to keep your license to practice in the state of Tennessee. But if you choose to continue this lie, we will take away your license to practice and you will be prosecuted for aiding and abetting a felon." *Shit. You don't hear a damn word I'm saying.* Wade ran his hand over his bald, wet head.

"I . . . I didn't want to, but . . . " bubbled from Bates's crusted lips.

Shit! He's in there. He hears me. "What did you do? You need to talk now, Dr. Bates."

"I watched doctor . . . Sum . . . ner. I didn't do . . . I only watched. Not my idea."

"Dr. Sumner told us everything, Bates. He said you did it all. He tried to stop you."

You did whatever the hell it is you're trying to say you didn't do.

Bates's legs moved. He tried to run. He lifted his elbows a few inches and dropped them onto the mattress, exhausted. He turned his head left and right. He stopped, exhausted. A monitor started beeping. One light started flashing. The IV bag was empty. Bates BP continued to climb. His heart rate continued to climb. His respiration increased. Bates was sopping wet.

"Talk now Dr. Bates, or go to jail and die a monster," Wade said inches from Bates nose. Each word lifted hair as spittle hit his cheeks. Beepers were wild. Nurses would come any second. Wade had to know what Bates wanted to say.

"This is your last chance. Summer told us everything. He said you did it."

"No . . . No . . . Elliott did it. I could not believe . . . what I saw."

"You could not believe what, Bates? What did you see?"

Talk to me you bastard. Talk now. Wade heard shoes shuffling down the hall. They were getting closer. "Believe what?"

Bates eyes popped open. The white tape broke from his skin and flapped above his red, raw lids. His eyes were bloodshot and wet and full of terror. His whole body trembled.

"Say it, Bates. Say it now," he yelled in Bates face.

"HE SAVED THE BUTCHER. IT'S ALIVE . . ."

On Batets last word he stopped shaking. Wade froze. He stared at the drenched, cherry red face and watched the medical examiner melt into his mattress and not move. All monitors flashed and beeped. All lines were flat. Henderson Bates stared at the ceiling.

The director backed away and stumbled across the hall into a vacant room. The *code blue team* rounded the corner and poured into room seventeen pulling lifesaving equipment and barking orders. The cluster of greens and stethoscopes were blind to everything around them except the monitors and patient. Wade went out the emergency exit and did not look back until he reached the last step and touched the cold metal door.

His heart beat in his throat.

He had to think. *Is Bates delerious? Is he in some kind of dream land? Could the Bluff City Butcher be alive? Did Elliott Sumner save that monter's life in the crawl space of the Bell mansion?*

He wiped his forehead with his sleeve and wept, something he could never let anyone see. This time Collin Wade had a good reason to cry. And he had all the time he needed. Nobody ever uses the ICU emergency exit. Most people died up there.

EIGHTEEN

"Courage is fear holding on a minute longer."
George S. Patton

The shadow stopped under his hotel door at the New York *Plaza*. From inside the dark room it appeared menacing or imagination.

The rasping sound. A key slid into the lock.

Maid service? No. They would knock. Did someone follow me from the lounge, see service elevator stop at six, hear stairwell door on twelve? No. How would they know my room? Maybe Kuzma sent you. Maybe change of heart—I'm a problem . . .

The shadow hung. The knob turned. *Maybe you don't know I'm here.*

There were two places to hide, the closet or behind the shower curtain. Elliott did not fit under the bed. He left the window. *I could hit you with the lamp.* He tugged the cord. The plug pinched in the socket behind the desk—*Too much noise. No time. And what if more than one?* He left the desk with the Bible. *At least it's hardcover.*

Everything happened fast. The lock popped, door whined, and lights came on. Metal hangers scraped the metal bar, drawers opened and closed, covers pulled off the bed, and mattress taken off box springs. The zipper on his overnight bag yelped. Clothes flew across the room. Then silence. Then panting. Then the crackle of parchment unfolding. Elliott held his breath. One minute later the lights were off and door muffled closed. Only the dank stench of the wet, dirty city loomed in his trashed-out room.

Each drawer was out. The covers were off the bed and mattress askew. Elliott's overnight bag sat atop a pile of his clothes. Unlike death scenes he worked, he knew what happened. He reached in his leather bag for the hidden pouch, and he felt his way into the deepest recesses of the lining. His fingers searched the compartment—the folded vellum gone.

It was given to him the night of December 23rd at the Bell mansion.

They pulled the Butcher off the snow-covered roof and performed a miracle in the dark recesses of the crawl space. After three shots of epinephrine in his chest, the Butcher's heartbeat returned. IVs were set and blood transfused. Bates maintained vitals with drugs. Elliott stopped bleeders, repaired organs, and sewed the abdominal wounds produced by the spire.

Elliott's objectives were resussitate and stabilize. He had to try to save his brother. He would be satisfied with one hour—sustaining life after the horrific incident would be impossible. On the night the Butcher impaled himself on the spire and later laid in his brother's arms, Adam opened his eyes one time and changed Elliott's life forever. He gave his Elliott a folded vellum. It would answer haunting questions. The day of reckoning was near.

Now, sitting alone in his ransacked hotel room, Elliott again questioned his judgement. Did he do the right thing the night he met his brother, the monster?

You're in bad shape, Adam. I'm going to get you out of here, away from these people. You must be still. You are dead to them. Got it? I remember. You nodded. You understood. The corner of your mouth moved. Then you pulled me close still with a strength of ten men. Your eyes were intense. Only I heard the words in my ear. I could not accept them. And for once in your life, you could do nothing. You said to

let you die. I said no. I said not this time, not when I am just beginning to understand the nightmare we lived forty years ...

Elliott shook his head and rubbed his eyes. His hands trembled. *Adam, I did not believe one week later I would discover a mystery bigger than yours ...*

In the attic Adam removed the folded vellum from his bloody sleeve and put it in Elliott's hand. *Now it is for you to finish, you whispered. Then you began to lose consciousness ...*

They zipped the crash bag. The IV was taped to Adam's arm, bags of blood were stuffed between his legs, and everything used to save his life were thrown inside. No one would know Sumner and Bates and Sumner's two medical assistants tried to save a monster.

Elliott made sure the restraints were tight. He would not risk the Butcher awakening and breaking free. He would not risk more people hurt. Elliott did not know his brother, only the monster of urban legend. But, he was sure Adam would not survive the night.

I didn't think much about you moving in the crash bag during transport. I assumed death before reaching the ambulance. No one could survive such massive injuries. I

remember the bloody vellum you gave me. I saw the Gilgamesh watermark—it was official and important. What did I hold in my hand? Why would our names be on a Gilgamesh document? And who are the coded names in the other boxes, the numbers, and the letters in the columns?

Now the vellum you gave me is gone, Adam. Missing . . . is not bothersome, Elliott thought as he stared at the patch of moonlight pouring over the floor by his empty travel bag. *Not knowing who took it and why is.*

Only we knew I had the vellum, and found a way into the gathering storm . . .

NINETEEN

"Welcome to my nightmare. I think you're going to like it."
Alice Cooper

The view from the twelfth floor overlooking Central Park cost eight-hundred dollars a night. Elliott sipped aged scotch from his well-traveled flask, and watched snow drift into the city. Leaving the room would be risky. The *interrupted visit* with Bernardo Kuzma, and the *unexpected visitor* in his room, gave Elliott plenty to think about.

Although the Russian's story seemed plausible, Elliott would treat it as fiction until proven otherwise. Developments since December 23rd were too bizarre, and conditions too hazardous, to rule anything out. Kuzma is the contact Elliott hoped he would find, one who could take him inside the veiled world of Gilgamesh. If Kuzma was legitimate, Elliott had a connection with a disenchanted board member at the most critical time for both.

He sat on the chair by the window and pondered Kuzma's incredible declaration about his own immortality. *Examples exist all over the world*, flashed through his photographic memory. *The Hydra's cells divide continually, no senescence stage. Tardigrades mastered biological suspended animation—they go dormant for unlimited periods only to reawaken when ideal living conditions emerge. All bacteria, at the colony level, are immortal. Turritopsis nutricula are immortal. Lobsters are more fertile with age. Planarian flatworms are immortal. The Bristlecone Pine lives over 5,000 years. The Llangernyw Yew 4,000 years. The Fitzroya cupressoides 3,600 years. And the giant barrel sponge 2,300 years. Okay! Immorality exists on the planet. It's not a new biological phenomenon.* Elliott

touched the cold, window glass and regained control of his runaway train. He learned the trick as a child. He needed a way to turn off the informational avalanche—every single fact and piece of information acquired over a lifetime and relevant to the topic on his mind.

Snow fell into the city but the streets were a shiny black. Lines of red and white light crawled in the late hour. Elliott put his head on the pillow, but his mind churned. *It is possible to possess a life-preserving genetic trait . . . a gene to perpetuate cell renewal by keeping the ON/OFF switch ON. Cell regeneration exists in all living organisms, replacing billions of aged and damaged cells, a well understood natural life process. It begins at conception, slows with age, and stops with death. Why couldn't immortality be a genetic trait . . . a gene leaving the renewal process running? Immortality is no more wondrous than the miracle of life.*

He didn't look at his watch when he put his head on the pillow. And he never turned on the lights in the room. Except for shoes and socks, Elliott was dressed when his cell buzzed in his pocket. Like the shadow under the door, the sudden intrusion startled him. He swung legs off the bed and sat up in a daze. He dug for the phone watching the snow fall in Central Park. Elliott pushed his toes into the cold carpet.

His screen glowed—*Wednesday, December 30, 2009, 1:17 a.m.* The phone number was the same one Kuzma gave him on the note. *Why would Kuzma call this late?*

"Yes?" Elliott said.

"Hello, Dr. Sumner." The voice sounded familiar, but not Kuzma's. Each artfully pronounced and painfully drawn-out word had all his attention. Elliott's pupils contracted and brow dipped. The hair on his neck stood up.

The voice belongs to someone I . . . "Do I know you?" Elliott asked.

"No," puffed back.

Elliott rubbed his unshaven jaw and pushed hair off his face. "But you sound . . ."

"We've *not* met."

"Are you sure?" *That should irritate you, but I need you to talk more.* "Give me your name, or I hang up. It's late."

"You won't hang up."

He's right. The voice—the inflection and pitch and strength behind the words—is familiar but not someone I've met.

"What makes you so sure?"

"I know of you. If you do not push, we both make progress."

"Your number, why do you have this phone?"

"In time . . ."

If you know of me, you know my capabilities. But they don't seem to matter to you, not now. "What is it you want to say?"

"You need to know about me."

"Okay. I need to know about you. Who are you?" Elliott asked.

"I was confused. Now I am sure."

"Good. You're not confused. I'm happy for you. Is that it?" Elliott poked.

"My hesitation is not relevant. It won't happen again."

"Don't be too hard on yourself." *What are you talking about?*

"I know what I must do. It is clear."

"I'm happy for you," Elliott chided. "What must you do?" *I need a mistake . . .*

"The time is here. I've been prepared for the moment. All has been anticipated."

You've been prepared for the moment, Elliott thought. That means others are or were involved. But who? How have you been prepared? And for what?

"Did an old Russian ask you to call me?" *Push away and ypu will give me more.* "If he did, it is really too late. We can talk tomorrow after I get some sleep."

"Seven days ago you met your father and learned you had brothers," he said.

"Thanks for sharing whats in every newspaper across the country."

"Did you ever wonder how an intelligent and powerful billionaire could not know he had three sons for forty years?"

No! I will not let myself. I'm comfortable living in denial. I'm not ready to go there. I've carried my empty beginings all my life. I wondered "why me" too long. Hope died many years ago. I'm not eager to open old wounds.

His breathing increased. The voice cracked. "Who has that kind of power, Dr. Sumner? Who has the authority and capability to keep such information from the Bell patriarch?"

"I don't know. Tell me."

"In time."

Elliott sat up in bed. "No. Tell me now. Why wait?"

The breathing slowed. The voice strengthened with the confidence of knowledge. He spoke as if he memorized the words. "In the spring Albert Bell will come to possess something of far greater value than his amassed fortune. He will have a decision to make, one that will impact the future of mankind."

"Sounds daunting," Elliott teased, unwilling to bite.

"You have the lead role, Dr. Sumner. Mine is to clear the way . . ."

"I'm moved."

Elliott slid off the bed and paced the cold carpet in his dark room. With the phone pressed to his ear, he reprocessed each word and searched for hidden meaning. "Tell me what Albert Bell will come to possess."

He stopped pacing and leaned his forehead to the cold glass of the window twelve stories above the sleeping city. "I'm losing interest. Tell me why I care about any of this."

"When Albert Bell is ready, he will tell you." The phone was quiet for thirty seconds. "I am a scion, not a demon."

Elliott's eyes scanned Central Park. He found a peculiar shadow. The large man wore a long coat and hat and stood in the shadows of a tree at the edge of the south avenue streetlights.

That's odd. No one is walking on the streets. Just cars crawling in the snow. Central Park is empty except for you, Elliott mused. It is too late and too cold and too wet to be out there. Even the bums have found shelter for the night. What are you doing? Who are you?

"If you're a scion—*one born into a rich family*—tell me more. I'm having trouble separating the two. There seems to be a lot of demons after me. You give me no reason to trust you."

"Soon you will have all you need."

"You're not a scion. You're a demon, or you are confused."

Elliott moved to the edge of the curtains and watched the shadow below. The tall man wore a long, heavy coat and a wide-brimmed fedora. On Elliott's last word the man's head cocked upward. Elliott backed from the window. *You're looking at the twelfth floor.* The head turned more. *You're looking at my window. That's a phone pressed to your ear.*

"You talk in riddles. This is a waste of our time," Elliott said. He muted the phone as the elevator doors opened. Elloitt crossed the lobby. He borrowed a random coat draped over a sofa at the edge of drunken laughter and piano music. He thought no one noticed.

"No riddles, Dr. Sumner. This must unfold one way."

Elliott darted from the Plaza Hotel toward Central Park. He had to keep him on the phone two more minutes. "Here's what I think," Elliott said. "This phone call is not about me. It's about you. You're having personal family problems. Believe me when I say I get calls like this all the time. People think I'm a psychologist. They mix it up with pathologist."

"This is not . . ."

Elliott cut him off. "You're trying to sort things out in your personal life with a surrogate, authority figure—me. Your pain inserted you into the Bell family tragedy. I understand. It is a series of emotionally charged events all over the news. You are confused. It happen all the time to good people. Our minds play tricks on us."

"Stop . . ."

"No. Please trust me when I urge you seek professional help. None of this is real."

"You were an *asset.* Now you are a *liability.*"

Kuzma used the exact words, Elliott thought.

"*He* must be stopped," cut through the phone like a knife.

"*Who* must be stopped?" Elliott loped through the falling snow. He was closer.

"The *Humbaba.*You are about to enter the *Cedar Forest.* I will clear the way."

You reference terms found in the Epic of Gilgamesh.

"Humbaba" is the mythological demon. The "Cedar Forest" he guards, the place of the Gods, the place forbidden to mortals.

He locked his eyes on the giant tree in the falling snow on the other side of a line of thick bushes that remained between him and the unknown caller. He was seconds away.

"It begins tonigh, Dr. Sumner . . . one less obstacle."

"One less obstacle?" Elliott said as he rounded the hedges, the thick snowfall transformed the night into a white fog of grays and blacks.

"January 14 . . . Barcelona, 9:30 p.m., the Palace Hotel. We meet there next time."

"Just tell me how you came to possess Mr. Kuzma's phone?" Elliott asked, not expecting an answer. But the phone went dead. "Hello . . . Hello . . . Wait. Talk to me. I have more questions." Elliott stopped on the sidewalk and stared at the smooth snow surrounding the tree. He plowed across and entered the dark canopy. His eyes were slow to adjust. Elliott was alone.

With his penlight he examined the boot impressions next to the base of the tree. The size, depth in the fresh snow, heel-toe weight distribution, and stance were enough for him to construct a preliminary biometric profile. The man on the phone is athletic. He is in his twenties, at least six-four and two-hundred-thirty pounds. The tracks left the tree north into the park.

His curiosity and determination left him no choice—he had to follow. Any delay would lose the trail in the falling snow. Elliott needed to know more about the man on the phone. He could be a scion or a demon. Either way, Elliott may learn more about Gilgamesh. And why did this man have Kuzma's cell phone?

Elliott followed the tracks in the snow, and at fourteen meters he saw a remarkable change in gait. The distance between imprints increased from one meter to three and to five. He had witnessed a similar and unnatural acceleration only one time before—the Butcher.

Thirty meters out the tracks left the snow and crossed the paper-thin ice on the *Pond* leaving nothing but faint, hairline fractures. Elliott picked up the tracks on the other side in the *Hallett Nature Sanctuary*. There were even fewer contact points in the fresh snow. The gait climbed above twelve meters. The speed had to be immense.

He focused on the scant trail in the falling snow and soon lost track of time. When Elliott reached the end, he lifted his head and found himself deep in the Central Park. New Youk City lights were in the distance. There were only faint reflections on his snow. He observed. *What kind of man are you?*

Ice crusted on his brow. With frozen hair and stinging fingers he stood in swirling grays looking into black. The last set of footprints were deep in the snow—the landing point. The assailant, in full weight-bearing mode, went in the thick stand of trees that denied the snow.

Elliott entered with only his feeble penlight. *Are you here? Will we meet this night? He moved slow.* He saw little. He heard wind cut through the naked branches and frozen leaves break under his shoes. Twenty feet in he smelled it—the unique aroma he knew too well. When Elliott lifted his puny beam the smell of blood and raw flesh thickened, and his world of grays and balck added a new color—RED.

He fanned his light. Blood covered the leaves on the floor of the snow-dusted stand. He moved forward. His lights found the bottoms of shoes. Elliott approached. He saw the legs to the knees . . . the thighs . . . the abdomen . . . the outstretched arms with palms up. But there was little blood, not enough to produce the thick, sweet smell of death. After fifteen years and thousands of autopsies, Elliott knew the smell of blood and torn human flesh and viscera. Then his light reached the shoulders covered in blood. The head was gone. Only a pool of blood.

Elliott cringed and backed away. He looked around. He felt something hard under his heel, maybe a rock to use to defend himself. He knelt searched. He found a cell phone—it was warm.

Something moved. It was large and close. Hunched over he watched the black figure glide through the slivers of black and gray. Elliott gripped the warm phone and watched it move away.

Is that you? Are you the scion or the demon who killed the scion?

Elliott pressed redial. His pocket vibrated . . .

TWENTY

"A person often meets his destiny on the road he took to avoid it."
Jean De La Fontaine

Dr. Quinn sat on the tailgate of his Ford pickup smoking a Chesterfield when Rudy Kohl drove out of the woods. Although the sun was still down, a Bentley silhouette is hard to miss. Quinn watched the "land boat" in the night and wondered why a sod farm? He was given directions and told to park in the middle of a forty-acre field of dormant fescue before six o'clock. But, it was not the first bizarre request from a board member. Quinn assumed it came with the territory. As the senior director of R&D for Gilgamesh, he spent half his life in secret meetings.

Kohl pulled up, turned off the lights, and got out leaving the engine running. Again, Quinn was not surprised. The man lived a life of extraordinary privilege—others did for him. This time Kohl was on his own—actually drove himself. That was a surprise.

"You should give up those damn things," Rudy grunted. He was a lot older than the seventy-eight years on his fake drivers license. "Give me one, and a light." He leaned on Quinn's truck and they watched the sun come up. Except for the bird chatter, the place was quiet and private enough; Kohl's people followed instructions to the tee. The fescue, a low maintenance crop in winter, would not get much attention until the spring. Regardless, to be sure they were not disturbed, someone on Kohl's staff bought the land including the hundred acres around it.

"That goddamn dirt road from the highway is pitiful. It's tight, full of ruts and bumps, and goddamn snow piles. I damn near ran off the thing a dozen times." Rudy sucked a deep one off the wet cigarette and grunted his face red. He was a homely, obese man who always wore wide suspenders, always had wet pits, never exercised on purpose, and was balding but in need of a haircut. Rudy had at least four billion people knew about.

"I suppose it was your idea to come here," Quinn said smiling inside. He enjoyed the rich old man's anguish. "You know that nobody does a thing unless you tell them."

"I said a quiet damn place outdoors, not a goddamn field in north, bum-fuck Shelby County." He dropped his cigarette butt, turned to Quinn and changed the subject to the reason for the little get together. "When did you know you had a problem?"

He didn't move except for the rhythmic crush of his molars. Quinn hung on the "YOU had a problem" part of the old man's opening comment. Kohl had always been quick to take credit and even quicker to distance himself from problems.

Quinn could be a stubborn seventy-two-year-old with little effort. Once a well respected physician, he stepped away from his practice to pursue an adventure. He always said he put his practice on the back burner. Each year he would fool himself into thinking it would be his last in a Gilgamesh laboratory. It didn't take long for the years to turn into decades and decades to a half century. Quinn got older. Kohl stayed the same kind of old.

"You know my life with Gilgamesh has cost me just about everything. I don't have a family or any friends. I'm an old man now. Missed life. Missed the world, Kohl."

"Always been your choice, Quinn. What about my question?"

There was only one man Quinn often thought about—his intellectual equal. They were in the honors program at the University of Texas and did post-graduate work together—genetics, organic chemistry, and cell biology. They went to Southwestern Medical School the same years. Quinn did his residency in internal medicine. Enrique Medino did his in obstetrics. Regardless, they spent a lot of time together in the early days, two brilliant and curious scientists ahead of their time in ways few could understand.

Medino's OB/GYN practice got attention during the day. Nights and weekends were dedicated to the laboratory, the experiments, and the rapidly emerging fields of genetics and biotechnology. For years Quinn joined Medino most weekends in Pecos, Texas. Their work was revolutionary and evolutionary, and did got noticed by Gilgamesh.

In 1957 representatives approached Quinn and Medino to present their grand plans—the wealthy members of the stealth organization wanted to unlock the genetic secrets to health and longevity. They offered the same deal to most of the top scientists in the world: their own laboratory, and unlimited capital and resources. Quinn accepted. Medino passed each year for the ten years they kept returning. The offers stopped. In 1982 Dr. Medino was considered a threat. In 1983 were Gilgamesh attempted to kill Medino but failed. Although always denied by Gilgamesh insiders, the same rumors persisted for several decades. Quinn stopped trusting Rudy Kohl in 1982. He knew Medino. The rumors were all true.

"This is the last time I'm giving you. When did you know you had a problem?" Kohl asked.

"Last week," Quinn said, holding back his contempt.

"What did you think you could do, hide it? Did you think we would not find out?"

"No. I did not hide anything. The truth is . . . I thought I could fix it."

Quinn sat in his white lab coat with the LIFE2 logo and name stitched over a breast pocket jammed with pens, felt-tip markers, magnifying stick, and small notepad. His wrinkled, gray flannel dress pants were stuffed in black rubber boots, and his coffee-stained sweater reeked of cigarettes—two packs a day, fifty-five years.

"Do I look like a man with ulterior motives?" Quinn said.

"We bet the farm, Quinn. You said it was in reach this time. You said we had the goddamn thing figured out. You said it worked—was reproducible. You said all we needed was a little time for fine tuning. Isn't that what you said to the board in September?"

Rudy yanked a handkerchief from his pocket and fidgeted with his pinsors. "Did I miss something?"

Quinn was only halfway listening. He stared at the distant edge of the field where the Bentley had emerged from the seldom traveld, gravel road. He could see a few feet into the morning shadows an eight point white-tail looking back at him. The buck had to be weighing its next move. *Was it safe to come out in the open? Or, should I hang here for a while?*

Quinn could see the muscular forequarters. They were twitching, strong and ready. And he watched the big buck sway his head left and right, and the eyes leveled on the truck, car, and two smoking humans in his field. He had to be thinking all those things were familiar but out of place. And the smells meant danger in his world.

What're you goin' to do? Quinn thought. *You're a wild animal. Everyday could be your last. There's always something or someone tryin' to kill you. You gonna risk this one?*

"What's the matter with you Quinn? You gonna say anything? You gonna defend yourself?" Rudy huffed stuffing his handkerchief in his pocket like a kid.

"I've told you the same thing for years. Do you really want to hear it again?"

"Told me what?"

"None of this stuff is predictable. It's leading-edge science. Genetic engineering, the human genome, telomeres . . . it is all new ground. The things we were doin' in the '60s was crazy science fiction for most of the world. We're still years ahead of everyone, and we're closer than ever to solving the puzzle, to controlling the genetic switch for infinite cellular replication—or as you like to call it, immortality."

"I don't buy *close* anymore," Kohl snapped back.

"We just hit a small bump in the road. We're still moving forward."

"From the goddamn beginning I gave you all the money, toys, and people you wanted. You spent billions on your research. You had access to the top minds, laboratories, and research in the world. And I gave you enough time.

"I keep trying to tell you . . ."

"I didn't do all that so you could get me *close*."

"I just don't know . . ."

"You cannot say you don't know, goddamn it." Rudy choked. Quinn seized the moment.

"If it only took money and resources, we would have found the biogenic secret to immortality many years ago. We have been focused. We are doing all the right things. But it takes smart work and a lot of luck. The variables we are dealing with are substantial."

"That is just a bullshit statement."

"We duplicated the *Bell Effect* with the triplets—longevity, genious IQs, eidetic memories, and remarkable sensory and motor skills. All three carried the unique *family* genetic trait for immortality. Before the triplets, the trait was limited to the first male born of each generation. After following them for four decades, we still don't know all their capabilities." Quinn's head dropped as he stepped out a butt. "And now, only Elliott Sumner is left."

"Exactly, two of the three boys are dead, Quinn. If you had been more accurate with your statements to the board, we would not have changed our timeline. All three would be alive today." Rudy spit and turned back to Quinn with rage in his eyes. "And what in the hell do you mean we still don't know all capabilities?

Quinn tried to slow the the runaway train. "I'm just saying . . ."

"The *Bell Effect*. You have not duplicated it since those three boys. And the son-of-bitch Medino stole our stem cells in 1968. The bastard made better use of them than you, Quinn. He duplicated it. He figured out how to turn on the switch you can't even find. And we're pretty damn certain he can do it in anybody. Medino had the biogenic solution . . . at least that's what we thought we stole from the bastard."

"When new ground is broken, scientists deal with new variables, even more opportunities to fail. All we can do is more research to answer the new questions."

"That's bullshit," Rudy spewed.

"Nobody can predict when the next success will come. That's why it is called an unknown."

"We would not have sacrificed Bellow in October if you told us then you had a problem"

"Go back to the transcript of the September board meeting," Quinn said. "I told you we were almost there. I never said we were there."

"Then Adam kills himself, for god's sake," Rudy mumbles. I never saw that one coming. Now Elliott Sumner is the last one standing. He's the most gifted and uncontrollable of them all. He's the true, first male born. He's the primary blood lion."

"Are you trying to kill him too?" Quinn asked not expecting a straight answer. He was always kept in the dark. He lived with unrealistic expectations piled on his shoulders and lies and rumors. Quinn's heart and soul left Gilgamesh a decade ago.

"We are on the beaten path to failure. You misled me and the board, Dr. Quinn."

"You have never dealt with reality. I cannot make you a scientist."

"Tell me, how did Dr. Enrique Medino get to the finish line before you?"

Quinn turned to him. With leveled eyes and bubbling ire he said, "He opened the right door. Dr. Medino was the lucky one. He won the genetic lottery."

"Why can't you make what you got work anymore? We stole the formula after Medino died. You had it working for six months. Why did it stop? What made it stop, Quinn? Did you make a mistake? Did your people screw up something."

"It stopped because you did not get everything," Quinn accused.

"What are you saying?"

"The cells regenerated perfectly for six months and stopped. I'm sure Dr. Medino saw the same phenomena. He had all the data in front of him. He could analyze it and determine exactly what adjustments to make. We don't have any of his research data. We only have his biogenic formula and his list of materials and a production process. I am forced to work backwards to find out what variable needs adjustment. It is possible the small piece of the puzzle will be found soon. In time I will . . ."

"It's too late for you," Rudy muttered.

"Dr. Medino did what all researchers do. He kept control of his research and his breakthrough. He knew you were watching, Rudy. He knew you would try to steal it from him."

"It was your job to take it the rest of the way." Rudy spit again.

"If you interfere now, know it was your covert operation that failed you, not me," Quin said with disgust and no more fight. "I am close. No one can get you closer."

"You should have known it was incomplete. We never would have made the moves we did. It is your fault our program is in jeopardy. You're the goddamn failure."

Quinn chuckled. "You're a dinosaur. You're from another world, unable to deal with reality. You don't understand limits. Never will." They turned to a flash of light on the edge of the field. A shiny black Suburban crawled from the woods onto the brown fescue carpet and paused. Quinn lit another. Rudy waved at the suburban. It approached.

"You're done, Quinn. HR will handle your termination." He huffed off to his coughing Bentley.

"You'll never get there, Kohl," Quinn chuckled. *You blithering idiot* . . .

Rudy slid onto his seat, slammed his door, and spun the Bentley around shooting fescue into the air as he sped off at less than five miles per hour, fishtailing and tires spinning all the way.

Dr. Quinn sat on the tailgate with a half smile. Although leaving Gilgamesh had always been an eventual probability, he always thought his last meeting with Kohl would end with him handing the old man his letter of resignation. On this cold morning in a field of fescue, it was neatly typed and tucked inside his breast pocket waiting for the ideal moment. Quinn decided halfway into the meeting termination would be better—an exit package he earned. Maybe he could enjoy his final years somewhere nice. Maybe he could have some of his life back.

The stag was gone. *Must have decided not to risk it. How ironic.* When the Suburban stopped, the Bentley disappeared into the woods.

"Hello, boys," Quinn said as two black raincoats got out with hands in their pockets and empty faces. Quinn had never met these people from human resources. His first thought was they were new. "Where's the paperwork, gentlemen?"

Rudy rolled down his window and sucked up some fresh air. *Another problem solved,* he thought. Although Gilgamesh had faced setbacks before, this would be their greatest. Medino's biogenic formula was incomplete and the creater was not around to fix it. To add to Rudy's woes, now two of the Bell triplets were dead—Adam Duncan and Jack Bellow—his lab rats and insurance policy for forty years gone. Now Gilgamesh had to perform with no net. Failure could send them backwards a decade. And Elliott Sumner was on his heels. The most gifted of the three would soon put the puzzle if not stopped. Rudy knew Elliott was the most formidable force Gilgamesh would ever face.

And the board. The founders were asking more question. They were unsure of their mission. They began to challenge Rudy's leadership. Too many people have died and the brass ring is still out of reach. Maybe the change in R&D would help.

When Rudy heard the hollow pop and rolling echo, he smiled. *Never liked loose ends or people who hurt me. Quinn's no longer a problem, and I have an interview for the next director at nine. Maybe this one can get us there. He comes highly credentialed. I should be at the LIFE2 facilities with time to spare.* Kohl looked at his watch and accellerated. He was rejuvinated.

Maybe if he had been paying closer attention to his driving he could have avoided the eight point buck charging the Bentley.

They said the timing of impact was perfect. The stag rammed Rudy's door, sending the Bentley off the road into a tree. It was unfortunate Rudy was not wearing a seatbelt. He got a nasty cut on his head, a bloody nose, and shattered his pincers.

They said Rudy made his big mistake getting out of the car. The lifeless buck laid on the narrow road by the steaming Bentley. After circling the enormous carcus with a few choice words, Rudy kicked the dead animal in the head several times. That was all it took to bring the buck back to its feet. And the path it chose was over the short, fat man with the bloody nose that just kicked him.

An hour later HR found Rudy lying in the middle of the road in the woods. He was bloody, muddy, and shivering. They got him to the hospital—three fractured ribs, a broken collar bone, and a busted ulnar were added to the list of minor head injuries.

They say Rudy Kohl was lucky the confused animal didn't kill him. That day the LIFE2 interview had to be rescheduled, and a memorandum circulated reporting after fifty years of service Dr. Joseph Quinn quietly retired and moved to Hawaii with a wonderful package. Like many of the LIFE2 executive team leaving the business, Dr. Quinn was never heard from again. They cannot seem to locate his new contact information.

Rudy Kohl refused to discuss the accident on the dirt road to the sod farm he acquired and sold one week later. Rumers got out that HR saw the eight point buck circle back to the scene of the accident. They said it looked like it purposely stepped on Rudy Kohl's arm before it eased back into the woods. The ulnar was crushed—his smoking hand.

TWENTY-ONE

"The meaning of life is that it stops."
Franz Kafka

E very morning of his seventy-eight years, Paciono Alucio Hernando looked over his emerald coastline and the crystalline waters of the Mediterranean Sea. As he gazed at the horizon from the balcony of the picturesque estate in northern Spain, he believed his life was perfect and he was immortal.

Aragon's stone pillars, ornate chiseled facade, gothic creatures, and piercing pinnacles climbed from the manicured lawns and lush, rolling hills in the northeast region of the Iberian Peninsula far away from the real world. Built in 1919 by his father, Carlos Salas Hernando, the estate was far more than a place for the privileged. For Paciono, now the family patriarch, Aragon was the place of a boy's innocent wonder, impossible dreams, and endless adventures. But all of changed one day.

They diagnosed pancreatic cancer in the summer of 2008, a

week after the abdominal pain, two after his annual meeting with estate legal and financial advisors—the family fortune had surpassed the sixteen billion mark. Paciono stood on his balcony that day willing to trade all his wealth for more life. But now he could see tall hotels on his once-empty coastline and the sea of tourists. Now smaller mansions were above the trees looking into Aragon. The suffocating sprawl, the night glow blocking the stars a night, and the yellow haze over the sun emanated from the second largest city in Spain. The world Paciono held at a distance was closing in on his boyhood refuge. His Aragon was crumbling, melting back into the earth from where it came. In another fifty years, all he knew would be gone and forgotten, like his dreams and his existence.

Few knew the wealth of the Barcelona philanthropist and entrepreneur. Most in the region thought him to be another, respectable millionaire. Family assets were artfully distributed around the world in a thousand ventures and a thousand shells under a thousand names. From the beginning Paciono was schooled in the art of *protecting family assets*, a mandatory skill of the privileged—one now deemed more important than wealth creation. He grew up in a purulent world of government grabs: blatant thievery from the producing, private sector with false promises of redistribution to benefit the masses. It was always about control.

Carlos died in 1951 after building the Hernando Empire. It was 1910 when he met Alberto Bella, the international cotton merchant and reason their family investment focus moved to textiles. In 1915, Carlos Hernando made another decision based on strong recommendations of the Memphis Bell patriarch. The decision to join Gilgamesh set Paciono's lifelong mission before his birth. It was the decision that stole his life. And it was the decision that would cost the family another $1.6 billion this year. But it didn't matter to Paciono this time . . .

* * *

At 7:54 p.m. the chartered jet landed at Aeroport del Prat Barcelona, taxied to a private hangar, and stopped on the tarmac fifty yards out. The lone passenger stepped from the plane wearing a black Chesterfield and wide-brimmed hat covering his face. He slipped a travel-worn strap off his shoulder and clutched the brown leather satchel to his chest while sliding into the backseat of the waiting sedan. It crawled away.

Ten minutes later they were downtown. Without a word, he got out and disappeared into a restaurant, walked to the restrooms, went out the backdoor, and disappeared in the alley. Three blocks away the hat and coat found a dumpster and he eased into a crowded bar. After a three drinks he left with a handful of pretzels for the taxi line. *Random* was perfect, like his beard of two weeks—just enough to cover features and not attract attention.

When he arrived at the El Palace Hotel, he checked in as Alfred Randle Montel, an American venture capitalist in Barcelona on holiday. It was 8:54 p.m. when he signed the registry—Elliott was ahead of schedule. If the New York connection was real, his visit to the Iberian Peninsula could provide a piece to the puzzle. Why had so many been killed for so long? Why Jack? Why did Adam jump on the spire? And why is Elliott's termination now urgent?

A Salvador Dali suite had been reserved in Mr. Montel's name. A change of clothes and the basic travel essentials were waiting. And the key to a black '98 SEAT Córdoba was taped to the back of a Picasso reproduction, *The Weeping Woman*. The car was tucked away on a side street two blocks north and one block west of the hotel.

Max Gregory was the only one in the loop this time. He gave Elliott his word. The fewer to know, the less the risk. The shrewd, retired CIA man reached the peak of his game. Max still had an vast network of talented people he used most of his life. Max guaranteed forty-eight hours no one would know the world-renowned, forensic pathologist was in Barcelona. Elliott Sumner had to move on before the end of day two or he could be compromised.

There was one. At 9:30 p.m. Elliott's cell phone buzzed.

Max was the first to receive phone calls to Elliott's private number. If they were on the approved list, it would be sent to untraceable VPN cloud and then Elliott—he answered only those calls with a 901 area code.

It was the voice from Central Park. "Go to the stone mansion on Darrer de Sant Joan de la Salle, north of Carrer d'Alcoi." He spoke with a crisp, triumphant tone. "There are a few. It is the oldest, biggest, and farthest from the road. Go to the north side and down the seldom-used dirt road. Park beneath the tallest tree."

"Where am I going?" Elliott asked.

"There's a rock wall and iron gate behind bushes. It is open. Cross the grounds in the shadows of the treeline . . . it leads to the east terrace. The door is unlocked."

You're using present tense—is unlocked. You're there now, waiting for me.

"Are you telling me to enter a private residence?"

"Inside, go to the third floor. There is a long hall and many rooms. Go to the last on the right, the best view of the sea."

You're looking at the Mediterranean. You're reveling. Do you live there? Or is this some elaborate scheme to kill me?

"Stop ordering me. Answer my questions," Elliott demanded as he typed the address and hit search. A reference popped up —*Aragon Estate, home of Paciono Alucio Hernando.*

"Is this your home? If no, why am I going there? You must tell me more." Elliott scowled. *Senior Paciono Hernando, a wealthy philanthropist and entrepreneur. What is your connection?*

"You have come to Barcelona for answers."

"But I'm not a fool. Tell me why here? Are you there now?"

"Yes, if you come now. No, if you wait."

Elliott grabbed the car keys and left the room holding the phone to his ear. *This is just like tracking the man in the park. Why Barcelona . . . ?*

"How long do I have?" Elliott asked.

"A short time. I must go. My travel is set."

"You're leaving Barcelona?" He asked running down the dark street scanning parked cars.

"You're about to enter the Cedar Forest, Dr. Sumner."

Here we go with the Epic of Gilgamesh *references.* "Look, I came a long way at great personal risk. I'm here in good faith, not knowing who you are or how you can help me. I came because you seem to know about Gilgamesh. You say you can help. I need a name."

"When we meet you shall have a name."

"You ask me to enter a private residence at night, unannounced. It will be protected, guarded. I risk being shot as an intruder."

"It is not guarded. Risk you must take."

"What makes you so sure I will?" Elliott asked.

"You need my help. You need answers."

"I don't need this kind of help." He said as he searched for his car.

"You will come. You are a hunted man. Time is running out for you and others."

Elliott found the black SEAT Córdoba. The key fit. He was alone.

"I don't know. Too many unknowns. You could be a

Gilgamesh soldier. This could be a trap. Your people failed twice. No . . . Not this way.

Tell you what. I came this far, you meet me halfway. After Central Park, I have no reason to trust you."

"You're playing games, Dr. Sumner."

"No. You're playing games. I still don't know who I'm talking to. I'm done tonight. You have my number. When you're ready to be reasonable, use it."

Elliott pocketed his cell and started the car. *I think I sold it.* The mansion was five minutes away. Elliott headed north.

TWENTY-TWO

"All men think all men mortal, but themselves."

E dward Young

"Good afternoon, Albert," Rudy Kohl bellowed, as he paraded into the study and up to the mahogany desk flanked by the infamous balcony doors. He had to look; twenty-two days earlier they had been pulled off the doorframe and tossed like frisbies across the room by the Butcher.

Albert smiled at Rudy and acknowledged William's frustration in the backgound, hands in the air and shaking his head. The short, round, bald-headed man standing in front of him was always a challenge. No matter what William did to manage his spontaneous visits, Rudy would break loose and barge in on Albert. And this time he had company.

"Well. This is a surprise." But it really was not. Albert got the *heads-up* call from the guardhouse at 3:05. Rudy was standing in front of him at 3:14. Albert had all of nine minutes to put away things and mentally prepare for the human tornado.

He rounded the desk to greet the diminutive man always somewhere in the background of his life. Rudy barely reached Albert's chest, but the plump bulldog always acted the giant. "I did not know you were in town."

"Been here a week. LIFE2 business, R&D matters. Staying at the Peabody this trip."

Two rather large men stood behind Rudy with stern eyes, tight suits on bulbous muscles, and as tall as Albert but built more like pro wrestlers.

"So you're not staying at your Memphis house?"

"Not this time. Peabody's more convenient to LIFE2 headquarters. You know, the walk is only a few blocks up Second Avenue."

"Yes. I know the walk well," he replied with a gentle pat on his shoulder and smile.

Although he didn't act like it, Rudy knew very well that Albert was the new Chairman of the Board of LIFE2, and he was quite familiar with its proximity of the Peabody Hotel. The changes with the board were made after crushing SEC violations —insider trading, clinical-study tampering, a hostile-takeover attempt, and the suspicious deaths of several investors including Jack Bellow, the president/CEO and the famed geneticist who developed the company's biogenic solutions for cartilage regeneration—Dr. Enrique Medino. In his new role Albert Bell was charged with the responsibility of keeping a close watch on the operation, and that included the meddling of the man standing before him.

"Like you to meet someone," Rudy said.

Albert eyed them from the begining. The two had lumbered into the room scoping the place out like they were checking for cameras and alternate exits. They had no interest in Albert Bell.

He was just a man standing behind a desk. Albert thought it peculiar they were with Rudy—not your typical associates. Their eyes were empty and faces flat. They had small, darting eyes and straight line mouths. Their buzz haircuts and thick necks projected a military background.

"Bentley Masher and Boris Tanner, this is the Bell patriarch," Rudy said as he scoped the papers and open files on Albert's desk.

Their hands were hard, leathery, and sweaty with callouses on the knuckles suggesting martial arts. Their grips were like their eyes, void of life and capable of bad things. There were no nods, no facials, and no words—just hollow eyes.

"My pleasure, gentlemen. Please sit. William, bring some refreshment for our guests."

Rudy interrupted, "Masher and Tanner will wait in the car. I'll have scotch." The two lumbered from the study, looking for trees to uproot. William followed with a scrunched face. Rudy flopped in a chair and pointed to the one next to him.

"Very well . . ."

Before Albert could sit, Rudy dropped his first bomb.

"Bernardo Kuzma is dead." He started digging in his coat pockets as he watched Albert for anything unexpected.

"I'm sorry to hear that." *He had to be in his late eighties now. How did he die?*"

"He was killed, Albert. Killed in New York City. Central Park. December 30."

"Killed . . . ? Two weeks ago? You're telling me this now? I've known Bernardo since I was twenty-five."

"We wanted to keep it out of the news. Needed time to do our own investigation. Our people inside NYPD did a good job for us keeping it under wraps. It's getting out now. People are starting to ask questions."

"What happened?"

"Cut his head off, Albert." Rudy enjoyed dropping his second bomb. He lit a cigarette and reveled in Albert's shock.

"Good god." Dazed, Albert got an ashtray from the mantel. "That is terrible. Why would anyone do such a thing to an old man? Bernardo was a gentle person."

Rudy blew a smoke ring and leaned back. "Bernardo left Moscow on December 28. His family said he was in the States to visit friends, and to take care of some business."

"Visit friends and business?"

"I'm a friend. I'm in businesses with him," Rudy said. "He didn't tell me he was in the states. He didn't tell anyone in the organization. His so-called friends in his little black book were all contacted by our people. Nobody knew he was here. He had one meeting. It was at the Plaza Hotel the same night he was killed in Central Park."

"Why were you contacting his personal friends and questioning his business matters? I'm sure he had his own reasons for coming over here. They don't need to include you."

"Nothing added up. His secret meeting in New York is troubling, Albert." Rudy took a long drag and flicked a long ashe into the tray. "Before I go there, tell me how far along you are with Elliott Sumner."

"What do you mean? Now you want to know about Elliott? Why?"

"It's been three weeks since the news broke—the next Bell patriarch. I want to know if you have brought him into the fold. Have you discussed family matters and business interests with him? Have you told him about Gilgamesh?"

"We were talking about Bernardo, not Elliott. What's the matter with you?"

"Please, just answer my question. They are related."

"Related? Impossible." Albert fell back in his chair. "I've not talked to Elliott. It's too early. We have plenty of time. You of all people should understand how I feel about the deaths of two sons I never had the opportunity to know. I'm not ready to move on, Rudy."

"It's time to get over all of that and deal with today and what you can manage. You need to sit down with the son you've got left and start talking. You better get with Elliott while you can. Things are getting confused out there. Do you know where he is now, what he's doing, Albert?"

"Slow down, and don't tell me to get over anything. I will grieve my losses my way. Elliott is not some small child I put on my lap and lead. He's a noted professional in high demand."

"I understand all that. Where is he now?"

"I don't know. He dosen't check in with me."

"You two are not talking daily?"

"Certainly not. I'm quite certain he's engaged in some forensic investigation." Albert leaned into Rudy's space. "And you didn't tell me what the NYPD thinks happened to Bernardo. Where was he killed? Was he robbed? And what do they think about the decapitation, or is that a term used when a throat is cut?"

"He was not robbed. Had a couple thousand in his wallet, diamonds on his fingers, and a $100,000 Rolex watch. I said Central Park. And yes, his head was cut off his body."

"*God!* I don't know why anyone would do such a thing . . . and to an old man."

"He was executed, Albert."

"Executed. Why?"

"Someone is sending a message. It took NYPD a week to confirm Kuzma's identity. The person who killed him took the head."

"His head was taken?" Albert got up, walked to the fireplace, and took his anger out with a poker and smoldering logs. He stopped when flames returned and his ire turned into revulsion.

"I have more disturbing news to share, Albert. If true, it is very bad."

Albert sat next to the old man. "What could be more disturbing?"

"Bernardo was meeting someone in the Plaza Hotel before he was killed. We do not know who for sure. However, Elliott was staying at the same hotel under an assumed name."

"You think Bernardo met with Elliott?"

"Yes. I do."

"Are you suggesting Elliott had something to do with Bernardo's death?"

"It is a possibility."

"Now I know you are losing it." Albert lit a small cigar. He was puzzled. William delivered the scotch. "Leave the bottle," Albert said.

"There are witnesses, Albert. People saw Elliott go into Central Park that night. And he was seen seen leaving the cluster of trees where Bernardo's body was found."

"You've got to be kidding. You don't think . . . ?"

"The coat Elliott wore that night, the police have it. Kuzma's blood is all over it, Albert. They have Elliott's DNA too. The NYPD has enough to bring him in for questioning. They're looking for him now."

"This just keeps getting better."

"Something's not right here," Rudy said with smoke drifting from his nose.

"Elliott was probably in New York City on a case. He would not know Bernardo. He would not meet with a man he did not know unless it was connected to his work. And Elliott certainly would have no reason to kill Bernardo, or anyone else for that matter."

"The NYPD did not know Elliott was in their city. And, Elliott did know Bernardo."

"Wait. I don't care about the NYPD, what they knew and didn't know. Elliott works cases that do not involve police early on. And I know he often works undercover to avoid the press. And what do you mean he knows Bernardo?"

"There was a shooting on the roof of the Peabody Hotel Christmas night."

"A shooting in Memphis Christmas night?" *So it's true. Tony said Elliott was shot on the roof of the Peabody, but he couldn't find proof it even happened.*

"You wouldn't know about this stuff," Rudy said. "It's a security matter. Some of our people made a mistake. We thought a man meeting Elliott Sumner was someone we had been looking for—a very dangerous member of a clandestine organization who killed several of our scientists. That night there was an unfortunate confrontation. I'm afraid Elliott was in the wrong place at the wrong time. He was almost injured. One man was killed that night. Turns out he was not the one we were looking for. All a big mistake."

"You say some of our people made a mistake. A man was killed. What are you talking about?" Albert demanded. "Our security people hunt and shoot people? My God."

"It's more complicated than that . . . and it's a long story. Just trust me when I say it was a mistake. Information came into Gilgamesh, a meeting on the rooftop of the Peabody after sundown. We were not expecting Elliott Sumner. Our security personnel were assigned to simply capture and turn over the target to the MPD. He started shooting. We responded."

You're lying to me? Elliott thought. "The target? Interesting choice of words." Albert downed his scotch and

spit the cube in the empty glass. "You've lost control of Gilgamesh. Your people could have just as easily killed Elliott. You should have pulled back when you saw he was there."

"They removed the body and our scrub team took care of the roof. No one will ever know we were up there, except Elliott."

"What happened to Elliott?"

"When our people got to the roof, he was gone. They think he hid in the hotel. We had to get out of there—no time to look and set things right with him."

"This is way over the line, Rudy. It is murder." He poured more scotch. "Who was the poor man killed that night?"

"For years we've watched Bernardo. He changed, Albert. He's been depressed over his deteriorating health . . . his aging and our inability to help. We kept close tabs on him. He had a friend arrange meetings for him, the meetings he did not want Gilgamesh to know about."

"Not everything has to include Gilgamesh. You were following a board member."

"That night on the roof of the Peabody Elliott was meeting with Bernardo's advance man. We think the New York meeting was set up then."

"So what. Elliott's the next Bell patriarch and my new-found son. Maybe Benardo wanted time with him. And frankly, I don't care. You have no right to stick your nose in someone's private affairs. Gilgamesh cannot kill people, for God's sake. What is the matter with you, Rudy? Have you lost your mind?"

"I understand your frustration and anger."

"I am more disappointed than you will ever know."

"Albert, the Peabody and morgue shootings have put Elliott on the offensive. I think he is weary of Gilgamesh. It is feasible to consider he could eliminate a Gilgamesh board member to send a message."

"Are you insane? And did you order a raid on the morgue to hurt Elliott?"

"No. It was Paciono Hernando. He ordered the raid."

"The Spain board member? How could he, and why?"

"He has the authority. Paciono has never been a fan of the Bell triplets. Because Jack and Adam were gone, he saw Elliott as a liability after the Peabody incident. He saw great risk to the organization and diversion from our mission. He's a desperate man, pancreatic cancer, only months to live. He's hoping for the life extending breakthrough we promised long ago."

"There is so much wrong here. I'm not sure I want to know anymore . . ."

"I came to put things on the table so there can be no misunderstandings, no mistakes."

"Jack and Adam are dead, my two sons I never knew. I've lost my wife. I've lost Betty Duncan, another son and daughter. Elliott is all I have in the world. Let me be very clear. If you ever plan to terminate Elliott, you best terminate me first."

"I don't want to lose Elliott either. He's the next Bell patriarch."

"I don't believe you, Rudy."

"You're upset with me. I understand. This is an emotion-charged time."

"You had no right to keep my sons from me. And, I have always been suspicious Gilgamesh had something to do with Betty's disappearance. Gilgamesh is out of control, Rudy. You best fix it or everything you hoped for will be lost."

"We are so close."

"Your dream of immortality is turning into something else. I believed Gilgamesh was an honorable society of privileged men seeking to do great things for mankind. I am now starting to wonder if any of it was true."

"We do want to do great things, Albert. All of this is a missunderstanding. We are close to the biogenic breakthrough we've sought for a century. The Bell triplets opened doors in 1968. For the most part, the ground-breaking genetic engineering experiments worked. But we have faced danger along the way.

Bad people—rogue governments and special interests—have tried to take what belongs to us. We had to find a way to protect ourselves. Over the years many of our people have been horrifically killed by very dangerous people. My single greatest failure has been my inability to open your eyes to this reality. Anyone who has dared to do great things has faced the looters and angry mobs of humanity."

Albert set down his glass and leaned into Rudy's face. "I understand danger. I understand protecting assets. Neither justifies killing people. Criminals are turned over to law enforcement. It is troubling you think Elliott Sumner is capable of beheading anyone. That kind of warped thinking tells me you are out of touch. More mistakes will be made."

"We do not intend to hurt Elliott. I want to do everything possible to bring him into the fold so there can be no misunderstandings by others in the organization. I'm concerned he has gone underground on a personal quest to penetrate Gilgamesh. I believe he sees Gilgamesh as a sinister entity. His mission could be evolving—destroy or be destroyed."

"Although I doubt that to be the case, I could not blame him after all he's been through."

"Albert, we need to reach a mutual understanding. I'm here to ask you to bring Elliott into the fold the right way."

"What did you do with Joe Quinn?" Albert asked as he reached over and stopped Rudy from lighting his third cigarette.

"Joe Quinn, he retired . . ."

"I want to talk to him," Albert said. "Can you arrange for that to happen?"

"No."

"Why not?"

"How would I know how to reach the man? I don't keep track of things like that." He pulled back and lit his cigarette. "I'm not a secretary."

"You know what's troubling?"

"No, but I'm sure you'll tell me."

"Why is it executives leaving LIFE2 disappear?"

"It's a big world, Albert. They make a lot of money and work hard. Maybe they want to be left alone. I'm sure if you made an effort, you could make contact."

"Maybe you're right." Albert had never attempted to find one. "Is it possible your attempt to extend life has become something else, Rudy?"

"Nonesense. The Gilgamesh mission has not changed. Our members have invested several billion over a century supporting our noble efforts to unlock the genetic secrets to immortality. Along the way we have protected our members and our assets like any other enterprise."

"Did Gilgamesh have anything to do with the deaths of the two deputies in the catacombs?"

"Absolutely not. We are looking into it as we speak."

"Why the interest?"

"They were killed in the same manner as many of our people over the years. We always assumed it was Adam. But he is dead."

"The deputies were working in a recently discovered room in the catacombs."

"Oh really. I didn't know that."

"Number nine . . ."

"Is that supposed to mean something to me?"

"There were a lot of Gilgamesh documents in number nine," Albert said.

"Again, I did not know." Rudy turned toward the fireplace.

"I recall father telling me Gilgamesh started to using the catacombs in the early 1900s when the Brent mansion was the the Bell mansion. I never ventured down there as a boy. I thought it was haunted." Albert chuckled. "But I remember a lot of strangers going in and out of the cellar with boxes. Always thought that odd . . ."

"What are you suggesting?"

"Maybe someone inside Gilgamesh didn't want certain records disturbed in room nine."

"I see where you're going with this. Rest easy, Albert. All Gilgamesh documents of importance are in code. Our secrets are safe. There would be no need to protect them further."

"But codes can be broken. In the age of computerization, thousands of scenerios can be analyzed in seconds. Maybe those secrets are not as safe as they once were."

"Gilgamesh is not involved, Albert. Our only interest is to find the killer of the two deputies. We may have another *Adam* running around—for God's sake. Your imagination is working overtime again. We're not the monsters you seem to think we are from time to time."

"I want you to investigate Gilgamesh personally. Someone could be out of control, Rudy. And I want you to send an order to board members. Make certain there is no misunderstanding. LEAVE ELLIOTT SUMNER ALONE."

Rudy nodded. "He's not so unique, you know."

"What's that mean?"

"We have others as gifted as your boys."

Albert knew he was outside the loop. Gilgamesh progress was rarely discussed, even at the quarterly board meetings. "This is the first I'm hearing this."

"You just met two. Bentley Masher and Boris Tanner are a lot like Adam—very strong and athletic. But they're not uncontrollable psychopaths. They're just angry all the time."

"Wonderful accomplishment, Rudy." Albert shook his head in his glass.

"The Bell triplets have always been special. They have always been our key to unlocking the secrets of immortality. Your sons were considered major assets of Gilgamesh. For that reason their universal protection was guaranteed. Now, two are gone and one remains. But Elliott is no longer our only asset. His actions can make him a liability. I don't want Elliott to become an enemy of Gilgamesh. I don't want him to be one we must stop to protrect our members and our assetts."

Albert's eyes climbed the old man. "So you agree with Paciono. Elliott as a liability."

He got up and rested a hand on Albert's shoulder. "I'm saying the world is changing. We all make choices. I hope Elliott comes home soon." Rudy pushed out his cigarette and left.

Albert stared into the dying fire for an hour with his scotch. The smell comforted him. It reminded Albert of his father, the man he most revered, the man taken from him too soon. The plane crash was on Albert's twenty-forth birthday. Devistated, he was too lost and confused to take on the vacated role of Bell patriarch. But Rudy Kohl insisted and Albert relented. Ever since that tragic day, Albert allowed Rudy to run his life from the shadows.

You are right, Rudy. The world is changing . . . and we each make choices. He downed his drink. *You just told me Gilgamesh is going to kill my son . . .*

TWENTY-THREE

"For an impenetrable shield, stand inside yourself."
Henry David Thoreau

His cell phone buzzed when he reached back to close the patio door at Aragon. He moved to the darkest corner of the first room and knelt below the furniture. Looking from under the dining table, he saw the soft light a hall and two rooms away—maybe a night light. Although the cold mansion seemed to be empty, Elliott had to assume he was not alone—he could die tonight.

He covered his phone with his hand and whispered, "Tee, it's been two weeks . . ."

"Hello to you, too," Tony shot back, and started in on him. Elliott could only listen and stay low watching for more signs of inhabitants.

"You need to talk to Max," Tony complained. "He's too goddamn secretive. Got real trust issues, Elliott. The old fart acts like I'm tryin' to turn you over to the cops. I'm very close to shooting the bastard."

Elliott smiled, "Don't shoot him, Tee. He's just protecting me. I asked him to keep me under wraps until I know more." A board whined upstairs. Elliott sunk in the dark corner.

"I still might shoot the corpulent creep. Where the hell are you, anyway?"

"Can't talk."

"You chasin' the Serpentine in London again?"

"No. Something new. What did you know about the Central Park killing."

"Right. I talked to my guy at NYPD. Don't mind telling you this thing is being held very close to the vest. Took my *inside buddy* a week to even confirm there was a kill. Took another week to get some poop. That is just bizarre."

"I wonder why?"

"I'm thinking a decapitation in Central Park would screw up tourist traffic to the Big Apple. Come on genius, you should know that. Sometimes you smart guys miss the obvious. I guess that's why you keep dummies like me around."

"It's more than marketing, Tee."

"Not every day do you lose a guy's head. Believe me, That's enough to go underground."

"Not buying it. Look deeper."

Elliott leaned around the door jamb and peered up the staircase. The black wrought iron handrail and balusters, dark granite treads, and risers curved up into darkness. Cracks in the dirty, white plaster, and the uneven walls revealed the age of Aragon. Halfway up was a round window. It glowed from an outside flood.

"What are you thinking?" Tony asked.

"Someone inside wants this quiet for a reason. You find out

who, and we'll find another way into Gilgamesh. I'm now certain the secret organization is involved."

"I hate to ruin your day."

"Ruin it."

"NYPD thinks you killed the guy."

"You're kidding."

"They're looking for you—Dr. Elliott Sumner, forensic sleuth gone wild." Tony chuckled and choked on cigarette smoke.

"Verr funny." Elliott backed into the shadows.

"I wish I wasn't."

"The NYPD thinks I cut a man's head off?"

"Well, I don't think they really believe you . . ."

"I've solved a dozen homicides for them over the years. They should know better. I did not even tell them I was in their city that night. I wonder how they found out."

Elliott started up the first flight of stairs, the creaking rizers marking his measured progress.

"People came forward—eyewitnesses," Tony said. "Some saw you leave the hotel headed for the park. Others saw you come out of the park an hour later. The NYPD has your overcoat with the victim's blood and your DNA. They found it in the damn lobby of the Plaza Hotel."

"It wasn't my coat. I borrowed it. Was kinda in a hurry. I returned it where I found it."

"Sweat, forensic man. The coat was soaked. Like you ran a goddamn marathon."

"I was following someone in the snow . . . a long way. I came upon the body."

"Well, you got blood all over you, Elliott."

"When I returned to the hotel, I put the coat back where I found it."

"You were not thinking clearly. There was enough blood on the coat to turn heads in that lobby. And people recognize you, Elliott. You're goddamn famous. You were identified. I cannot believe you did not think to ditch the goddamn coat. You'd make one lousy killer."

I had to get out of there fast. My meeting with Kuzma was compromised. My room was ransacked and the vellum taken. The guy on the phone was in the park—he ran like a cheetah. Then I trip over a headless corpse. I was losing it. My demons were stirring.

"You were followed up the back stairwell to the twelfth floor, Elliott."

I knew it. "I Had a lot on my mind, Tee." Another board ached. This time it was the third floor. "I didn't look back that night," he whispered.

"The police pulled up to the Plaza minutes later. They did a room-to-room search on twelve. You were registered with a fake name and gone. It did not look good, my friend."

Elliott reached the second floor of Aragon and moved to the darkest wall where three halls converged, each pitch black and musty cold. *No one's been living in this house for a while . . .*

"Why did you leave that night? Why not stay put?"

Maybe the caretaker's quarters are downstairs. It would explain the light and better climate in the old place.

"Elliott, talk to me," Tony pushed.

"You know why—my demons, people hunting me. I live in the shadows now," he whispered as he eased around the corner to the third-floor staircase. There was another soft glow above.

"I get it, but police types don't like people running from dead bodies with blood on their clothes. We think guilty, case closed, hang the bastard."

He climbed hugging the wall.

"Like it or not, you're always in the news busting serial killers. The BCB case is all over the place now. Bigger than that, you're the next Bell patriarch. Elliott, you're a goddamn billionaire super hero. People know you."

"Well, that's just . . ."

"No, well-that's-just about it. You need a disguise."

"You're right," Elliott whispered. A shadow moved at the end of the hall.

"Now it's even more critical," Tony said. "You got Gilgamesh and NYPD lookin' for you. And if you're outside the country, add FBI, CIA, and INTERPOL."

Elliott eased toward the soft glow where the shadow moved. He smelled furnace heat falling from the room. There was enough light to see carpet in the center of dusty wood floors. The plaster walls were like the stairwell. They were lined with oil paintings—dark landscapes with soldiers wearing red coats riding white horses swinging sabers. They were in heavy gold frames and perfectly spaced. He moved toward the last doorway on the left, the west side of the Aragon mansion.

Elliott held his phone tight to his ear and whispered "Did you and Max look at the Butcher kills like I asked?"

"Yes. It's still early, but you are right. I gotta admit I thought you were losing it the day I put you on that crop duster. There is something odd going on. I get back with Max next week to pool our findings. We will have the answers then."

Elliott stopped. He was not alone. "Got to go." He started toward the last door, the place where the voice on the phone had said they would meet.

"Wait," Tony said. "About the dead man in Central Park."

Elliott stopped a few feet from the door jam—the room with the best view of the Mediterranean. He pushed his back flat against the wall. "Hurry. What else?"

"Do you know a Bernardo Kuzma . . . ? Elliott—are you there . . . ?"

TWENTY-FOUR

"By doubting we come at truth."
Marcus Tullius Cicero

"Bates told me they saved Adam Duncan's life in that attic on December 23rd." Director Wade said in a matter-of-fact manner as he rifled through the papers on his desk. "I have the order somewhere."

"What in the Sam Hill are you talking about? Bates is in a coma. Been in one since December 26. Still is now. How'd you get that man to tell you anything?" asked the sheriff.

Taft tried to avoid downtown as much as possible. And he dispised visiting MPD headquarters—nothing good ever came of it. They had their way, he had his. But out of the spirit of cooperation he went once a quarter. This time Collin Wade had left three messages over three days. G.E. couldn't put it off any longer. He had some late-day business to attend to at the county courthouse. MPD was a few blocks away.

"I know he's been in a coma. Went to see him anyway. Went to The Med to talk."

G.E. struggled out of the hole in the old leather sofa. Got to his feet and walked over to look out Wade's third floor window. The empty courtyard was lit up and a trolley passing by. "The last time I was in that courtyard, you guys had to go public with the Bluff City Butcher. You remember, Wade?"

"Yes, I do. That monster just killed three more people and hung a sick, three-headed corpse off the Hernando de Soto Bridge." He looked up at the ceiling and got quiet for a few long seconds. "That was hell. Changed my life that day."

"I'm startin' to worry about you again. You've been under a lot of pressure, been making some bad decisions based on, I don't know what."

"What're you talkin' about?" He turned to Taft with eyes pinched down and a lips pursed.

"For years you refused to accept there was a serial killer in Memphis. You looked for every reason under the sun to explain it away. You stopped listening to your people. You gagged Tony Wilcox, probably the sharpest knife in your drawer, best homicide guy I know next to Deputy Pilsner. And you didn't even take the professional advice of the top serial-killer hunter in the world—Elliott Sumner. Hell, he didn't have to help you boys, but he did. And the mayor forced you into a collaboration with *The Memphis Tribune*. Wanted to get outsiders to take a look at a decade of cold cases in the region. That was just another slap in the face, another example of your screwed-up way of looking at this whole Butcher thing."

"Wait a minute. I agreed with the collaboration after I discussed it with Albert Bell. He had some good ideas and then he brought in the Carol Mason girl."

"Come on Collin, you had to agree. Albert owns the goddamn *Tribune*. He's close to the mayor. What makes you think that program was the mayor's idea? That's my point. It's like you got something else driving you. And now this. It's a bunch of malarky."

"I supported the process." Collin Wade joined G.E. at the window.

"No you didn't. You gave a Pulitzer Prize winning investigative reporter more shit to deal with than was reasonable. She broke the Bluff City Butcher case wide open on your watch. And you still tried to avoid dealing with the whole thing. But the Butcher wouldn't let you—not anymore. He hung the guy on the bridge after he sewed on a couple more heads. That got your damn attention. You couldn't bury that one."

"As the director of the Memphis police department, it is my job to consider all possibilities and all options. Not to just react. What is it with you guys second guessing me?"

"Bullshit Collin. It's your job to take the bad guys off the streets. You got hung up in needle-dick paper and process."

"I think it's a little more complicated than that."

"No, it really isn't. And what about hooking up with that Dexter Voss character? You let that man get too close over the years. You stopped listening to reason and following police instincts, the stuff that got you to the top of your profession, responsible for 2,500 people and a $250 million annual budget."

"Voss was the regional director for the FBI. My job includes cooperating with that office like I do with the county sheriff and other law enforcement bodies."

"Yeah, cooperate . . . that's bullshit, Collin."

"That's what I did, G.E."

"No, you put your damn brain in your bottom drawer. Voss was trouble and we all knew it. After we exhumed the Medino family, we were able to prove the man ran them off the road and doused them with kerosene. The guy was rogue, trying to steal Dr. Medino's research."

"I must admit it flushed out the Butcher. He killed Voss on July fourth."

"And you had your head so far up your ass you didn't even consider the fact the Butcher might have some kind of relationship with Dr. Medino. Your people had all the information. The suspicion was there, but you were MIA, Collin."

"Okay. I made some mistakes. Everybody does. I'm human. But I'm telling you this time it's different. Dr. Bates told me . . ."

"Nobody's allowed in ICU to talk to Bates," Taft barked. "Especially police business. All of them up there are rigid protectors. Damn ICU nurses take courses on how to keep people like us out of their hair. Some scare hell out of me, frankly." He smiled. "Guess it's all about saving the guy lying in the bed. Everything else can wait a while. That's how they see it."

"I wasn't born yesterday. I got into ICU without them knowing. There was a code blue, a heart attack somewhere up there. People were running around. Doors opened and attention was diverted. I slipped in and found Bates private room. I was with him five minutes. I left out the emergency exit, the staircase to the back of the place. They never saw me, G.E."

"Oh, that's great. The Director of the MPD violates rules of The MED. Shit son. When did you do that?" G.E. tugged on his silver handlebar mustache and peered over the tops of his bent pair of reading glasses.

"December 29. Was after eight. The night we got all that snow. I got off the phone with the interim M.E. He got me to thinking about the Butcher—you know—the way those deputies were attacked with a knife in the catacombs."

"It's January 14. Over two weeks later. Now you're just getting around to talking about this?" They stayed at the window. Another trolley crawled by and took their attention like two kids playing with a train set under the Christmas tree.

"Dr. Bates was in a coma—messed up bad. I thought I'd ask some questions, push a little. You know Bates and Sumner were in the attic at the Bell mansion with the Butcher for twenty minutes after they pulled him off the roof."

"He was dead on the roof. Your point?"

"At the time I didn't think much about it. I thought the Butcher bled out on the roof, too. I assumed he died long before they got to him."

"A lot of people saw him die, Collin. Nobody could survive a damn seven-foot spire stuck through their gut like that . . . and lose all that blood. Not even a mythical monster."

"I simply asked Henderson Bates what they did in the attic. He laid their, but his monitors started to go crazy. They were beeping and flashing. My words were having an impact. Bates could hear me. I changed tactics. Pushed a little harder."

"Oh boy, this ought to be good."

"I got up close to his ear and whispered Sumner *told us everything*. I said Sumner *turned state's evidence* and got a reduced sentence—aiding and abetting a felon. I told Bates he was going to lose his medical license and die in prison if he didn't talk now."

"You said that to a man in a coma? That's damn pitiful. That's sick." Taft's lips thinned and eyes squinted as he looked at Wade's reflection in the glass.

"Yeah, well that little threat lit up the monitors even more. His heart rate and blood pressure went through the roof. God knows what else it did."

"You could have killed the man," G.E. said.

"Then Bates eyes popped open. The tape on his lids ripped from his cheeks. He said Adam is alive. He said Sumner saved the Butcher's life."

The two stared out the window in silence.

"Bates sank into his mattress and stopped moving," Collin

Wade said. "I thought I killed the man. When the little alarms went off, I got out of there before the doctors and nurses showed up. I waited in an empty room untill I could get out the emergency exit without being seen."

"You're a sick man, Wade."

"Why? Because I was doing my job." He pulled papers from a file on his desk. He glanced at the cover page and passed them to G.E. "The judge seems to think I have something?"

Taft read the bold title out loud. "COURT ORDER . . . EXHUMATION . . . ADAM DUNCAN." His eyes left the page and crawled up Wade. "You told this story to a judge?"

"No. Not the story I told you. I made the case that a serial killer was released by the medical examiner outside the rules of law—a blatant violation. Adam Duncan should have been brought into the county morgue for a proper inquest, a full autopsy."

G.E. Taft stared at Collin Wade. "My God . . ."

"Adam Duncan's manner of death was *apparent suicide*. The man was the Bluff City Butcher. We got it wrong before—Jack Bellow—and the man killed a hundred people in six states. No medical examiner has the right or the authority to ignore the law, G.E. Bates can't just release the corpse of a monster to a private funeral home at the death scene."

"You need to get a grip, Collin." G.E. started for the door tucking his loose shirt back into his pants. "I'm worried about you, son."

"Wait. I'm doing this, G.E. I want to see that body. I'm going out to the Bell estate to serve these papers. I was hoping you would come with me to show solidarity." Collin Wade passed by G.E. Taft and put his hand on the door. "Please, listen to reason."

"I wouldn't waste my time if I were you," G.E. said, his nose inches from Collin's face.

"Albert Bell may be a powerful man, but this is a court order.

I'm going to have that body exhumed from the private burial site on the Bell estate. We're bringing in that corpse for a proper inquest. I've got to know he is the BCB and he is dead. I have to see with my own eyes, G.E."

"You're still afraid of that man. You think he's still out there, don't you?"

"I'm just doing my job. You need to do yours. Come with me, G.E."

"Let it go, Collin. You're chasing ghosts. Adam Duncan died on the roof at the Bell mansion on December 23rd. His corpse left in a crashbag. His blood stain runs down the side of the Georgia marble, three damn stories. They can't get it out of the rock. You know how much blood it takes to run down three stories?

"A lot."

"And there is another reason you need to give it up," G.E. said.

"If you were honest about it, you'd agree there is no good reason to give this up."

G.E. smiled. "Adam Duncan's body was cremated and spread over the Mississippi River on Christmas day, Collin. Your court order gives you the right to go dig up a symbolic urn."

Wade's face went white. His hand slid off the door and dropped to his side. He stared at Taft but no longer saw him.

G.E. patted Collin's shoulder and strolled down the shiny linoleum to the open doors of the empty elevator. Looking back at Collin Wade's catatonic stare he thought,

Goddamn Bluff City Butcher is still alive. He pressed the button. As the elevator doors closed he smiled. *And I think I know where Sumner's got the wounded bastard . . .*

TWENTY-FIVE

"It is easy to see, hard to foresee."
Benjamine Franklin

T he scion killed Bernardo Kuzma. Who else could it be? But
now Elliott had no time to give it. When he leaned in the
doorway he saw the pool of blood steaming in the Iberian
moonlight.

Aragon's best view of the Mediterranean is over the trees off
the balcony of the master bedroom. The chair had been
positioned perfectly—*a 19th century Santo Domingo loller with
mahogany arms and legs and vintage French woven damask,
material and pattern from the court of Louis XV.* Elliott bit his
tongue to control his photographic memory, the wild stallion
kicking down the barn doors of his brain to escape the inferno of
data. The chair faced opened French doors, its back to the room
entry and Elliott. *I'm exactly where he wants me to be . . .*

White sheers floated and settled as a cold gust of sea air

entered the room and diseminated the familiar, sweet smell of torn flesh and blood. From the doorway Elliott saw someone sitting in the high-back chair. With the new knowledge, he studied the room.

The small lamp in the corner and full moon provided scant light. Between the mahogany, baluster legs of he saw the backs of a man's legs and shoes. The heels touched and were flat on the wood floor in a pool of blood—*too much blood for a man to lose and live.*

He walked a wide arc processing every detail with his back scraping the wall. There were few places to hide: the far side of the 18th century Catalan bed, or in one of three closets with the louvered doors, or in one of two bathrooms, or on the balcony. When Elliott rounded the chair, he stopped moving. Only his eyes revisited each potential hiding place for another presence. Then he looked back at the man in the chair. His head was gone.

Now there were two—Bernardo Kuzma and a man at Aragon, both decapitated. This one wore a black pinstriped suit and white shirt that now matched his red tie. Blood gushed from the jugular and pulsed from the carotids before the head and heart knew it was over. Elliott adjusted his stance to better examine the bloody viscera while monitoring the balcony—now the most expedient avenue for a surprise attack.

He saw blood in the early stages of coagulation. Less than an inch had been absorbed by the edge of the oriental rug. The lethal pass of the knife occurred minutes before Elliott arrived— probably when he crossed the grounds or knelt in the dining room on the phone. The creaking boards and moving shadow belong to the killer. He may still be at Aragon.

Elliott saw it two times before, both times in Memphis. The first was in 1982 on the bluff of the Mississippi River. The second was in 2009 on the Hernando de Soto Bridge. Each involved three victims. All were beheaded by a uniquely skilled knife-wielding killer. The victims lost their heads with the single pass of a blade. The left-to-right transverse path severed the soft tissue passed through the vertebral space between C6 and C7. Elliott could confirm the man before him Aragon experienced the same high velocity, transverse sweep passing between C6 and C7.

Tracks were faint, from the edge of a right boot, trace blood. Although invisible to most, not to Elliott. The soft line pointed to the balcony. The distance from the body was similar to the gate in Central Park. Elliott stayed over the headless corpse—the scion killed like the Butcher killed in '82 and '09. *Either you're on the balcony or you used it to leave Aragon. Why bring me here? Do you want me to see your kills? For what purpose? Are you working up to me . . .?*

At first the sirens meant nothing. They were distant, maybe a normal part of a Catalonian night. Then he saw the silhouette. Now the dark man stood at the center of the balcony and the sirens grew louder. Elliott straightened and turned to the man holding the long knife in his left hand. He saw moonlight on bulging deltoids and a thick neck . The hair was short. The man was six-five, two-hundred-forty pounds. His right hand held onto a dripping—probably the head. He fit the biometrics of the mystery man in Central Park. Elliott was looking at the scion.

"Why?" Elliott asked.

"You still don't know," he said.

"Why did you bring me here, to kill me?"

The scion laughed. "You are in this. We have more to do." On the last word he fell backward over the balcony railing.

"Wait! Who are you . . . ?" Elliott ran onto the balcony and looked over the side expecting to see the scion lying on the ground—injured or dead—three stories down. But instead, the scion was running north into the woods. Then Elliott felt something cold and wet on the ledge. He picked it up and held it under the moonlight—the bloody knife.

"Que esta' en esta lista? Hablame. Tengo un arma."

Elliott translated as he stepped to the edge of the balcony. *You ask who is here. You want me to give myself up. You have a gun.* Elliott could not survive a three story fall. He was trapped. The voice in the hall approached. They would see the dead man soon.

The room lights came on. Elliott crouched and watched through a crack. The old man rushed in waving a gun, then he saw.

"No. No. Por favor, Dios. No. Senior Paciono Hernando . . ." He caressed the hand of the corpse and touched the gold ring. Elliott watched the old man sob and heard police cars pulling into the driveway at Aragon. He was cornered.

Shuffling shoes and police radios grew louder. Elliott looked over the railing a second time. The small cluster of saplings were within range. *If I can jump out far enough, they could break my fall. I have a chance. I can't stay or I will die in a Spanish prison or worse . . .*

Elliott turned back. The old man now stood a few feet away. His eyes went from Elliott's eyes to the bloody knife. The old man raised the gun in a wobbling hand.

Elliott spun and jumped.

As police entered the room he crashed through the sapplings and dropped to the ground. Injured but conscious he found his legs and started moving. He stumbled, got up, and ran north across the moonlit grounds. Looking back at Aragon, he saw police crowding onto the balcony. The old man pointed. Shots fired. Turf exploded. Elliott dove into the woods.

He ran as fast as his sore body would allow. He ran in the dark woods with no knowledge of terrain or obstacles. He could fall off a cliff or run into a fence or explode onto a lawn of another mansion, but one with guards and dogs and more guns. He also considered he could get lost in the Iberian woods north of Barcelona. He could lose the police and wander around for days with no food or water. He was injured—bruises and cuts. He was bleeding. And Elliott understood the dangers of open wounds and infection. And there was law enforcement. The Barcelona PD had the clear advantage. They knew the area. They had the resources. Now they were motivated to find a killer who cut off a man's head. The BPD would set up a perimeter north of the Aragon.

Elliott could not go south or he would meet his hunters. If he went west he would land on the coast of the Mediterranean—no place to hide or move without being seen. They would be looking north and east. The sirens were

all around him.

Who called the police? Elliott thought as he pushed forward. No one could know we were inside the empty mansion. No one would could know a man died tonight at Aragon.

The flashlights behind darted closer. The police were on Elliott's trail. They were moving faster than he could with his sore leg. They would catch up soon. Dogs were barking. Elliott reinjured his leg with the jump from the balcony. His bullet wound from the Peabody, compliments of Gilgamesh, already started to bleed.

It had to be motion detectors, silent alarms, and surveillance cameras. They have me on video with the knife in my hand. He couldn't keep going at this pace.

I should stop. I did not kill anybody. I was lured to Aragon by a killer . . . by the kind of people I hunt. Elliott slowed. He lost ground to his pursuers. *But the old man saw me holding the bloody butcher knife too. And I am running from the police. I'm screwed!*

"Detener! No corra ni vamos a disparar," the police shouted.

Great. They are going to shoot if I don't stop. Elliott kept moving.

"Sabemos que esta' Elliott Sumner."

How do they know me? He approached the end of the woods. There was a drop off into a black abyss.

If I stop now, they're going to shoot me anyway. I have no choice but to jump. If I give myself up, I could rot in a Barcelona jail until executed for this heinous crime. And who is Paciono Hernando? They have me holding the knife.

The steep slope dropped a hundred yards to a road or a river or more abyss. The flashlights danced in the woods sixty yards behind. Barking dogs were closing. The shooting started.

Elliott jumped into the abyss.

He rolled forever. The slope, covered with thick brush, cushioned his fall on the hard dirt, loose gravel, and sand. He was fortunate to miss most of the boulders and trees. At the bottom, disheveled, disoriented, and in an exhausted stupor Elliott got to his feet and took a physical inventory. His arms and back were scraped and bruised. His head and leg were covered in blood. His whole body ached.

The flashlight beams got brighter on the ridge he just left. Too his left headlights popped on and approached. Elliott stood on the gravel road in pain and ready to surrender. He had no more options. He would take his chances with the BPD. After all, Elliott never ran from police. He was a forensic pathologist and upholder of the law. He had to trust the system. And, in his current state of shock and exhaustion, he convinced himself he could get the truth out—the scion who killed in New York City and now killed in Barcelona.

NYPD thinks I killed Kuzma. Now it appears I have killed again . . .

The headlights got closer. Elliott covered his eyes. *Albert can get me a good lawyer, he thought. Max has connections everywhere. He can get this straightened out. I can explain why I was here, why I was in Aragon late at night.* He rubbed the blood off his forehead and raised his hands above his head as the car approached. *They could just shoot me on this dark, lonely road.*

Surely the police car sees Elliott's hands, empty and high above his head, no weapons. He dropped the knife on his way off the balcony. It is over now.

Most want to believe police, faced with a surrendering suspect, do their job; apprehend and take the assailant to jail for trial by peers. But the night is dark. The gravel road is remote. The assailant is unknown, a foreigner, a runner. There would be no witnesses. The horrific killer, a sick monster who cuts off a man's head, is cornered.

The legal process always begins in the field. Sometimes it ends in the field, too. No one is prepared for pure evil. No one knows what they will do if they have the power to stop it.

Standing on one leg, the other bent and blood soaked, Elliott pushes his hands higher and waits for the bullet to the head. Headlights burn his eyes and get bigger. Flashlights shine down from the ridge.

The police car nears popping over the new gravel. Elliott hears the whine of the engine and smells the hot exhaust. He opens his eyes as the car slows. It is not a police car. It is a black

SEAT Córdoba. It is his car. Now nothing makes sense. Not the flashes from the ridge, the explosions, the echoes, and the bullets hitting the gravel around him. The car stops. The door swings open . . .

"Get in Elliott!"

"Carol . . . ?"

TWENTY-SIX

"Present fears are less than horrible imaginings."
Shakespeare

"We have one stop to make first," Tony said as he left Austin Peay and snaked through a north Memphis neighborhood. "I know where Mike Primeaux lives."

"This damn thing came out of left field." Sheriff Taft pulled his seatbelt tighter. He never liked *riding* in a car. Always wanted to drive. Wilcox would not allow it.

"I was skeptical 'bout the whole thing from the start." Tony hesitated at the stop sign and jerked the car left.

"What do you mean?" G.E. asked.

"Why would Elliott and Henderson disappear and suddenly a door in the damn roof pops open. Shit, I watched William (Albert's butler) take his skinny ass out on the roof, three stories up and a damn snowy slant. He helped Elliott's handpicked paramedics pull Adam Duncan's body into the attic. Well hell, I ran all over tryin' to find the way up. Couldn't find a damn door. Next thing I know they're wheelin' a dead body in a crashbag across the courtyard. I watched them put it into the ambulance— no lights no sirens. Fooled me. Damn ambulance crawls off into the night. Like everyone else, I assumed they were heading to the county morgue."

"So did I," G.E. mumbled.

"But I saw Elliott standing in the snow after it pulled away. He watched it. I know the look. Elliott was up to somethin'. And he was not tellin' anybody about it."

"When Director Wade told me what Bates said in ICU, I thought of you."

"What the hell does that mean, G.E.?" He tore down a narrow neighborhood street looking at row houses. "I don't recognize this damn place."

"I don't mean I thought of you in a bad way. I thought about the night Elliott saved your life in your condo. Last August. The Bluff City Butcher sliced the hell out of you, boy."

"Oh yeah . . . that night. I don't like to think about it."

"You died that night, Tony. Your buddy performed a miracle with those two tight-lipped paramedics your talking about. They brought you back from the dead, boy. Patched you up and gave you back all the blood you poured onto your wood floors. If I were you, I'd not talk bad about them."

Tony halfway listened. He focused shaking off the memory of the terror and excruciating pain and the eyes of a monster that still visit him in his dreams most nights. "I'm not pissed off. I'm worried the whole damn thing can get back out of control. We don't need anymore serial killers running around Memphis."

"Whoa boy," G.E. yelled. Tony cut the wheel sharp missing a parked car. G.E. tightened his seatbelt. "You ok, son?"

"Shit." Tony shook his head and accellerated.

"You reliving that night?"

"The pain was real bad, G.E. Can we just change the subject?" Tony asked.

"Never will understand how Elliott got to you in time." He rolled down the rear window. Tony took another sharp turn, throwing him against the door. "Slow down. son."

"We always knew the Butcher was coming for us. Just didn't know when or where. We couldn't stop the bastard, so we came up with a plan," Tony said. "Elliott handpicked his two paramedics, people who could handle anything medical-surgical and keep their mouths shut."

"The Mike-and-Mike team?"

"Yeah. Primeaux and Hinton. We figured I'd be first to be knocked off. The Butcher would want to save Elliott. The freak always wanted to prove things to Elliott. Our plan was simple. I get attacked by the BCB. Elliott and his paramedics save my life to fight another day. In the Butcher's eyes, I am off the table—no risk. He's not watching for me.We wait for the Butcher to go for Elliott. I'm waiting in Elliott's shadows. We get the drop on him. We needed an advantage—surprise. Everything we tried had failed over the last ten years."

"You're crazy, Wilcox."

"It'a no different from baitin' a trap to catch any other vermin."

"In this case Elliott was the bait and the vermin was a monster. You're lucky I showed up."

They pulled up to the curb in front of a small ranch with two bikes in the front yard. Tony went to the door. When it opened, Mike tried to close it. But Tony stuck his foot out.

"Mikey, Mikey, come on now. Is that any way to be." Tony pushed open the door. "The jig is up, my friend." Still in his hospital scrubs and holding a chicken leg, Mike stepped outside and closed the door. Tony reached for the chicken leg. Mike jerked it back. "Okay. Be that way. I'm sorry to interrupt your dinner with the family."

Tony took in Mike's muscular five-seven frame, dark crew cut, sharp eyes, and clean shaven face—a retired Navy Seal rock. "What jig would be up, Detective Wilcox." Mike stood his ground. Tony did not frighten him. Even though Mike could whip Tony, the reason Tony was safe was because Mike saved Tony's life and had a rule not to break things he fixed.

"You boys going to kibbitz or are we going to go?" Taft yelled from the backseat window.

"Is that Sheriff Taft?" Mike asked as he passed the chicken leg.

"Yes. Don't worry. We are subterranean right now. At least until I ring Elliott's neck and we agree on what to do about this damn mess." He took a big bite.

"What mess?"

"Oh, I don't know, mister-loose-lips-sink-ships. Let me help you. Remember when you guys saved my life in my condo? The Butcher was watching to make sure you took a dead body out. You did not want to disappoint him. You put me in a big, black, crash bag with my blood units and you took me away in a slow ambulance without lights or siren. Bates prounounced me dead and later faked my autopsy. If you recall, you guys took my half-dead body to a secret medical facility in Millington. Ring any bells?"

"You were there. What about it?"

"We know you're up to your old tricks. We know *Adam Duncan* is alive, Michael. We know he is in Millington now."

"Who is we, and does Dr. Sumner know you're here?"

"We . . . is me and Sheriff Taft. No . . . Elliott does not know we are here, nor does he know we know Adam is alive." Tony lit a cigarette. Mike revealed nothing.

"Here's what's gonna happen now. You're one of Elliott's paramedic confidants. I respect the arrangement. But now the proverbial shit has hit the proberbial fan and you're going to get it all over yourself if you don't work with me and Taft."

"I take my orders from Dr. Sumner."

"This is not the damn military, Primeaux. You're not taking orders from anyone. You're a free-thinking citizen who can go to prison. *That* is how the courts are gonna look at this mess. Now, here's the deal on the table. I am going to Millington tonight with or without you. It would be in your best interest to come so you can explain medical shit to the Shelby County Sheriff and a MPD Homicide detective. After I go up there and get my hands all dirty with this gargantuan secret of all time, and since I am keeping all this shit from my superiors, effective tonight it is all on me . . . not on you and the other Mike anymore."

"I don't know . . ."

"You do know aiding and abetting the most prolific homicidal maniac in American history can be a very serious matter, unless you come clean with a Memphis Homicide Detective. This is your only ticket out of jail."

"It's been a month since I spoke to Dr. Sumner."

"He is busy and we now need to make sure Adam is not going anywhere until Elliott gets back. I don't think you and the Millington team can control this guy. I can't risk putting the Butcher back out there. You coming or not?"

Michael grabbed the chicken leg and took a bite. "Let's go. You'll never find the place."

"You need to call Hinton."

"No. He'll find us. He has ways."

Tony nodded. "Good."

"You should know he's unconscious," Michael said. "Been

like that since the Bell mansion. May never come out of it. He's losing ground."

"Is he confined?" Tony asked on the way to the car.

"Yes." Michael stopped Tony on the sidewalk. "Dr. Sumner visited his brother every day before going out of town December 29th. Each time he asked for more restraints."

"Shit. Let's go . . ."

TWENTY-SEVEN

"The only difference between me and a madman is that I'm not mad."
Salvador Deli

"This is not where I was." Tony pulled into the abandoned parking lot somewhere in Millington. The storefronts were boarded and covered with grafitti. Unintelligible signage fell off weathered headers. Brown weeds draped over crumbling asphalt, and trash fused to every corner.

"Drive to the back," Mike said. G.E. felt for his gun.

Tony turned onto the dirt road and followed it to the alley. The back side of the abandoned stores was fenced, overgrown, and trashed. "Where the hell are me going?" G.E. asked.

"Pull up to the garage door in the middle," Michael said.

"One in middle?" Tony asked. It went up. Hinton stood inside and motioned them to enter.

"What the fa . . . ," Tony muttered. The door closed behind.

Hinton stepped up. "Hey Mike. Your wife wants you to call. Said you left without a word." He turned attentions to Wilcox and Taft. "We've been waiting for this day."

"How did you know we were coming?" Tony asked.

"Gentlemen, you are required to leave your weapons in the car if you want to go any further. It's policy here. There are no exceptions."

"Damn. I hate that," Tony grumbled.

"Whose policy?" G.E. blurted. "Never mind. Fine." They both tossed their guns in the car.

"I assume you spoke to Primeaux's wife. Put this together," Tony pushed.

Hinton nodded. "I figured since Mike didn't tell her where he was going, he had a good reason. Then I figured he was bringing someone up here. It's been uncomfortable for us for a while now. Dr. Sumner left town. Been too long with him gone."

"Where the hell are we?" Taft huffed.

"Relax G.E. Give it time." Tony hid his own impatience.

They left the garage through one of four nondescript, metal doors. Inside the ten-by-twenty cinder block room was a hanging lightbulb. The walls were lined with file cabinets, stacks of dusty boxes, mangled store shelving units, and piles of random junk. Once Primeaux joined them, Hinton made the call on his cell. "We're ready."

The lightbulb got brighter. A ginding noise grew beneath the floor. Three metal file cabinets lifted five feet and revealed a narrow staircase. After they entered, the file cabinets lowered back into place. They were sealed in a metal room.

"This is like some damn spy movie," G.E. said. "Where're we going?"

"This isn't the place I was at," Tony said.

"This operation is different. Available to a very narrow patient base," Hinton said.

The metal door in the metal room at the base of the stairs had two number-pads. Hinton punched a code into one as Primeaux did the other. They hit the last number at the same time. A wall slid open like a massive door. White light poured in from behind thick, translucent glass walls as they stood in awe watching shadows move on the other side.

"We're entering the adminstration area—the brains of the operation," Hinton said. This facility has three med-surg suites and ten-bed ICU." They followed.

"I'll be damned," Tony whispered as he stepped onto the white linoleum. The surgical suites behind glass had walls of screens, dials, and flashing lights. They passed the entry into intensive care where a dozen in green scrubs and masks walked between isolation rooms where patients were out of sight. The medical staff was oblivious to the foursome's presence.

"Guess these people are too busy to be concerned about visitors around here . . ."

"I'm Dr. Franks, the medical director." They turned to find an elderly doctor holding a clipboard and pen. The thin, bald, pale man in the white labcoat projected confident efficiency. "And you must be Tony Wilcox, Memphis Homicide. And of course, Sheriff G.E. Taft."

They stood looking at each other for an uncomfortable five seconds before Dr. Franks continued. "Well then. I understand you're here to look in on a guest, Mr. Adam Duncan," he said while flipping pages on his clipboard.

"Yes," G.E. said. "Where the hell is the Bluff City Butcher?"

"G.E. please," Tony interupted and stepped between the sheriff and Franks. "I don't know how much history you get on your patients, but we are eager to look in on Mr. Duncan."

"Yes. I understand . . . of course." Dr. Franks removed a

stapled document from his clipboard. "Before we visit Adam Duncan, there are a few matters to attend to. First, both of you must agree to the terms and conditions that govern your privileged entry into this stealth medical facility."

"That will not be a problem. Dr. Franks." Tony turned and gave the evil eye to G.E. who kept trying to nudge him out of his way.

"Both of you must sign this document—a nondisclosure agreement. Gentlemen, you cannot talk of this facility, its location, or its people and practices. Upon your departure, you must forget eveything you have seen and heard. Sheriff Taft, Detective Wilcox, if this a problem for either of you, we must respectfully escort both of you from the facility at this time."

"This is not a problem for either of us." Tony took the form and signed. He passed it to G.E. showing his teeth. Taft grabbed the pen and signed.

"Very good. Now, we checked-in Mr. Adam Duncan the night of December 23, 2009." Dr. Franks cleared his throat and waited for G.E. and Tony to make eye contact. "I say the year because some of our special patients have been here for several years. In our environment we need to communicate accurately at all times or mistakes can be made and people will die."

"What kind of people are here?" Tony asked craning his neck around a pillar.

"The highest-value, low-profile government, business, and scientist types who play a vital role in the safety, security, and future of our country. Each patient admitted to one of our stealth medical facilities has been physically or psychologically compromised. They are brought here to recieve the best care in the world, and to be protected. We have a 100 percent success rate."

"100 percent success rate for what," G.E. grumbled.

"Protection. We have a seventy-two percent medical success

rate. Unfortunately we have not found a way to keep our national treasures alive indefinately." Franks chuckled.

"Gee. A special place for special people," G.E. muttered as he

pushed his glasses back up his nose and caught Tony giving him the stink eye.

"When I say special people, I mean they are national assets comparable to top-secret technology. We need them back out there helping us as soon as possible. We do not want them falling into the wrong hands."

"How many places are there like this?" Tony asked.

"I'm sorry. That information is classified."

"Not a problem."

"I can tell you we are a private funded global operation. Our function is to benefit our country and selected friends on an exclusive basis."

"Okay. No more questions. Tell us what you need to tell us, but take us to the Butcher now." G.E. was busting at the seams. He could not stand the banter and meandering process.

"We are on our way, Sheriff Taft," Dr. Franks reassured.

"Dr. Elliott Sumner is a well respected man and very close friend. His unique skillsets and high intellect have served our nation on many an occassion. I am certain few know of his significant contributions. I must share the President of the United States is most appreciative. Dr. Sumner gets anything he wants or needs, no questions asked."

"That explains a lot," Taft said shaking his head.

"We're not here to judge our special patients or sponsors. We are here to bring people back from catastrophic medical conditions. We utilize the most advanced science and technology on earth—much still in the research mode." At an increased pace, Dr. Franks led the group through ICU. They entered a long, wide hall that sloped down. "Sorry for the long walk, gentlemen."

"Where do you keep him? Hell?" Tony quipped.

"He's in the secured area," Primeaux answered.

At the bottom of the long hallway the floor leveled the next thirty feet. They stopped at an iron door with rivits. Dr. Franks peered through a sliver opening and unlocked it. They went inside. Lights activated with motion sensors.

Fat iron bars, from floor to ceiling, ran the width of the room. They were corroded and caked with layers of old paint. Tony wrapped his hands around two bars and pulled. They were solid in spite of the aged appearance. "Where'd you find these, the Titanic?" He squinted into the shadows on the other side. There was a thin spray of light on the giant metal bed bolted to the cement floor. Adam Duncan laid still on his back. Six cameras fed a bank of monitors on the far wall outside the bars. Leads and tubes—EKGs, EEGs, IVs, Urine Collection, Respirators—ran from portals under the bed to Adam.

"My God," Tony said. "He's enormous."

G.E. stared at the most dangerous man he had ever come across in his lifetime. The monster he thought was dead laid there with arms shackled. The inch thick, u-shaped irons were bolted to the iron bed: both wrists, elbows, ankles, and thighs. And there was a two-inch thick metal bar over his neck. Adam's large head was dark and chiseled like some greek god. He had a long, straight jaw line and overhanging brow. His black, oily hair hung off the bed.

"Are you sure this man's alive?" Tony asked.

"Yes. For the moment," Dr. Franks said. "Mr. Duncan is unconscious." They witnessed his occassional and explosive breathing. "He's been off the respirater two weeks—some progress."

"He's in a coma," Hinton said. When they turned to Dr. Franks for an explanation, they saw him fiddling with monitors and pulling strip-reports from printers.

"I've never seen a man survive the amount of trauma and blood loss this man has endured," Dr. Franks said as he continued to survey the screens with most current patient vitals—respiration, heart rate, blood pressure, O_2 saturation and more.

"From this station we can monitor the progress of a confined patient. In Mr. Duncan's case, lack of progress. He's been unconscious since arrival. He's non-responsive. In a steady decline that we can't seem to reverse."

"How often do you go in there?" G.E. asked pointing inside the cell.

"Our medical staff enters twice a day for feeding—a tube down the esophagus—and to change dressings, repair equipment, replace tubing, and to give a sponge. Mr. Duncan receives what he must have intravenously: vitamins, minerals, nutrients, electrolytes, medications. Those IV lines are closely monitored. They must remain functional 24-7. I go in once a day for physical examinations and therapeutic injections. We do not move Mr. Duncan, ever."

"What are you looking for, the examinations?" Tony asked.

"We treat tissue damage and distressed organs due to severe blood loss. We are finishing wound drainage procedures. He has essentially healed from the massive abdominal injury. He's a very fortunate man on that account—no damage to his spine. We now syphon off minimal fluids from the abdominal cavity. He is infection free. Infection was one of our primary concerns in the begining. His wounds have healed."

"Infection?" Tony asked.

"I believe you know Mr. Duncan was injured in October of last year," Dr. Franks said. "He was shot in both shoulders and received an abdominal knife wound." Tony looked at G.E. and winked. "He survived those wounds easily. However, he fell into the Mississippi River following the traumatic confrontation. The river introduced nasty bacteria into his sytem left untreated for sixty days. Mr. Duncan was septic before his December injury—the spire."

"Can we go in there for a closer look?" G.E. asked. Tony wenced.

"Certainly." Franks unlocked the cell door. They entered and surrounded the metal bed.

"You can see Mr. Duncan is amply restrained. It is impossible for any man to break those iron shackles, especially in such a weakened state. I do not understand the restraints. However, Dr. Sumner forbid us from removing them under any condition." He touched Adam's arm. "He has been in this supine position ever since arrival more than a month ago."

"Look at the muscles on this guy," Tony said. "For a sick guy, he looks like he just got back from the damn weight room."

Dr. Franks knelt to inspect tubing under the bed. "I have no explanation for muscle tone. Seems to be even more pronounced than when he arrived. I have know idea why."

"I guess he's gonna live," Taft said.

"Muscle mass is not a life or death determiner. Unfortunately we expect Mr. Duncan to stop breathing sometime next week. His life-sustaining systems have been compromised for too long, even though his numbers are good. Very odd. Seems our medical interventions are not achieving any of the desired results. Everything we do tends to work to his detriment. Standard treatments have the opposite effect we expect. Mr. Duncan's body rejects our help. I'm afraid his body is shutting down, gentlemen."

"Is it possible he's in hibernation kinda like a bear? Maybe everything's slowing down to conserve energy and focus on repairs his way," Tony said.

"Interesting concept. I don't know the answer. Why do you suggest such a thing?"

"I saw his brother do the same thing in Dallas, August 2008.

Elliott had some kind of emotional overload that triggered a cardiac arrest. He was dying in ICU at Parkland Hospital. The docs saw the same things—none of their treatments helped. Only hurt. And I remember them saying all his numbers were good but he was dying."

"What did they do for Dr. Sumner at Parkland?" Dr. Franks asked.

"Stopped all treatments. Left him alone except for IV nourishment and hydration. Elliott fixed himself in twenty-four hours. He went from death's door to a full recovery in a day."

"And you think Adam and Elliott are made the same way?" G.E. asked.

"Hell, they're paternal twins. I'm no medical expert, but I'd say there's a pretty good chance what works for Elliott works for the Butcher, I mean Adam." Tony looked down at the massive frame of the man who tried to kill him not too long ago.

"I knew they were brothers," Dr. Franks said. "But I did not have a medical history on Elliott Sumner. I agree with your assessment, Detective Wilcox. It makes good sense. I have always thought Adam Duncan unique, something we've not seen before."

Tony's wandering eyes noticed a change in Adam's breathing pattern. No longer were there occassional and explosive gasps. Adam's chest now lifted and sunk with a smooth and steady motion. *He's breathing with control,* Tony thought. *Maybe it's part of his breathing pattern.*

His eyes moved from Adam's chest to his large, muscluar hand—the one that held the butcher knife and killed more than a hundred people. When Tony entered the cell Adam's hands were open. Palms were down and fingers spread. Now his hand is closed into a fist. Then Tony saw the white knuckles.

At the same time, Hinton and Primeaux saw something. Maybe they saw what Tony saw. Eyes met. In unison they stepped away from the metal bed. Dr. Franks was oblivious, kneeling and untangling lead wires.

G.E. straightened up when Hinton, Primeaux, and Tony moved. G.E. saw them back to the wall. Pushing his glasses up his nose, he stepped away unsure but cautious.

It is unclear when Tony first looked at Adam's face in the cell. When he did, Adam's eyelids were open a quarter inch, his brow dipped and nostrils flared.

"There's the problem," Dr. Franks said as he moved deeper beneath the bed reaching for the loose lead he hunted. "I knew there had to be a . . ."

"Ah . . . Doc," Tony said in a craking voice. "How certain are you he cannot get off this bed?" Tony backed further.

Dr. Franks stood triumphantly, the faulty EKG wire reconnected. He discovered he was alone next at the bed. Before he could answer Wilcox's question and return his neatly folded hankerchief to his breast pocket, Adam's right arm broke from the bed. The iron shackle flew across the room, pinged off the wall, and clanged across the floor.

Adam pulled the two-inch-thick metal bar from his neck with a single thrust. He broke his legs free and his left arm. The iron shackles rained down on the cold cement floor like broken glass. When Adam sat up his heavy, black hair fell down his back, his angry eyes sharpened, and his lip raised showing his eye tooth.

The five were small. Four were now against the wall. Adam eyed each as he pulled tubes and wires from his body and threw them to the floor. Rubbing his wrists and leveling his head like a wild animal ready to pounce, the Bluff City Butcher took control of Adam Duncan.

Dr. Franks stood at the end of the bed with his mouth open. He stared at his patient coming alive, growing before his eyes, transforming into something wild, something could have never imagined. Elliott's insistence on shackles and iron bars now made sense to the doctor.

The table would never hold the Butcher. As Tony explained, the monster of Memphis urban legend healed himself. On that night in Millington, the Butcher came alive and *the skies roared*.

TWENTY-EIGHT

"Courage is ten, nine is the ability to escape."
Unknown

"How's the leg today?" Carol asked as she walked up behind Elliott and wrapped her arms around his waist. Sipping coffee and looking at the Mediterranean, he reached back and squeezed her thigh.

"I guess I'll live," he said with a weary but playful tone.

She sank into his back. Carol loved Elliott more than she ever dreamed possible.

The small shack southwest of Marseille was long forgotten by locals. Elliott and Carol found it by chance while hiding their borrowed vehicle. Entangled in the thick coastal foliage of the lush Languedoc-Roussillon region, the one room abode had melded with the terrain over the decades. They discovered its tattered roof stopped enough of the wet weather, its walls stopped enough of the snooping critters, and its rusted, pot-belly stove burned enough of a log to cut the edge off a crisp January night in southern France.

"First time I sewed up a doctor." She rubbed his stomach.

"You did a good job for a rookie. Lucky for me you brought some of the essential medical supplies. Do all women carry such a wide assortment of sutures, needles, antibiotics, and wound dressings in their purses?"

"No. Just us special ones."

"I see, Miss Mason. Every time I look at my wonderful scar, I'll think of you."

"You better. Those are my initials on your leg. You belong to me now."

They held onto each other, and the moment, avoiding the negative thoughts. Elliott's growing dangers and mounting deadly forces were begining to take a toll.

They got rid of the SEAT Córdoba the first day and borrowed a small Ford pickup with two mountain bikes in its bed. They stayed on side roads and headed north to Paris until running out of gas. After hiding the truck, they pedaled west to the outskirts of Toulon where they spent a few nights in a quiet barn—Elliott and his injured leg needed rest.

On day five Carol found the 1955 Austin-Healey tucked under a tarp in the back of the barn. After some tinkering, they rolled it out and replaced its dimensions with bales of hay. The undisturbed layer of dust on the tarp suggested their use of the sports car would go unmissing for a long while. When they reached the coast of the Mediterranean, they hid the sports car near the abandoned shack—the rapid departure option in place. As they sat on a cliff looking over the Mediterranean Sea, they drew some comfort from knowing they had enough to eat for a week and wheels good for two-hundred miles. But Elliott had more on his mind.

"I'm still not comfortable with you being here," he said staring at the water.

"We've been through this, Elliott. When you love someone, you take the bad with the good. That's how it works." Carol rubbed his back.

"But this is not your *typical bad*," he said. "My life is not easy to share."

"You didn't ask for the *bad* in your life, Elliott. And I knew what I was getting myself into the day we met. I fell in love with you, a man who just happens to be a forensic investigator who chases really bad guys for a living. Someone has to do it, Elliott. And you're pretty good at it."

"But now I'm into something a lot more dangerous than hunting serial killers."

"I'm not leaving. You can't do this alone. That's why Max and Tony are in this too. The girl you're crazy about is a lot tougher than she looks."

"I can't do this with you." Elliott broke from her arms. "I can't risk you getting hurt because of me. The danger is growing. The unknowns are everywhere."

"If I did not save you in Barcelona, the mission would be over. Every day from that day forward I bought for you, Elliott. Max and I bought for you. You cannot do this alone."

"You know me. Everything about me is multiplied a hundred fold. It's how I'm built. My feelings for you are not typical, they are overwhelming. My worries are big, too. Not only do I put you in harms way, your presence puts me in harms way. They use you to get to me."

"I am just as much in love with you, Elliott. I worry big about you too? You have a lot to learn about love and women. For a man with so many gifts, there are many things you do not understand. You've lived alone a long time. You don't know what it is to be committed to another person. It's time you feel the greatest power in the world, the one all of us feel if we want to. Love and sharing is worth all the risk, Elliott."

He pulled her to him and kissed her. She held his face and looked in his warm eyes.

"Stop worrying about me. This is life. Our feelings matter. Don't let anyone take that from us."

"I just don't like it," he said. "But I love and trust you completely . . ."

She dropped down and rested her head on his chest. "We've been on the run seventeen days," Carol said. "This place has worked well for eight days. No one snooping around."

"I expected them to look for me in the small towns, especially around Spain's border. We were heading north when we escaped that Barcelona firing squad."

"They're hunting a genius, forensic sleuth, Elliott. They're weighing everything. What will you do to throw them off. If we do the most expected, we're probably safest," Carol chided.

Elliott smiled. "Guess they bought into all the lame news reports over the years."

"Stop. You're a genius. I bet their looking in the big cities, France's interior."

"Probably Paris first and then moving out. In a few more days it should be safe for us to go to Paris. There we can get Max to send a plane." Elliott sunk. "Then I'm back to square one."

They sat on the flat rock that jutted out over the crystal blue water fifty feet below. The morning sun hit their faces and cut the edge off the cold. "We have work to do. We need to compare notes before we lose our details." Carol started digging in her massive purse.

"I never forget details, remember?" Elliott teased.

"Well, I do, mister genius." She fumbled in her bag, her hair falling forward and parting to reveal her neck. Elliott leaned over and kissed it. She kept digging as she reached up and rubbed his cheek. They made love two times in the last eight hours. Number three was close.

"So you broke Max. He told you all my secrets. Impressive. He's CIA. Supposed to be unbreakable."

"In all fairness he was worried about you, Elliott. He didn't like the way Barcelona got on your agenda. It didn't pass the smell test. I pushed very little. He made sure I had enough to keep us both alive if necessary—city, hotel, car, and timeline. My job was easy. I hopped into your trunk and waited. You did the rest."

"I must admit I was relieved you were at the bottom of my hill. I was out of gas . . ."

She found her notepad, pushed hair behind her ear, and flipped pages. "We need to talk about Aragon. But first, let's talk about Gilgamesh. We have both been doing research. Let's compare notes. You wanna go first?"

"Sure. It's a clandestine society of billionaires looking for the secret to immortality."

"A novel idea," she scoffed.

"The most popular quest of mankind since we learned we were mortal. This group got serious about it a long time ago—early 1900s. Their focus is on a biogenic solution. They're not looking for the proverbial fountain of youth, some magic fairy dust, or the holy sceptor."

"What do you mean, biogenic solution?"

"There's been great progress in mapping the human genome —learning what individual genes do, the proteins they produce, and the tasks they perform. Everything from promoting health to fending off disease and controlling the aging process. Gilgamesh has been engaged in genetic engineering—managing genes—long before the rest of the world. Now the world is catching up. That reality may be a driver. It may explain their desperation.

"*Desperation* because they are getting older and don't want to die?" Carol theorized.

"That could expain their aggressive behavior, but it would not explain their active role in hunting and terminating people. I suspect Gilgamesh has convinced themselves they need to find and control the genetic secrets for continuous cell regeneration. If they alone hold the secret, they control mankind. They could be very close to accomplishing their century old mission."

"Seems apocalyptic."

"Exactly," Elliott said rolling his eyes.

"And somehow the Bell triplets are a threat." Carol flipped a page and made a note.

"We need to start at the begining. What do you know about the formation?"

"Gilgamesh was started by Alberto Bella."

"Albert Bell's grandfather?"

"Yes. Alberto came from Italy in the late 1800's. He grew up in the textile world. When he got to America, he became one of the first international cotton merchants. Alberto purchased fertile land in the Mississippi River Valley and planted cotton. He contracted with other cotton farmers for their crops. Soon he controlled a portion of the world cotton supply."

"I knew cotton was the foundation of the Bell dynesty, but did not know that story."

"Alberto did more than grow cotton and contract with other cotton farmers. He did something new at the time. He got farmers to abandon other crops to plant cotton on an exclusive basis. Alberto guaranteed the sale of these crops before the farmer put one seed in the ground. He removed *risk* from the farming equation."

"So that's how you become a billionaire."

"He also introduced irrigation in sections of Texas and

turned wastelands into cotton producers. There are a lot of Texans committed to the Bell family still today."

"And Alberto Americanized. Changed his name from Bella to Bell, and he became a respected, southern gentleman and billionaire patriach," Carol said.

"That takes us to Gilgamesh—the entity. Alberto and his closest billionaire friends started it in 1915. Gilgamesh was a typical, philanthropic venture. Their mission to serve the common good focused on improving healthcare delivery for the masses."

Carol looked up from her notepad biting her pen. "And how did this noble cause turn into a sinister quest?"

"I suspect they had an *eureka* moment," Elliott said. "We may never know the whole truth, but it would be safe to assume their healthcare discussions emersed them in the bottomless pool of challenges faced when attempting to cure disease and improve the quality of life for a poor and unruly population of misfits."

"You believe they were that cynical?"

"Enormously privileged people are very different from you and me. Try to imagine a life where you could have anything you wanted anytime you wanted it. I suspect in their minds making real progress with the masses became an impossible proposition. However, it did not stop them from wanting perfect health and immortality for themselves."

"That's a depressing scenerio," Carol said.

"It follows that each breakthrough produced another secret and fueled their paranoia and need to protect assets. It is the metamorphosis of a rich man's club into a dangerous entity."

"Their dream became an obsession . . ."

"And a nightmare for everyone else."

"Do you know anything about their sturcture and membership?"

"Bernardo Kuzma said they had 200 members, ten percent of the 2,000 billionaire population in the world with a combined net worth of $4.3 trillion. To give you a sense of magnitude, it's equivalent to the GNP of Japan, the fourth largest economy in the world."

"Guess we can assume they are well financed."

"My quest to stop Gilgamesh is tantamount to the Virgin Islands declaring war on the United States." Elliott sipped his coffee and squinted in the sun.

Carol let his comment pass. "What about structure?"

"It's simple. Two-hundred paying members led by a twelve member board that does everything and anything they want. The members meet once a decade. They tithe ten percent of their net worth at that time. It keeps their family in line for breakthroughs."

"What about the board, how are they chosen?"

"Six board members are original founders—the old guys. The other six are scions, direct descendants of the six dead founders. Board seats stay in families of the founding twelve."

Carol pushed hair from her eyes. "That would mean Albert Bell is on the board, Elliott. Albert's father is the son of Alberto Bella."

"You are right. His father died in 1956. Albert Bell took a seat on the Gilgamesh board when he was twenty-four."

"Fifty-three years on the Gilgamesh board," Carol said. They stared into the water wrestling with their personal knowledge of the man and the new, troubling information.

"He has not been open with me," Elliott said.

"You know Albert. He must have a good reason."

"I can't go there. I must assume the worst. There's too much at stake."

"There are others pursuing the secrets of immortality. Gilgamesh is not alone. Is it possible we're looking in the wrong place? Are we jumping to conclusions? Maybe another entity unknown to us is behind everything."

"People invest in new technology all the time. They take chances and naturally want to possess their creations and discoveries. The problem is not always mission oriented. The problem can emerge after something is obtained and great value is established."

"You do not have indisputable proof Gilgamesh is stealing and killing to protect assets."

"I think I do. When the ends justify the means, things spin out of control. Gilgamesh had something to do

with Dr. Medino going underground with his research and his death?"

"And the theft of his research?"

"Yes. Gilgamesh is behind Jack's death and connected to Adam, the horrendous things he did and his suicidal leap off Albert's balcony."

"Now they are coming for you?" Carol asked. "You're accusing Gilgamesh?"

"Yes, I am."

"Do you have an idea why they are hunting you?"

"Bernardo Kuzma told me something the night he died. He said they once viewed me and my brothers as assets. Now, I am a liability."

"I can't imagine why they would view you as assets and liabilities. To your knowledge they have not been involved in your life, right?"

"I have an idea why. They are nearing the realization of their dream. They're desperate to protect it. My brothers and I threaten their dream. Two of us are gone. I am the last obstacle."

"The rooftop of the Peabody and Shelby County morgue, you believe Gilgamesh was behind them. You believe they were attempting to terminate you, their last obstacle?"

"Yes. They lost touch with reality a long time ago. Like the serial killers I hunt, this secret society has reached a point of no return. I think their board is convinced I'm a major problem. Why else could they justify such aggressive and overt actions against me." Elliott finished his coffee and smiled at Carol. "Maybe I am the only one left who can stop them."

"You're in France because of this mystery scion. Could he be a Gilgamesh soldier on a creative mission to kill you and a few board members along the way?"

"I don't think so. The scion is in his mid-twenties. He's smart and profoundly athletic. He has an agenda and is determined to stay on some macabre schedule. He has a negative history with Gilgamesh. I get the sense his mission triggered around the time Adam left Albert's balcony. I am now certian he killed Kuzma and Hernando."

"It almost looks like he's setting you up, Elliott. Now you're being hunted by the NYPD, Italian and French police, FBI, CIA, and INTERPOL."

"He could be setting me up. It's possibe. But he says he's helping Albert and me overcome obstacles," Elliott said.

"But what obstacles and why?" Carol asked.

"Albert will come into possession of something of great value. My personal involvement is required for success. I have no idea what he's talking about."

"That's about as cryptic as you can get."

"He references *The Epic of Gilgamesh*. I'm entering the Cedar Forest where I will face the Humbaba. You're familiar with the *Akkadian* poem. It's considered to be the first, great work of literature. Written around 1200 BC?"

"I had it in college. Read it again after I saw the Gilgamesh logo for the first time. Maybe this scion character views modern day Gilgamesh as *gods* and you are the *demigod* Gilgamesh who enters the Cedar Forest and drops trees . . . kills board members."

"Sounds screwy enough to be right," Elliott said.

"Kuzma and Hernando are dead. Two Gilgamesh board members."

Elliott tossed a stone as far as he could and turned to Carol. "He said he *was prepared* for this moment."

"What do you think that means?"

"It means *someone* prepared him . . . someone who knew this day would come."

Elliott sat back down after scanning the thick foilage between them and the road.

"Prepared. He was given a mission. He knows his enemy. And, he has been taught to kill. I examined both Kuzma and Hernando . . . the decapitations. They were identical in every way. I've only seen it once before."

Carol stopped writing. "The Bluff City Butcher?"

"This scion was in the Brent catacombs. I think the dead deputies were an accident. It served no purpose but to force him into his mission."

"My God, there's a new, deranged serial killer out there?"

"I tracked him across Central Park the night Kuzma died. He moved like Adam. It was not human." Elliott turned back to the sun. "And he used a knife exactly like Adam."

She reached for his arm. He turned to her. "Is there something you're want to tell me?"

"I'm ready to talk about it now. I had to try to save my brother."

"That night. You and Dr. Bates in the attic of the Bell mansion. I asked you if there was anything you could do. He was in such pain. But he died on the roof that night. I saw."

"We got a heartbeat. It took a while, but I got him back. We transfused blood. A lot. I stopped all the bleeders, repaired torn organs. I sewed him up, Carol. We didn't take him to the county morgue. There's a place. It's in Millington. A secret place medical facility. They do wonderous things there. Things beyond common knowledge. Cutting-edge things.

"My God, Elliott. The Bluff City Butcher is alive. Is he the scion, Elliott?"

"No. He's been unconscious ever since."

"Unconscious . . . ?"

"There was one moment of clarity in Albert's attic. We finished sewing him up. We replaced most of his blood. He was breathing normal, but very shallow. He could die any moment. When we put him in the crash bag to take him out, his eyes popped open. Adam grabbed my arm. That's when he gave me the vellum."

"The same vellum I lost the night he took me from Beale Street?"

"Yes. He gave it to me. It has a table with dozens of initials and bizarre codes."

"And Gilgamesh watermark," Carol muttered.

"Yes. I had it with me in New York City. I was going to study it after meeting with Kuzma. I had a few questions. It was in a safe place. It was taken

from my room at the Plaza."

"Someone came into your room when Kuzma was killed. Where were you, Elliott?"

"There. Hiding in the dark, the bathtub."

"You could have been killed."

"That piece of vellum holds the keys to solving this mystery. If I can break the code, I could understand the scion's plan and find a path into Gilgamesh."

Elliott took Carol's notepad and flipped to a clean page. "Give me you pen. I'm going to recreate the table. I put this off long enought. We're going to figure this out now."

"Elliott. Is it at all possible that Adam is involved? You said he is alive."

"It is impossible. Adam is dying. When I left, he was in very bad shape. I expect him to be dead when I return to Memphis."

Carol nodded. She grabbed her leather purse and dug around in it. "Before we get into the table, I need to give you something from Max." She pulled out a plastic bag. There were four cellphones—a red, blue, green, and black one. "I know you've not missed your phone the last few weeks. I think it's safe enough to have our lifeline again."

"I enjoyed crushing mine when we crossed the border. It was therapeutic."

"Good for you, honey." She winked and he pushed her.

"Max gave me these phones. He anticipated the need for stealth communications would arise. That man has a lot of gadgets. You're to use one phone a week. At the end of a seven day period you can crush it and get a new one. Activation is easy. You hold down the pound-star keys and enter M A X. Pick a color."

Elliott selected the blue one. When he hit the last letter in the sequence, the phone beeped three times and said, "Hello Elliott. This phone will be activated in twenty minutes. You may use it for seven days then destroy."

"Okay 007, you're good to go." She tucked the others back in her purse.

The recreation of the table on the vellum was limited only by Elliott's graphic skills and writing speed. Every detail was burned into his memory. Twenty minutes later he neared completion. And his cell phone came alive.

Carol picked it up. "You recognize a 901-853-0390 number?"

"Wonder why Tony's calling me . . . ?"

TWENTY-NINE

"I'm not good at secrets, so don't tell me any."
A.J. Mclean

E lliott passed his scribbled rendition of the vellum table to
Carol as she passed him the phone. "Hey Tee. What's up?"
He watched her handle the paper like a first doll.

"Goddamn it Elliott. Don't *hey tee* me. I have been dialing
this number for three days. Where the hell are you?"

"My phone had an accident. I need to stay under the radar.
Max got another one to me—I just activated. You're my first
contact with the outside world in fourteen days." He smiled at
Carol as she held his handiwork up to the sun. "I'm in France."

"Fucking France! Well good for you. I'm sure you've got
damn good reasons to be over there. We've got some big ass
problems over here—in little ole' Memphis, Tennessee. And I
can't tell a damn soul about em but you."

"Okay. You've got me now."

Carol caught the tone. She turned an eye and ear from the vellum. She saw Elliott's eyes sharpen and the muscle in his jaw roll. In the quiet on the cliff she heard Tony on the phone.

He barked, "I don't know whether to apologize for butting-in, or to be pissed-off because I was once again left outside the loop. This is about the Butcher, Elliott."

"What do you know about Adam?"

"Every goddamn thing, Elliott. I know you, Bates, and your goddamn paramedic buddies saved Adam's goddamn life in Albert Bell's attic on December 23rd. I know you guys took him to Millington and put him in a goddamn secret medical facility. And I know he's been in a coma ever since."

"Breathe, Tony."

"Me and Taft went . . ."

"G.E. is in this too?" Elliott asked.

"Yep. Actually, Taft's the one got me into this shit in the first place. I was minding my own goddamn business. Seems Director Wade squeezed the miricle out of Henderson Bates. He then met with G.E. Wanted him to join him on a visit to Albert's to exhume the body."

"Henderson came out of his coma?"

"Not really. Wade somehow slithered his chubby body into ICU without permision. He climbed into Bates face and told him you cut a deal for a reduced sentence. Said you admitted you and Bates saved the Butcher's life in the goddamn attic that night. Wade threatened Bates. Said he would take his medical license away and put him in jail for aiding and abetting a felon, interfering with a homicide investigation, and for the manipulation of an inquest and legal documents. He screamed all this shit into his face, Elliott. I guess at some level of consiousness the bullshit scared Bates out of his coma. He told Wade you saved Adam Duncan's life!"

"Wonderful," Elliott muttered. "That's all we need now." Carol touched his arm.

"Don't worry about it, Elliott. Your secret's good with us. And Wade's not gonna do anything either."

"I find that hard to believe."

"Don't get me wrong, it's not because he's a nice guy, the prick."

"What did you do, Tony? Why's Director Wade going to leave this alone?"

"I did nothing wrong," Tony said. "Wade had a goddamn court order to exhume Adam's body.

G.E. told him not to waste his time. Said he'd be diggin' up an empty urn. G.E. told him Adam was creamated, his ashes dumped over the Mississippi River. But that's not why I've been calling you for three goddamn days."

"I know. You have bad news about Adam. I was expecting . . ."

"G.E and I went with your boys to that secret medical facility in Millington, the one under the abandoned storefront. We signed our goddamn lives away down there, but that's another story. Dr. Franks took us to see the Butcher, I mean Adam. It was not a pretty sight."

"He's dead, isn't he? That's why you're calling. To tell me my brother's dead." Elliott looked up at the sun. "I knew I should have stayed. I could have made a difference. But I did all I could. Adam was on the edge of death every minute of every day."

"Elliott . . . Elliott," Tony tried to cut him off but he kept going.

"Dr. Franks said it was out of our hands. He convinced me they could manage the care process better without me. I was hovering, in the way. There was nothing more I could do. That is why I took on this trip, New York and Spain. It was important. It couldn't wait. Adam ran out of medical options. It was up to him. And God was not going to help him . . ."

"Elliott. Stop talking now," Tony demanded.

"I'm sorry."

"How many times have I told you to avoid tangents when you're worried about something. I know you're thinking when you ramble on like that. But ramblin' just messes up your superhero image. It's like a nasty stain on your cape. It makes you less interesting. Makes you normal like me." Tony chuckled. "Are you smiling yet? I need you to relax so we can talk."

"I do that—ramble when I'm upset." Elliott pinched the bridge of nose and shook his head. Carol smiled and kissed his arm. He had many great gifts, but his big heart was his weakness, his Achilles heel, and the part Carol fell in love with.

"I'm sorry. I'm listening, Tony," he said.

"Adam is alive, Elliott. You could say he's pretty much back to his old self. He's back on his feet and meaner than ever. One very scary dude. It's a damn miracle, I guess one could say."

"Adam's alive. He made it." With eyes dancing Elliott turned to Carol. "He's alive. Adam's alive." She moved an ear to his phone.

"Elliott? Are you there? Did you hear a weird buzzing sound. Lasted a couple of seconds?"

"Heard nothing. Adam's alive. That's a miricle and the best news I've had in weeks. It is good news, Tony. I know you have your doubts, but trust me. I will explain later."

"You'll need to do just that, Elliott." The phone fizzled static followed with a set of three beeps. "Adam's stronger than I remember too, Elliott. Didn't think that was possible."

Those an odd comment to make now. "What's the matter, Tony?" Elliott asked.

"And he's mobile. Yes, he's stronger and mobile." Tony forced a laugh. "You know what? It was funny not one of those smart docs in the goddamn underground hospital was ready for what happened."

"Tony. What happened?"

"We were all in there, Elliott. In the cement room with the bars. You know the place. You've been there many times. The place at the end of the dark, fucking tunnel. Like the hallway to hell, Elliott." He cleared his throat. His voice cracked. "We were all standing on the wrong side of those fat, fucking, metal bars, the ones that could stop a gorrila, right."

"Tony . . ."

"The Butcher was bolted to the fucking, metal bed, Elliott—his arms and legs, and goddamn neck. He was in a goddamn coma, Elliott. Had not moved since the day you put him there. It was G.E. He was the fool that suggested we go inside the goddamn cage."

"Tony, what happened? Did Adam hurt somebody?"

"He woke up, Elliott. He popped out of those metal shackles like they were fucking pipe-cleaners. I've never seen anything like it, except in the fucking movies."

"Adam broke his restraints?" Elliott said.

"Adam is alive and up?" Carol asked.

"That man is a real monster, Elliott. He pulled himself out of those shackles like King fucking Kong. The damn metal clamps rained down as he sat up. We were helpless standing there. G.E., me, and your two Mikes, we backed away. Poor Dr. Franks didn't move. He just stood there a few feet from the Butcher. The old guy was in shock—frozen."

"He didn't hurt anybody," Elliott whispered. "Tell me he didn't hurt . . ."

"Adam pulled his tubes and wires out. He pushed his hair back and got off the metal bed. He looked at all of us real slow, like he was daring us to try anything that would make his day. His big goddamn eyes were alert, not angry like in the begining. I can tell you none of us were gonna give him any trouble. Shit, we didn't even have our goddamn guns. I had a fucking pen . . ."

"What did Adam do. Tony? Where is he now?"

"I thought he was going to rip Dr. Franks head off."

"Tony. Focus. What did Adam do?" Elliott tilted the phone so Carol could hear.

"He walked up to Dr. Franks, just standing there at the end of the bed. Adam's goddamn chest and head were way above that little doctor. Adam had at least a hundred pounds of muscle on him, Elliott. He put his hand on Franks shoulder. They looked at each other for a long minute. Franks smiled and nodded. Adam walked out and locked the cell. He did not hurt any of us, Elliott. I can tell you G.E. and I thought we were goners—The Butcher never like us. I guess because we were always trying to kill him. Adam looked at Hinton and Primeaux. You could tell he liked them. He knew they took care of him, Elliott. He knows a lot of stuff. I could tell."

"So you survived as I would expect," Elliott said.

"How'd you know he wasen't gonna hurt anybody?"

"I'll explain later. Where's Adam now, Tony?"

"That's another reason why I'm calling. We don't know where he went. It was nighttime when this all happened. He got out of that place with no problem. Primeaux thinks he memorized the place, was conscious when they brought him in. He was playing opossum all that time, weak but lucid. Where do you think he went?"

Elliott looked over the Mediterranean rubbing his chin. "He went to the river. He could find himself a log and float back to Memphis. I think he went home, the catacombs."

"I don't think so. That place is crawling with Shelby County deputies and Memphis police. I don't see him getting past them."

"Don't kid yourself. There's a lot more ways into the

catacombs than we know. And there are a lot more uncharted tunnels and rooms. Adam could run around down there the rest of his life and we wouldn't know."

"You think he'll kill again? Do I need to take this inside?"

"He will not hurt innocent people, Tony. Gilgamesh soldiers are another story. Remember, he attempted suicide. He did not want to live anymore. I don't know how he feels now."

"He may go after the people that drove him to suicide," Tony said.

"Tell Max we spoke. Tell him I want him to share the new information uncovered on Adam's life in Texas, specifically the incident that brought him to Memphis."

"Can you give me some now? I won't see Max for a few days."

"Gilgamesh sent people to Texas in '82 to kill Betty Duncan and Adam. Dr. Medino came to their aide. He got Betty out of the country and brought Adam to Memphis. You remember the horrific killings on the bluff in '83?"

"Hell yeah, the beginning of the Bluff City Butcher legend. Killed three college students and kidnapped the Weatherford girl."

"That makes no sense. Adam was fourteen in '83. Max has evidence pointing to Gilgamesh. They did it to get the resources of the MPD looking for Adam. They made it a heinous act so the police would shoot first and asked questions later. They wanted Adam dead."

"But there were eyewitnesses," Tony said.

"Never were. All fiction. They killed the four and staged everything. Max has proof."

"Damn. They had the whole city looking for the Butcher for years."

"Gilgamesh made one mistake. They did not factor in Adam's unique qualities. They were dealing with a gifted, genius psychopath. Their aggressive tactics only helped Adam focus on them. Adam spent a lifetime hunting Gilgamesh operatives, the people who tried to kill him and his mother, the people who forced them to live apart, and the people who killed Dr. Medino."

"I don't get the Adam-Medino connection. How did that even come about?"

"It's still a mystery. We do know Dr. Medino brought Adam to Memphis." The phone fizzled and popped. Elliott continued. "Adam and Medino formed a bond. I think Adam protected him ever since.

We're still piecing all that together."

"FYI, Max and I are looking into the *Butcher victim* backgrounds. If there are connections, we will find them. I guess you still believe Adam's victims are stealth, Gilgamesh soldiers."

"Gilgamesh is a century old operation. There are a lot more people on their payroll than we we know. I'll bet most don't even know they're paycheck comes from Gilgamesh."

"How much you want me to share with G.E.?"

"He can know everything. That man's solid as a rock. Tell him Adam's not the one who killed his deputies. Adam's not going to be a problem for him. On the contrary, he may help us find those responsible his way."

"There's a chilling thought. When are you back to Memphis?"

"I'm on the trail of the man who killed Bernardo Kuzma. He may be the one that killed the deputies in the catacombs. He has the skill sets." The phone fizzled again. "We better get off."

"Be careful. Talk later."

As Elliott set the phone on the rock, a flash of light caught his eye. There was movement in the brush behind him. "Someone's coming," he whispered. Carol pushed everything into her bag. "Get down on the ledge now." When she dropped out of view four men with guns broke from the brush fifty feet away. "They see me," he whispered. "Go. Hide now. I'll be okay."

Moving along the face of the cliff on the narrow ledge, Carol clung to the rock wall grasping roots and crags. Her path descended. The ledge narrowed. Her footing was treacherous. It was a hundred foot drop to the rocks below.

"Hě toi. Ne pas děplacer ou vous allez mourir [Hey you. Do not move or you will die]."

THIRTY

"Control your fate or somebody else will."
Heinrich Von Pierer

They pushed through the thick gorse, heather, broom, and braken with guns out. Elliott sat still on the flat rock and kept his back to them. Spreading out, the four stopped a few feet away. Elliott turned his head. Now only one pointed a gun at him —he did the talking.

Two were tall and thin with long hair. The one with the gun was short and clean shaven. He spoke English. "If I were you, I wouldn't do nothin' to make me shoot ya, Dr. Sumner. I know you're a bad guy, so don't give me no trouble. You're worth as much to me dead."

The fourth and biggest had a beard and small eyes. He stared at Elliott and said, "No Drake. We only get paid if he's alive."

"Don't use names you idiot. Just shut up." He turned back to Elliott. "Ignore that peon. He has no knowldege of the deal." He smacked him in his chest. "I don't know why I brought you, Carl. Great French though. Seriously, cut that shit out."

"I don't intend to give you trouble." With his heel, he backed his cell phone into a rock crevis and turned his body tamping down the weeds.

"Don't move. What ya think you're doin'?" Drake yelled.

Carl kicked Elliott. "Put you're hands behind your back. I will shoot ya."

"Don't kick the man, Carl. Shit! Don't do a damn thing unless I tell ya. Got it?"

Carl backed away and spit. "Yeah."

"Go ahead and tie his hands behind his back. Sumner, put you hands back there now."

Elliott heard Carol scraping against the rock moving down the ledge. "Who are you guys? What's this all about?" he yelled. His explosive demand stopped the other two from walking to the ledge. "And you two. You look familiar to me. You know I'm a serial killer hunter, right?" The two turned and froze pointing at each other.

"You ain't ever seen me, mister," one said.

"Or me," the other said. Elliott was successful distracting them and giving Carol more time.

"We ain't no serial killers and we ain't never heard of you."

"All of you are Americans." Elliott prodded.

"Would you two imbecils shut your pie holes. You don't answer his questions. What the hell's the matter with you." Drake pushed Carl from behind. "Hurry up. Tie up the son-a-bitch so we can get out of here and get our money."

When Carl finished tying, he grabbed the knot at the wrists and yanked. He enjoyed delivering pain. He dragged Elliott backwards off the rock into the tall grass. The two skinny ones resumed their trek to the edge. *I hope you got out of sight baby. These guys aren't real bright. Unpredictable.*

"We're not here to answer your questions doc, so shut the hell up unless you're asked somethin'," Drake ordered. Carl pulled Elliott upright. He stumbled turning Carl and Drake from the line of view of his hidden phone. "Who was you talkin'too? We heard talkin."

Don't ring . . . please. "I was talking to myself." *Please don't see Carol . . .*

"We pinged your phone, Sumner. Who were you talking to on the phone, and where is the damn phone now?" Carl tugged the ropes for emphasis. Drake stood in his face holding the gun on his nose. The two skinny ones were at the edge of the flat rock. "Check the man's pockets, Carl. Find the damn phone."

"I don't have it anymore. I tossed it in the woods when I heard you coming." Carl kept rifling through Elliott's pockets.

"That's great. Who was yau talkin' to?"

"If you must know, I was talking to the police, a homicide detective back home. He's talking to the local police here now. I turned myself in. Gave them directions. They should be here any minute. Probably not a good idea for you guys to be here."

"You're lying," Drake said.

"You're not French. You're American. You should know I don't lie." Elliott smiled. Carl hit him in the stomach and grabbed his face and squeezed.

"You keep this shit up, I let Carl hurt you." Drake looked around. "Let's get out of here," he barked. "If he did talk to the police, we don't need to mess around here too long."

"I hope you and your friends know what you're getting yourself into. The people in this are dangerous. They promise things. When you deliver, they erase you. They can't risk having you around talking about things. Best you rethink this. Leave me here for the police. Just say you couldn't find me so they won't have a reason to . . ."

Carl hit Elliott in the stomach again. Elliott doubled over.

Drake pulled back the hammer on his gun and put it to Elliott's head. "Shut up or I'll shut you up."

"Drake. There's a rock ledge over here." Both men leaned over the side. "If someone else was here, they could take this ledge and get away."

"Shit. I'm surrounded by morons. Both of you get out on that ledge. One go one way, the other the other way. Move. We got to hurry."

They started to hang over the edge to get footing. "I don't know about this. It's really narrow, Drake. Looks dangerous."

They looked down. "Yeah Drake. It's gotta be hundred foot drop to those rocks down there. I don't like it either. Maybe it's a bad idea."

"If you guys want any of the money, you go. We can't have any loose ends. That's the deal." He turned to Carl. "We take Sumner to the car. We finish tying him there. Sumner, I will shoot you if you do anything I don't like. I don't make money if you get away. So who gives a shit if your dead in the weeds."

"I'm not going anywhere. But you could lose a guy on that cliff if . . ."

The blood curdling scream came on Elliott's last word. It faded into an eerie silence. Drake ran to the edge of the flat rock. Both men were missing. One was lying on the jagged rocks a hundred feet down. The waves lapped over his lifeless body. Pools around him turned red. He was dead or dying. Either way he was no more use to Drake.

Carl held Elliott by the knot and shoulder. "Someone fall? Was it my brother?"

"No. It was Palmer. He's gotta be dead. Shit . . . shit . . . shit."

"Where's Branch? You see Branch?" Carl asked.

"He went the opposite way. He's around a bend in the rock. I don't think he can see us from there." Drake cupped his mouth. "Branch. Where are you? Are you okay?"

"I'm okay," Branch yelled back. "Is Palmer okay? Thought I heard him yell."

Drake shook his head. "Palmer's fine. Saw a snake. You see anything yet?"

"Looks like someone's been over here. See some roots pulled out. Can't be sure. I'm moving good, but it's gettin' tight."

Drake yelled, "You find someone, kill them and toss their body over the side. You got five minutes. Police Nationale are on their way. Meet us at the car. If you're late, walk to the hotel and don't let anyone see you."

This was the only chance he had. Elliott butted Carl's head knocking him to the ground, and he ran into the thick brush. He heard the explosion. The bullet grazed his arm.

"Next two go into both legs, doc," Drake said while taking aim.

Elliott stopped.

"Let's go. And don't touch Sumner, Carl." Drake lead the way. Elliott followed. Holding his bleeding head Carl pushed Elliott every step of the way. When they reached the small clearing, Drake pulled rope from the trunk and tied Elliott's ankles and knees. They tied a rope around his chest and arms and shoved a dirty rag in his mouth.

"Put him in the backseat. We give Branch three more minutes."

"I don't like standing around like ducks in a pond," Carl said. He kicked the back tire rubbing the bloody knot on his forehead. "That guy has a hard head."

"We're waiting on your brother," Drake said.

"He can find his way back to the hotel. He's a big boy," Carl scowled.

"Your call."

"I say we go now . . ."

The sedan crawled out the dirt road onto black asphalt and

went north. There were no cars on the quiet stretch of road for the next hour. Elliott, tied up like a Christmas turkey in the backseat, could only pray Carol found a way out.

She reached the end of the ledge and managed to jump across a four-foot gap to a narrow landing. The short distance across seemed twice as far when looking into the hundred-foot abyss. Grabbing a fat root on the other side when landing, Carol swung into an eroded crevice that turned out to be a cave on the face of the cliff. It was dark and draped with matted webs.

I can't go back and I can't go up, she thought. And I'm more than ten feet below the edge of the cliff I can see. Maybe this cave goes somewhere. I hate spiders . . .

She heard the tumbling gravel and groan. Easing back into the webs, she peered out. A man with a gun, glued to the rock, wall was inching toward the gap. Carol backed deeper into the cave with eyes closed and hands swatting anything that crawled. The thick webs broke on her back and neck and head and legs. Then she dropped to her knees in the cold, damp darkness. Her knee found a sizeable, loose rock. Althoug heavy, it wide and flat and would serve as her only weapon. Twenty feet in she looked back and saw him. The man stood at the opening of the cave leaning and looking in with his gun. *Maybe you don't know I'm in here . . .*

"I know you're in there," he shouted, like he was in the car picking up a teenager after a dance. "I see your tracks in the dirt, and them spider webs are all broken up." He paused to laugh at the stupidity of his prey. "I'm known for my trackin' skills, mister. Best you come out now. You can join your friend. Nobodys gonna get hurt. We're just doin' a job. Gotta deliver your friend to some people."

Won't hurt me? Then why the gun, Daniel Boone? Carol sank further and leaned on the cold dirt wall. She crouched enough to hide but still maneuver some. *Your not real bright. If you only wanted Elliott, why risk falling off this cliff looking for me? You must be freelance, contracted by Gilgamesh, not one of their trained soldiers. I'd be dead already. They don't like loose ends. Nobody takes a loose end with them. They dispose of them . . . This is it for me.*

The explosion was louder than she expected. Although she knew it was going to happen, she was not ready for the magnitude of noise coming out of a small handgun, and the eye burning smoke that spewed into the cave behind the bullet that went into the dirt inches from her side. Carol got lower. She tilted up her flat rock, a shield for her head. The second shot came. This time it exploded the dirt inches in front of her, and part of the cave rained down from the rolling concussion that left her ears ringing and the world a muffled memory.

He's going to empty his gun in here. He's bound to hit me. I need to charge him with this rock. It's my only chance . . . But before she could get up from her knees, the third shot rang out. This time there was no explosion of dirt or richochet—there was a squeal deep in the cave. She heard the whining, and yelping, and snorting for the first time. Carol got as close to the dirt wall and floor as possible. She sucked her legs under her torso as the sounds of movement from the depths of the cave approached.

I can smell you . . . my god. What are you? She pressed the side of her head into the dirt floor behind her flat rock and looked up with only one eye. The darkest shadow in the cave now stood next to her. She could see its large head looking out the cave at the man with the smoking gun. Its head swung to her. It snorted. Something dripped on her face and arm. She didn't move, but she gagged and closed her eyes and thought, *oh God . . . now I've done it.*

The forth shot changed everything. Carol's eyes popped open after she was sprayed and when the squealing rage left her side charging the shooter—he had no idea what was coming his way.

She lifted her head and watched the dark dimensions grow and close out the light. Then there were two more shots. They came in rapid succession. The angry shadow was not slowed. It took shape when it erupted from the cave into the sunlight and the shooters chest.

They both disappeared . . .

THIRTY-ONE

"If the enemy is in range, so are you."
Unknown

"Y ou need to pull over. What were you doing . . . speeding or something?"

"No, I was going slow. It's gotta be something else. What about Sumner?"

"He's not going anywhere." Drake looked in the backseat. Elliott laid there tied and gagged on the floor.

"The cops will see Sumner. What are we gonna say?"

"You're driving. You gotta be the one to get out of the car and go to them. They don't need to look inside the car. Give me your damn gun and act natural," Drake said to Carl.

"I don't like this." He pulled his gun from his waist and slid it across the seat. Drake pulled his and put both under the seat.

Carl pulled the sedan off the road and got out before the squad car parked. Leaning back on the the center of the trunk, he waited with a stupid smile and blood on his head. The two police officers got out at the same time and approached with hands on their guns.

"Is there a problem, officers? I don't think I was speeding." One walked up to him.

"American?"

"Yep. American. Don't speaka the Frencha."

The officer spoke in perfect English. "I need to see identification, please."

Carl complied.

As he examined the visa he asked, "What happened to your head?"

"Oh that." He rubbed it. "I was under the hood. Slipped. Hit it on the radiator."

The officer pulled his gun from his holster and aimed from the waist. "If I were you, Carl, I'd stand very still and not say another word." The second officer moved around to the passenger door pulling out his gun. He tapped the barrel on the glass. Drake held his hands up and shook his head.

"Hands on you head now." He opened the door, pulled Drake from the car, and pushed him to the ground on his stomach. "Spread your legs and keep your hands on your head."

"What is the problem here?" Drake asked.

"Stop talking," the officer shot back.

"Now you can join your friend. And Carl, do exactly what he is doing."

"But what did we . . ."

"No talking," the second officer said. "And don't try anything stupid. You just might get out of this mess." He watched Carl lay down next to Drake.

The hunter green Austin Healy came over the hill. It pulled alongside the parked sedan and stopped. Carol got out, pulled Elliott from the driver's side backseat and loaded him into the roadster. She got back in and they drove away. She would untie him on the road.

They both watched the rearview mirrors in silence. One policeman leaned inside the sedan as the other kept the two on their bellies. The unregisterred guns would be found and the two would be detained and prosecuted.

"You're full of surprises," Elliott said as Carol untied his wrists with one hand, shifted, and steered with her legs.

"There. You got the rest." His wrists were free from bondage. She passed him the blue cell phone and shifted into four. "You forgot this."

"Oh. Thanks. You found it."

"I managed to get back. I figured you would find a hiding place for your new toy. Was pretty certain you had to find it fast and you're not a fan of throwing things randomly."

Elliott smiled looking straight ahead. "I didn't want those bad people to take it from me." He rested his hand on her exposed knee. "I'm sure there's a great story behind the blood spray, torn dress, spiderwebs, and cave moss."

Carol leaned into the mirror. "I don't have moss on me."

"Before I forget, we need to tell Max his system failed," Elliott said. "The bad guys pinged my blue phone." He saw the corner of her lip go up. Carol kept an eye on the road and the shrinking images in the mirror.

"You know that'll drive Max nuts."

"Exactly. Now.

You going to tell me what just happened or keep it to yourself?" Elliott pulled the ropes from his ankles and knees.

"You remember that little ledge you made me get on? It had a dead-end and someone with a gun was coming. So, I had a choice to make—confrontation or spiderwebs and cave."

"Ah . . . sounds like you chose well."

"Let's just say it was the spookiest, ickiest thing I ever did."

"There are those big people words," he teased.

She shifted into fourth and pressed the pedal. "At the end of the ledge was a cave on the side of the cliff. I had no way out. I had to go inside. Next thing I know he's standing at the entrance shooting into the cave. Well, long story short, he upset the owner."

"Wonderful. And you're in there with the owner."

"I was between it and the gun. He kept shooting. I again had no options. I was ready to charge him, take my chances. Then that thing came up next to me. I think it was curious about me but pissed-off at the guy making all the noise. The next shot hit it." She swallowed hard. "It sprayed blood on me. The thing charged the man. They both disappeared."

"Unbelievable." Elliott rubbed her thigh.

"I didn't know what it was until I got the nerve to leave the cave. I looked over the edge. The man with the gun was on the rocks a hundred feet down. I'm sure the fall killed him. Next to him was an enormous, wild boar. I never saw one that big. I didn't know they were in France."

"A *sanglier*. You survived a French, wild boar. I'm very impressed. They're known for their aggressive nature. It must of sensed you were not a threat."

"Elliott, it was standing on the rocks next to the man. I don't know how it survived the fall."

"The shooter was its cushion. They're smart, hardy beasts. I'll bet they've learned all sorts of maneuvers along those cliffs. Probably not the first time it fell off them. Now, tell me why the police nationale allowed you to drive up and remove me from the sedan without a word."

She smiled with her eyes straight ahead. It wasen't often she could show-off to the renowned serial killer hunter she adored. "I came across those two gentlemen and used my *lady in distress* approach."

"I've heard of the *damsel in distress . . .*"

"Same thing. I told the two young officers we were from America on our honeymoon. We were having a wonderful, romantic picnic and these men harrassed us and took my husband from me. They were going back to the hotel to get money wired from the states. I said they threw our keys away, but I found them. I needed their help."

"But they did not call it in or the place would have been swarming."

"Oh no. I said I just wanted my husband back with no hastles, or our honymoon would be ruined. Then I gave them each hundred dollars, U.S., and suggested they detain the bad men for carrying weapons probably unlisenced. I did not want the hastles of pressing charges."

"And the *policea* were good with that . . ."

"No. They called it in. But I forgot to tell you I called Max before I talked to the two young officers. Their superior told them to do as I asked. I guess Max made a call."

"Max has connections in Toulon? I'm impressed."

"He's well connected."

"I'm proud of you darling. But, unfortunately, we're not out of the woods yet. I think we're heading into more problems. Gilgamesh is starting to look in the small towns."

"And the police are not looking for you. Your name didn't mean a thing to them."

"Thanks for the confidence builder."

"I don't want people to care about you, sweet man."

"Don't you think you're being a bit possessive?" He squeezed her knee again. "Gilgamesh is not networked into the small towns. They use local thugs."

"They want this kept off the grid."

Elliott pulled up his pant leg. His calf wound oozed from the bandage. He applied pressure. "Riding in the back of that car I heard them talking."

"Anything useful?" Carol kept an eye in the mirror. So far they weren't followed.

"They were taking me to Eligio Tasso Peters. The table on the vellum. It's a code, *ETASP*. The center column, fourteen from the top. On the line of five boxes the first had the number 539. The second had the letter S. The next box, a letter *F*. The Last box was empty."

"The *F* may be the origin country—France," Carol said.

"The 539 is a date reference—9 for 1900, 53 for 1953. Most likely the date Elgio became a board member. Twelve of the twenty lines are highlighted." Elliott turned to Carol. "We have a list of the Gilgamesh board members. That's why the scion took it. He's killing Gilgamesh board members . . ."

"He's cutting down trees in the Cedar Forest," Carol muttered.

"On line ten, center column, the letter sequence is *B K U Z*. That's Bernardo Kuzma. And the date he told me he joined Gilgamesh was 1949. In his column-one is the number sequence 499. And in his column four there's the letter *R* for Russia. It all fits. Code broken."

"I don't have your eidetic skills, Elliott. You're going fast now. I can't see the columns and boxes like you. I remember pieces like your name, Jack Bellow, Adam Duncan, and Betty Duncan."

"Right. Then there's that. Don't have a clue why those names are on that table."

"Is the wealthy Aragon Spaniard on the list?"

"The line nine under Kuzma—letter sequence *P H E R*. The country of origin is *S N* for Spain. He joined the same year as Kuzma—1949. We need to go through this and reconstruct as much of the board as possible. We'll get it to Max. He can run it in origin countries looking for a billionaire fitting the letter sequence."

"Now we know for a fact Gilgamesh is coming for you," Carol said.

"And my mystery scion is hunting their board members."

"Looks like the *hunters* are the *hunted* and don't like it. Since you've now been at both deaths, it is possible they think you are the one hunting them, Elliott."

"I suspect if the four that found us were Gilgamesh A-team, the police would be in a ditch somewhere and the package—me— would be delivered."

"I'm afraid you are right about that." She watched the car behind hold its distance.

"When those bad boys don't check in, Gilgamesh will know there was a problem."

"They will know our general where-abouts," Carol said.

"Not a lot of roads around here to monitor. Or old, hunter green Austin Healys . . ."

"Now you're just being negative."

"We need to trade up, darling. See the hospital coming up?"

"What do you want me to do?"

"Go in that parking garage. Let's go shopping." When they turned off, Carol kept an eye on the car behind them. It continued northbound.

"I just remembered. You've got a voice message. Could be important. Didn't know your password to check." Elliott pulled out his cell and started punching.

"You know it's not good to keep secrets from the one you love," Carol said as she turned into the three-level parking garage and started to crawl. It was dusk. She left the lights off. There were no people.

"I have trust issues," he said as he pressed the phone to his ear with a wink. After twenty seconds he pocketed it and pointed.

"There. The dark sedan with the tinted windows. Drop me. Put this on the top level and come down." Carol dropped him and took off. By the time she returned, the new car was humming and passenger door open.

"You picked a snazy one," she said as she got in and her dress hiked up her legs. She knew Elliott would enjoy the moment.

"Only the best for you, my dear." Elliott crawled out the back of the parking garage.

"Are you going to tell me about the message?" Carol asked.

He pulled onto the road heading northwest. There were no cars in the area. After shifting and getting up speed he said,

"We're going to Nevers, France. It's a small town on the banks of the Loire—population 43,000. It's about a hundred-fifty miles outside of Paris, the Bourgogne Region. It appears I could just as easily stayed with my captors."

"What do you mean?"

"My phone message, it was from the scion. He promises me an unforgettable evening with Eligio Tasso Peters. Said he'll see me there."

"My God, Elliott. He's going to kill another board member. He's on a tight schedule."

"We need to get me to be the Church of Saint Etienne on time, preferably before nine if Eligio's going to have any chance to survive the night." Now that Elliott was driving, Carol could pull out the reconstructed table from her purse and study it.

"While I go to church, you can get a copy of that to Max," he suggested. "Oh, and by the way, we're being followed. That car has been behind us since the hospital."

Carol looked back. "No. They've been with us a while longer, Elliott. They passed us when we pulled off. Must have doubled back. Qu'est-ce tu as comme voiture?"

"Can I lose them? I love it when you speak French. Une voiture rapide . . . très vite." He smiled. "I don't know if you noticed. We borrowed a *Bugatti EB* 110. The predecessr of the Veyron, everything to the extreme: V-12, 592 horsepower, 0 to 60 in 3.2 seconds. It has a top speed of 216 mph."

"I can't believe it was sitting in a hospital parking garage." Carol studied the vellum.

"Probably an orthopedist—carpenters of the body. Those boys like fast toys."

"You still didn't tell me if you could lose them, dear."

"Short answer is *yes*."

Elliott down shifted and threw-out the clutch bolting the car forward. Carol sunk in her seat. Her eyes watered on each side of her face as she smiled and gripped his arm. Two minutes later they were alone. Elliott fish-tailed off the highway onto a side road. Navigation said it added ten kilometers—snakey. Their tail didn't have a chance of catching up.

"I always suspected you could be a fun guy," she said.

"By the way, my password is easy to remember . . . C A R O L."

THIRTY-TWO

"He is most powerful who has power over himself."
Seneca

I t was the first time Albert allowed a Gilgamesh board meeting in his home. He made an exception only because he had to know what was going on and the extent of Elliott's involvement. It had been a month since they spoke, and Gilgamesh board members were dying. Albert's last meeting with Rudy was disturbing—the inference Elliott was out of control.

The limos started to arrive at the Bell mansion before seven. William met each guest in the courtyard and escorted them to Albert's study. The somber mood—like a funeral—filled the winding halls with whispers and long faces as if they were on their way to see the corpse. In the study they greeted each other with fleeting eyes and nods, and helped themselves to a drink and seat at the conference table.

Rudy acknowledged no one. He sat at the end of the table with his head down. Everyone knew to leave him alone. After the last sat down, Rudy got to his feet. He stared at the empty notepad in front of him in silence. Even the three on the speakerphone on the other side if the globe sensed the moment had arrived. Their heavy breathing faded into the ebbing static.

Rudy raised his head and looked around the table stopping at each attendee. He cleared his throat and spoke with no emotion. "Since I have served as your chairman, there have been only two times I've invoked the emergency meeting privilege—once in 1925, when our founding chairman, Alberto Bella, passed away and I accepted his seat by letter of authority. The second time was in 1968, when we successfully dipped our toe into the uncharted waters of immortality the first time." He paused for effect as much as to take a big swallow of scotch. The room was quiet except for the raspy breathing and gurgling stomachs of old men.

"I wish I was bringing us together to share more exciting news on the progress of our great research, but it is not why I've asked for this meeting. It is a sad day for Gilgamesh. I have terrible news to share. No more time can be allowed to pass. Action must be taken . . .

"On December 30, Bernardo Kuzma died. Most of you knew he was in his late eighties struggling with cancer. His death would not be a surprise to any of us. The proud Russian and valued member of our board since 1949, the humble scion who followed in the footsteps of his father—Andrei Kuzma, a Gilgamesh founder—Bernardo was killed in New York City."

The room groaned.

The speakerphone crackled alive. "Killed two months ago? You're telling us this now, Rudolph? Are you certain Bernardo was killed? Is there a possibility your information is in error? And why did you wait so long to tell us of this most terrible tragey, Mr. Chairman?"

The buzz on the phone silenced. The room slumped in their chairs.

"Francisco . . . gentlemen . . . I am sorry to deliver this shocking news. And, I am sorry for the obvious delay in notification. I wish there were a way to soften the blow, but there's not. I held this information so it could be look into, investigated, to confirm what we now know to be true. We kept it under wraps for sixty days, out of the news. We had to know the facts. Eliminate rumors. Gentlemen, I am sorry to tell you Bernardo died by a knife in Central Park on the night of December 30."

"Rudolph, may we ask questions?"

"Howard Carson, Seattle, has a question," Rudy announced.

"What was the motive? Was Bernardo robbed? You said an investigation. Tell us everything you found—I am sure I speak for all members of the board. Why and how was he killed. And where was his protection, for God's sake? We know Bernardo traveled with bodyguards."

"Robbery was not the motive. Bernardo was executed."

The room gasped . . . and then whispers.

Rudy continued. "He was taken into the park late at night. Gentlemen, his head was cut off. It took the NYPD two weeks to verify identity. His head was taken. It has not been recovered."

"Decapitation! Head taken! Why would anybody do such a thing?" Carson emoted.

"I'm afraid there's even more bad news. On January 14, Paciono Hernando was found dead in his home in Barcelona. He and his family were away on holidy. Paciono returned to Aragon for reasons unknown. We continue to search for answers."

"Could there be a connection, Rudolph?" Carson asked.

"Paciono was killed the same way—a knife, head cut off and taken."

"Paciono's head taken? Lord have mercy . . ." The room fell silent.

"Who would do such a thing to old men? Is there a message, an explanation, demands?"

"Mr. Stein, the only message is the decapitations and removal of heads," Rudy said, his chin pushed on his chest and eyes darting around the table as if searching for the guilty ones.

"Did your investigation turn up anything? What do we know?"

"For those on the phone, the question comes from Meir Stein, Israel, the presiding officer over our Dead Sea research facility. The answer. I can share some disturbing information now emerging. However, I do not want to jump to conclusions. Before I go into the evidence, I must tell you there have been others."

"Oh my God. Peters and Wilkens are not here tonight." The voice broke on the speakerphone and the revelation flowed through the room. Rudy Kohl stayed on script.

"I called this meeting because it is now clear we must do something to protect ourselves. We must find and stop the entity targeting our board of directors. This is a significant breach."

"Who else, Rudy? It's Peters and Wilkens. Right?"

"Yes. I am sorry to tell you Eligio Tasso Peters died this week in Nevers, France, and James Wilkens died last night in London. They both died like Bernardo and Paciono—their heads were cut off with a knife and taken."

The chilling information ignited even more chaos in the study. The horrific deaths of four Gilgamesh board members generated unfathomable shock, stark sadness, and crippling terror.

"We are being hunted," Carson shouted.

Stein jumped to his feet. "I'll be damned if I'm sitting still for this."

"I'm with you. Someone is killing board members. How can it be anything else? We need to dissolve the organization immediately and increase our protection," Fransisco said.

"Slow down everyone." Albert spoke for the first time. His words had an immediate calming effect, counteracting Rudy's carefully orchestrated efforts to create a frenzy from which to lead his board to another of his self-serving conclusions. "Let's hear more, and from everybody."

"Yes. I agree, Albert. We haven't heard a word from Mobutu Ali, Robert Armstrong, Ningpu Wu, or you for that matter. What are your thoughts at this juncture, based on the terrible information we've learned?"

"Is Mobutu speaking here. I not surprised. One day this come. We very close to reaching objective of long life. We know someone want to take. We always know we protect us. Not to change now. We go on offense. We hunt this madman. That what I think."

"Ningpu Wu speak here. I not in favor of offense. Concern four members dead tonight, secret members. No one to know our names. I very, very upset how killed. Very, very angry person. They very mad at us. This look like Butcher man. The Adam Duncan twin, is he alive? I know he very angry with Gilgamesh. I hear he dead. But we not sure."

"Robert Armstrong—Chicago. I'm like Bernardo Kuzma, a scion, my father an original founder. When he died I took his seat. I don't like what's happening at all. Clearly someone's killing us off. I want to know more about who could be hunting us and why. Once we have those answers we can take the necessary actions."

"Yes. We are too close to achieving our goal to be deterred

now," Carson said. "A lot has been invested for a long time. I would hate to walk away now."

Rudy got up and walked around the table, stopping at Albert's chair. He rested his hands on Albert's shoulders and spoke with more emotion than he had conjured up for the entire meeting. "I'm sorry to say we do have information on the killer. It's very disturbing, but in an odd way makes sense." He patted Albert's shoulder and walked back to his chair.

"What do you have, Rudolph?" Armstrong asked lighting a cigar.

"Our people have found Dr. Elliott Sumner presence in the vicinity each time a Gilgamesh board member is killed."

"You can't be serious," Albert exploded. "You're not pushing this forward with the board."

"You say Dr. Elliott Sumner killing board members?" Mubutu asked.

"I'm saying we have physical evidence putting him with Bernardo Kuzma the night of his death. Dr. Sumner was seen entering Central Park and returning from the location where Bernardo's body was found. The NYPD obtained Dr. Sumner's overcoat. It is covered with Bernardo's blood and his DNA."

"There is another explanation for that, Rudy. Someone's setting up Elliott."

"Albert, I expect you to defend your son. I would have a problem if you did not."

"This is not about defending my son. This is about dealing with reality."

"Facts. Barcelona. We have video and eyewitnesses that put Elliott Sumner at Aragon the night Paciono is killed. Dr. Sumner is holding the bloody knife on the terrace fifteen feet away from Paciono's headless corpse. They said the blood was still steaming on the floor. He ran from police. You tell me Albert, what was he doing there alone with a knife in his hand?"

Albert spoke with authority and respect. "I don't know, Rudy. Can you tell me for certain Elliott Sumner was not on a secret assignment with the government, FBI, CIA, or INTERPOL? Just maybe he was investigating a linked case. He is a world renowned forensic pathologist known for hunting serial killers all over the world. Does your information allow for the possibility Elliott was lured to Aragon by the killer to create confusion, a smoke screen? It's absurd to suggest Elliott Sumner is even capable of committing such heinous crimes. He has no history of such. He is a law enforcer. There's absolutely no basis for the wild accusations set forth tonight."

Rudy huffed. The room turned to him. "As I said, Elliott Sumner was seen by the groundskeeper standing on the balcony a few feet from a headless Paciono Hernando. He was holding the bloody knife that later authorities confirmed to be the murder weapon. And Albert, Elliott ran when the police arrived. He jumped from a third-story balcony and escaped into the woods. That's not the behavior of an investigator or innocent man. No sir. He risked his life jumping to avoid capture."

"You're wrong. Elliot is being framed. He behaved just as any innocent man would. He was set up, trapped. Every one of us would have ran under those terrible circumstances."

"I wouldn't be there in the first place," Rudy muttered so everyone could here.

"Any innocent man caught in horrific circumstances would be confused. If Elliott left the scene, he had a reason. He needed time to sort through the puzzle he stumbled upon. For anyone to assume he is the killer, well, I have a serious trust problem."

"They have him on video sneaking into Aragon. Sneaking Albert. Alone. Nobody else is on the video that night except Paciono , the groundskeeper, and Dr. Sumner. Truth prevails, Albert."

"I am shocked you would bring these wild claims to the board," Albert fumed.

"I'm sorry, Albert, but these are indisputable and incriminating facts. The evidence is overwhelming and significant. I cannot stand by and risk another board member's life. The police in four countries are hunting Elliott Sumner because they believe he is the killer."

"I will tell you and each board member this. You know me. You know what kind of man I am. I tell you this night Elliott Sumner did not kill these men. Elliott Sumner is not capable of such heinous acts. He has no reason to do such terrible things."

"That is just not true," Rudy said. "Elliott Sumner has killed before, several times as a matter of fact. He has killed monsters, serial killers. He almost killed the Bluff City Butcher with a butcher knife, if you recall. No Albert. The man is capable of killing."

"That is very different. They were trying to kill him. He was defending himself. In every case Elliott was cornered. He had no other options. He acted like any other man would under the same circumstances."

Rudy shook his head and rolled his eyes. "If Dr. Sumner believed Gilgamesh was trying to kill him, it too would be self-defense, Albert. He would be defending himself against us, the Gilgamesh Board of Directors."

"Bolivar here. Was Dr. Sumner at Peter's and Wilken's deaths?"

The quiet room leaned closer.

"We have video of Dr. Sumner stepping out of a dark sedan at the Church of Saint Etienne, the place where Eligio was found dead. It was the night of February 1st. There is additionl video showing the sedan enter the city of Nevers around eight o'clock. He had an accomplice, a driver. Eligio was killed around nine.

Dr. Sumner got back in the car on Rue Abbe'Boutillier at nine-thirty. He was carrying something."

"Was it Eligio's head?" Armstrong asked.

"We don't know. It was too dark to assess."

"What do we know about James Wilken's death?" Carson asked.

Rudy sipped his scotch and leaned back in the chair for the first time. "We have nothing that puts Sumner with James Wilkens."

"That shoots a hole in your theory, Rudy," Albert pounced. "Clearly you don't suspect Elliott had a partner. Someone else is doing this, gentlemen. Someone who knows where the cameras are. Someone drawing Elliott into their view. If Elliott was involved, do you really believe a man of his intelligence would be so exposed?"

"We do have Dr. Sumner in London, Albert. We just don't have him at the Wilkens place as of yet. Scotland Yard is investigating as we speak. I'm afraid we will see him there, too."

"Is there any other evidence of anyone else involved at these murders?" Armstrong asked.

"There are images of others, but nothing concrete . . . and nothing of interest to the investigating bodies."

"We are fooling ourselves to think Elliott would do this. The real killer is out there."

"I must agree with Albert," Mutubo Ali said. "To take man's head off is very serious thing. Very difficult for educated, civilized man do. Dr. Sumner is man of medicine and law, man of big reputation, a forensic expert in world. I do not believe this man could do this."

"I, too, have trouble with the theory," Meir Stein said. "Beheading is a savage act. It is an awful, uncivilized thing to do. A man would need to be sick. We have four dead. Taking four heads is beyond perverse, it is evil. Dr. Sumner would need to be someone else completely, and he would need to have one hell of a reason to behave in this heinous way—the motivation and committment is more a third-world mentality than the actions of a respected and educated man. We need to keep looking . . . for our own good." Meir turned to Rudy and said, "And we must make sure Dr. Sumner knows Gilgamesh is not hunting him."

"He would need incredible motivation," Armstrong muttered.

Rudy cleared his throat. "I'm afraid Dr. Sumner has motivation."

Heads turned.

"What motivation, Rudy?" Albert scoffed.

"He believes we are trying to kill him, Albert."

"Are we?" Meir asked.

"No," Rudy puffed. "But Dr. Sumner is convinced Gilgamesh killed his brother, Jack Bellow. He also thinks Gilgamesh sent Adam to kill him. When Adam learned, in this very room, he was the son of Albert Bell and brother to Jack and Elliott, he committed suicide. In a round about way Elliott blames Gilgamesh for Adam's life and death. Now, he's convinced we are hunting him."

"His brothers are dead—it is a fact. He would have good reason to believe we are trying to kill him to eliminate the Bell triplets," Armstrong said.

"We are trying to kill him," Ningpo said. "You tell truth, Rudolph Kohl. You tell about the Peabody roof and county morgue incidents. Both times Gilgamesh soldiers try to kill Sumner. I know because Mr. Wilkens tell me he order to be done on Peabody roof. Mr. Wilkens never like Bell triplet program. He never like genetic engineering experiment. He say two of them gone. Now it time to get rid of number three. I know Mr. Hernando order attack at county morgue in Tennessee. He also think action necessary and important to protect Gilgamesh. He say Dr. Sumner not asset. He say Dr. Sumner liability."

"Mr. Wilkens told you this, Ningpo?" Rudy asked. "And Mr. Hernando told you this, too?"

"Yes. And they tell to Mr. Peters, too. Mr. Peters agree—Sumner need to go."

"Is all this true, Rudy?" Albert asked. "You tried to tell me in January. You said there was an error. You said someone ordered Elliott's termination. Do you remember saying that?"

"Yes." Rudy rubbed his chin as the room waited. "But this only proves what I've been saying tonight. Elliott Sumner has good reason to believe Gilgamesh is hunting him. He is motivated to react very aggressively.

"The *survival instinct* is a very powerful thing. *Retribution* can change a man into a monster. What you just heard is sufficient motivation to kill and to send a chilling message."

"I disagree. It is not motivation to kill for a civilized man. It is not near enough motivation to remove a man's head, Rudy. However, it is ample motivation for a man of justice and principals to pursue and stop Gilgamesh."

"I understand your heartfelt view, Albert. But as the chairman of this board, I cannot risk leaving this alone. Therefore, I make a motion we vote on an action to protect the eight remaining board members by neutralizing Dr. Elliott Sumner. I am sorry, Albert. He has a legitimate reason to kill our board members. The evidence placing him at three of the four death scenes in three countries is irrefutable and conclusive. It cannot be ignored . . ."

"I second the motion. Sorry, Albert. People are dying and there are no other suspects," Carson said with his head down. "We must protect ourselves."

Albert jumped to his feet. "Don't do this, Rudy."

"If we do not move on this aggressively, our next board

meeting will be very small or non-existent. Everything we have worked for will be lost. We have the resources and capabilities to protect our members and emerging biotechnology. This is not for you or me to decide, Albert. It is for the Gilgamesh board to decide. There's been enough talk. It is time to put it to a vote."

"What are you proposing?" Meir asked.

"Termination of the threat posed by Elliott Sumner. Find him and eliminate any further risk to the board and our interests. My motion has been seconded. All in favor, raise your hand."

He counted those in the room. "And on the phone? Aye or nay?"

He listened as each man spoke. "The motion has passed by a majority . . ."

"This irrational action is wrong. It is illegal and unacceptable, Rudy," Albert said. "This body has no right to hunt and kill anyone." He looked up and down the conference table. "Who do you think you are? Your opinions and fears do not give you the right to be any man's judge, jury, and executioner."

Heads stayed down and the phone was silent. Now only Rudy eyed Albert.

"Who else have you killed in the name of Gilgamesh? I've been a fool. I trusted you. I never questioned you . . . even when I had suspicions." Albert backed away from the table. "I will not allow you to take the life of my son."

"You have no choice," Rudy said. "You are bound by the doctrine of the organization you've been a part of since 1956. You took your father's seat, and you took a solemn oath. Your father understood the importance of our work, as we thought you did. Think about what you're doing here today. Departure from the rules and tenets of this body has consequences."

"I am disappointed and angry," Albert said. "I honored my oath of secrecy and allegiance even when I doubted the works and behavior of this body. It is my fault. I did not look deeper."

"This board has always had the right to protect our members, Albert. Your personal interests cannot take that away."

"You sicken me. I am not going to permit this. I can only hope all of you realize how wrong you are before it's too late."

Albert left the study.

Rudy shuffled papers as whispers filled the room. He looked up. "I'm sorry for that, gentlemen. But I would expect nothing less. Elliott Sumner is Albert's son. Albert cannot see the obvious. Albert is understandably blinded and immune to the risk we all share. Dr. Sumner is not a threat to him. He is a threat to each one of us."

"Rudolph, maybe he's right. Maybe we should leave this in the hands of law enforcement. Maybe we should each bolster up our security and give them all the information we have so they can do their job," Armstrong said.

"Four of us are dead. Four board members of a stealth society of billionaires securing the secrets of immortality. We can't sit down with police. We are not supposed to exist. The police in four countries are stuck. Their efforts will shift to us—questions will be asked . . .

"There are eight of us left. We are next, Mr. Armstrong. I don't know about you, but I do not want my head cut off. The evidence is overwhelming. Dr. Sumner wants to kill us because he has been hunted—mistakenly or not. Like Adam, Elliott Sumner has a dark side Albert refuses to recognize. I did not want to say that in his presence. He has lost a lot. But, in time, Albert will see. He will come around. He is a man of truth.

"Now. My motion is that Gilgamesh immediately eliminate the impending threat—Dr. Elliott Sumner." Albert stood. "I will now ask each of you to vote—no action or action, meaning termination. I will call your name. First, Mr. Stein . . ."

"No action."

"Howard Carson."

"Action."

"Robert Armstrong."

"No action."

"Francisco Boliver."

"Action."

"Ningpo Wu."

"Action."

"Mobutu Ali."

"No Action."

"We have three *no action* and three *action* and Albert is a *no-vote*. My vote will decide." Rudy turned to the window, hiding his smile. "My vote is *action*. The motion passes. I will take it from here, gentlemen."

Rudy turned to the group. "I urge each of you to travel with personal bodyguards 24/7 until additional arrangements can be made for your increased protection. I need twenty-four hours. So, please be cautious. Dr. Sumner's skills are substantial."

"What happened to Bernardo Kuzma's bodyguards."

"They were killed. Their bodies were found not far from Bernardo."

"How were they killed?"

"A knife . . . cut their throat, and stabbed in the chest and groin—their heads left intact."

"Rudolph, if Albert voted this evening the termination order would fail. Don't you think someone should go get him so he can vote?" Armstrong suggested.

"No. It would be contrary to protocol. Albert knows the rules. His departure is a *no vote*. And gentlemen, let me remind you all voting matters are confidential. The TEA report will show a termination order was approved on this day. It will not reflect individual votes. As in our founding tenets, we act as one. There are times we go with the majority regardless."

Armstrong pushed, "But this is the son of a board member,

Rudy. I think an exception to the standing rule is in order. We should . . ."

Rudy interupted. "I will talk to Albert. I know him. He will come around when he accepts this dangerous and unacceptalbe situation. The evidence is real, gentlemen. Unfortunately his son is a killer that must be stopped before others in this room die. Elliott Sumner has the same emptiness we have seen with Adam. But Elliott Sumner is a smarter, more sophisticated killer."

* * *

As the last limousine pulled from the mansion, a storm rolled into Memphis. Albert sat alone in the dark on the west patio, the most difficult place to find in the mansion. It was tucked away at the end of a labyrinth of corridors and stairs. William stepped outside with a fresh carafe of coffee and a silver case—inside a pack of Marlboro.

"Are they gone, William?" Albert asked, his head studying the turbulent night sky.

"Yes, sir." He offered a cigarette. Albert took one. The lightning danced in his eyes. "I see a storm is coming, sir."

"Yes. I've been watching it develop," *for a lifetime, he thought as he* sucked the flame into his cigarette. "This one is going to be different, William. There's something unique about lightning bolts that stay in the sky."

"Yes, sir." He stood next to Albert watching the chain reaction, lightning flashing from the east to the west inside bellowing clouds piled high above the city.

"We're surrounded by great power and even greater danger, yet we continue to believe we're in control." The grounds of the Bell estate fell still. The soft winds vanished. The eerie silence seemed a strange contrast to the churning night sky.

"Difficult meeting tonight, sir?" he asked. William knew Albert sat on the west terrace when he wrestled with a problem.

"Yes. But a meeting I needed to have. One I wish I had years ago." He inhaled and stared at the light show as he exhaled.

William watched too.

"The trees, the bushes, each blade of grass—they're leaning west, sir."

"Very observant, William. We're never as alone as we think."

On his last word a blast of cool air crossed the west patio, slid over the manicured hedges, and hit a cluster of young trees. Elliott and William watched the explosion, leaves stripped from delicate branches and sprayed into the sky. Just as sudden, the wind disappeared and the supple, green leaves rained down on the lawn where they would die. Their life would be over in seconds. Each leaf would shrivel and die alone. They had no other future.

"*The skies roared and the earth rumbled . . . then it became deathly still, and darkness loomed and there rained death,*" Albert said as he turned from the leaves to William.

"Very nice. A quote, sir?"

"The *Epic of Gilgamesh*. It is an old poem about a man's quest for immortality."

"Much like your club, sir."

"Yes. Like my club, William." He smiled but weeped inside.

"Does the man find it, sir?"

"Find it, William?"

"Immortality, sir. Does the man in this poem find immortality?"

"No, William. And many miss the life they have. And many die along the way."

"I see. A very depressing poem, sir . . . this *Epic of Gilgamesh.*"

"Yes. It is, isn't it?" Albert took another long drag from his cigarette.

"I would not worry about the storm, sir." William got up and turned to leave. Albert grabbed his arm. William paused, maybe a forgotten service.

"Tonight is not just another night," Albert said. He let go of his arm.

William nodded. He backed into the house and closed the door leaving the patriarch alone.

"I'm not worried about this storm, my dear friend. The skies roar . . ."

THIRTY-THREE

"Life is just one damn thing after another."
Elbert Hubbard

W ilcox got the call at 2:20 a.m. He arrived at the Peabody Hotel seven minutes later. The only reason the streets were quiet was the late hour. Inside he found a beehive of activity.

The seventh floor emptied, all except three rooms: one a crime scene and two breaking and entering. Hotel guests were interviewed and relocated to the Marriott. All were instructed to stay in town until the Memphis policee said they could leave.

Paramedics could do nothing for the guest in room 714. They found him sitting in a chair facing the window and best view for the impending sunrise. But this guest would not enjoy the morning splendor—his head was missing.

"We got a name?" Tony barked. He leaned over the back of

the CSI agent bagging the hands for the headless victim. "Is that your vomit over there CSI person?"

Alex interrupted. "Yes, it is Mr. Granger's vomit. He did aim it away from the victim."

"Wonderful," Tony muttered as he looked into the raw, bubbling, neck wound.

MPD assigned Alex Harris to Wilcox in 2008—the sharpest rookie detective with the top, most disorganized and wildly unorthodox, homicide investigator in the midsouth. It was unclear who Director Wade wanted to rub off on who.

"Ningpo Wu . . . He's visiting from Japan." Alex spoke while writing in his notepad.

"I think I could have figured out *Japan* on my own, Sherlock," Tony said.

The headless neck was a perfect, transverse, horizontal, bloody plane with holes—trachea, esophagus, carotids, and jugular. The single pass was evident, and similar to the dismemberment Tony saw in the catacombs. He also picked up on the similarity to the Butcher's kills.

"Are you writing down *everything-under-the-sun* as usual, Harris?" Tony nagged.

"I'm trying to restrain myself, sir," he replied with all seriousness.

"I doubt that's working for you. Tell me who saw and heard *anything . . . please?*"

"No witnesses. Nothing seen or heard, sir."

"Surprise." *Why not just one goddamn time in my life, he steamed.* "So Mr. Wu dialed room service and asked for a head. They said they were out and then what?"

"An unknown caller contacted the front desk, an outside line, at 2:04 a.m. The caller said it would be a good idea to send paramedics to room 714, words verbatim. Hotel management called 714—no answer. They went up and knocked—no response. They let themselves in and then backed out of the room and contacted MPD."

"This shit is not good, Harris. I can handle routine shootings and stabbings, but cutting off heads is bullshit." Tony looked around the room for anything. "Who was Mr. Wu in town to see? Do we have a name?"

Before Harris could answer, they were interrupted by another CSI agent leaning a head into the room.

"Detective Wilcox, you need to come now."

At the end of the hall they stood in front of a door marked *storage*. The CIS agent opened it like opening a casket on a freak show. "We just found this."

"Shit. Another surprise," Tony puffed. "I assume the paramedics have been here—the man's dead. I don't want him moving when I get in there."

"Yes sir. Paramedics said warm but no pulse."

"You boys have enough pictures? I need to poke around?"

"We're done, detective."

Tony knelt and eased into the closet. He never liked his alone-time with a corpse. When he touced the body, a first responder leaned over him and whispered,

"We would have found him sooner, but the door was locked."

"Thanks for sharing," Tony grunted. "Now go away. . ." He gathered himself and yelled, "Harris. Get me a goddamn . . . Thanks."

Alex rested a flashlight on Tony's shoulder.

"Asian descent too," He muttered.

"Harris, don't always say everything passing through your brain." Tony moved the light around. "This man's a sumo wrestler. Gotta be a little over five feet and more than three-hundred pounds. Solid as a rock. And look at those mitts—a little cut on the knuckles. Looks like he got one off before he got filleted. CSI needs to bag em."

Harris yelled down the hall, "CSI. We need to bag the sumo wrestler's hands."

"I was referring to a body type. I don't know if the guy's a sumo wrestler."

"Sorry. A little misunderstanding."

"I don't know about you sometime, Harris." He reached in the back pocket for a wallet. "Bet this guy's Wu's bodyguard. Shit. No wallet. No ID."

Tony opened the bloody shirt. "He took a knife in the jugular, heart, and groin. Looks like he bled out in the closet only —very efficient. I like tidy psychopaths." Tony backed out and waved at a cluster of CSI waiting.

"I'll ask you again . . . do we know who Mr. Wu came to visit in Memphis?"

"Yes, sir. The front desk said three limousines were in service tonight."

"Don't tell me all three went to the same place."

"Yes. The Bell estate on Walnut Grove," Harris said as a man in a tan suit approached.

"Excuse me. You are Detective Wilcox?"

"Yes I am. Who needs to know?"

"I'm Daniel Morgan, the hotel night manager. I was instructed to come see you."

"Great. What can you tell me about this mess in your hotel, Mr. Morgan?"

"A terrible thing. We've completed our guest inventory. I think you should know there are two unaccounted for, not counting Mr. Wu. I believe they are connected . . ."

"They used the same limo service and went to the same location."

"Yes. Same limo service and same destination." Morgan seemed surprised Wilcox knew.

"Was it the Bell estate?" Tony asked.

"Yes, Detective Wilcox. You are very good."

"Let's just keep this between us for now. Tell me about the two missing guests."

"We checked their rooms. They are not there, detective. It seems odd."

"Names please?" Tony asked. "Harris, write this down."

"Mr. Howard Carson and Mr. Meir Stein. They were one floor up, rooms 824 and 832. As I said, both suites are empty, beds undisturbed."

"Are you certain they returned to the hotel this evening?"

"Yes. The limousine service completed before nine o'clock. The three enjoyed cocktails in the lobby lounge until midnight. They retired at the same time, one check. Oh yes, Mr. Wu's bodyguard left with them as well."

"Did Carson and Stein have bodyguards, Mr. Morgan?"

"No sir. Only Mr. Wu, a heavy set, short, Asian man. He stayed outside Mr. Wu's door day and night. The man did not have a room here. It must be an oriental thing. That reminds me, the bodyguard is missing too."

"Right. Anything else, Mr. Morgan?" Tony asked with his head moving somewhere else.

"No. I want you to know we will cooperate fully with the Memphis police."

"Thank you." Tony backed away and found Harris by the closet. "I want you to process the rest of this crime scene. Pay attention to details, down to the gnat's ass. Surveilance video could take a few days to get—we need a close look. I'm going to visit Albert Bell before anyone else. I want to know what was going on at his humble abode. Call me if you trip over more bodies."

"May I say, sir, this looks like the work of the Bluff City Butcher."

"No. You may not say."

"But sir."

"Harris. Think. The Butcher died on the roof of the Bell mansion—December 23rd. You were there. You saw it with your own eyes. Don't get weird on me. I got no time for it."

"But sir, I've seen his work. I studied it. I compared it to historical cases. Nobody kills like that man. Nobody handles a knife like the Butcher—the power, speed, and accuracy. I don't like what I'm lookin' at tonight—neck slashing, heart puncture, and groin clip nailing the femoral artery, and single sweep decapitation."

Tony could not reveal his new knowledge. Although the Butcher was alive and running around somewhere, Tony trusted Elliott when he said Adam would not kill anybody but maybe Gilgamesh people. "The Butcher is dead, Harris. Stop with the theories."

"Then we have another, skillful, knife-weilding killer in Memphis. I would hate to think we had to deal with . . ." They were interupted.

"Excuse me, Detective Wilcox," Morgan insisted. "We have some video in security you will want to see right now."

"You already have something? Come Detective Harris." Morgan led the way.

They took a quiet ride to the basement of the Peabody Hotel. Tony prayed he would not see Adam Duncan on hotel video. Harris was right. The stabbing of the bodyguard and killing of Ningpo Wu looked like the Butcher's work.

There's no way you killed the two sheriff deputies in the catacombs, Tony thought. You were in a coma in Millington at that time for certain. But they died from neck, chest, and groin wounds . . . and a severed arm as flawless as the decapitations I've seen you do . . .

The security office was dark. Behind the tinted glass and security locks were armed guards and three banks of monitors.

Each floor had a minimum of one camera but usually five. And cameras were on all building exits and inside the Peabody garage with a panoramic view of the four roads boxing in the property. When Tony entered, a path opened to the bank of monitors and a short, curly-haired man with thick glasses and sleeves rolled above his bony elbows.

"Detectives Wilcox and Harris." he said. "How many cameras you got?"

"Raymond Burser, head of security, fifty cameras."

"Good. What do you have for us, Burser?"

"We've started our review of video at the time the man in 714 was found. We are going backward in time looking for anything that could help. We found something on the eighth floor first, detective. It is related to the two gentlemen who disappeared—rooms 824 and 832. This took place at 12:35 a.m."

They watched a large man in the main hall pushing a commercial laundry hamper. "This is not ours. It's a *Lavex*. We use *Luxor* at the Peabody."

"Great. Our killer brought his own hamper on wheels," Tony mumbled.

"Let me slow this down here . . ."

Tony

was more interested in the man pushing the Lavex—tall, broad shoulders, walking with a familiar, lumbering gait and slight limp. The black hair was pulled back into a pony tail. The head was down. "He's avoiding your camera. We need more."

"Do you have another on the floor," Harris asked.

"Yes. Unfortunately we suspect he knew. By the service elevator. it was crushed. We do have a brief image . . . and then boom. Maybe a second of a blurred face."

"We need it. Harris, get it to the FBI ASAP. They can do a lot with a second."

They continued to run the video. The mystery man wheeled

his laundry hamper to room 824 and went in. "He accessed with a master key," Burser said "Let me advance."

The door opened. They watched the mystery man push the Lavex and drag a man from 824 to 832. He lifted him up to the door.

"We believe it is Mr. Howard Carson. He's in room 824."

"The bastard's holding him sideways at peep hole level," Tony muttered. "He's presenting a recognized profile, hiding the face with the closed eyes." The door opened to a crushing blow. The man entered with the laundry cart and Carson's lifeless body. They watched the door close and waited a few minutes. Nothing.

"What about Ningpo Wu, room 714. You got anything yet?" Tony asked.

"Not yet," Burser replied as he moved to another monitor. "

We started at the top and bottom floors and are converging so we don't miss anything. We've been hung up on the elevators. So far we have him getting off only on eight. That's what we just shared. There's a lot more video to go through, detective."

"Have your men identify all crushed cameras. Then check video feeds on working cameras in their vacinity. The son-of-a-bitch is too big to hide."

"Will do . . ."

"Harris, get a team up here and help these boys. I want a face. Carson and Stein could be dead and stuffed in a closet somewhere. And I want the goddamn laundry cart. Get as many Memphis police down here as Wade will give us to look in every hotel room, closet, and cubby hole—time is not our friend."

"Got it." Harris ran out with radio at his mouth.

"Burser, what do you have before midnight on the seventh floor? I have a hunch our man killed Wu before going up to eight," Tony said.

Burser moved to another monitor and fast-forwarded to the bodyguard standing outside the door of room 714. "Okay. This means Mr. Wu is in his room now."

As they watched the door opened. The bodyguard turned and dropped to the floor.

"I'll be damned," Tony sighed. "He was waiting in the room. The poor bastard's probably dead already."

They watched him drag the bodyguard to the storage closet. "Only the back of his head."

He opened the door and dragged Wu's bodyguard into the closet. Before he closed the door the bodyguard jumped to his feet. "Here we go. A battle," Tony said.

Facing the camera at the end of the hall, the bodyguard assumed martial arts stance. His hand shot out, and the man's head whipped back. Burser had to turn away from the screen. One eye stayed. "Oh God. That poor man. That . . . knife."

They all stared in amazement and shock. In the ensuing blur of motion the man's arm swept the blade finding the bodyguard's neck, heart, and groin. Before the blood flowed from the gaping wounds, he pushed the dead man into the closet and watched him collapse. He locked and closed the door and slid the knife under his coat.

"What's he picking up?" Burser asked as they watched. "I didn't see him with it before. It's a backpack." He entered the stairwell. The door closed behind.

"He has Ningpo Wu's head in that backpack," Tony said.

"Oh my God . . ."

"This goes nowhere," Tony instructed. "No talking to friends, family, or media. Everyone got that?" They nodded in their trance. "This is an active investigation. These videos belong to me now. Burser, you can continue to comb through everything, or you can wait for our guys to do it. I will understand. This stuff is not easy. I gotta have a face. A big man with a ponytail is not enough to go on."

"We're in this, detctive. We never had anything like this. He could still be in the building."

"Harris will get the FBI in here. They've got capabilities. Video is full of surprises. Even when you think you got nothing, it could be something. I want you working with them . . ."

Harris met Tony in the basement hallway. "The hotel is crawling with Memphis police and some dogs, sir. I'll get back upstairs with the medical examiner. If Mr. Carson and Mr. Stein are here, we will find them, sir."

"Harris, the sooner you get the FBI to do their magic with the video, the better. The killer made a mistake. We gotta find it."

"They're on their way," Harris replied eager to meet Tony's expectations.

"Good. Now call the Bell estate. Let them know I need to see Albert. Do not tell them what's happened down here. Keep the goddamn lid on this, the media out. Tell them someone is dead and there are suspects in the hotel. That'll explain the attention and lock down.

Tony jogged up the stairs from the basement into the Peabody lobby. It was like a circus had come to town. He lifted the collar of his raincoat and eased out the exit avoiding questions. Stopping in Second Avenue under an awning five feet from his cruiser, he lit a sorely needed cigarette and inhaled deep.

Damn you Adam, this better not be your work. I swear I'll kill you this time . . .

PART THREE
DEADLY NEPOTISM

THIRTY-FOUR

"A man often meets his destiny on the road he took to avoid it."
Jean De La Fontaine

The buzz in the Patterson House cocktail lounge slowed down around eleven on weeknights. Regardless, it stayed open until three in the morning for the regulars. Marcus Morino came late. His shift at the CHGR always ended at ten. This night loose ends kept him. Now, sitting at the bar, he ordered the *Moscow Mule* to honor a friend he heard just died.

"El Diablo, please." The bearded man in the raincoat sat one stool over.

Marcus waited for his Mule and politely nodded.

"The Diablo is one of my favorites," he offered, as he pulled a leather pocket calendar from his coat and started to flip pages and shift crumpled notes from the front to the back.

Looking straight ahead, the man with the beard said,

"Lunazui Reposado, Creme de Cassis, Lemon, and Ginger Syrup . . . what's not to like?"

"I'm impressed. Another connoisseur of the cocktail circuit." The bartender set the Moscow Mule in front of him. He smiled and raised his glass.

The man with the beard said, "Connoisseur . . . a person who is especially competent to pass judgment in an art, particularly one of the fine arts, or in matters of taste. A discerning judge of the best in a field. Yes. I accept the use of the word."

Marcus watched him over the rim of his Mule not quite sure what to think.

"Prairie Vodka, Lime and Ginger Syrup. A very nice drink, but not your usual." The man with the beard kept looking straight ahead sipping his Diablo. Marcus set down his glass for a closer look. Still unfamiliar.

"I'm sorry, do I know you?"

"You like the Benton Bacon Infused 4 Roses Bourbon, Maple Syrup, and Coffee Pecan Bitters."

"Right, the Bacon Old Fashioned cocktail. You must come here often. After a long day, I find that particular drink best settles my nerves." Marcus dismissed the mystery. He assumed the man with the beard to be just another Patterson House consumer.

"Why the switch? Why go to the Moscow Mule?" he asked.

Marcus took another sip and sank on his stool. "I just learned a man I met is dead. He is an old Russian. I didn't know him well, but we spent quality time together. I will miss him."

"Where did you meet Bernardo Kuzma? Did he come to Nashville?" The bearded man turned to Marcus for the first time. His eyes were penetrating and familiar. Confused, Marcus looked straight ahead into the mirror. He saw a clear path to the front door. He could push his stool into the man and run if needed. If he had a gun, Marcus would not avoid the bullet in the back. He knew the day was near.

"Excuse me, but how do you know about Mr. Kuzma?" Marcus asked with his pivot foot sliding from the stool to the floor.

"How is your postdoctoral fellowship program working out for you at CHGR? I would imagine it's not as challenging as you'd hoped. I don't know, is computational genomics ringing your bell, Marcus?"

"You know my name? You know what I do? Who are you? Something about you is familiar, but I don't recognize . . . Have we met?" He leaned onto his pivot foot.

"Your father would want you doing more than deciphering the genetic basis of human traits and their integration into diagnostics, treatments, and the prevention of human disease. I bet he is rolling in his grave wondering why his son is not taking his lifelong work forward."

"Who are you?" Marcus got ready to escape.

The man with the beard reached for his arm.

"I'm Elliott Sumner, Marcus *Medino*." Elliott watched the blood leave his face—Marcus wobbled. Elliott held him on his stool and watched him stare into his empty glass. He needed time.

"How did you find me?" He mumbled.

"I did not know you existed until December 30th. Bernardo told me about you before he died in New York City. He said Dr. Enrique Medino had a son still alive—Marcus. He said he contacted you concerned that he could find you. It meant Gilgamesh was not far behind.

"It's been a while since your father died. What are you doing hanging around the Vanderbilt human genetic research program? Are you trying to commit suicide?"

"I did not know know what else to do. I thought it was so obvious it was safe."

"Right. The *hide in an obvious place* strategy. Over the years that strategy allowed me to catch a dozen psychopaths."

"Really."

"I don't mean it like it sounded."

"I've been in Nashville since 2004, Vanderbilt since 2007. I thought I blended, just another research fellow. No one knows Dr. Medino had a son."

"It worked for a while. But like Bernardo said, if he could find you, others could. Gilgamesh did not want your dad around. They don't want his sibling walking the planet either, especially one with an interest in genetics."

"I know who you are, Dr. Sumner. My father said one day you would come for me. He said if you did . . . he would be dead. You know he made sure my life was erased. All records of my existence were destroyed at birth. I was the chosen one in the family. I was given a new identity so I could work with him. He needed someone he could trust completely."

"I know something about growing up without your family. It's not much fun."

"My mother knew. I saw her a dozen times in my life. But my father's work was ground breaking, important to humanity. The risks for him, and everyone around him, were enormous. That's why we did it. I sacrificed a normal life so if my father was successful, the greatest evolutionary leap for mankind had a chance. They killed him, Dr. Sumner. He was right. His work was important. He had success. Bad people came out of the woodwork. They tried to steal it from him for years. They would stop at nothing."

"You lost your family that night in November. I know you were devastated."

"I wanted to kill myself." Marcus waved for another Moscow

Mule. "I found myself in a hotel room with a gun, but couldn't do it. If I had gone through with it, I would let *them* win. My father's work would have no chance to benefit humanity. It is what drove him, advancing the human species in a limitless universe. In that hotel room I decided to pick up where my father left off. We spent a lot of time together at the farm and in Memphis where he did his groundbreaking work."

"Do you know if anyone saw you coming and going between?" Elliott asked.

"There were underground tunnels at both locations. At the farm tunnels run from the woods into the barn and house. I suppose someone could find one of them. If they did, I could not tell. I go to the farm all the time."

"I assume in Memphis you spent your time in the Brent mansion catacombs."

"Yes. I read about it last October. They found one of the entrances into the catacombs. There's a lot of stuff down there. The place is enormous, like a giant ant farm. My father took me there twice a month. I know the catacombs well."

"I won't ask you what your father did down there, until later." Elliott finished his drink and waved a finger at the bartender.

"Why are you here?" Marcus asked. "Am I in danger?"

"Gilgamesh could be nearby. Things are happening. I think we need to pool our information and get you somewhere safe. Gilgamesh seems to be nearing their own end game. They're getting desperate."

"How do you know?"

"They are tying up loose ends, one of which is my termination. I suspect another is your location and termination, Marcus. They are approaching their end game."

"So they must believe they've found the secret to biogenic imortality, too?"

"I don't know what they believe. I do know there is a sense of urgency. I believe they killed my brothers. I've been running around the world trying to find out more about Gilgamesh and the person seemingly on a mission to execute board members. So far everything is just out of my reach. Finding you alive means—for once—I've gotten ahead of them.

"Some of my investigation implicates your father. If I know more about him, his work, and his associations it may help. Gilgamesh has enormous power and agenda to control immortality. If it exists and they accomplish their mission, it will effect everyone."

"I'm glad this happened. I've been lost, unsure of my next steps. My father said if you came to me it would be important. He said I can trust you."

"I never met your father. I don't know how he would know that."

"He knew you, Dr. Sumner."

Elliott ignored the comment. He forgets nothing. "I do believe we may be able to help each other. Maybe you say something that puts me on the right path."

"We have the bar until three. Probably a safe place for now. It's not bugged. One of the last things my father gave me was this lapel pin." He pressed one end. "Is it blinking green or red?"

"Green," Elliott said with a quick glance.

"It detects listening device, analog and digital. Green means no bugs."

Elliott nodded. "Good. I'm starved. Have you eaten?"

"No. Allow me." He waved at the bartender. "Jessie. Give us two shrimp corn dogs with the curry ketchup. And bring my friend a Moscow Mule. I'll take one more, too."

Elliott watched the mirror behind the liquor bottles. He could see out the front picture window. Across the street a car sat. It arrived when Marcus came in . . .

THIRTY-FIVE

"The impossible is often the untried."
Jim Goodwin

"He said he wasted his life chasing immortality." Marcus closed his eyes. "He was scared, didn't want to burn in hell for the things Gilgamesh has done. I hope he found peace"

"My time with him in New York was brief," Elliott said looking in the bar mirror. "I heard the pain and desperation, too."

"How Mr. Kuzma die?" Marcus asked with no knowledge of the horror in Central Park.

Elliott took off his raincoat and surveyed the lounge. They were the only two at the bar. Three elderly couples were at tables. The night staff was now a bartender and a waitress. The next two hours could be uneventful if the car parked across the street is nothing.

"Bernardo died at night. I know he went fast."

Marcus raised his glass. "Good. That helps. To Bernardo Kuzma . . . may he rest in peace."

Elliott sat. "Tell me more about your father, his work and history with Gilgamesh?"

Gathering his thoughts, Marcus stares into the bar mirror. Although he knew this day would come, his often rehersed words were now inadequate. He knew his father more than most sons, and he knew Elliott Sumner's veiled beginings more than Elliott Sumner. His words could do unrepairable damage or bring meaning in an ocean of pain.

"My father was a smart man," Marcus boasted. "His IQ was off the charts . . ." Marcus sipped his drink with the fond memory of a father and icon. "All his life he had one obsession—genetics. He believed DNA held the secrets of life for the universe."

"I agree," Elliott said in his crystal fllute glass. His eidetic memory exploded through a quivering cell membrane, and dove into an amber sea of cytoplasm shooting by mitochondria, glogi bodies, and endoplasmic reticula. In a tiny fraction of a second he entered an undulating nucleus and touched strands of DNA. Before the double helix moved to the molecular level, Elliott bit his lip and regained control.

"My father graduated University of Texas El Paso Medical School. He did his residency in the obstetrics specialty."

"OB/GYN, I never would have thought . . ."

"He opened a clinic in Pecos, Texas wiht an underlying objective to support his research. Obstetrics was ideal. He had unlimited access to cord blood, no questions asked."

"Of course—stem cells. I should have known," Elliott said rubbing his chin.

"Tell me, when was Dr. Medino in Pecos, Texas?"

"1967 to 1970. I am one of the very few who know why you ask that question."

"You are? Enlighten me," Elliott said.

"You were born in Pecos, Texas, Dr. Sumner. My father delivered you . . ."

Elliott froze. His mind shot ahead making all the relevant connections.

"One day a woman appeared in my father's clinic. She was alone, very pregnant, and very desperate. He didn't know she gave him a fake name until later. She told a reasonable story about an abusive relationship in El Paso and her need to leave. My father didn't push. He knew without his help she would die. She was days away from giving birth to triplets. As you know, that can be a dangerous and complex procedure."

"Of course," Elliott said, wanting for the woman's name to validate Marcus's story.

"She did not deliver for another week. My father earned her trust. Soon she wanted to talk—she needed to talk—to someone. She was scared and alone. That's when she told him her real name, and said she was hiding from very powerful people.

"My father gave her a place to stay, food, and medical care. He told her she could stay as long as she needed. He would help when she was ready and able to leave."

He could not wait any longer. "What was her name," Elliott boomed.

Starteled, Marcus answered. "Betty Duncan." He let it sink in. He was just getting started and felt he had to manage the flow or delicate information. He feared Elliott could be overwhelmed. Marcus knew the stories of his breakdown in Dallas and attempted suicide. He shared those same dark feelings after his family was killed in Memphis.

"Who was she running from?" Elliott asked. "Was it Albert Bell?"

Marcus spoke with a calm but firm tone. "She was running from Gilgamesh . . ."

It made no sense. Why would Gilgamesh be involved? Elliott

recently learned of Albert's association with Gilgamesh. He would not expect him to use them to locate the woman he had an affair with . . . the woman he made pregnant?

"Why was Gilgamesh looking for Betty Duncan?" Elliott's mind raced crashing into the myrid of illogical walls.

"Please, Dr. Sumner. I've gotta tell this my way. I have a lot to say, things you might not know—important things. I will tell you, but in my way. You gotta trust me."

Elliott doubted he could sit still as Marcus shot a spotlight into the black abyss of his life. But Marcus could hold pieces to the puzzle. "I will try."

"Good. Thank you." He sipped his drink as the bartender delivered their food. When they were alone again, he said, "My father asked Betty Duncan about the father of her babies. He explained the medical risks—blood type, compatibility issues, and consequences. That's when she told him about Albert Bell." Marcus paused to give Elliott time to process.

"I know Albert Bell and Betty Duncan are my biological parents. I wanted to see if you did."

"My father saw that as a gift from heaven. Even back then everyone knew about Albert Bell—the international cotton merchant and billionaire patriarch from Memphis."

"Of course," Elliott sighed. "Future financing for Dr. Medino's cherished research. I get it." Marcus let the comment go.

"Albert Bell had no idea Gilgamesh and Betty Duncan knew each other, or that they were looking for her. He had no idea she was in danger. Albert thought she left him because of his decision to return to his estarnged wife before learning of her pregnancy."

"The Gilgamesh connection still makes no sense," Elliott said slamming down his glass."

Marcus ignored the outburst. "From the begining Miss Duncan struggled with her decision to be a part of a *surrogate mother* program, one she later discoverd was an secret and illegal, genetic-engineering research program."

"Are you saying Gilgamesh contracted with Betty Duncan to carry Albert's child?"

"Yes, but for research. Betty Duncan thought she was a surrogate mother. Albert Bell did not know Gilgamesh and Betty Duncan were working together."

"It's hard to swallow that the topic never came up between Betty and Albert," Elliott scoffed

"It did not because it was part of the Gilgamesh contract with Betty Duncan. Albert Bell could *never* know the mother of his child. She was bound to secrecy."

"My God. This is unbelievable."

"It was over forty years ago, Dr. Sumner. Put it all into perspective. Betty Duncan was young. She had desperate financial needs. There were other reasons my father never shared except to say they were Gilgamesh manufactured problems. Gilgamesh targeted Betty Duncan from the start. They disrupted her life putting her in the position to accept their offer. Miss Duncan did not know Albert Bell, except for his public persona. She was led to believe she was having his child because he needed a son. The surrogate mother program Gilgamesh offered was confidential, lucrative, and would require only one year of her life."

Elliott downed his drink and pushed the glass to the edge of the bar. "When in fact it was a secret, genetic-engineering research project using Albert's sperm," he fumed.

"When Betty found out their real purpose, Gilgamesh scrambled to mend fences. They explained the research was a small part of the surrogate mother initiative. Albert did need a son—the next Bell patriarch. The research was secret only to circumvent obstructive federal regulations and keep things out of the newspaper."

Elliott stared at his empty glass at the edge of the bar—*we were assets and are now liabilities,* he thought. *What was the reseach? What changed the value equation?* He blinked back into reality. "She was on the run because Gilgamesh lied to her?"

"That was one reason. The other was Betty fell in love with Albert. Before I get much further, allow me a moment. I want you to know my father was not looking for easy money. Gilgamesh recruited him for a decade before he met Betty Duncan. He rejected all offers. He did not trust Gilgamesh. My father wanted to be left alone with his research. That meant he had to finance his work alone. When he learned Betty Duncan carried the first male born from the seed of the Bell patriarch, he knew he would deliver the next Bell patriarch, the sole heir to the Bell fortune."

"I understand his motivation," Elliott said.

"Scientists need benefactors."

"When they found Betty Duncan in Pecos, Gilgamesh offered my father unlimited funding with total freedom."

"With strings . . ."

"None at that time. But my father still rejected them. He knew whatever he discovered they would want to control. His vision was to share with the world."

"Why do you feel it necessary to tell me this, Marcus?"

"Because some things my father did are wrong and inexcusable. As I emerse myself in his research and world, I see how it impaired the judgement of a good man."

"I do understand. If his principals kept him from Gilgamesh, he still needed capitol. Moving from cord blood to fresh, human tissue and specialized testing equipment would be even more expensive an endeavor. It would'nt hurt to know a billionaire. Where did things go wrong?"

"He pretended to collaborate when they caught up to Miss Duncan. He had no other choice. He wanted to see things through and needed access to information he otherwise would not have. Betty Duncan had a legally binding contract with Gilgamesh. Failure to meet the terms, they would prosecute to the full extent of the law."

"She could have given damaging information on the illegal research," Elliott said.

"She had no proof. They would deny all such allegations. It was her word against billionaires and their high-priced lawyers."

"I understand. Continue. What else do you know?"

"Gilgamesh bought it. The believed my father was on board. They shared incredible information on the triplets, the research, and their goals to enhance lineage and extend lifespan. They told him about selection of the ideal vessel and postpartumn surveillance of progeny."

Elliott leaned closer and whispered,

"Ideal vessel and postpartum surveillance—really?"

"I don't know much about either. I know Gilgamesh employed an elaborate screening process to select Betty Duncan as the best vessel to share genetic material and carry progeny from the seed of Albert Bell. Following birth, you and Jack were randomly dispersed. Betty kept Adam. All of you were covertly monitored your whole life."

"Did your father say why Jack and I were dispersed and Adam stayed with our mother?"

"Gilgamesh conducted many prenatal tests. One revealed Adam possessed a genetic marker for psychopathy trait. They believed a genetically engineered psychopath could be extremely dangerous. Their protocol called for postpartum euthanasia."

"My God. Turns out they were right. But postpartum termination is a homicide?"

"Betty Duncan convinced them to give Adam a chance. She pledged her life to ensure Adam's environmental stimulation suppressed the undesirable genetic expression. She argued his genetic assets outweighed and would prevail. They agreed with stipulations. If Adam exhibited the negative tendencies, he would be terminated."

"That's why they came for him in Carollton, Texas," Elliott mumbled waving at the bartender for two more drinks.

"I don't know much about Texas, but I do know the existence of the *euthanasia protocol* only confirmed my father's feelings about Gilgamesh."

"They were playing God."

"He let the Pecos collaboration contract expire and backed away. They tried to get him to stay, but he said he had health and family issues. It was an amicable separation."

"Why did they want him dead?" Elliott asked.

"There were many reasons. They knew he had

Betty Duncan's cord blood. But more important, they knew he had stem cells from each of the triplets. Gilgamesh monitored my father for thirteen years. They followed his progress. I think they always intended to steal his research."

"Why were the triplet's stem cells important to Gilgamesh?" Elliott asked

Marcus leaned back on his stool for the first time. He had been working up to the moment from the start hoping Elliott would give him some sign he knew. Only one couple sat at the tables. The car was still sitting across the street—there were two shadows inside.

"You really don't know do you?"

Elliott leaned back with an eye in the bar mirror. "Enlighten me."

"I'm sorry. Why would you know? My father knew because of his research. He only told me. Gilgamesh would never divulge . . ."

"Knew what, Marcus?" Elliott turned from the mirror and leaned closer.

Marcus whispered, "You possess a rare genetic anomaly. Your cellular replications are infinite."

"That is nonsense," Elliott scoffed as he reached for his drink.

"Dr. Sumner . . . it is the truth. You and your brothers are immortal. Every cell in your body is replaced with a new one indefinately."

"Bernardo tried to tell me," Elliott said under his breath staring in the mirror.

"Mr. Kuzma is not a geneticist, but he knew. All gilgamesh board members know. You are immortal, not superhuman. You can die from external factors—trauma, poison, and infection. You are immune to disease. Given the time, all injuries heal regardless of the extent of damage. You can bleed to death because you cannot reproduce blood fast enough. You can drown or suffocate. You may not want to deny this reality, but I know you know."

"Did your father tell you whether this cellular replication phenomena was a genetic engineering accomplishment or surprise?"

"He said it had nothing to do with genetic engineering."

"So it just presented . . . ?"

"It's a family trait, Dr. Sumner."

"The Bell family?"

"It is a genetic anomoly passed on to only the first male born of each generation."

"So Gilgamesh replicated the trait in three."

"Yes," Marcus said. "They don't know how it happened. After the Bell triplets, it's never been repeated to my knowledge."

"Albert Bell, his father and grandfather, were the first male born of each generation. Did Dr. Medino know—do they possess the genetic anomaly?"

"Albert Bell's father possessed it—he died in a plane crash. Alberto Bella also possessed it—he died from a respiratory infection. Jack Bellow did, and he died from gunshot injuries and drowning. And, of course, Adam Duncan committed suicide—he bled to death on the roof at the Bell mansion. That leaves only two with this rare genetic anomaly—Albert Bell and you."

"It makes sense. Gilgamesh needed to control or stop your father. Dr. Medino had the Bell family genome in his lab. He was competing with Gilgamesh, a race to reproduce immortality," Elliott said.

"Both used the Bell family genome in their research," Marcus said.

"They searched for the DNA segment responsible, the immortality gene. After their one success—the Bell triplets—they kept us around for

study controls. Now I see why we were viewed by Gilgamesh as *assets*." Elliott waved for another drink and turned to Marcus. "But I don't recall ever being followed or giving up a blood or tissue sample growing up."

"You were watched with the top surveillance technology know to man—24/7."

"I suppose that would be possible."

"Everytime you went to a doctor or dentist you were sampled, Dr. Sumner. You were just not looking for it."

"Of course—unsuspecting guinea pigs," Elliott muttered.

"Gilgamesh was desperate. For decades they ran into dead ends. They were paranoid. They were sure my father was ahead of them, would cross the finish line before them. Gilgamesh could not allow it."

"Maybe they got there," Elliott said. "Maybe that's why my brothers and I are liabilities. They no longer need their guinea pigs."

"Or because they fear you like they feared Adam," Marcus said.

"I'm not a threat like Adam," Elliott said.

"I'm surprised you don't know more about your uniqueness."

"I spent a lifetime denying it. We all have our burdens, Marcus. For me, being different was terrifying." He looked in his glass. "Abandonment by my biological parents crippled me in ways I could not set aside." He turned to Marcus. "But I can assure you, I'm not like Adam."

"In 1982 Dr. Medino reunited with my mother and Adam . . . Carollton, Texas. Why?"

"Gilgamesh was on their way to kill them. Adam did something terrible at school. He attacked a teacher. Almost killed him. It was a very public event. Adam broke the rules. Gilgamesh was going to terminate both of them."

"Munson . . ." Elliott whispered.

"Adam went on a rampage. He killed his step-father, a police officer, and his common-law wife. My father arrived after the horrific event. Betty was unconscious—didn't see anything. I think her husband beat her. My father helped Adam bury the dead. The three left. He put Miss Duncan on a plane to Mexico and returned to Memphis with Adam."

"Adam lived under the Brent mansion," Elliott said.

"Mr. Brent was an investor in my father's research—a wealthy hermit."

"Did your father know Adam was a psychopath?"

"Yes. But he had Adam's complete trust. He tried to rehabilitate him, but found it to be an impossible task. Adam was too powerful in so many ways—physical and mental.

Gilgamesh kept sending people to kill my father. Adam protected him. Gilgamesh was determined. They lost a lot of people."

"And your father benefited. Access to fresh human tissue."

"I don't excuse it. He had his research and no control over Adam. My father warned Gilgamesh, but they never let up. He rationalized self-defense and use of the human tissue for the greater good. They were at war with an evil force, Dr. Sumner."

"I guess no one benefitted from this nightmare," Elliott said.

"My father got there, Dr. Sumner."

"Got where?"

"The biogenic secret to immortality?"

"You can't be serious."

"Cells know how to replicate, Dr. Sumner. They decide to stop. We don't know what turns off the process. Immortality is no more astounding than life itself . . ."

"That's a profound statement, Marcus. My head has been burried in medical pathology and forensic books for so long I forget to be amazed."

"He developed the TGO-STASIS program, an assessment tool. 'T' for telomere maintainance, 'G' for glycation and helix supercoiling and 'O' for oxidative stress reduction. His theory was simple. DNA is immortal. How can he optimize the cellular environment around it? DNA damage leads to cell death. How can he protect DNA."

"Sound logical."

"Based on the TGO-STASIS program, he ran thousands of formulations to stimulate the ideal cellular environment and put the replication process on auto-pilot. Without all the science, after many formulations and failures one worked. He said it was luck to find it. That's when he got with your brother Jack and started the LIFE2 company."

"I assume you don't have the final TGO-STASIS formula."

"My father had two electronic storage files, one at the farm, and one with Jack Bellow. The one at the farm is gone. There is evidence it was destroyed. A security virus is released."

Elliott finished his drink. "I need to get you out of Nashville. Don't look now, but a car has been parked across the street since your arrived. I don't know if they're here for you or me. But their patiently waiting for us to leave the Patterson House."

Marcus held up his Moscow Mule to toast and glanced in the

mirror. "I've seen that car before. It was outside the lab today, windows overly tinted, not cool around here."

"Take off your coat. Hang it on the chair and go to the bathroom." Elliott slid two hundred dollar bills under his plate. "Go out the back door and two blocks east. Stay in the shadows until you see a black Lexus."

"Got it."

"One last question. Is Betty Duncan alive?"

"Yes. South America."

"Go."

THIRTY-SIX

"I do not seek. I find."
Pablos Picasso

Carol turned onto Shady Grove Terrace and headed south. Max was in a rental house, still looking for a permanent place in Memphis. He said she couldn't miss it—on the right just before a bend. The graystone two-story with a five-car garage sat under a dozen giant oaks a few acres off the road. He kept the iron gate open. If she had missed Tony's unmarked cruiser tucked under the ivy-infested canopy, she would have missed the meeting.

Amazed, she crawled up the long driveway, parked behind Tony, grabbed her box of files from the backseat, and pushed the door closed with her foot. When she turned, Max was standing in his robe and slippers in the deep gravel. "Well good, you found me. It wasen't so bad."

"Really, Max." She shoved the box into his stomach. "You

could tell me your little rental is a palatial estate. I didn't know there was this kind of money in the PI business. I see Spyglass has been very good to you."

They started to the door. Max looked back at Shady Grove Terrace. A car slowed by the gate and then accellerated up the road.

"Please, press the red button inside, to your left," he said like asking a child to pet the friendly dog. Carol followed his eyes to the closing iron gate close. "It wouldn't stop anyone, but it makes trespassing more of a pain in the ass." Max turned back to Carol with a boyish grin on a weathered face. "So, you like my rental?"

She rolled her eyes. "I'm impressed. It's more than I expected."

"Young lady, you've got to remember I'm older than God. Anybody who lives long enough can accumulate things."

"Yeah, like money," she teased. "I think your stint in the CIA was good to you. Maybe a little profit center." She poked her finger in his belly next to the box he struggled to balance.

"You got me. I give up. Stealing from the government." They laughed into the den.

"And who do we have here?" she said to Tony's head deep in a pile and surrounded by stacks of papers and a flickering computer screen. He looked at them and turned to the screen.

"I've been all over this shit. I think Elliott's right, goddamn it."

"Don't you know Elliott's always right? What are you talking about this time?"

"Max and I have been looking at the history, every Butcher victim 1983 to 2009 . . . all one-hundred-sixty-seven of them.:

"The ones we know about," Max added from the doorway.

"Why are you doing that?" Carol asked.

"So far we've linked seventy-two," Tony said with his nose inches from the screen.

"I'll ask again, why?"

"So far, seventy-two Butcher victims went to Atlanta, Georgia for nine days at some time in their recent life. Not eight. Not ten. Nine days. They flew on the same airline from all over the country. Some went there different years, but all went to Atlanta on one of four days in their given year . . . the first day of each quarter—January first, April first, July first, and October first. And they all departed on the ninth day." Tony leaned back in his chair rubbing his head.

"I don't get it," Carol froze at the desk.

"They each stayed the first night at the Airport Holiday Inn, disappeared the next seven days, checked back into the Airport Holiday Inn on day eight, and departed the morning of day nine," Max injected.

"So did thousands—no—tens of thousands of other salespeople in Atlanta on business. They went for a week, fellows. They stayed at the Airport Holiday Inn so they wouldn't miss their morning flight. It happens all the time." Carol sat on the chair across from Tony's glare. She leaned in and said, "So what, Mr. Homicide Detective."

"Miss Mason, do you really think we are dumb idiots?"

"Now Tony, let's be professionals. Carol knows we are not dumb." Max patted him on his rigid shoulder and moved a stack of files off his chair.

"Maybe Tony's assessment of opinion is more accurate than the BS he's selling. Or is there more, detective?"

"I don't think all the salespeople visiting Atlanta-damn-Georgia were picked up by the Mercer Limo Service and taken to a place in the country, a damn dairy farm. What do you think about that, Miss *Memphis Tribune* Investigative Reporter Pulitzer snob?"

"I don't think I like your choice of words, a dairy farm?" Carol stopped poking in her box.

Max puffed on a new cigarette and jumped in before Tony could give another smart answer. "The dairy farm is owned by Mr. Rudolph Kohl. He's a billionaire out of Germany. Now he claims Amsterdam as primary residence. Spends a great deal of time in Memphis, LIFE2 investor nosing around. Kohl recently purchased a place near the Botanic Gardens, Audubon Park. We've got people watching him now."

"There's a lot of comings and goings," Tony said under his breath with his eyes on the screen. "Rich types, and some of your muscle men type . . . bodyguards with weapons. All is perfectly legal, but we're talking big time surveillance and protection assets 24/7. I think Mr. Kohl is afraid of something."

"And hiding something," Max said.

"What do we know about the *dairy farm* outside Atlanta?" Carol asked.

"I have some of my CIA buddies aiming a few excess satellite resources, off the clock if you know what I mean. Early assessment, we believe we have a training facility. Some things we can see, but most happens inside the unusually large barns and out-buildings. We did a high altitude drone fly-over and heat sensor scan. There was a lot of activity inside the barns—group meetings, pairs and singles moving about . . . obstacle courses, shooting ranges, and such."

Tony passed a paper to Carol. "In December Elliott told me the Butcher was not who we all thought he was."

"What's that mean?" Carol asked.

"The Butcher's killing Gilgamesh soldiers." He took one of Max's cigarettes. "Elliott's convinced his brother's not such a bad boy after all. He's killing bad boys."

"He's been consistent on that point—a stealth army. I just got back from running around Europe with Elliott hiding from them," Carol said.

"I thought he was nuts in December. Now, I'm changing my

mind. Adam's a bad guy, but it appears most of his kills are graduates of the Kohl's dairy farm outside Atlanta."

"What's this world coming to?" Max said with a smirk.

"We were in Spain, France and England—thanks to Max getting us out of some tight spots. I got back last week. There is no question Gilgamesh is hunting Elliott."

"But why?" Tony asked lighting his cigarette.

"He has a few theories, but none he wants to share yet. Still gathering information like a good forensic investigator."

"And where is the genius sleuth today?" Tony asked.

"Nashville. Something about Dr. Medino."

"Without knowing more about Gilgamesh, it's difficult to move forward," Tony said.

Max stared at the ceiling as he spoke. "Let's consider what we have new. We have a well-resourced global entity—Gilgamesh. They are dedicated to put in place an army of stealth killers. They are now hunting Elliott Sumner. They have some interest in Dr. Enrique Medino who had an interest in genetics and immortality. Adam Duncan has been killing their soldiers for decades apparently. And we recently learned Dr. Medino brought Adam Duncan to Memphis in 1969.

"I think we can agree Gilgamesh is on a mission to control immortality—if that's even a possibility. It follows the Bell triplets put their mission into jeopardy," Carol said.

Tony blew smoke. "They must be close to reaching their goal. Two down one to go."

"Eliminating their remaining threats . . ."

"Makes a hell of a lot of sense," Tony said.

Max got up and looked out the window. The car he saw earlier passed the gate again. "I wonder what it is about Elliott that has Gilgamesh so desperate?"

"In the beginning they were on the offense," Carol said.

"Now they're on defense. Their initial reason to eliminate Elliott could have changed."

"They think Elliott is hunting them," Tony said. "I'll be goddamned. The hunters are now the hunted. This is taking an interesting turn."

Max stepped into the next room to dress. Carol yelled,

"You both know about the unknown scion he spoke to in New York City? This guy lured Elliott to Barcelona promising information on Gilgamesh. Elliott was led to a mansion—Aragon—a a certain time. When Elliott arrived, he found the owner dead, Paciono Hernando."

"Like Mr. Kuzma, the Spaniard was beheaded," Max yelled from the bedroom.

"They have Elliott on video at two crime scenes. After Barcelona he was lured to Nevers, France," Carol said. "When he got to the next location, there was another beheaded, Eligio Tasso Peters."

"Who are these people?" Tony asked as Max entered the room fixing the knot on his tie."

"You didn't need to put on a suit and tie, Max. This is a casual meeting," Carol said.

"It's just what old people do young lady. I don't own casual clothes, just suits and pajamas and a robe. Now get back to the people losing heads."

Carol passed a copy of the vellum to Tony and Max. "This will answer your question. This is a recreation of a table on a piece of vellum given to Elliott by Adam before he died, right Tony?" *We don't need to burden Max with too much information now.*

"Ah, yes." *Now I know something the old CIA fart dosen't.*

"This table has the Gilgamesh watermark. It is an official document. Max, I tried to get this to you from France, but ran into complications."

"Best you brought it yourself, my dear."

"It was stolen from Elliott's room in New York the night Kuzma was killed. Elliott recreated it from memory. He wants us to decipher as much as we can and let him know as soon as we can.

"We now know Gilgamesh is run by a twelve-member board. Look at the center column: 'BKUZ' is Bernardo Kuzma, 'PHER' is Paciono Hernando, 'ETASP' is Eligio Tasso Peters, 'JWIL" is James Wilkens . . ."

"Ningpo Wu, Howard Carson, Meir Stein. I'll be goddamned. One dead and two missing in Memphis," Tony sighed. "Someone's killing their board."

Carol looked up. "Rudolph Kohl, your Atlanta farm Tony. He's on the board, too."

"And Albert Bell. My god," Max mumbled. "That is disturbing."

"Who is this scion?" Tony asked. "Looks like he's killing these guys."

"We don't know. But the more we get from this table, the better chance Elliott has to get ahead of the scion and Gilgamesh. We need to stop both."

"The TEA column is curious," Max muttered. "And those letters in column two . . ."

"Gilgamesh is working up to something," Carol said. "They're moving fast trying to find and stop Elliott. They're making mistakes."

"Appears the scion is having success. My three and your four means seven of the twelve board members are dead or missing."

"A quorum," Carol said under her breath.

"We will increase surveillance at Kohl's residence," Max said. "And, I'm afraid we will need to add surveillance at the Bell estate. The time has arrived for a sit down with Albert. If this 569 number is a date, it could only mean 1956. Albert has been a

Gilgamesh board member for a very long time. I don't understand why he never shared that information with me."

"Are you okay with this, Max?" Carol asked.

Tony said, "Can you go wherever this takes us, Max?"

"I can assure you both we will find Albert to be in complete opposition to any unsavory and illegal actions of this group . . . or he will be in the dark like the rest of us. I have known this man for thirty years. Albert Bell is the most honorable man I have ever had the pleasure to call a friend. To answer your question, Anthony. Yes. I can function without prejudice. I am CIA."

"Elliott wants desperately to believe those words, Max. But he must be cautious until he's sure. There is too much at stake," Carol said. Tony went out front to take a phone call.

"I understand." Max leaned closer. "There are other things you know when you get to be my age, young lady. You learn to listen to the voice you've been too busy to hear most your life." He got up and left the room. He yelled back, "And you need to visit the privy more frequently."

Carol took the opportunity to walk outside to talk to Tony alone. He got off the phone and joined her in the driveway. "How's the Peabody homicide going for you, off the record."

"Not good. Two are still missing. No leads. No evidence. This scion is well trained."

"Did you talk to Albert?"

"That morning. He was straight up with me. Always has been." Tony lit another cigarette and took a long drag. "Said the three were at his home earlier that evening, a business meeting. Said he left them in his study. Something about an unresolvable disagreement. He did not share it was the Gilgamesh board."

"Did he say what the disagreement was about?"

"No, and I didn't push. He told me more than he needed, legally speaking. I did get the sense it was of great concern to him. He was distracted. Never saw him like that."

"I don't understand."

"He said, in all his years he never walked out of anything. He took great pride in his ability to resolve disputes among honorable men."

"Maybe he's not dealing with honorable men," Carol said. "Was Rudolph Kohl at the meeting?"

"Yes. Albert gave me a list of attendees, including those on the phone. I was looking at the initials on the vellum. I'm sure it was a Gilgamesh board meeting. I'll give you the list when we go back inside."

"Good. I'll get them to Elliott." She looked over her shoulder to make sure Max was not nearby. "You think Adam's involved now? Is he killing these people?"

Tony stepped out his cigarette and squinted into the morning sun. "

Considering what the Gilgamesh clan is up to now, I'll bet we'll see Adam . . . and the Bluff City Butcher will be more involved than his tamer half."

"That would not be a good thing. We know what the Butcher is capable of."

Tony's eyes sharpened as he leaned into Carol's face. "He is much stronger now. I don't think he can be stopped by anyone . . ."

THIRTY-SEVEN

"The wisest men follow their own direction."
Euripides

Rudolph Kohl sat in the backseat of the powder blue Bentley convertible. He had on his Teddy Roosevelt pince-nez glasses. Although balding, he parted his remaining hair close to the middle. Rudy was stuck in a time long ago. He never liked flying and never got used to digital watches, computers or liberals, and when he could, he preferred relieving himself the old fashioned way, on a tree. Pulling up to the Bell mansion reminded him of his Isabel—she loved the place.

They sat in the west garden. It was morning, not yet hot and humid. The shade draped over the terrace. Where the sun found a way through the foliage, morning dew disappeared. William made sure hot coffee, cold juice, blueberry muffins and real butter—Rudy's favorite—awaited him. It wouldn't be long now.

"Are you still upset with me?" Rudy asked as he buttered a muffin.

"Upset? Are you serious?" Albert flipped his newspaper and snapped it into position. "What you're talking about doing is wrong and cannot happen."

"When your father died in that God awful plane crash, I had to make decisions for the good of the family, part of which included Gilgamesh. It already existed forty years, making progress, breaking new ground. Your role as the next Bell patriarch would be pivotal."

"I'm questioning my participation in Gilgamesh. I trusted you, took things for granted. The other night I witnessed what I always suspected but did not want to believe."

"We can talk about it now, Albert."

"Where do I begin?" Albert put down his paper. "I've seen the documents from the catacombs . . . the Gilgamesh meeting minutes. I know how to read coded narratives."

"What have you learned that troubles you, beyond the board's concerns with Elliott? We can discuss and resolve all of it."

"Let's begin with you taking control of my life in ways I will never get back."

"Like how, Albert?"

"Even now you avoid it. There are so many lies you're afraid to start the discussion. Okay, I'll start. All my adult life I was led to believe my wife stopped loving me the day my father died in that airplane crash. You led me to believe she could not live her life with the next Bell patriarch. It was a lie. She never said that, did she? You moved her out of the way so you could use me in your experiment."

"It was not an experiment. It was ground-breaking research possessed only by Gilgamesh. It was time. We needed to give you a family with extraordinary gifts, something special, something the world had never known. You are special Albert. You know that."

"You arranged for me to meet Betty Duncan in El Paso. She was a Gilgamesh approved vessel recruited to carry my child. Your scientists manipulated my genes without my knowledge. They impregnated Betty with three, genetically engineered embryos to ensure one survived. But you got three. And you kept my sons from me forty years. And you let me believe Betty Duncan did not want to be with me."

Albert looked into Rudy's eyes searching for meaning. *How could you do this to me?* He had to reconcile a lifetime, compare his interpretations of major events to new facts revealed on dusty documents from the catacombs. *Have I been diminished? Or am I like everyone else, a collection of truths, lies, and awakenings that define me in life?*

"Betty Duncan did want you. She could not resist you. She loved you, Albert. That was a very big part of the *vessel profiling program*. She had all the genetic traits we were looking for, and she was drawn to you like you to her. She wanted to be with you forever but . . ."

"Being together did not conform to Gilgamesh protocol?"

"Unfortunately, it is true. You were the first. We could not risk emotional ties. We were in uncharted waters. Our research . . ."

"That is reprehensible," Albert muttered.

"Hindsight is always different. At the time it was all about the boys." He popped another muffin into his mouth as William refreshed the coffee and left. "Albert, I'm sorry for the lies surrounding your transition to patriarch. You were not ready for the whole story."

"You kept my sons from me. It is forty years I will never get back."

"Honestly, I am surprised you didn't see the similarities.

Elliott, Jack, and Adam were so much alike physically—tall, athletic, penetrating eyes, chiseled jaws, and the way they carried themselves. Each had an incredible presence like you Albert. It's not something you learn. It's something you have . . .

"Albert, they were you in so many ways. You knew Jack and Elliott for more than a year. You never asked. I thought you did not want to see, so I left it alone. What purpose could it serve to tell you now?"

"After I knew they were mine, I could see." Albert pinched the bridge of his nose and squinted. "Maybe I was in denial. Like I am about Gilgamesh."

"As we expected, the boys had unmeasurable IQs, eidetic memories, and unparalleled analytical skills. Elliott possesses the most advanced sensory systems of any man. He may have many more gifts not yet discovered. Jack is our perfect visionary—he could see the future and take the leap. He was the consummate entrepreneur and leader. Adam could have been a world-class athlete. His incredible physical attributes were closer to those of a wild animal than man. But, as you know, Adam had severe mental problems."

"I guess Gilgamesh didn't have all the bugs worked out," Albert said over his coffee cup and staring at the man he now dispised.

"We found the recessive, psychopathic gene sequence late. It was missed in Betty's profile. Maybe you know we were going to euthanize and Betty convinced us she could help. You know the rest of the story. Adam eventually killed. We gave a lion a genius brain."

"How can you sit there and talk about a man like an animal? Adam was a person with a mental problem. He deserved a chance at life. You are not God."

"Let's get to the crux of the matter. You do not share the board's concerns about Elliott. We believe he is hunting us,

Albert. We voted. We must defend ourselves. Five board members are dead. Two are missing. Elliott has cause. And he has been implicated. My God, he has been at each crime scene with blood on his hands. I wish there was another way."

"Elliott is not hunting Gilgamesh board members. He is being set up. I cannot be a part of an organization that believes they have the right to kill anybody, much less my son."

"That's why we are meeting this morning. I want to stop all of this. I want to meet with Elliott and talk to him—avoid making a mistake. We have always been reasonable, fair minded people, Albert. If what you say is true, I will promise I will reject the board initiative. We will stop all this talk. Gilgamesh is not about killing. We are about extending and improving the quality of life. And we are closer than ever to achieving our century old mission."

"You think you now possess a genetic secret to immortality?" Albert asked.

"Our new director of R&D believes we are weeks away. We've been able to merge our research with Dr. Medino's."

"How did Gilgamesh obtain his research?" Albert leaned closer to emphasize his focus. "Did Gilgamesh have anything to do with Dr. Medino's death? Don't lie to me."

"Absolutely not. After his death we purchased some digital files containing his unproven biogenic formula, bill of materials, and synthesis protocol. Our people authenticated the data. It cost a great deal of money, Albert. Much later we discovered it had been stolen."

"Stolen? I'm not surprised. Tell the truth. You always disliked Dr. Medino. I recall you discrediting the man and his research at the board meetings I attended."

"Medino stole DNA from the Bell family—the triplets. He's a theif, Albert. He spent his life trying to duplicate something that did not belong to him. That was the reason for the mistrust and conflicts over the years—the scoundrel."

"And his formula, you think you can reproduce it, and it works?"

"We believe we can reproduce it. We do not know if it will work. We're running into transcription problems. Medino had cell replication failures at the six-month mark. We believe he fixed it, but the fix never made it into the data we purchased. Our people are working on it. There could be a light at the end of the tunnel. Our mission could be complete."

William appeared on the terrace. "Excuse me, sir."

"Yes, William."

"Your nine o'clock is here, sir."

"Good. Give me a few minutes and then bring him out."

Rudy got to his feet. "I'll be in the greenhouse playing with the orchids."

"That would be good. I'll send William for you when I want you back, not before."

"Yes, of course. I'm looking forward to meeting Elliott."

"I will not be satisfied until Elliott is safe and I know the history and workings of Gilgamesh are legitimate. I've been kept in the dark too long."

"I understand." Rudy left the terrace and disappeared into the greenhouse. William brought Officer Starnes outside.

They embraced. "Hello, my friend," Albert said holding Willie's arms at his bulky shoulders. *You're still chiseled granite, the strongest person I've ever known—until Adam.*

"Mornin' Mr. Bell."

"You look wonderful, Willie. You look as young and strong as the day Rudy introduced us, what, twenty-five years ago?"

"I think you're right with twenty-five, Mr. Albert."

"So nice to see you. Please sit. I understand you have something for me."

Willie pulled a thin leather box from his pocket and set it on the table.

Albert turned the box so he could read the embossed word on center of the leather cover. He smiled, placed his napkin over it, and took a sip of coffee "Do you know what this is, Willie?"

"No sir. But Mr. Jack said give it to you when things settle down some. He said if the bad people got you too, I was to give it to Dr. Sumner." Willie looked down and rubbed an eye. "And Mr. Jack said if they got the doctor, I was to break it into a hundred pieces and throw them pieces into the muddy Mississippi River."

"You're a good man, Willie. I'm glad Jack had you as a friend." Albert said. "When did he give it to you?"

"That day at the Exchange Building. I member October 15, the day the people who put money in Mr. Jack's company stole it from him and pushed him out."

"LIFE2 was taken from Jack and Enrique Medino that day, the founders were overthrown."

"Yes sir. Mr. Jack had to get one last thing in his office that night. Police came lookin' for him. All hell broke loose. Next thing I know, Mr. Jack says meet in the basement. I did."

"That's where he gave this to you?" Albert asked.

"Yes, Mr. Albert. Then he hugged me hard and went down the sewer pipe. I put the lid back over the hole. I think he knew then. We never gonna see each other again, Mr. Albert."

"I wish I had known Jack was my son." Albert sunk in his chair.

"I didn't knew neither."

"When we look back over our lives and get to see our story, I guess it's normal to wonder why we failed to get around to a lot of the important things."

"Yes sir. Seems like life happens and sometimes we just don't keep up."

"You took care of him without him ever knowing, Willie. At the end, he was blindsided by people he thought he could trust. He came to you. Hold onto that my friend."

"Yes. I guess he did that didn't he, Mr. Albert." Willie smiled with wet eyes.

"Can I do anything for you, Willie?"

"No sir. I'm Good, Mr. Albert." He got up from the table. Albert stood. They embraced. Willie left. Albert could hear him whistling his way through the mansion. He sat down and pulled the napkin off the thin, leather box and ran his finger over the words on the cover—*Gilgamesh Never.*

This must be one of the hard drives Rudy mentioned, the one they couldn't find. The one with Medino's corrected forumlation. Albert looked up at the clouds. *You have given me a task you believe I can complete. I won't let you down son. It is the only thing I have to give you.*

Albert saw William standing in the shade next to the patio door. "Is Elliott here?" Albert asked.

William approached and whispered, "Yes sir. But first, Max phoned."

"What did he have to say?"

"Sir, Miss Betty Duncan has been contacted. Max said to tell you she never married. The Texas records are fraudulent. She left Texas. She wanted to disappear."

"I see," Albert said dropping his head.

"Sir. Miss Duncan wants to see you."

Albert sat up. "She does? Where is she? Do we know anything?"

"She is in Peru, Sir. She is afraid but does not want life to end this way. Her words, sir."

"We will make travel plans later."

"Very good, sir. And, Dr. Sumner has arrived. He is in the study."

"William, bring Elliott to the terrace. I want him to meet Rudolph Kohl in the light of day." He reached for the leather box. "And put this in a safe place." Albert disappeared into the mansion.

Albert watched Elliott walking inside the mansion, passing the line of long windows on his way to the terrace. *You are a handsome man, and a good man. You will be a much better patriarch than I* . . .

Rudy surprised Albert pulling out his chair unannounced.

I did not send for you. You have never respected me. I have been blind for so long, Albert thought.

"So. Here comes the famous Dr. Elliott Sumner," Rudy spouted in a haughty tone.

Albert got to his feet and watched Rudy track Elliott from window to window. *You watch my son like a wild game hunter waiting for your prey. You can't even hide it* . . .

"This will be a day to remember, Albert."

Elliott stepped onto the terrace.

"Yes, I am quite certain it will be . . ."

THIRTY-EIGHT

"But logic never could convince the heart."
Colin Raye

Wearing a blue sport coat, tan khakis, and white cotton shirt with opened collar, Elliott approached the two men with an air of comfortable professionalism. He stopped to greet William at the door leaving him with a smile. Walking taller than his six-four stature, Elliott took in his surroundings as he approached the table. The sprawling grounds of the Bell estate were perfect for a sniper. He was getting used to being hunted. Before he would sit down, he would know all the risks, rank them, and position himself for undetectable vigilance.

He met Albert's hand first. "Hello. It's good to see you again."

"Elliott, I am so pleased this worked out, your schedule and so forth. Allow me to introduce you to . . ."

" . . . Rudy Kohl. Good to meet you." When they shook hands, Elliott's swallowed Rudy's small, clammy paw. Elliott watched the discomfort creep into the foggy eyes of the old man, the overwhelming disparity unacceptable. Rudy pulled back.

"I've heard great things about the acclaimed Dr. Elliott Sumner, the famous forensic pathologist who single-handedly rounded up fifty serial killers over the last decade," Rudy said with a scoffing tone.

"I wouldn't pay too much attention to newspaper headlines, Mr. Kohl. No offense meant to the *Tribune, Albert*."

"He smiled. None taken, young man. You're comment is quite accurate."

"I'm just one of thousands of pathologists in the world looking at dead people."

"Please, let's sit," Albert suggested. Elliott took the chair with his back to the mansion. Servants appeared and cups were filled followed with an awkward silence for Rudy.

"What brings you to Memphis, Mr. Kohl?" Elliott asked as he stirred his coffee.

"Business. And you? I would think traveling around the world looking for dead people, solving mysteries, and catching bad guys would give you little time in Memphis."

Your first slip. Looking "for" dead people is not the same as looking "at" dead people. This will be another learning experience. "At the moment my professional duties are in far more demand than I ever imagined or prefered. I'm sure things will slow down soon."

"How can you be so sure?" Rudy said.

"Experience." Elliott sipped his coffee with eyes locked on old man.

"I for one look forward to that," Albert said. "I would like to spending more time with you."

"Yes, Albert. That would be nice. The world needs to slow down."

"You won't need to do forensic investigation work anymore.

As the next Bell patriarch, you won't have time." With a twisted smile Rudy dropped a fistful of sugar cubes into his coffee.

"That's not an accurate statement," Albert said with authority.

"It is true," Rudy shot back.

"No, actually, it is your incorrect assumption. Elliott will continue to make decisions about his life as always. We have ample time to talk about family matters. And those discussions will be between Elliott and me," Albert said firmly.

Rudy didn't look up from buttering his muffin and chewing the one in his mouth.

He swallowed and spoke with most of the muffin in his teeth. "A Bell patriarch has enormous responsibilities. It is a full-time job running a diversified, multi-national enterprise. Managing billions takes training and active participation."

He turned to Elliott. "I don't know much, but have you spoken with Alberto Bella yet?" He stirred his coffee with a butter knife and squinted one eye at Elliott, watching for the slightest reaction. He would get none.

"Certainly, Albert's grandfather. That would be you." In the silence that followed, Elliott lifted his cup and took a swallow. Albert winked so only he could see.

"Ha! Very funny. And that would be me, you say? Interesting, Dr. Sumner. Now tell me how you would even begin to come to such a conclusion? The man died in 1925. I was just testing your knowledge."

"No you weren't. And to answer your question, it is simple logic."

"Simple logic, you say? What does that mean?" Rudy asked still trying to hold onto control of the moment slipping from his grasp. His attempt to shock and confuse, to control the morning, were foiled. Now he was forced to stay the course, to play out his hand.

"Do you really want to know?"

"Yes. I would really like to know."

Elliott leaned into Rudy's space. "The science of reasoning is about the principles governing inferences. Deductive reasoning reaches a conclusion that follows a set of premises. The conclusion must be true if the premises are true."

"Must be your forensic training. What premises do you believe true in this instance?"

Elliott leaned closer. "Actually, I learned about deductive reasoning in the fifth grade. You behave like a patriarch in this house. Albert, the gentleman he is, allows it."

"That's all you have?" chided Rudy grabbing another muffin.

Elliott stayed in Rudy's face. "You wear pense-nez glasses. You dress and comb your hair like Woodrow Wilson. You could admire the man, but your attention to detail comes from a more personal experience, one only possible from knowing the man well. And then there is your approach to me: aggression, dominance, disdain. Your sense of superiority is deeply rooted in your lifelong struggles with incompetence, the less than perfect men to fill your shoes, to follow your plan. Your world was surely disrupted—chaos—when your son, Albert's father, left you. When his plane went down in the Gulf of Mexico. Albert was twenty-four, too young, not ready to be the next Bell patriarch. It wasn't supposed to be that way. You faked your death twenty-five years earlier. You became Rudolph Kohl, no family responsibilities. But no, it all fell to you as usual. You had to make Albert ready, and you did. And now there's me, the unknown, the unpredictable scion, the brother of the Bluff City Butcher, the man who could ruin everything you've built over a century . . .

"And you eat like a man with no concern for health when you should know better. You are confident you will live even though everyone around you subconsciously thinks of their own mortality several times a day. By my calculations, you will be 164 in September because Bell patriarchs are immortal. Am I close . . . Alberto Bella?"

Albert sipped his coffee to hide his smile, impressed with the genius of his son, and his knowledge of the history of the family. Elliott poured a fresh cup. Alberto sat with his mouth open long enough to reveal his shock and confusion. He had never been beaten so soundly, and so quickly. He set down his fourth muffin and pushed his plate away. "It appears you are as bright as they say, Elliott Sumner."

"He got it all right, Alberto. A little knowledge and maybe three minutes of observation," Albert gloated. "I shall hope one day you could teach me *deductive reasoning son*. It could come in handy." He chuckled.

"I very much look forward to it."

"*Disdain* is such an aggressive word. I think *annoyance* is a better fit," Albert said. The breakfast cart rolled onto the terrace. His primary mission was temporarily sidelined, but he needed time to think. Alberto said nothing during the meal.

"Why no questions from you all morning, Elliott?" Alberto asked.

"I'm sure you have an agenda," he said. "I will let you get to it."

"You do understand as a first male born Bell you carry the rare genetic trait that promotes longevity."

"Yes. I heard about that."

"I'm sorry, but I would think knowing you are immortal would be somewhat invigorating. You don't seem to be moved by that incredible anomaly or the Bell money for that matter."

"I'm sorry. I don't mean to appear ungrateful," Elliott said.

"What do you know about Gilgamesh?" Alberto asked.

"Enough."

"Are you killing our board members, Dr. Sumner?"

"No." He sipped his coffee and studied Alberto, the sweat

beads on his forehead and nose, the slight tremble in his hands—
the reason he moved them under the table. But he could not hide
the quivering eyelid. It took the morning to work up to the
question, the reason Alberto came.

"Why should I believe you?" He wiped his dripping mouth
and leaned back in his chair. Probably a position he took
countless times, calculated to intimidate.

"It's not logical. What would be my motivation? And how
could a man of medicine and law turn against everything he
knows abd cut off men's heads? I find the question absurd.
Gilgamesh is being hunted for reasons you know, Alberto, not
reasons I know. With all your wealth and resources, I would
expect much more out of your organization. I don't need or fear
your technology or your money. Remember, I'm immortal. I'm
the next Bell patriarch."

"You can't argue that pure logic, Alberto," Albert said.

"You've been seen, Dr. Sumner. There is proof. You were
with Bernardo Kuzma when he was killed. You were with
Paciono Hernando when he was killed. You were with Peters in
Nevers, and Wilkens in London. You were in Memphis the night
Mr. Wu was killed and Stein and Carson were taken from the
Peabody. How do you explain that—concidence?"

"I'm disappointed. Am I the best your people can come up
with? Gilgamesh has been hunting me since December 23rd. No.
I'm the one with the questions. Why is your organization hunting
me? You're the chairman of the board of a billionaire's club trying
to kill me. I'm sure you can answer my simple question. But we
both know, you will not."

"The incidents in December were a mistake."

"And Barcelona, and Nevers, and London, those were
mistakes too?" Elliott asked.

"You must admit, the evidence is compelling. You have been

running, and you keep showing up when one of our board members gets his head cut off."

"One thing I've learned in my travels is Gilgamesh has many enemies. Your club has not been playing nicely in the *immortality research sandbox*. If I were you, I would start dealing with the profound reality of a hundred years. Who are the enemies you've created? Someone has taken the time to prepare. They have studied each of you. They are on a mission to destroy you. This someone is not going to stop until they are done . . . or until someone stops him. The time spent hunting me is wasted time. He is coming for you, Alberto Bella."

"Do you know this man?" Alberto asked brushing crumbs from his lap.

"I know he exists. I don't know his identity. I've been trying to find him while avoiding your aggressive members and stealth armies."

William came out on the terrace. They stopped talking.

"Excuse me, Mr. Kohl. You were to be reminded of your eleven o'clock appointment. Your driver has returned and is waiting."

"Thank you,William. I'm sorry, gentlemen. Our new director of R&D seems to have something of great importance to share. I've put him off. I'm afraid it can't wait any longer."

Elliott nodded. Albert stared at his coffee mug.

"Why did Alberto Bella have to die. Why invent Rudolph Kohl," Elliott asked.

"Too many questions. The world would never understand a man living 164 years."

The three stood. "Well then, this has been an interesting discussion, gentlemen. I shall take what you've said to the remaining members of the board. Albert, I will call you later this week." Alberto reached back and grabbed another blueberry muffin while staring at Elliott. He nodded and disappeared into the manson.

The two sat in silence until William returned to confirm they were alone.

"Sir, the powder blue Bentley has departed. The gates are closed." William handed him a folded linen napkin. Albert set it in his lap.

"Elliott, you're not safe."

"Simple logic?" he said with a half smile.

"Alberto Bella seeks advice from no one. If he had any intentions of leaving you alone, he would have said so this morning. The man shoots from the hip. He never takes things to the board for a decision. He plays the board to do as he wishes. He should not need time to think."

"You know more about *deductive reasoning* than you may think, Albert."

"I've been a fool. Since the last board meeting and the death of Ningpu Wu, I've had the opportunity to read numerous Gilgamesh documents brought to me by Miss Mason, a wonderful, intelligent, and high-sprited girl." He looked up and smiled. "She reminds me of, well, maybe that discussion is best left for another time."

"Carol Mason is the most unique woman I've ever met, and quite the handful."

"The Gilgamesh documents, Elliott. You must believe me when I say there is much I did not know. I was put on the board in 1956 when my father died. But my participation was rare and superficial up to 1995. Even then I attended only to please my grandfather. I thought their dreams were wishful thoughts of people with more money than they could ever spend. The science I heard about was bizarre and farfetched. I never saw a lab. I suppose I was too busy managing the family businesses, and too trusting. Or I was in denial. I just don't know.

"Don't Albert . . ."

"I'm ashamed of myself. Elliott, I believe the founder scions have been kept in the dark as well. I believe the original founders still alive have their own agenda."

"I want to believe you."

"I know you need more." He looked at his lap. "Jack wanted me to have something. It was brought to me this morning by his trusted friend, someone least likely to be watched by dangerous people."

Albert produced the linen napkin and opened it. He turned the leather case so Elliott could read the embossed words. Elliott reached over and ran a finger over the words. "You have it. Jack got this to you."

"You know about this?"

"Yes. I learned of its existence just this week."

"And I learned this morning it is Dr. Medino's biogenic solution for infinite cellular replication, the formula Alberto has been searching for. This could change everything."

"If it is real, everything makes perfect sense—my life, the Bluff City Butcher, the scion, and Gilgamesh. I learned of the mission long ago. I thought it was a dream of old men. My progress to the proper conclusion was slowed because I could not believe it real."

"This could be dangerous in the wrong hands, Elliott."

"The ultimate weapon."

"How so?"

"Immortals are gods in a mortal world. Special interests like Gilgamesh, sinister governments, and other covert entities will stop at nothing to control such a magnificent breakthrough intended for all of mankind."

Albert covered the leather case with the napkin. "Not only are you in danger. If this is the solution to immortality, it is clear why I too must be terminated."

"After Dr. Medino we were the only remaining risk. They killed Jack. That night in December they used Adam to do the rest of their work. I'm sure that after he took care of you and me and other enimies, Gilgamesh would terminate him. When Adam let us live, they had to change their plan. They were not prepared for the unknown, the scion."

"But why kill Jack Bellow? He was no threat. He was a businessman."

"There had to be a reason. Something happened. Maybe they believed they achieved their goal—their own biogenic breakthrough. Think back. Do you remember anything said in a board meeting or a communication?"

"Yes. Dr. Quinn, director of R&D, reported a milestone . . . six months of success. The cellular reproduction of major organs: heart, kidney, liver. But I had seen similar progress reports over the years. They were never successful long term. They always failed for one reason or another. This time, Dr. Quinn said they were in the final stages of qualifying biomaterials and formula refinements."

"When was that?" Elliott asked.

"September 2009, a special board meeting was called."

"Jack was killed in October. Adam lured me to Mud Island in October."

"Dr. Quinn resigned the end of year," Albert said. "He disappeared. I think he was terminated. I can't get Alberto to tell me. But he can't make eye contact on the topic."

"Dr. Quinn overstated. The refinements failed. A new director was brought in to pick up the pieces, salvage, and accelerate. They lost two of the Bell triplets before they were on safe ground."

Out of the corner of his eye, Elliott saw a flash of light near the west wall of the estate.

"Albert, Gilgamesh began their termination process too soon, to close loose ends to ensure their exclusive control of biogenic immortality. When they learned their science was incomplete, they were too far along. Plans were adjusted. They were desperate to regain order.

"They were desperate to send Adam that night," Ablert said. "And later, to attack you on the Peabody rooftop and at the Shelby County morgue."

"They killed Jack too soon, Albert. That night Adam turned on them. Alberto's world

was spinning out of control. That's why I am hunted now. I am their greatest risk, the most uncontrollable factor in the equation. When I'm gone, they will terminate you. Only Alberto will carry the Bell family immortality gene sequence."

"But why keep us around if he has a viable sequence?" Albert asked.

"Lack of potency . . ."

"I want you to go to Peru with me," Albert said. "It's related. It may make all the difference, if we have some time left. I want you to meet your mother."

Elliott's eyes narrowed. He leaped from his chair and pulled Albert to the ground. A water goblet exploded. A coffee cup exploded. The Georgia marble under the kitchen window shatterd.

Blood flowed on the terrace . . .

THIRTY-NINE

"A mother understands what a child does not say."
Unknown

The Peruvian sun leaked between peaks of the Andes and streamed into his room at the Hotel Santa Cruz. He stirred early after a late night. His circuitous route from the States challenged Gilgamesh operatives just enough to keep them close and on their toes. He would lose them at the right time. They would kill him after he led them to his mother, Betty Duncan.

Elliott stood in the blinding sunlight in front of his mirror. He repositioned his new hat in search of the perfect look. He found the Dorfman Pacific fedora in an obscure haberdashery a few blocks from the hotel, another prop in a carfully constructed plan. His monitored selection would sell his unwanted guests on the importance of the purchase. Elliott wore it from the store, at dinner, and all night as he meandered the bustling streets of the South American city.

Behind him, next to the bed, were two black Osprey Talon 44 backpacks. He purchased them in Colombia on the way down during the two-hour layover. At the time, one was folded and stuffed into the other—no one would expect a purchase of two. He still had plenty of room to transfer all his travel possessions, and he made sure they saw him discard his tattered suitcase. Now, he moved one to the bed—it was tightly packed with hotel pillows and wadded newspaper, and it was the one he grabbed on his way out the door, his fedora tilted on his head.

At seven o'clock on a Tuesday morning in Lima, Peru, the downtown sidewalk traffic moved like a massive school of fish battling upstream. He had not factored-in the chaos that crippled the efforts of his stealth trackers. Elliott stopped several times to window shop and to give them time to catch up.

He stopped for a coffee at the pre-selected, outside cafe on schedule. After he enjoyed his breakfast under the Peruvian sun, the flirtatious waitress topped his second cup with a wink. Elliott stepped inside the café to use the facilities—his cherished Dorfman hat, Osprey backpack, steaming coffee, and open newspaper holding his table and the attention of his stealth friends. When they found the pillows, Elliott had left the city.

He boarded one of a hundred flights departing Lima that morning. His small, commercial airline flew to Peru's second largest city—Arequipa—a critical leg of his journey, one he had to take alone. When arrived, he did everything necessary to lose himself in another sea of a million strangers before Gilgamesh could locate his new city.

If they had done their homework they would have known Elliott was not a hat man.

For show, he took the short ride from Rodríguez Ballón International Airport to the Casa de Avilla Hotel Turistas. He paid the taxi, grabbed his real backpack, and walked into the lobby, through the kitchen, and down the alley. The teal Chevy pickup waited at the 2400 block of Luna Pazrro. The keys were beneath the only triangular chunk of concrete in the bed. He would find a crude map tucked behind the passenger-side door panel. Max had people everywhere.

Dark tinted glass and a musty truck cab would be home for the next six hours. Half of that time was dedicated to driving around the city to be certain he was alone. Elliott left Arequipa southwest for two hundred kilometers. He left the main highway onto a maze of dirt and gravel roads scribbled on the map. A red line snaked across the penciled lines, and there were child-like drawings of landmarks—a church, railroad tracks, bridges, a grocery store, creeks, and several donkey trails. Elliott ignored everything except the faint pencil lines with the occassional slash. That route would end somewhere in the foothills of the Andes. Albert and Max told Elliott to park and wait. Someone would come after sundown . . .

"You Elliott?" The words floated from somewhere in the thick scrub.

"Yes." *Even if I did everything right, I could be talking to Gilgamesh, he thought.*

A tall, thin man stepped out with a hand in his pocket and a dirty straw cowboy hat pushed back on his jet black hair. His black shirt was tucked in his worn jeans with a hard crease. He had a holster strapped to his leg and a hand on the gun pointed at the dirt.

"I'm Paul." He looked around. "Friend of Miss Belford . . ."

"Sorry. Don't know a Miss Belford. Who are you?" This could be a major problem. Elliott held his ground with his eye on the gun. If it moved he had to charge.

"We've been calling her Belford for so long, I forget." The English revealed Paul did not grow up in Peru. "Dr. Elliott

Sumner. You've come a long way. Betty Duncan prayed for this day."

"Take me to her, Paul. I don't have much time." Elliott started moving backing to his car. Paul's hand moved on his gun. Elliott stopped.

Paul snapped his holster.

"I'm driving."

After twenty minutes of dirt roads and mountain passes and convoluted treks across fields without in the dark, Paul drove up to a small cabin nestled in an Andean forest. It had a wide porch with a rock walkway through lush, flower gardens.

"Go ahead," Paul said. Elliott got out of the truck and watched it disappear into a barn on the horizon. He turned to the cabin and saw the shadow with a rifle on the roof and another by a tree. He knew they would have been missed by most, and wondered how many others he missed.

Elliott stood at the door with his hand clenched ready to knock. Not until that moment did he think about himself. He was about to meet his mother for the first time in his life. She was the person who broke his heart the most, the one who abandoned him, left him in the dark abyss of confusion and self-doubt. In a fraction of a second Elliott felt the emptiness and crippling pain that comes from being alone in the world.

All the way from Memphis he thought about helping Albert Bell and stopping Gilgamesh. Betty Duncan could know something that makes a difference. And Elliott had a message from Albert to deliver—he loved Betty more today than the night in El Paso, Texas, in 1968.

The door opened. He lowered his hand. *My mother* . . .

He expected a small, sixty-five-year-old, gray headed woman, but saw a beautiful, mature lady. She lunged for him. She embraced Elliott. She held him tight around his waist, her head buried deep in the massive chest of her son. She trembled as she wept in his arms. Then her hand touched his face. And then her other hand. She held his face lifted her head. Her big eyes swallowed her son. It was the first time she held him since he was a baby. Then she smiled, her face radiant, full of life, and beautiful. He saw the lines of sadness and despair.

"You are here," she said. "You are the man I hoped you would be."

"How do you know me . . . ?" Elliott whispered.

"I could not be with you, Elliott. I could not be in your and Jack's lives. But I could watch you from a distance, never risking contact. If Gilgamesh knew, you and Jack would be . . ."

She led him inside the cabin like a little boy. She opened a cupboard and removed a thick album. She took Elliott to a sofa by the window looking into the garden.

"I have lived many places since 1982, the year they sent their people for me and Adam. Dr. Medino helped. After a few years, I pulled myself together. But I realized I could never return." She opened the album and placed it on Elliott's lap. "I have been following you since 1985."

Elliott turned the pages stuffed with newspaper clippings. There were photographs of him at all ages, each taken from a distance—behind a fence or around a corner or out a car window.

"I have but a few friends," she said. "They loved me. They understood I was hiding from dangerous people."

"Why . . . ? Why did you leave me and Jack? Why did you only keep Adam? What was wrong with us? Did we do something to you?"

"No, no, no, my son." She grabbed his hands. "The only way they would let you and Jack live was if I stayed out of your life. Adam was a problem for them. His genetic tendencies worried them. Genetic engineering was a new concept in the '60s. Adam confused and frightened Gilgamesh. They were going to euthanize Adam after birth. They would not risk their program with the Bell triplets. There were others. They had objectives."

"There are more like us?" Elliott asked.

"I don't know. But I convinced them not to hurt Adam. I convinced them to give me Adam so you and Jack could have a life away from their laboratories. They had terms."

"What terms?"

"You and Jack would be abandoned, taken in by unsuspecting families. You would be watched. Any sign of aberrant behavior like Adam would be handled by Gilgamesh. I could not be in your lives . . . only Adam's."

Elliott held his head. "This is too much to take. It is all so crazy."

"I know. I'm sorry. I was young and stupid. My family was very poor. I agreed to be a surrogate mother, Elliott. I was approved to carry three embryos. They gave my family a lot of money, and I was going to be able to finish at the university after one year with their program. They made it sound important . . . something to help a couple unable to have children."

Betty's head dropped. "They expected one embryo to survive. They said it was normal procedure. I would deliver the child and go away, but . . ."

"But what . . ."

"I fell in love with Albert and my three babies. I did not want to do what they asked. I ran away. I wanted to have my babies. I wanted to tell Albert everything."

"That's when you met Dr. Medino?"

"Yes. Pecos, Texas. He took care of me. He helped us."

Elliott got up and paced. He turned to Betty. "Why now? Why did you contact Albert?"

"Your father found me. A man, Max Gregory, talked to me. He helped me find the courage to risk more, to leave the shadows.

He told me Albert never married. After all the years he still loved me. I always loved him, Elliott. I can't hid anymore. I don't know if Albert and I can have a life together. I just want my life back."

"It's even more dangerous now," Elliott said.

"Yes. I know. But you're a strong man now. You are stronger than I could ever be. I know you can protect yourself. I have lost Jack and Adam. I can't live any longer not knowing you."

"Gilgamesh is more active than ever before. Their board of directors are being terminated. Seven of the twelve are dead already."

"I know who is doing this, Elliott." She got up and opened a drawer. She removed a rolled document. "You need to see this."

The door opened. "Betty, we need to go *now!* Cars crossing the field." Paul ran to the window. Betty opened the closet and pulled out a bulging backpack, slid her albums into a pocket, and zipped it closed.

"This is my life, Elliott." She threw it over her back. They went out the back door as headlights swept across the gardens and cabin . . .

A hundred yards away they pulled a tarp off a jeep. Paul drove. As they neared the edge of the field behind the cabin, two men pulled dense, sagging limbs off tall bushes opening a path. After they passed through the limbs snapped flush with gunfire echoing in the mountains.

He navigated the narrow pass for several miles without lights straddling the edge of a sheer drop-off into churning streams hundreds of feet below. The pass widened into numerous dirt roads and trails. They took one. An hour later they approached the empty, paved highway. Paul turned on the lights and went south.

"Did you see?" Betty asked.

"Adam has a son . . . Kayne," Elliott said.

"Kayne was why Gilgamesh came for us in 1982."

"I don't understand. I thought . . ."

"They did not allow damaged progeny to breed. They would not risk another *Adam* in their program. Kayne is the ultimate symbol of my failure to control Adam," Betty said. "Gilgamesh came to Texas to terminate Kayne, Adam, and me. We were liabilities."

"I've heard that word before . . .

"Kayne would be twenty-seven today. Who raised him?"

"Adam would not allow me to take Kayne in 1982. Dr. Medino, Adam, and Kayne went to Memphis. I was put on a plane to Mexico. Dr. Medino promised he would look after Kayne. He was all Adam had in life. Adam trusted only Dr. Medino, and he protected him always."

"What about Kayne's mother, where was she in all this?" Elliott asked.

"She was fifteen, Elliott. She died giving birth."

Headlights came out of nowhere and got brighter. They crouched down in the seat. "Kayne is killing the board members," she said. "Kayne lived a life of constant Gilgamesh attacks. Adam stopped them all, but at a price. He taught Kayne how to protect himself."

"Kayne thinks Gilgamesh drove his father to suicide," Elliott said. He leaned close so only Betty could hear. "If we survive the nightmare down here, you've got to promise me you will not return to the states until I tell you it's safe."

"But Elliott, I must be with Albert. He is older now. I want him to know how much I love him before he is gone. I want to know my only surviving son before I die."

"Albert is not old. He is immortal—trust me. And Adam is alive. He is in hiding. Now that we have our mother back, I do not intend to lose you again. Promise me you will wait."

"Adam's alive," she gasped. Then she put her hand on Elliott's strong chin and looked into his eyes. "I promise my son."

"Hold on people," Paul yelled. "We're taking a shortcut." The jeep took a sharp left off the asphalt mountain road. The headlights closing from behind attempted the turn, shot off the road, and disappeared. Seconds later they heard the explosion. The valley glowed . . .

FORTY

"Insanity is a perfectly rational adjustment to an insane world."
Thomas Szas

"It's a quorum, Dr. Sumner," the scion said. Elliott had not heard from him since Nevers, France, and he only saw him once—Aragon. "There's a board meeting tonight you don't want to miss."

"I'm not doing this with you . . . *Kayne*," Elliott boomed.

"You know my name. Good. You found Betty Duncan."

"She wants you to stop. Too many have died. She has pain, too. We all have pain. But this is not the way."

"This is my enduring achievement. I am almost finished."

"No, Kayne. This is your death sentence." Elliott glanced at his watch—3:00 *a.m.*

"Let the dead spend their time being dead. The living should have life without demons."

"A quote fom the *Epic of Gilgamesh* does not give you

permission to kill. It is mythology, not real. You cannot fight a real war alone, not anymore." Elliott pulled on his jeans and stepped into his kaolins. *I know where you are. I'm ten minutes away . . .*

"My father was strong, but not wise. He fought demons all his life—those in his head and those all around him. They wore him down. He could not go on. Now it is my time. My father prepared me like no other. I will finish this war against evil men. My father, your brother, knew this day would come."

"I don't know the life you had in the catacombs, but I do know my brother lived in the shadows of life denied truth and family. His narrow and painful view of this world twisted and distorted everything good. He lived an angry and incomplete life . . . until the end, Kayne."

"Like an animal in the wild, my father survived. He protected the few from the many, the good from the bad. He dispised the civilized world that allowed this insanity."

"There is a price paid to be civilized, Kayne. We are surrounded by the uncivilized. We will always seek to remove these men from our world, but there are right and wrong ways to do it. Scions can not become demons in the process . . ."

"There is a quorum. The Gilgamesh board meeting is in session. They will reveal a century of transgressions. They will give truths you were denied when you met with Alberto Bella. I told you I would clear the way. I have been to the Cedar Forest. I have cut down the giants so all can see. I stand at the gate. My work is almost done."

Elliott got into his car. "Kayne, hear me. I know how to stop Gilgamesh. Not like this."

"No. Go where you first met my father. I am waiting. The board is in session."

"Have you talked to your father, Kayne? Have you asked Adam?"

"My father is dead. I watched him die. You did nothing to help him." Kayne's voice broke.

"Adam is alive . . ."

When Kayne disconnected, Elliott pressed speed dial and turned off Madison onto Front. "Come on Tee. Answer the phone."

"Shit, Elliott. You know what time it is? Oh God. You're into something."

"Meet me at Mud Island now. The *No Boat Launch* sign at the north end? This time you better get your people out there fast. I think we're gonna find the two missing Gilgamesh board members . . . and much more."

"I live on Mud Island, goddamnit. Can't some of this scary shit happen in another Memphis neighborhood?" He stepped into his pants. "Give me three minutes. I'll call MPD from there —too many too soon can fuck it up. Wait at the top of the trail. Elliott—damn it—do not go down alone." Tony jumped into his car strapping on his gun.

Elliott knelt on his haunches at the top of the trail until headlights turned into the abandoned lot. The island was almost pitch black, the full moon hiding behind a thick bank of clouds. Elliott smelled the river a hundred yards away, the unmistakeable smell rolled off the turbulant river and flowed up the walls of the ravine into his face.

"Welcome back from South America. I assume your trip was productive. Now, what the hell do we have tonight?" Tony stepped out his smoke as Elliott got to his feet.

"I spoke with the scion. His name is Kayne. He's Adam's son."

"Jesus Christ and Mother Mary. Don't tell me the Butcher has a son? You're a damn uncle? This just keeps getting better." Tony shook his head like he was regaining consciousness.

"Well, I guess the old man passed on his cutlery skills." He checked his gun. "Hope I have enough damn bullets. But if he's anything like his old man, I won't need em. He'll just carve my ass up after I shoot him six times."

"Are you done yet . . . ?"

"Sorry, but you gotta see the irony in . . ."

"Just follow me," Elliott sighed.

They went down the narrow trail into the ravine. Nothing behind the forgotten sign had changed. Elliott remembered each twist and turn as it snaked through the bone-white, gnarled piles of river debris, wild scrub, and rotting garbarge. River rats and other vermin scrambled out of their path as they eased forward slow and low.

When they got to the end of the trail, Elliott leaned and eye out of the tall scrub. He saw the clearing on the east bank of the enormous river. He was at the place where he met the Bluff City Butcher—the place where he thought he would die. Instead it marked the begining of the end for the monster of urban legend. Two months later, Elliott learned the man he hunted was his brother. Five months later, he learned his brother had a son. Gilgamesh would not allow defective progeny to breed—Adam, Betty, and Kayne had to be erased. But they underestimated Adam. Many died. And they have fortotten the son of a monster. He now hunts them.

The small fire burned in the center of the clearing. The moon broke out of the clouds. The silver water of the Mississippi slid behind sparce trees, their long shadows falling in all directions like witnesses. The Gilgamesh board members came into Elliott's view. They were in a half-circle around the flickering fire.

"What do you see, Elliott?" Tony whispered with his gun and eyes on the trail.

There were seven, their heads looking down on the fire from seven feet above.

"Elliott," Tony whispered with more urgency. He lowered his

gun, reached back and tugged Elliott's shirt. He knew they were surrounded by danger, and he would not wait for an answer. Tony poked his head out of the tall grass.

"God! No!" Tony sunk back down into Elliott's face. "Listen to me. We will go real slow. Tell me what in the hell I'm looking at. What is this carnage about, Elliott?"

There were seven poles in the ground, each with a head on top.

"It's a quorum, Tony."

"What in the fuck is a quorum?" he shot back.

"A majority. Enough of a twelve-man board to vote on actions that bind, Tony. I'm quite certain we're looking at the missing heads of seven Gilgamesh board members. You just found the two missing from the Peabody."

"This is very sick shit, Elliott. I thought the three-headed ruse on the Hernando de Soto Bridge was bad. This is even worse. Are you sure the Butcher didn't do this?"

"I assure you, this is Kayne's work. And, he could be here."

"How do you know?" Tony poked his head above the brush for a three-sixty. "I don't see anything out there but heads on sticks."

"Kayne doesn't know Adam's alive, Tee. He's doing this on his own. I don't know if Kayne even knows what he's doing anymore. He's in a confused state—loss of his father and Dr. Medino, and a lifetime underground with no human contact and no mother . . . only enemies and death. I think he's sorting things out."

"Well let's give him some room!" Tony scoffed. "Really Elliott. You're the thinker around here. I don't want to understand some sick bastard that can do this kind of perverted shit."

They stared at the eerie scene. "In all fairness, this is your gig for a while. You didn't have to call me. I'm goddamn amazed you did, *Lone Ranger*. What do you want to do before I get people crawling like ants out here?" Tony asked.

"Let's get out there. I need a closer look."

"Not a good idea, Sherlock. Maybe I should make the call first." Tony started to reach for his cell. Elliott got up, took a pair of latex gloves from his pocket and snapped them on as he walked into the clearing.

"Well shit." Tony jumped up and followed with his gun out, the barrel down, his finger on the trigger. "How many pairs of those damn things you got on you?" he asked. Elliott held a second pair behind him. Tony snagged em and popped em on as they approached the carnage.

The seven heads were in a half-circle around the fire facing the river. Elliott clicked on his penlight and moved in to examine the first head in the arc. Tony kept his back to the river watching their surroundings. The wind rolled across the river foilage lifting and sinking it as if the island was alive. *Hope that bastard can't swim, Tony thought* as he checked the water's edge along the bank and hit speed dial—MPD. *You got maybe five minutes, my friend.*

"Wilcox here. Need you at Mud Island, clearing on the river bank. Take the trail behind the *No Boat Launch* sign at north end. You'll see my car. Follow the trail to the bank. Get CSI down here. And get the new M.E. out of bed. This is one ya gotta see up close and personal . . . seven heads on poles around a campfire—really quaint. I think our missing persons, Peabody, are now accounted for . . . Well, part of them anyway. Get me a perimeter up STAT. I don't want anyone getting off Mud Island by land or water." *That'll get everyone's blood flowing . . .*

Elliott studied a head inches from his nose. "They've been preserved. Looks like dry ice. They're beginning to thaw. Been out here an hour . . . two at the most. Time enough to unpack, stage, and clean up. Each neck reveals the smooth, single pass of the knife. I'm sure forensics will confirm identities of the board. They were all killed with same knife and same hand."

"What is this setup all about, Elliott? Looks like a sick ritual."

"Kayne said a board meeting. Said the attending members would reveal transgressions of the last century, but I don't see . . . Wait . . . What's this?"

Tony leaned over Elliott's shoulder as he shined his penlight on a coiled strip of paper stapled to the neck skin of a thawing head. "It's a damn note. Unroll that puppy," Tony said.

Elliott held one end and pulled the strip. It uncoiled like a shade. The narrow strip of vellum had the Gilgamesh watermark. It unrolled to twelve inches, an inch wide. "What is that?" Tony asked. "It looks like a list of names and some letters . . . *T E A*."

Elliott leaned in. "There are three words—*threat, exposure,* and *advance.*"

Elliott focused as Tony surveyed the nearby brush.

"I count twenty-one names, each preceded with one of those letters," he whispered. "At the bottom it says, '*I am responsible for the deaths of these innocent people.*' The signature belongs to James Wilkens. This must be his head, Tony."

"What do you make of this?" Sirens got louder on the island.

"James Wilkens was the Gilgamesh board member in London—killed. You remember the vellum table I told you about? The fifth column heading was *T E A*. Now I know what it means."

"A list of kills directed or carried out by the board member," Tony said.

"If this is an accurate accounting, Wilkens was responsible for twenty-one people dying, their names listed here. Kayne made Wilkens sign the *admission of guilt* and cut off his head."

"Judge, jury, and executioner," Tony scoffed.

"The names can be validated. We can confirm or reject. Check the next one."

Elliott uncoiled the next strip on the next head.

"This is Howard Carson. On his *T E A* list I count twenty-eight names. He signed it, too."

Tony glanced at the other five. "They all have the coiled thing stapled to their neck, except this one" Tony stood next to a head dripping blood. "This has three of those strip things."

Elliott uncoiled one. "This is Meir Stein. It has the letter S for scion. Stein is a descendent of a Gilgamesh founder. He has a lot of names listed as well."

"Check the second strip on his neck."

"It says Rudolph Kohl, and his T E A list. There are forty-three names, but no signiture."

"If that short, fat bastard killed forty-three people, I'd like to beat the living . . ."

"Tony. Focus. We don't know what any of them did. Right now we have heads and lists of names and signatures from men who had no other choice. And Kohl is still alive."

"I'm sure this is just another sick game of another monster," Tony said. "Or, your genius brain has it all figured out. If you do, connect some dots for me."

"Let's look at the third strip." Elliott unrolled the delicate paper. It was the longest so far. They saw flashlights bounce down the narrow trail from the parking lot. Two-way radios squawked orders and a rustling crowd neared like a heard of grazing cows.

"Talk to me, quick. What's it say?" Tony asked.

"This one is for Alberto Bella. It's not signed either." Elliott leaned closer. "It says his head will roll next."

"Talk to me, Elliott?"

"This can't be right—all the names, the cities, and dates of death. The others didn't have DODs, Tony."

"How many, Elliott?

"Two-hundred-eighty-nine on Alberto's *T E A* list."

"Holy shit." Tony's face grazed the next head. He jumped. He got blood on his cheek. "Can I get anything from this crap?" Tony asked.

Elliott shined the light on him.

"Don't move." The beam passed over his cheek to another strip of vellum, but this one had the board member name in bold letters on the outside of the coil. "Tony, this is for Albert Bell." Flood lights popped on and a frozen crowd of badges appeared.

Tony turned to them.

"Welcome to the party. Dare I remind you, don't touch a goddamn thing until the M.E. and CSI work their magic." He and Elliott backed away from the spectacle with eyes on Albert's vellum. It was now an official crime scene—no more touching.

Detective Harris broke through the crowd.

"Sir, tactical has surrounded the island. If there's anyone here, we'll get em." He turned to a head a few feet away. "Is he looking at me, sir?"

"I feel much better now, Harris." Tony turned Alex from the head. "Keep everyone back. There could be tracks in the sand. We don't wanta screw up any more physical evidence."

The cluster of badges gawked at the seven pale, dripping heads atop the seven-foot poles. Lapping flames casted an orange/yellow light on the matted hair and glazed eyes of the dead with looks of terror—the frozen facials right before the blade severed their spines.

As heads thawed, melting saliva and phlegm, blood serum, gastric juices, and vomit dripped from severed orifices like a gentle rain on a summer day. Each drop of body fluid pattered on the dry sand and disappeared like hundreds of forgotten stories on the banks of the old river.

Elliott backed away. Tony controlled the crime scene. The MPD lights stole the darkness. Power generators broke the eerie silence. The macabre scene morphed into a theatrical display—a circus had come to town. Helicopters pounded above, motorboats stirred waters, yelping dogs and bobbing lights moved in gnarled brush, and desperate sirens screamed in the night.

You're living the Epic of Gilgamesh aren't you, Kayne? You think you've been to the mythical Cedar Forest. Elliott searched for an unexpected advantage, a way to stop the carnage, and then it caught his eye. The silhouette on the horizon stood beyond the commotion. Across the Wolfe River feed on the bluff above the trees, the dark man owned the gray, morning sky. Elliott saw Kayne. He kept his word. Gilgamesh revealed a century of transgressions. He said there would be a quorum—but they were dead with declarations.

The silhouette could have been a tree. But soon the tree was gone.

The skies roared and the earth rumbled, then it became deathly still and darkness loomed. There rained death . . . The verse played in Elliott's head. *Alberto Bella miscalculated the strength of those he hunted—Adam and his scion. Gilgamesh is now Kayne's Cedar Forest. Your board members are now Kayne's trees to drop to let the light in. And you are his Humbaba. Kayne is coming for you now, Alberto. The Epic of Gilgamesh is the oldest story told, the struggle of men facing their own mortality and evil in our world. Adam gave Kayne the map and the skills to do what he—the real monster—no longer could.*

Elliott walked up to the head with Albert's vellum. He looked around and pulled it off. *No one watches or questions the forensic guys, he thought.* Elliott slipped it into his pocket and aimed his penlight at a neighboring head—misdirection. He backed away. But Elliott did not know where Tony's eyes were that night. He only heard the director of the MPD barking orders and calling the name as he emerged from the trail.

Elliott eased into the chaos and disappeared . . .

"Wilcox, I thought I told you to personally get me on

anything and everything like this. What happened, detective? I did not get my call from you."

The director had found Tony standing in the shadows at the water's edge, a smoldering cigarette hanging from his lip. Tony was a smart cop. He took the best position to watch his crime scene. He missed nothing . . .

FORTY-ONE

"There's none so blind as they that won't see."
Jonathan Swift

William escorted Max to the second floor of the Bell mansion, a walk they had made many times over the last year. This time there was an urgent meeting at eight and he was late. Following the early morning carnage on Mud Island, Elliott said it was time to put heads together. Kayne was known and in Memphis—there were two of the five surviving Gilgamesh board members in town. A strike could come at any moment.

"Albert, you really should get lights in this room," said the silhouette holding the briefcase in the doorway to the study, the glowing hallway at his back. If they had not recognized the voice, they never would have known the silhouette was Max. He would be a mystery until he reached the mahogany desk at the far end of the room.

Elliott and Carol were sitting with Albert. They watched the shadow of Max approach flanked by softly lit oil paintings and a small lamp next to the sofas by the dead fireplace. When he got close enough, the antique globe lamp on the corner of Albert's desk touched his pinstriped suit, starched white shirt, and royal blue tie . . . and smiling teeth.

Max saw Elliott and Carol in jeans and Albert in a open collar summer shirt.

"Oh dear, am I overdressed again?"

"Goodness no, Max. You always look impeccable," Albert said as he stood to greet his old friend and trusted PI. Reassured, Max set down his briefcase, brushed his lapels, and straightened his tie. "Hello, Miss Mason. You are a joy to an old man's eyes."

"Thank you, Max. You're always the gentleman."

"Dr. Sumner, very good to see you safely returned from Araquipa." Max went to the vacant leather chair on the left side of Albert's desk, Carol and Elliott on the right.

"Well sir, not everyone has a CIA icon managing his travel arrangements." Elliott walked around and embraced Max. "I'm very grateful."

Albert's study would forever be the place where he met the Bluff City Butcher, and where he learned he had three sons. And the study was the place where Elliott found his father and learned he had brothers, one the serial killer he hunted for a decade.

Even though the balcony doors were repaired months ago, Carol would forever remember the strengh of the Butcher. He pulled them from their hinges and tossed them across the room like garbage can lids. Then he leaped into the night. But now, on a warm April night, the balcony doors were open. There was no whipping, snow flurries like that December night. Now they were wide in hope a cool breeze would find its way into the stuffy room of the sprawling mansion.

"Max, we waited for you. You didn't miss a thing. It's

important we all get on the same page tonight. My travels in Europe, Nashville, and Arequipa have shed new light on a very dark world." Elliott cleared his throat. "Adam has a son . . ."

The three erupted with a flurry of questions.

Elliott held up a hand with a smile.

"I'll get to all questions, but please let me cover some of the most important things first. Later we can drill down. We have precious little time . . .

"His name is Kayne. He's the scion I spoke to in New York City, the one I followed through Spain, France, and into England. Kayne is killing Gilgamesh board members. His mother died in birth in Carrollton, Texas. The birth launched Gilgamesh into action. They would not allow defective progeny—Adam—to reproduce. Their death squad intended to kill Adam, the child, and Betty Duncan. But they escaped. Others did not.

"Kayne went with Adam to Memphis. He grew up in the catacombs and had a lifetime of bad experiences with the predatory organization. Adam taught Kayne everything. Believe me when I say . . . Kayne's skills with a knife are the same as Adam's."

"What happened on Mud Island, Elliott?" Albert asked.

"At three this morning Kayne invited me to a Gilgamesh board meeting on Mud Island. He called it a quorum. He said they would reveal a century of wrong-doings. Tony and I went. We found seven Gilgamesh board members, Albert. Their heads were on poles around a fire."

"How sickening," Carol said. Albert's eyes stayed with Elliott.

"Kayne attached strips of vellum to each head. The vellum contained disturbing information, lists of names. Next to each name was a letter—*T* or *E* or *A*. They stood for *threat, exposure* or *advance*. The names listed are people killed by or under the direction of the referenced board member. Clearly these victims of Gilgamesh were classified as a specific problem type. The list of names were signed by the respective board member."

"A list of names for each of the seven board member?" Albert asked.

"Yes. And each name has a city and date of death. The individual board members were responsible for between twenty and fifty deaths, according to this strip of vellum. One had no names listed, but Kayne judged him guilty for being an attending member of the *T E A* committee. Alberto Bella had the longest *T E A* mortality list."

"How many, Elliott," Albert asked leaning forward.

"Two-hundred-eighty-nine . . ."

Carol and Max gasped. Albert dropped his head. "Albert. Your strip of vellum was attached to Meir Stein's head next to Alberto's."

"Excuse me, sir." William entered the study holding a box. He had never interrupted one of Albert's meetings in the forty years. It had to be important.

Albert waved him in. "Excuse me Elliott. What is it, William?"

"I'm sorry to disturb you, sir. This was delivered to the gates just now. There's blood on the outside of the box, sir. I thought you should see it right away. It's for you."

Albert stood as William set the box on the center of the desk. "Elliott, would you please do this?" he asked.

Elliott examined the box before touching.

"This is blood."

"Should we call the police?" Carol asked as William left the study.

"Not yet." Elliott opened the flap as the three watched. He peered inside. "Albert, do you know an African American with a tattoo—*Memphis State Tigers*?"

"Yes I do. Willie Starnes. The night watchman at the LIFE2

Corporation, now retired. He is a dear friend of the family. Willie has that tattoo on his hand. He watched over Jack for twenty years. Why do you ask?"

"I'm sorry, Albert. Willie's hand is in this box."

"No. He should not . . . He's a good man. Why would anyone do this to Willie?"

Elliott removed a blood soaked paper clutched in the severed hand. Carol and Max stood in silent shock. "It is a message for you, Albert."

"Please. Read it."

"*Life is a series of choices. Willie for the leather box. You decide tonight.*"

"Why would Kayne hurt Willie Starnes," Max asked as Elliott perused the severed hand.

"This is not Kayne's work. This is an amateur. They hacked it off," Elliott said.

The phone rang and Albert pressed speaker. "William here again, sir. We seem to have company, the Memphis police, three in the lobby. Director Wade is on his way up. I could not stop him, sir."

Elliott closed the flaps and slid the box to the side. Director Wade walked into the room as if he owned the place. "So he did get a call to you after all. I thought my people could keep him off the phone for at least two minutes while I found this place. I should have cuffed him."

"Thank you William." Albert cut off the phone.

"Although you are always welcome in my home," Albert said, "please sir, you cannot walk in like this. I must ask you wait downstairs until I complete my meeting."

Wade walked up to the desk pulling a folded document from his breast pocket. He tossed it on the leather blotter in front of Albert.

"I think you need to see this, Mr. Bell," he said leaning toward the open box.

Albert opened the multi-paged document.

"A search warrant. Why, sir?"

"I suggest you read on, Mr. Bell. You and Dr. Sumner will find page two of particular interest." Director Wade stood defiantly with his hand at his waist under his coat. Carol moved the box to her chair. Wade's eyes followed her as he waited for Albert to finish reading.

"Arrest warrants for Dr. Sumner and me? I can't imagine what this could be about, Director Wade. I will need an explanation, sir."

"I'm sure Dr. Sumner has already shared confidential police information concerning a crime scene he attended earlier today . . . Mud Island."

"That would be an unsubstantiated assumption on your part, Director Wade," Albert shot back. "I'm sure there's been some terrible mistake."

"It seems there were seven heads on sticks, some secret organization you belong to, Mr. Bell. I think you call yourselves Gilgamesh—some perverse club of the privileged with sick rituals. Now we have another killer out there. Don't worry, we'll find him. But what I found to be most interesting this morning were these little strips of paper hanging from the heads of the dead people. Each had a list of names of people killed by your members over the years."

"Whatever are you talking about?" Albert asked.

"We have already validated and linked twenty-four cold cases in the last six hours. I'm sure we'll find these *kill lists* are accurate—very damning information Mr. Bell."

"And what does it have to do with me or Dr. Sumner?"

"Mr. Bell, you are a member of Gilgamesh. You held their last meeting in your home. I thought it odd we did not find your vellum strip out there. I took a closer look . . .

"Dr. Sumner, do you remember when those big flood lights popped on this morning and interrupted you and Detective Wilcox, the first responders to this horrible crime scene?"

"Yes. Of course I remember," Elliott said.

"You forensic guys think you know everything. Well apparently you didn't know when the lights popped on, the cameras started rolling. The crime scene went live, Dr. Sumner. We have you on video pulling off one of those coiled vellum strips and putting it in your pocket. Now, I'm not as smart as you, Dr. Sumner. But I'm pretty sure the one you took belongs to your new found father. As a loyal son, I'm sure you have Albert Bell's TEA list in your possession.

"And your buddy, Detective Wilcox, well we have him on video too. He's standing in the background watching you. He did not stop you, Dr. Sumner. He failed to report the incident to his superiors. You both broke the law tampering with a crime scene. Now, Anthony is in a cell his poor decisions. He's sitting next to the cells I'm saving for you two."

Elliott reached into his pocket. Director Wade whipped out his gun. "What do you think you're doing? Take your hand out slowly. I may be on a desk now, but I still know how to shoot." He raised his gun as Elliott pulled his hand from his pocket in a closed fist.

The study seemed darker than usual. The stark light in the hall poured in the open doorway. A soft breeze from the balcony tickled the arrest documents Albert dropped on his desk. "I can explain," Elliott said. Max and Carol's eyes moved from Elliott's fist to Albert.

"As a professional courtesy, I left my officers downstairs. I thought we could do this like gentleman," Wade said. "Open your hand, Dr. Sumner."

He opened it palm up. Sitting there was a coiled vellum. On the outside was bold print all could see. It said in capital letters— ALBERT BELL.

Elliott whispered, "I think you should look at this now, Director Wade."

Holding the gun, Wade snatched the vellum tube and took one step back. His face pursed in doubt and eyes squinted as he unrolled it and read to himself . . .

The first explosion was deafening. Wade jerked up straight. His eyes widened and he dropped in front of Albert's desk. The second explosion came when Wade hit the floor. Elliott's right shoulder flew back from the impact. He rebounded and struggled to balance—his shoulder soaked with blood and arm hanging limp. The next filled the room with more burnt gunpowder and more confusion. This time Elliott's left shoulder flew back spinning him around. When he regained footing, blood flowed from both shoulders and both arms hung. Elliott's eyes rolled as he swayed and attempted to focus on the new shadow in the room. Carol reached for Elliott as his legs buckled. He blacked out. She held him close, guiding his fall into his chair . . .

FORTY-TWO

"When the game is over, the king and the pawn go into the same box."
Italian Proverb

The room smelled like a shooting range. When Collin Wade dropped, they all saw the silhouette in the doorway. Albert recognized him immediately.

"I've never liked policemen," he boasted. "They always get in the way of my business ventures." He walked into the room as he had so many times before. There were three. One backed into the hall and disappeared. And one took over the vacated doorway—a much larger and dark, menacing figure.

He held the long-barrelled, smoking gun at his side and pushed Director Wade with a foot. There was no response. He stepped over the body and up to the mahogany desk. When the light washed over his pale face and toothy smile, the others knew.

"Sorry about shooting you, Elliott, if you can hear me."

Elliott Sumner was unresponsive, and Carol was covered in his blood and in shock.

"Just the shoulders for now. I really don't need your brand of super-heroics tonight—such a brood of resourceful men . . . the infamous Bell triplets."

"Alberto, what are you doing? Have you lost your mind?" Albert yelled.

"You remember Bentley Masher?" Alberto Bella pointed to the doorway over his shoulder. The enormous silhouette nodded. "And you remember Boris Tanner, I'm sure. He left to take care of the other police in case things get a bit more dicey up here."

"You're insane," Albert scoffed as he looked over at Elliott in desperation. His son opened his eyes and focused on Alberto Bella, the shooter now in clear view.

Alberto pointed his gun at Albert's face. "I must admit—Dr. Sumner—I've been quite impressed with your ability to avoid our stealth armies since Christmas. If we had inspected the crawl space at the Peabody the first night, maybe things would have been easier for everyone.

"Oh. And congratulations on your Peruvian adventure," Alberto chuckled. "You had our South American contingency chasing their latino asses all over the Andes."

Elliott stared. Carol glared.

"Alberto, stop. Shoot me if you must, but leave these people alone," Albert pleaded.

Looking over at Elliott he said, "You were the strongest and smartest, you know. Or maybe you don't. You and Jack were always so reluctant to search for your gifts. I never understood that odd behavior. You had the same physical capabilities as your demented brother. I didn't factor in how much you two would want to be like normal people. What a shame . . .

"I truly hope I won't have to shoot you tonight, Albert. If we can conduct our business efficiently, you can get medical attention for Elliott. He just might have a better chance than this one." Alberto looked down and pushed the director with a foot.

Albert pushed back his chair and leaned closer to his grandfather standing on the other side of the desk with the gun. "What are you doing? You shot Elliott. My God. And you shot the Memphis police director in the back. You have gone mad, Alberto. You need help."

Carol applied pressure to Elliott's wounds. Max glared at the beast considering options.

"Let's not waste precious time calling me names and placing blame. Am I the only one with a sense of urgency tonight? If we pussyfoot around the real issue, your precious Elliott loses more blood. I'm afraid that would be it, Albert. He will die, the end of the blood lions. No more sons to carry on the Bell dynesty. Elliott will join Jack and Adam if you keep putting off."

Alberto smiled and turned to Max. "Mr. Gregory, I'm sorry you have to be here for this unfortunate family matter. I have no quarrels with you—or Miss Mason for that matter. But if either of you interfere with these proceedings, I will shoot you.

"I'm sure by now everyone in the room knows about my two vellum strips—the TEA scores of Alberto Bella, alias Rudolph Kohl. I think you can see I have accumulated a lot of experience in protecting my assets. I am a skilled marksman."

"What have you done to Willie?" Albert asked. "He has nothing to do with any of this."

"Let's not start the process with a *lie*, Albert. Willie did not tell me the truth when he had the chance. Thus, he lost one of his hands. Amazing. He decided to be truthful when he regained consciousness and begged for a tourniquet . . . and to keep his other hand."

"I don't know you. I've never known you," Albert seethed, his eyes filled with rage.

"That's not important now, Albert. One day you will

understand all of this. I know you have it—the leather box. The day Willie Starnes was given it by Jack Bellow, he failed to bring it to me. That day Willie chose a side. That day he got involved . .
.

"Now, if Willie lives, he will need to learn how to write with his left hand. But his time is running out, Albert, faster than Elliott's. I had to say no to the tourniquet. I suppose he's doing the best he can to slow down the blood flow . . .

"*I want that box now,*" Alberto Bella demanded.

"You can have it." Albert said. "I don't want anything to do with it."

"Get it," Alberto Bella spewed.

"First, you must promise the killing stops. You will leave this family alone."

"You're in no position to negotiate terms, Albert. You saw my bodyguards—my Adam doubles. And there's my gun, of course. But I will agree to your terms when I have the leather box in my possession. The killing may never stop, but I will leave the country. No one can stop Gilgamesh then."

Alberto lowered his gun. Masher's massive silhouette in the doorway spread his legs signaling the room that he was ready to charge if necessary.

Eyes moved back to Albert. "Very well." He opened the top drawer and looked down. The leather box sat next to his loaded gun—the safety always off. He read the embossed letters one more time—GILGAMESH NEVER. Albert considered he could get one shot off.

"I met Kayne today," Alberto Bella gloated with eyes locked on his grandson. He knew Albert always kept a loaded gun in his top drawer.

"You never told me about Kayne," he prodded. "The boy paid me a visit this morning. I guess it was after he put on his show on Mud Island. I didn't realize he was the one hunting us."

"What are you talking about?" Albert said buying time.

Elliott opened his eyes and groaned.

"Kayne got greedy. He wanted to move too fast. He wanted my head on a stick now. He wanted to add me to his collection— all the bad people in his sick, demented life. Well, we were waiting for the little bastard . . .

"His head's in my freezer and corpse floating down the river —fish bait. You know, the Mississippi River is a magnificent 2,320 mile creation. Did you know it drains all of thirty-one states and two Canadian provences—the fourth longest river in the world? It serves many purposes, Albert. One is burial without fanfare and investigation. You drop a body in the swirling, muddy waters and it is gone. We've used it often over the years."

"Your the monster," Elliott said as Carol compressed his wounds.

"Kayne's the monster," Alberto gloated. "The scion of defective progeny. He was as stupid as his father—both titanic failures. Adam never understood vulnerabilities. They both lacked patience. Kayne blamed me for his father jumping onto the dreadful spire. He blamed me for that demented creature's suicide. It was the one time Adam Duncan did me a favor—he ended the reign of the psychotic Bluff City Butcher. Now give me that goddamn leather box!"

"Albert. Give it to him," Carol pleaded. "Elliott's losing too much blood."

Albert reached inside the top drawer and put his hand on his gun. He closed his eyes and moved his hand to the leather box that held Medino's biogenic formula. When his fingers touched, a hollow groan came from deep within the Bell mansion. The empty echo rolled down the hall and into the dark study. Eyes left Albert and moved to the door. Alberto Bella turned, raised and cocked his gun—but Bentley Masher was still standing there, and the menacing shadow in the doorway seemed even larger then before. The unfolding crisis was now hopeless. Dr. Medino's biogenic solution for immortality would be in the sinister hands of Gilgamesh and everyone in the room would die.

Alberto Bella's grin widened. He uncocked his gun with a twisted, maniacal snicker. Other eyes stayed on Masher as he began to sway. He stopped and fell forward into the room, crashing onto the hardwood floor like a giant sequoia. Now a much larger shadow filled the doorway, and it did not move.

The massive deltoid muscles touched the door jams and head grazed the lintel. Long hair fell onto bulbous shoulders, and the long coat hung below his knees. A knife with a ten-inch blade found the scant light and glinted in the dark. It pointed down in his left hand.

"Who are you?" Alberto Bella demanded as he turned and squinted. "Speak now or . . ." Then he saw what he could not believe. "No! You are dead," he yelled with contempt. Alberto cocked his gun and raised his arm.

At Alberto's feet Director Wade stirred, his cheek pressed to the floor and body unable to move. He heard the madman above him, the one who shot him in his back. But one eye found the giant silhouette in the doorway across the dark room. *I know you . . . Now I fear you will be the last thing I see in this world, Collin Wade* thought.

Albert Bell froze. Elliott lifted his head. Max stepped back. Carol wrapped her arm around the man she loved and was losing.

Director Wade pushed through the fog of pain to make sense of it all, and the shadow at the door into Albert Bell's study. *You are here for him, he thought, the man that killed your son and 289 others on strips of vellum. You are here for the man who ordered the deaths of Jack Bell and Elliott Sumner. And you are here for the man who shot me in my back . . .*

"Are you *bulletproof*, you ugly bastard? Your unhinged boy was not," Alberto crowed as he took careful aim challenging the

Bluff City Butcher to charge. He already hit his mark three times this night. He would not miss his biggest target.

The Butcher stood silent thirty feet from the gun aimed at his head.

"Don't shoot Adam," Albert pleaded. "Leave him alone. You've killed enough. I have what you want. Take it and go . . ."

But Alberto stayed with his bead under the Butcher's head. It was what he really wanted. His dream turned into a nightmare long ago. Alberto Bella knew his true need could never be satisfied—he was already immortal and a billionaire. He knew his quest for total control could never be achieved. But now, the Bluff City Butcher was at the other end of his gun. Killing the monster would give him the adrenaline rush he yearned for, he had to have. Killing was control.

"Those are heart-warming words, Albert. But I should have done this in 1968, when we knew we created a freak." Alberto pulled the trigger. The explosion filled the room and a fat ring of white smoke followed the bullet halfway across the study. Nothing moved. Sound returned and breathing and more pain and anquish. But the Butcher did not drop.

No one saw him move. They did not see his head shift inches to the left and return. They did not see the Butcher's eyes and intense focus. They did sense the man in the doorway was very different—still not all of the Butcher's skills were known.

Alberto Bella missed. When the sound faded and the reality hit, he pulled the trigger again. This time they saw. It seemed almost casual. It was precision. Alberto Bella missed again. But he had six and the third shot would be different. He lowered his bead. Through the hanging smoke he centered on the Bluff City Butcher's massive chest.

Director Wade was barely alive when he found his last ounce of strength and delivered the unexpected kick to Alberto's knee. The timing was perfect. The muzzle moved and the Butcher descended from a thirty foot leap into the third blast. His knife pierced the exploding smoke and plunged deep into the center of Alberto's cold heart. When the Butcher's feet crashed to the floor, the room quaked and the giant, mahogany desk hopped and the oil paintings fell from the walls. Kneeling above, he pulled his bloody fist back with eyes locked on Alberto Bella's eyes that danced and disappeared into his head. The smoking gun dropped to the floor. The real monster that thought he was a GOD was dead.

The smoke-filled room was still. The Butcher stood up and threw his hair back with a swing of his head. He wiped Alberto's blood on his black leather coat looking down at the man who hunted him all his life, the man responsible for the deaths of his son, his friend Dr. Medino, and the Gilgamesh minions. When he lifted his head, his raised lip dropped over his teeth and his furrowed brow melted away, and the burning rage left his eyes. The Bluff City Butcher was gone and Adam was in the room.

He walked to Elliott, his knife in his hand still dripping blood. Petrified but determined, Carol shielded Elliott from the monster she did not know. Undeterred, he pushed the knife under his belt and gently moved her aside with the back of his hand.

Elliott was on the edge, awake but weak and unable to move. Elliott's shirt was soaked with his blood. Inches from his face, Adam looked at his brother's wounds. He placed his hand on Elliott's chest and looked into his eyes. "You will live." He turned to Albert. "Call for him."

Albert jumped to the phone and dialed 911. He looked at his sons, two men so different but his feelings strong for both. "Yes, this is Albert Bell. The Memphis police director has been shot. And Dr. Elliott Sumner has been shot. There are more. Send ambulances to the Bell estate on Walnut Grove. Please hurry."

Albert and Max went to Wade as Adam watched, kneeling

next to his brother. Soon the sirens screamed in the distance crawling onto the estate grounds.

"Adam, you need to go," Elliott whispered.

Adam started to stand. Elliott reached for his arm. He stopped. "I'm sorry about Kayne. I know this has been your war alone, for that I am sorry. Only a few will ever know. Adam. Hear me now. Gilgamesh has lost. It is over . . ."

Adam looked at Carol. She no longer feared him. She nodded and did not back away. Adam looked at his father. Albert smiled and his eyes weeped.

Elliott saw the wound. Adam took a bullet in his chest. The third from Alberto's gun entered an inch above his heart. "Adam! You've been hit . . ."

Adam looked down and touched his wound—it was not bleeding. "This is not bad for me." He got to his feet towering above all, and left through the open balcony doors.

The police cruisers surrounded the mansion and paramedics poured into the study. Director Wade was in critical conditon— and the first taken out on a stretcher. Albert returned to his desk and the open drawer. He closed it with his hip—*No one needs to see . . . my gun.*

Albert looked out the balcony doors into the night and thought, *my sons may not be that different after all.* Then he looked at Elliott, *and our secret is safe.* Their eyes met. Elliott winked as they rolled his gurney out of the room with Carol's hand on his chest where Adam's had been.

EPILOGUE

"What would you do if you weren't afraid?"
Spencer Johnson

"I met Marcus in Nashville." Elliott stepped over a crumbling log swarming with termites. "Watch your step here." He led Albert around a dark hole and behind an upended stump, once a giant oak. The exposed roots were covered with spider webs and mold and an alien-like, greenish orange fungus that only added to the uneasy feelings in the unfamiliar surroundings.

"And you trust this fellow is who he says he is?" Albert asked, as they descended into the musty, overgrown ravine. The thick bed of dead leaves and slippery undergrowth made their trek more treacherous than expected. They had five minutes before the place would be pitch black.

"Yes." Elliott stopped. "But I asked Max to take a look. Last night he got back to me and confirmed Marcus Moreno is Marcus Medino, the son of Dr. Enrique Medino."

"I don't know how Max does it. To my knowledge he's erred only once over the years," Albert said as he moved through the ravine and overhanging brush like a man half his age.

"Max did make one small error, I suppose . . ."

"December 23rd, 2009, I learned I was the father of three, not one," Albert muttered.

"I did not see that one coming either." They plodded onward.

"I suppose Marcus is one we need with us now."

"I think so, Albert."

They stayed on the edge of the dry creek bed. When they rounded the bend, it came into view behind thick foilage. It protruded from the bank marking the end of the ravine. The ten-foot diameter cement pipe seemed out of place.

"Interesting. In the middle of nowhere," Albert quipped as they stared.

"Marcus said there were seven, like spokes of a wheel with the Brent mansion the hub. The pipes were laid by Alberto in 1930, when they built the house."

"The first Bell mansion in the midsouth. I don't recall much about it. I was born two years after its construction. We moved to the east Memphis property in 1950. I was seventeen and spent little time at home in my growing years—boarding schools and all." Albert's head dropped. "Father was gone six years later."

"I'm sure it was a difficult time for you," Elliott said.

"I wonder if he had not been killed in a plane accident, would we be doing this?" *Did you share Alberto's obsession?* Albert reflected.

Elliott thought, *no harm in thinking the best now.* "You have no reason to doubt he was a good man. I don't believe you would be the man of principal you are without his influence."

Albert appreciated the words from his son. "We better move on, young man."

Elliott led the way through the thick shrubs. "Marcus needed help getting to Memphis. Once he got here, he knew he would be safe. The Brent catacombs is the place his father brought him often—an underground maze he knows well. He told me about the hidden entrance in this pipe."

"Dr. Medino anticipated the impending dangers his research would bring."

"And he recongized at an early age his son shared his dream and possessed the intellectual assets to carry it forward if he was unable. Preparing Marcus as he did reveals great foresight."

They reached the pipe entrance. Elliott climbed inside and shined a light into its depths reaching back for Albert's hand. "We have a hundred yards. You up to it?"

Albert grabbed Elliott's hand and got hoisted into the pipe. "I am."

Thirty feet in it was dry and the matted webs ended. There was no debris or signs water evered flowed in the cement pipe. It was tall enough to walk upright.

"Have you noticed Director Wade in denial about that night?" Albert's voice echoed.

"He needs to forget. The whole experience was too traumatic."

"Understandable . . ."

"Kayne's remains have not been found, and his head was not in Alberto's freezer. We may never know what really happened to him."

"Director Wade would rather face Kayne than tell the mayor the Butcher is alive."

"Dr. Bates will struggle as well," Elliott said as he examined scuff marks on the cement several inches above his shoulders. "He will regain his memory. He was in a coma a long time. Still healing. He's a professional trained to live with horrific information."

"Collin Wade, on the other hand, is blocking it. I read those protective mechanisms can be tricky. I'm no doctor, but denial is sometimes a good thing."

"Yes it is. Denial will help Director Wade deal with Adam's little visit in all its splendor," Elliott said.

"There's something we need to talk about, Elliott—my vellum strip. I saw it when the director retrieved it from you clenched fist. It was still sealed. Why did you not open it?"

Elliott stopped and turned to Albert.

"That night on Mud Island I saw seven heads on seven poles. I did not see yours, Albert. Kayne went halfway around the world to kill Gilgamesh board members when he had one five minutes away . . . yet he never hunted you. In fact, he told me he was on a mission to clear the way for you and me. That night on Mud Island I took your *T E A* strip for one reason."

"What was the reason, son?"

"To give it to you along with my apology for ever doubting you."

"Don't do that to yourself, son. There was no way you could have known. I was still a mystery. You could not have known Gilgamesh was never an interest of mine. You could not have known my participation was random and symbolic, that I thought it was the folly of wealthy old me. My disconnect is inexcusable. People died because I did not pay attention. Maybe they would be alive today. I must take responsibility for that, son."

"Rudy Kohl—Alberto Bella—was a secretive man, Albert. He was driven and led men who lost their way in life. He went to great lengths to keep the *T E A* program from you. He knew you would never allow it, like I knew you were a good man."

"There is one perplexing matter that remains, however."

"What is that, Albert."

"If I too carry the family genetic trait for immortality, I too am a blood lion. Why was I not a target like you and your brothers?"

"You were a target at the end. You were when you walked out of a Gilgamesh board meeting when they showed themselves. Up until then Alberto needed a known and respected man for his new world, one he would have after harnessing the biogenic solution for life extension. Remember, he manipulate you for a very long time."

"He did manage to keep Betty and you boys from me for forty years."

They continued into the depths of the cold sewer pipe. The scuff marks above Elliott's shoulders were consistent and curious. "If Dr. Medino's research was successful, we have in our possession the most world changing breakthrough for mankind, Elliott."

"And we would have a lot to consider. But, I seriously doubt we are holding the secret to immortality."

"Maybe we should destroy it. Maybe it is something the world cannot handle."

"Destroying it is certainly an option, probably the safest one."

"Is that our decision to make?"

"It may be the only way to keep it from falling into the wrong hands . . . the evil few who would use it for their own purposes," Elliott said.

"Or, we could reduce its inherent value."

"And how would we accomplish that?" Elliott asked.

"If everyone has it, the value to the evil few is gone."

They reached a dead end. Albert's cell phone chimed. "It's Max."

"Amazing that works down here. You better take it. We have time." Elliott turned to the wall and counted seven bricks down from the top center, five right, and another three down. He pushed the brick. A half section of the wall released an inch. He pushed it open and motioned Albert to follow on his phone.

The room with a dirt floor was colder, darker, and danker

than the pipe they left. Elliott pushed the brick wall back into place and shined his penlight. The space

was longer than wide and had a seven-foot ceiling with a patchwork of rotting boards. The earthen walls were partial brick and stone. Random beams were draped in webs and the fungus they saw along the creek bed. Elliott's light got lost in the floating dust. He called out to Marcus. There was no response.

"Guess we wait here. What did Max have to say?"

"Betty is on her way to Memphis," Albert said as

Elliott and his flashlight turned to him. The weak beam stopped behind Albert. A shadow took shape. The head touched the rotting boards and eyes caught the light. "The three Gilgamesh board members have been seen."

"Where?" Elliott asked.

"Cape Town, South Africa. They're resurrecting Gilgamesh. This is not over." Albert saw Elliott's eyes drift over his shoulder and up. "Did you hear me?"

"Yes. Albert, your other son is here . . ."

ABOUT THE AUTHOR

STEVE BRADSHAW is a forensic field agent and biotech entrepreneur writing his unique brand of mystery/thrillers. Steve's training and experience investigating thousands of unexplained deaths for the medical examiner's office, and as the founder-President/CEO of an innovative biomedical device company enables him to put his readers on the front row in the fascinating worlds of fringe science, modern forensics, and the chilling pursuit of real monsters.

Steve enjoys sharing his experiences and perspectives as a forensic investigator, President/CEO, and mystery/thriller author. Visit his website and join MEMBER GUEST so you can interact with the author, get insider information and updates, arrange for an author visit, and to be the first in line for new releases.

For more information:
www.stevebradshawauthor.com
steve@stevebradshawauthor.com